The
Restaurant
Critic's
Wife

ALSO BY ELIZABETH LABAN

The Tragedy Paper

The Grandparents Handbook

The
Restaurant
Critic's

Elizabeth LaBan

Wife

LAKE UNION
PUBLISHING

Published by Lake Union Publishing, Seattle

www.apub.com

Amazon, the Amazon logo, and Lake Union Publishing are trademarks of Amazon.com, Inc., or its affiliates.

ISBN-13: 9781503947757
ISBN-10: 1503947750

Cover design by Emily Mahon

Printed in the United States of America

To my husband, Craig, who made me
the restaurant critic's wife . . .

FALL

CHAPTER ONE

Something is rotten at Via Rizzo. It's not necessarily the food, which was tasty though often inconsistent. It's the false advertising. The menu claims that the pasta sauce is crafted from an old family recipe, when in fact it is factory made. It went down easy enough; my wife finished her plate. But I knew better, and the chef didn't deny it. Why lie? I asked him in a phone interview. "People don't want the truth," he said. "They want an illusion of romance. It tastes better."

—Sam Soto

I am standing in a dark alley behind a restaurant. One hand rests on my pregnant belly and the other shields my nose from the smell of rotting food. I watch as my husband disappears into a Dumpster. I hear him push garbage around. The odor gets stronger. I put my other hand up to my nose and hold my breath.

"I found them," Sam finally says in a loud whisper. His bushy hair emerges, followed by the rest of his head. He looks at us with bright dark eyes, then flashes his know-it-all grin. He reminds me of a ferret who just snared its prey. "That chef is lying."

I glance at my mother and her old friend Elaine, our dinner guests, waiting impatiently on the sidewalk. My mother pats Elaine's light-pink cashmere sleeve as I straighten my arms, still trying not to breathe, and offer them a weak smile. I can't believe this is happening.

Two hours ago, I imagined we would have a smooth evening at Via Rizzo, one of the trendy new restaurants on Philadelphia's Avenue of the Arts. When we walked in, my mother smiled warmly at the creamy marble floor and the crystal chandeliers. She nodded politely to the two trickling fountains that greeted us at the entrance to the dining room. She practically sighed with relief when she saw the well-dressed waiters. At first I wanted to ask if she had worried that we would take her and Elaine to a dump. Little did I know we'd end up at one.

My hopes of helping my mother impress her friend with Sam's job went out the window just moments after we got here. As soon as we were seated, the two women ignored the menus and launched into the story of how either one of them could have ended up with the other one's husband.

"If Martin had asked me to dance first, and Joseph had asked you, it would be a very different world," Elaine said with a high-pitched laugh, playing with the orange-and-pink silk scarf that circled her wrinkly, long neck.

"You don't have to tell me that," my mother answered warmly, placing her soft, plump hand over Elaine's perfectly manicured one. For a moment they were quiet, each, I was sure, remembering her now-dead husband. No matter who was telling the tale, it always began with the dance. I had heard this story many times before and dismissed it, but this was the first time it occurred to me that they were probably right. A simple detail like deciding which stranger to ask to dance or, in my case, deciding where to eat in a strange city, can change your whole life.

I tried not to be distracted. I knew my mother expected our full attention for this story. I was tense because Sam wasn't listening. As the women paused for feedback with big lipstick smiles, he looked away and mumbled into his sleeve where a tiny microphone was hidden.

"Bad choice of music," he said. "And it's too loud in here. But it smells good—like roasted garlic and fresh bread. The walls are a sort of mint color—no, I would say more of a lime sherbet." He clicked the pocket tape recorder off but continued to look around. For a second the women looked confused; Elaine's tastefully frosted head and my mother's very round one turned to face him, thinking, as any normal people would, that he was addressing them. They quickly realized he wasn't.

I tried to compensate by giving our guests my full attention, but Elaine looked down and brushed crumbs off of the silky white tablecloth. My mother actually glared at me.

"S—" I began. "Um, he gets distracted," I finished apologetically, catching myself before I made the error of uttering Sam's name in public. "He's working."

I was a little annoyed at my mother for wanting it both ways: wanting to show Sam off to a friend she hadn't seen in years and expecting normal conversation at the same time. She's been out with us before; she should know better. Most people are intrigued with Sam's job; why didn't Elaine seem to be? And considering our guests never have to pay a cent for these meals, there should be a little room for unusual behavior. I guess my mother wasn't in the mood for unusual behavior tonight, not in front of Elaine anyway.

Once they had gathered themselves after their perceived slight from Sam, we ordered tons of food: appetizers, *primi* pastas, five main courses, and a bottle of wine. Sam had some say in what they chose, and they were expected to share a portion of their food with him. But they still had more food than they probably ate during the course of a normal day. Who cared if the man they were eating with talked to himself throughout the meal?

Sam always has to record information about the restaurant so that he will have details when he sits down to write his review. But finishing a meal by the Dumpster might be too much to ask of anyone.

My husband is the restaurant critic for the *Philadelphia Herald*. Six months on the job and we're still adjusting . . . to everything. Thanks to Sam's position, we eat a lot. That's the good news and the bad news. There's other bad news, too.

To say Sam is serious about anonymity is an understatement. Our starting fresh in a new city where presumably nobody knows his face yet has made him, to put it lightly, a crazy man. His rules are extensive. Number one: never make a reservation in his name. Number two: call restaurants only from borrowed or random phones—never home, office, cell, or any other line that might be traced back to him or anyone associated with him. Number three: never, ever utter his name at the table. Number four: when necessary, wear a disguise. My mother had promised me that she'd briefed Elaine on the rules.

It took only fifteen minutes for Elaine to forget.

"Oh, Sam," she trilled, putting her hand on the arm of his food-splattered blue blazer. She touched something sticky and pulled away, looking at her fingers.

"Sam?" she said a little louder, wiping the stickiness off on her white linen napkin. She glanced at Sam. He was focused on the different types of bread in the silver bowl that had been placed on our table, finally picking a flour-dusted roll. He tore off a piece and put it in his mouth, chewing slowly. It was a skill, really, to be able to not react to your own name. I wished Elaine could have appreciated that.

Sam's mission is to have the same dining experience that anyone else would have. Makes sense. In New Orleans, where too many people had gotten to know him before he started reviewing restaurants, he saw it as an honest challenge. Since our move to Philadelphia, however, it is becoming an obsession for him, and it has started to affect our lives more than I ever expected.

Unlike Sam, when we first moved here, I was occasionally surprised to find myself being a little loose lipped. It seemed harmless with people who were unlikely to ever actually meet Sam. Sharing stories about review meals and Sam's sometimes-humorous attempts to remain unknown gave me something to talk about in a city where I barely knew anyone besides my husband and three-year-old daughter. At first I liked the way people's eyes lit up when I told them what my husband does.

But the last time I got my hair cut, my hairdresser barely said hello to me before he asked why Sam was so disappointed by a sushi bar that had opened around the corner from the salon.

"I was there last week," Scott said, whipping the scissors through the air. "It was terrific. Did Sam try the live scallop? Or the rainbow roll? They were terrific."

"I'm not sure," I said, waiting for a good time to tell him how I wanted him to cut my hair. "I—"

"Now that I think about it, Sam is pretty tough on Asian food," he said, almost to himself. "He didn't like that new Chinese place either—oh!" He nicked my ear with the scissors. "Sorry!"

"That's okay," I mumbled.

"But I did agree with him about that steak house," he said, brightening up. "The porterhouse was terrific."

I never did get to tell Scott that I wanted my hair a little shorter that time. When I left I was just happy I wasn't bleeding or bald. It was then that I decided I was probably better off following Sam's rules and pretending I'd never heard of him.

In New Orleans, where we had a regular, trusted babysitter, I used to join Sam on review meals once every few weeks. But since we've been here he hasn't wanted us to give him away to anyone, not even a babysitter, so I've spent a lot of time at home eating chicken korma delivered from a cheap Indian restaurant on Walnut Street while Sam enjoys the delicacies of the city. When my mom said she'd be here to catch a glimpse of her very pregnant daughter and to see her old friend Elaine, who was in town for her high school reunion, I begged Sam to let me ask Sunny, a new babysitter I'd found, to take care of Hazel. He reluctantly agreed, but I had to tell her he worked for a bank. She was already there when Sam got home from work. Sam had given me a concerned look, mumbling something about vaults and accounts before going upstairs to change.

"When is the baby due, dear?" Elaine asked me, taking a sip of her manhattan.

"Tomorrow," I said, not really wanting to talk about it.

"Tomorrow, and you're out to dinner with us tonight?" she said, her eyes lit up like the chandelier over our heads. "How nice! Eunice, I thought you said you had to be back in Rye tomorrow. What if that baby comes?"

"Oh, I doubt he'll come tomorrow," I said. "I don't feel any different."

"Well, you never know," Elaine said smugly. I couldn't help but notice how different Elaine was from my mother. I knew they were college roommates, but I wondered what held their friendship together for all these years. Then I thought about how different my best friend, Cece, and I must appear to people lately: Cece with her silk Parisian scarves always adorning her lovely neck, and me gearing up for another year of the burp cloth being my most frequently worn accessory. In fact, almost every single thing she is right now, I am not—working, always traveling, single, free.

Thinking about Cece made me miss her. So instead of talking about the baby, I tried to think of a way to steer the conversation away from me. I was afraid my mother was going to ask about a hotel project I sort of fibbed about, possibly giving her the impression that my work life had not come to a screeching halt. I didn't want to disappoint her, but I certainly didn't want Sam to wonder what I was up to.

My mother likes Sam enough, I know, but she has been so proud of my career I don't want to let her down by telling her the truth—that I am one hundred percent unemployed.

"So, Elaine, do you work?" I asked. I wanted to kick myself. What a stupid question; she'd probably turn it around on me. But then I looked at Sam, who was staring right into my mother's eyes and describing the yeasty holes of the bread into his gold cuff buttons, and I knew it didn't matter what I said. He was on another planet. My mother looked so bewildered.

"Oh, no, Lila," Elaine said. "I might not look it, but I am well beyond retirement age."

"Oh, well, what do you do with your time?" I asked.

"I see the grandchildren whenever I can. I have seven now. If I see each one of them during the course of a week, there goes my week! And I keep busy in other ways, too. I take an adult education program at the community college, and I go to the movies once a week with my friends. We have a standing date," she said.

"That reminds me," my mother said, and I held my breath. "Did Lila tell you about the relationship she formed between the local colleges in New Orleans and the Addison hotels in the area to teach students about hotel management?"

"Mom, I don't think Elaine cares about that," I said. Of all the things I've done, that is not the most interesting. But leave it to my mother to take any chance to show me off.

As my mother told the boring story, I tuned her out and wondered why she felt a need to bring up things I did years ago. She should take a cue from Elaine and spend more time with her granddaughter. But she has always been career focused. Well, at least since my father died. No matter where we are, I always think she would rather be offering guidance to the high school students she works with. I know that's why she was so excited about that long-ago education program I set up in New Orleans. Her rule to live by is that if you're engaged in a rewarding line of work and always reading one good book or another, you will generally be in a better mood.

I don't disagree with her. But what am I supposed to do? Leave Sam when I have a toddler and I'm nine months pregnant? Refuse to try to make his new job—his dream job—everything he wants it to be? In New Orleans, I was already established, and it was easy to find a great nanny and work part-time while Sam worked at the newspaper, covering local government and then, for what he considered those magical months, filling in for the restaurant critic there. But when we made the move he asked me—and he really did ask; it was only later that I wondered what would have happened if I'd refused—if I would lie low for a while and not get a job. He wanted me to keep my name out of the news. Basically, I think, he didn't really want me to talk to anyone. And it made me wonder: other than the obvious—that Hazel needed to be fed, kept clean, made reasonably happy—what would keep me going and in an acceptable mood at this point? I'm not even reading a good book.

Daily motivation is something that I never used to even think about. After college, I earned a master's degree in hotel management. I rose from doing publicity for a local hotel, to doing it for a large chain on a local level, to eventually heading publicity and crisis management for the entire chain. I spent seven years pretty much living out of a suitcase, planning big promotions and events, supervising hotel openings, and battling crises at hotels all over the world. I was never bored, never floundering. I loved working in front of a crowd, getting my name into the newspapers, appearing on local evening-news shows. I couldn't imagine what would ever happen to make me slow down. I glanced over at Sam, who was still muttering to himself. I took a deep breath.

"And Sam, will you take some time off when the baby comes?" Elaine asked, again putting an emphasis on the word *Sam*. I tried not to cringe.

As usual, my husband wasn't paying attention to us. He was focused on a plate of lamb chops that was being sent back to the kitchen from the next table.

"Sam?" she said even louder, before I had a chance to answer for him.

"Well, I know a lot of fathers are doing that these days." She took another swig of her manhattan, realized there wasn't much left, and finished it off. A small circle of waiters had formed off to our right. Elaine noticed them and signaled to the group.

"Yes, madam?" one of the waiters asked, hands behind his back.

"Another manhattan, please," Elaine said, handing him her empty glass.

"Of course," he said, taking the glass out of her hand.

Uh-oh. Did Sam just give her a dirty look?

"Excuse me," I said. "I'll be right back."

I was doing okay up to that point, even though I couldn't stand the silences when Sam didn't respond to Elaine. But suddenly I needed a break, because it was now pretty clear things were going even further downhill than I had realized.

I don't entirely blame him. Usually we order just wine, but he said Elaine and my mother could each order a cocktail tonight. He didn't say they could order two. The newspaper pays for all the meals, including beverages, but Sam is careful not to abuse that. He's rarely questioned about his expenses, but he gets annoyed when he thinks someone is taking advantage. Especially someone who keeps calling him Sam.

When I stood up, I forgot to leave room for my extra-large belly, and as I tried to wiggle out, I knocked a glass of what looked like champagne off of the table next to us. So much for being inconspicuous. The diner looked annoyed as three waiters from that same group rushed over to try to remedy the situation. I murmured an apology and got away as fast as I could.

After I peed, managed to pull my huge-but-now-too-small pants back on, and washed my hands, I sat on a fancy tan-and-black striped chair trying to relax. Then I caught a glimpse of myself in the mirrored wall. I counted to five slowly, waiting for the scare to send me into labor. When it didn't, I took a good look. It was definitely not the image that comes to my mind when I picture myself, which is still the working version of me: crisp clothes, tight bun, perfect makeup, one beautiful necklace or another. Now my belly was big enough to comfortably house the growing baby, my three-year-old, and our cat. I was wearing a huge lime-green blouse with ribbons straining to remain tied in the back. I had puffy eyes, a too-eager smile, hair that looked more like a little girl's than Hazel's does, a pale face with no makeup, and no jewelry. I quickly decided that the company at the table was probably better, at least better to look at.

The appetizers were there when I eased myself back into my seat, and the mood had not lightened. Elaine wouldn't share her baked clams.

"But I have to taste one," Sam said to Elaine. "It's my job."

"I can't have someone eating off my plate," Elaine said.

"I don't have to eat off your plate—just put one on my bread plate. I won't come near you," Sam said through gritted teeth.

Elaine picked up a spoon, used her napkin to wipe imaginary dirt off of it, and gave Sam half of the top of the baked clam. Then she took a big gulp of her new manhattan.

"This is a little sour, Tom," my mother said. Startled, I glanced at her and noticed her cheeks were flushed red. At first I thought she was trying to play along by calling Sam by a different name. Then I followed her gaze out the big windows overlooking Broad Street. It took me a moment to focus on the back of the figure crossing the street: tall, dark head, familiar uneven gait.

"I mean Tim, or Fred." My mother was trying to cover for her mistake, having called Sam by the name of my ex-boyfriend Tom. Sam didn't even notice. When I looked out the window again, the man had turned the corner. I sighed and tried to shake it off, turning my attention back to our dysfunctional dinner table.

"I'll get to your salad in a minute, Eunice," Sam said. It sounded like he was trying hard not to spit.

"No, but Fred, you don't understand; I can't eat it," my mother said with her full lips pursed, her cheeks no longer red.

"You don't have to eat it; you just had to order it," Sam said, surprising me with the sudden patience in his voice. Where did he find that? "There will be plenty of food for you."

I waited, but no one put anything in front of me. Despite the way the dinner was going, I was hungry.

"I don't have anything," I said, trying not to whine. Sam was having enough trouble. "Where's my tomato and bread salad?"

Sam likes to let the meals move forward without comment, witnessing all the mistakes that might happen to the average diner. He rarely sends food back to be cooked more, and he never complains if food is served cold. He simply takes notes.

Sam looked over at my empty place.

"Let's give it a minute," he said.

I pouted. I didn't want to give it a minute. I was nine months pregnant and very hungry.

Finally, when everyone else was almost finished with their appetizers, a waiter came over and noticed I had nothing. He glanced at me, then at my belly, and gave me a questioning look. What, did he think I ate the salad and swallowed the plate?

"Where is your food, madam?" he asked, like it was my fault.

"I never got it," I said.

"I am so very sorry," he said. "I will have it to you in a jiffy."

"These are very good," Elaine said of her clams after the waiter sprinted away.

"Yes, from what I could tell, they were," Sam said.

"So, Sam, Eunice was telling me a little about your work," she said. "But I haven't heard what else you do. I mean, this isn't your full-time job, is it?"

Sam and I looked at her, then at my mother. Sam went right back to his plates.

"No, Elaine, it *is* his full-time job," my mother said, clearly embarrassed. Maybe she had made some crack to Elaine about not understanding how someone could make an entire living out of critiquing restaurants—something she had uttered to me at various times during the last few years—and Elaine had misunderstood. My mother glanced over her shoulder to make sure nobody was listening. Then she lowered her voice. "I don't know what I could have said to make you think this isn't his only job. Remember I told you he works for the *Philadelphia Herald*? He works very hard."

My salad finally arrived. Obviously the waiter had forgotten to put in the order the first time around. It was delicious, full of moist chunks of crusty bread and juicy red tomatoes. It was perfectly dressed, and I enjoyed every bite. I laughed for the first time all night when Sam slowly took a piece of tomato, then bread, then tomato, and chewed with a studious look on his face, as if to show that he does, in fact, work hard. It was lost on my mother and Elaine.

But Sam disappeared again when our pastas arrived. He took small spoonfuls of the tomato sauce, sat back, then took another taste. Elaine fidgeted in front of her near-empty plate. It went on for a good three minutes. At this point we didn't even try to talk to him. I thought my mother and Elaine were finally getting used to it. We watched as Sam dipped bread in the sauce. He took a twirl of spaghetti. He scooped some sauce onto his finger. Finally, he looked at us.

"It's canned," he announced with the gravity of a NASA scientist announcing life on Mars.

"I don't think so," I said. "The menu said homemade. Wasn't there even a story about the sauce on the back of the menu? It's the chef's grandmother's recipe from Trieste."

"Trust me, Lila," Sam said, interrupting me. I could feel my face turn red. I glanced out the window again, looking for another glimpse of Tom or whoever he was, but there was nobody on the street.

"I've had this exact sauce before; I'm sure of it," Sam continued, softening a little.

"Okay," I said. I just wanted to stop talking about the stupid sauce.

Elaine looked at me, then at Sam, then back at me. I assumed she was judging our little quibble. But Elaine surprised me by overlooking our exchange. I thought the manhattans had finally loosened her up. She even dared to ask Sam another question.

"Did you major in food writing in college?" she asked. "If there is such a thing?"

"Forestry," I said quickly, expecting Sam to ignore her.

"Forestry?" she repeated, confused.

"It's a long story," Sam said. "But the long and the short of it is that I always loved food and cooking and writing. Forestry wasn't my choice. It was my father's. He has always been obsessed with the great outdoors. Some parents dream about their kids becoming doctors or lawyers. My father had other ideas."

"He wanted Sam to be a park ranger," I chimed in.

"Director of a national park," Sam corrected me, laughing. For the first time all night, he looked my mother and Elaine full in the face, offered a warm smile, and shrugged his right shoulder. For a few minutes we were normal people at a normal dinner having a normal conversation. Then the next course arrived.

I had the lamb shank with chanterelle mushrooms and peas, but I looked longingly at my mother's filet mignon wrapped in pancetta, with caramelized onions and crispy potatoes. Sam had the monkfish. I took bite after bite of his chive whipped potatoes while he concentrated on the other dishes. And Elaine had a lobster risotto that was just okay. When she didn't complain, I started to wonder if she had ordered a third manhattan without our knowledge.

I was sure of it when dessert arrived and Elaine willingly shared her crème brûlée with Sam.

"I haven't had this many carbohydrates in years," she said to my mother as Sam looked over the bill. "Come to think of it, I haven't had this much food at one meal in years."

Everyone always says something like that at the end of a review meal with us. The truth is, I never used to eat this much either. Lately, however, I always do, and tomorrow or in a few days or whenever this baby comes, I am going to have to stop.

We paid and were out the door. But Sam said he wasn't finished reporting yet.

"What do you mean?" I asked, eager to get home, eager to be rid of our company before my mother started to grill me about my phantom hotel project.

"I need you guys to cover for me," he said. "I think the Dumpster is down that alley; I'm going to check on the sauce."

"Sam, you can't do that—that's trespassing," I said as calmly as I could, trying to take some control. "There are probably rats back there!"

But the next thing I knew, he was squeezing down the alley to the back of the building, pulling me along. My mother and Elaine stood primly off to the side. Once he was in, I left him and walked over to them. The smell was overwhelming.

Now Sam's still rooting around in there. I'm too repulsed to talk. All I can think about is how he'll ever get clean enough to come into the house. All that garbage, all that raw meat, all that filth in his hair. I hope I don't catch anything from him that I can pass on to the baby. I turn and walk to the sidewalk and watch the cars speed by on Spruce Street, willing the familiar nausea away. That's all we need to end the perfect evening—my spewing chanterelles and whipped potatoes on the sidewalk.

A small calico cat scurries out of the alley. Sam probably surprised her at the Dumpster. She hesitates for a second when she sees us, and I notice how skinny she is. My mother gently shoos her away, and she runs off down the sidewalk. Poor kitty. I have an urge to go home and cuddle our kitty, A Streetcat Named Desire, whom we rescued from a similar fate in New Orleans. I sometimes secretly worry that I have stronger maternal feelings toward Desire than I do toward Hazel.

My mother, who until now seemed unable to move, joins me at the edge of the sidewalk. Elaine trails behind. My mother clears her throat.

"Are you feeling okay, Sweetie?" she asks, putting her arm around my lower back. It feels good.

"Yeah, I'm okay," I say. "Just a little tired, and Sam is a little stressed about work."

They both nod, accepting my explanation.

"Don't be mad at Sam," my mother says after we're quiet for a minute. "If they're lying about their sauce, it would be good if Sam proves it, especially because they make such a big deal about it with that story on the menu. They shouldn't be able to get away with that. People shouldn't lie."

"I guess," I say weakly, unable to shake the bad feeling that what I said to her about work was as good as lying.

Finally we see Sam shimmying back through the alley, picking something off of his sleeve, and carrying a huge bright-yellow can of Mama Donna's Homestyle Sauce that is leaving a trail of red behind him. It looks like blood.

Mama Donna's is a local brand. Good, but definitely mass produced. And definitely not the chef's grandmother's recipe from Trieste. To my surprise, my mother and Elaine walk quickly toward him.

"There were tons of them," Sam says, sweaty with excitement. The two older women cheer, and I try to suppress a smile. Sam has such a strange way with people.

"I think there are at least thirty," Sam continues, shooting the women an appreciative grin. He looks at me and I look away. He is not deterred. "There's no way they make their own. When I interview that chef, I'm going to ask him so many questions about the recipe that I'll get him to step into his own sauce. Does he think people are that stupid?"

"We were," I mumble to myself. But nobody hears me.

We begin the walk home. My mother wants Elaine to see our new block before they head to their hotel, the only indication tonight that she is proud of my life since I stopped working full-time. Even though we now have a three-story, four-bedroom row house, and plenty of room, my mother chooses not to stay with us. She got used to staying in hotels when she visited us in New Orleans and we were in our tiny shotgun on Burdette Street. Now I'm torn between being annoyed and the overriding feeling of being grateful. She promises that it's because she wants to extend her time with Elaine, and she'll stay with us next visit.

Elaine is asking Sam about our street, and he's answering every question. The restaurant and the meal are behind him; he is finally in the company of our guests. Plus, I think they bonded at the Dumpster.

"So it sounds very social," Elaine says, brushing something brown off of Sam's back.

"Thanks," he says. "Rumor has it that there's a knitting class, a babysitting cluster, a make-dinner-for-the-new-mother alliance, a reading association, a baked-good-of-the-month club, and I think a crafts corner," he tells her. I glance over just in time to see him wink at her. She actually giggles. I have to admit I like listening to him talk, and

I'm a little surprised by the fact that he paid attention to what people have said about our new neighborhood, and that he gets how ridiculous it is. It won't do me any good anyway, considering Sam barely wants me to tell our neighbors what our last name is, let alone hang out with them. It's a wonder he didn't suggest we buy a farm outside the city. Sometimes I think it wouldn't be so bad if Sam could just go to an office, obsess about banking or the law all day, and come home to us. But for some reason, this job seeps into so much of our lives. Maybe it's the food—the fact that we are literally ingesting his work.

"That's lovely," Elaine says. "It reminds me of the cul-de-sac outside of Cincinnati where I raised my family. I drew tremendous comfort from my neighbors."

In the end it might be better that Sam doesn't want to socialize with our new neighbors. I don't seem to have much in common with the other moms on Colonial Court. I feel sometimes like I moved not just to another city, but to another decade—the 1950s, maybe. And as far as comfort goes, claustrophobia seems more likely.

"Do you think your neighbors will bring you food when the baby is born?" my mother asks. I'm not sure why she cares.

"Well, someone brought us blueberry buckle the day we moved in," I tell them. "And another neighbor shares all of her baked goods with whoever will take them."

The sound Elaine makes is a little like purring; maybe she is remembering the old days in Cincinnati. I don't tell them how strange it felt to have The Blueberry Buckle Lady open our door and call in, then bring me a dish covered with a red-and-white striped linen towel. A cold wind gust catches us by surprise, and I stretch my coat to cover my bulging stomach. My mother cinches the belt on her royal-blue raincoat.

"It sounds like the kind of place you could live in forever," Elaine says with a sigh.

"I guess," I say.

"There must be lots of kids," she continues. "That will be great for Hazel."

"We're really still just getting to know everyone," I say.

"You have how many bedrooms?" she asks.

"Four," I say.

Elaine nods, calculating the possibilities, I think. I hold my breath, wondering if she is going to ask how many kids we want, but thankfully she doesn't. Already I know that it is a preferred topic of conversation on Colonial Court, so much so that I can't help but wonder if the women here have babies so they can add them to their collections. *Are you going to have any more?* is right up there with *Do you think you'll ever move to the suburbs?*, *How long will you breast-feed?*, and *Did you get your two-year-old into the right preschool?* It's nothing like the questions I used to face: *How can we recover from a hotel fire that caused three million dollars' worth of damage? How can we draw customers to an island that was recently in the news because of violent political uprisings? How do we keep a high-rise hotel running when two of the three elevators need to be replaced at the same time? How do you deal with reviews on TripAdvisor that inaccurately say your hotel has bedbugs?*

I usually had the right answers to the hotel questions. On Colonial Court, I worry that I am going to have the wrong answers. We've been here for almost two months—we spent our first four months in Philadelphia living in a big apartment building where it was easy to avoid most human contact. It seemed like we could go for days without talking to anybody but each other. The night before we moved onto Colonial Court, Sam reminded me about how important it is that we keep a low profile. He even mulled over the idea of using my maiden name and pretending that he did something else for a living. Luckily, I convinced him that in the end that was sure to draw more attention. Besides, chances are we would forget and slip up. So I don't have to lie; I just have to pretend I have plenty of friends and don't have time for any more, which of course is the biggest lie of all.

We turn onto Colonial Court and everyone stops. It is impossible not to notice the tiny white lights strung through all the trees, bright in the cool night air. The neighbors have a strange tradition of leaving the holiday lights up all year, adding, I think, to the residents' vision of Shangri-la. And even in the dark you can't miss the cheery flower boxes. Many are holding orange and yellow mums. Some have little scarecrows and wooden pumpkins stuck in the soil.

We knew this was a family-oriented block when we chose it. What we didn't know is that we were moving into sorority headquarters for stay-at-home moms. Every sunny day the street is full of children and mothers. They have it down to a science. One mother stands in the street while the others sit and talk. When a car turns onto the street, the standing mother walks toward the car with her hand up, crossing-guard style, while the others gather the children and the tricycles, balls, and sidewalk chalk and move everything off to the side.

There are bake sales and lemonade stands. Calendars are pushed through mail slots telling families when it is their turn to help an ailing neighbor. Topics are constantly being debated: Is it okay to walk the dog around the block while the baby is sleeping inside? Do olives and pickles count as vegetables? The mother who has a newborn—I forget her name—sits on her stoop and nurses the day away. She doesn't even pull down her shirt when the mailman walks by.

When Sam isn't around, I take Hazel outside and let her play. I haven't told the neighbors anything about us yet, and they seem content leaving the depth of our conversation to my pregnancy. I don't think they would be interested in what I have on my mind these days anyway. That sometimes when I wake up, my first thought is which hotel do I have to deal with today, and then I remember Hazel will need her Cheerios soon and will want me to find *Sesame Street* on TV. Or that when we were in New Orleans and our babysitter, Judy Beth, would show up around ten o'clock in the morning and take Hazel from me so I could go deal with one crisis or another—and in that city there was always something—I would feel like I had been let out of jail. Well, maybe not jail, more like house arrest.

The women have been welcoming enough; as far as they know I fit their profile. After all, I haven't worked since we moved to Philadelphia. But there is something about all these endlessly cheerful women reducing their world to one block that makes me a little uncomfortable. From what I can tell, they are doing exactly what they want to be doing. I haven't heard anybody mention checking e-mail, keeping up with the news, what they did before they had children, or going back to work. I don't know how they can stand it. I'm not sure I can.

My mother and Elaine finally get their fill of Colonial Court. I invite them in but, thankfully, they decline. They want to get back to the hotel. They don't want to miss the eleven o'clock news, and my mother has to get an early train back to Rye in the morning. Unless, of course, I go into labor before then.

"Next time I see you, Lila, we'll have a new baby," my mother says, barely able to get her arms all the way around me.

We wave as they head toward Nineteenth Street. I am so tired when we finally close the door behind us that everything I held in to talk to Sam about disappears from my mind. Sunny is waiting for us in the kitchen. She says Hazel was great and is fast asleep. Sam walks Sunny home, and as I head up the stairs, I hear the first bursts of a cry. Shit. I can't wait to stretch out in bed, and I have to finish my book. Sam doesn't know it yet, but I might go to the block's book group on Monday night. Now that I'm actually reading the book, though, I'm not so sure it's for me. The selection this month is *How My Breasts Saved the World*.

I stop and listen, hoping Hazel will quiet, but she only gets louder. She definitely knows something is brewing around here. We told her about the new baby a few months ago, and we try to mention him casually, hoping she will get used to the idea. But I think she's afraid she'll go to sleep one night and wake up to find that another baby has taken her place, and her world will be suddenly changed. I know just how she feels.

I push open her door and see her standing up in her crib, reaching for me. For a brief second I consider picking her up and taking her upstairs to our bed, but I know I shouldn't do that.

"It's late, Sweetie," I whisper. "Little girls should be sleeping. Put your head down."

She shakes her head again and stretches her arms out to me.

"No, Sweetie, it isn't playtime, it's sleep time," I say in what I think is a confident voice. Do I smell a poop? I sniff the air. I do smell poop. I flick on the light to change her diaper. That must be the problem. I sigh and pick her up, snuggling her as best I can with my big belly. I pull back her pajama bottoms and look down her diaper. No poop. Hmm. I flick off the light.

"Noooooooooooo," Hazel wails. "Keep that wight oooonnnn."

"No, Sweetie," I try to say gently, cursing myself for thinking I smelled poop with my overactive nose. It must have been a lingering smell from the Dumpster. "It's sleepy time. Daddy and I haven't even gone to sleep yet."

"Noooooooooooo," she cries, pointing to the light switch. "I is not sweepy."

"Yes you are," I say firmly, trying to force her squirming body back into her crib. She bangs her elbow on the wooden rail and wails even louder. I try again. This time she complies but continues to whimper.

"I'll sit here for a minute," I tell her, perching on the edge of the chair next to her bed.

But every time I try to get up, Hazel rouses herself out of what I'm sure is a deep sleep and cries. Finally, Sam pokes his head in.

"Is she okay?" he whispers. I can see he hasn't changed his clothes yet.

"Yeah, but she won't go back to sleep," I say.

Sam walks into the room, and Hazel sits up and makes giggling sounds. He reaches for her.

"Sam, you're pretty filthy," I say as gently as I can.

He looks down at his clothes and nods.

"You can stay sitting up, Sweetie," he says soothingly to Hazel. "Daddy will be right back."

"Kaykay," she says with complete trust.

Sam manages to shower and come back in a few minutes. As soon as Hazel sees him, she stands up and tries to get to him. He lifts her up and she melds into his body. He takes my place on the rocking chair.

"You go rest, Hon," he says. "I'll get her back to sleep."

"Okay," I say. "Thanks."

I hear Sam singing "You Are My Sunshine" as I close the door.

Once I'm in our bedroom, I immediately start to relax. This cozy room makes dealing with all this more bearable, I think. It is the perfect size, bigger then Hazel's room but not too big. I love the subtle yellow color we chose. As I twist the pole on the blinds, I look out our window and take in the zigzag lines of the Philadelphia skyline.

I climb into bed and open my book. How can breasts save the world? Can they fund the renovation of a beach resort? Will they keep a hotel afloat after two hundred guests contract food poisoning from the breakfast buffet? I don't think so. I decide not to go to the book group. I put the book down and I turn out my light. I'm starting to drift off when Sam comes in. By the time he climbs into bed, I have completely forgiven him for his craziness, and I'm glad to have him next to me.

"Hi," I say, turning to face him. He smells clean and he feels warm. "Is she asleep?"

"Yes," he says quietly into my ear. "Finally."

"Sam," I say.

"What?"

"I'm going to need some friends, you know. I can't not work and not have friends."

Sam pulls away from me a tiny bit and pushes himself up on his elbow. He looks tired.

"I know," he says. "But can we just take it slow? I mean, we have no idea if someone on this block owns a restaurant, or if someone's aunt or father does. You can say hello to people—just don't talk too much. Inevitably people are going to ask questions. Please, just until we know more about the neighbors. I'm only going to have this chance once."

"Not everyone out there is waiting to find out what you look like," I say, trying not to sound mad. "Most people probably don't care."

"I hope you're right," he says, lying back down, not the least bit put off by my slightly mean comment. Then he pushes back up onto his elbow.

"Look, let them talk, get a sense of them," he says seriously. "If you come across someone who never eats out and never reads the paper, then I'd be comfortable if you got to know that person better."

I turn onto my other side, away from Sam. He scoots close and hugs me from behind and rubs my stomach. It takes me a while to relax. The stomach rubbing helps. I am finally drifting off for the second time tonight when I am roused by the other man in my life—the one growing inside me. He flips and swims and makes me feel like he is going to turn me inside out. I open my eyes, settle myself deeper into the mattress. I can hear Sam's breathing slow, and I'm surprised when I feel my eyes get heavy again. Maybe I will get some sleep tonight. I fall into a deep, comfortable slumber. For twenty minutes. That's when I am startled by Sam's voice.

"From a can, it's from a can," I hear him mumble loudly in his sleep. "Not fresh. Dumpster. Can."

I roll over, annoyed at how many times my sleep has been interrupted in less than an hour. *Interrupted sleep,* I say slowly in my head, *interrupted sleep.* I want the rhythm of it to lull me back to my drowsy state. *Interrupted sleep,* I say again, knowing it won't work. I give up. I'm not getting sleepy; I'm getting angry again. Interrupted sleep, huh? I feel like I'm living an interrupted life.

CHAPTER TWO

Transitions are never easy, and that has been the case since Joseph Breen took over the once-golden oven at La Noix. The classics still shine. My wife's Dover sole was as good as ever, as was the rack of lamb. But Breen's contemporary dishes suit La Noix poorly, like an old maestro trying to shed his classic tweed for a Hawaiian shirt. For the record, I'm not yet taking this one-time culinary gem off my map. Breen is new, and everyone deserves a little time to settle in.

—Sam Soto

I pull the huge orange fleece top over my head, then try to stretch it to fit my nine-days-overdue pregnant belly. I tie the pumpkin stem hat to my head, but think better of it and stuff it into my coat pocket.

At least Hazel looks adorable. It took only three costume changes and two tantrums to turn her into the cutest witch in the history of the world. She is wearing a black gauzy dress with a bright-orange velvet sash, black tights, and a big black witch's hat. She is carrying a miniature broom.

"Can I see?" she screeches for the fifteenth time, twisting away from me as I retie her sash.

"Yes," I say finally. And I watch as my three-year-old enchantress wiggles and jumps to catch a glimpse of herself in the mirror in our living room. Her huge brown Mallomar eyes widen with delight.

It is a few days before Halloween, and we are going to a costume party given by Hazel's friend at a hotel on Market Street. Really, it is being given by my friend who happens to have a child whom Hazel likes. Maureen has been the one thing keeping me sane during these last months. I knew Maureen in graduate school, but we had lost touch.

Hazel and I first ran into her and her daughter, Pamela, at the playground last summer. Maureen was about eight months pregnant; I was almost four months pregnant, and at first we had smiled at each other in sympathy for what the other one was going through. Then I looked at her again. We had been in school together. In fact, we had worked on a project together, something silly about making banquet halls festive.

"Hey," I said, so happy to see a familiar face. "I know you."

She looked at me, and for a split second I thought I had made a mistake.

"Flowers, balloons, keep the music loud, what else?" she asked, naming the list we presented to the class. I laughed, easing Hazel off the slide and walking over to the swings where she was pushing her daughter.

"I think we said a lot of chocolate desserts," I said, holding Hazel's twisting hand. She managed to pull away before I could stop her, walked in front of the swing Maureen was pushing, and got a kick in the head that knocked her off her feet. Maureen immediately grabbed her daughter to stop the motion. I ran to Hazel, who was stunned and not crying. I didn't know what to do and felt embarrassed by my negligence. But then Hazel started to cry, and Maureen found a grape lollipop in her purse. A few minutes later, our girls, who it turned out were exactly the same age, ran off giggling.

"She's fine," Maureen assured me, gesturing for me to take a seat next to her on a bench. "One time Pamela fell off that twisty slide and was knocked out for a few minutes. It was so scary."

"Did you call an ambulance?" I asked, relaxing a little.

"No, but I called the doctor," she said, digging into her diaper bag and pulling out a brown bag. She lifted a delicious-looking sandwich into the air, unwrapped it, and offered me half. I took it. It was turkey with olive salad. It smelled like New Orleans. "She was fine. But that whole night I was supposed to keep waking her up to make sure she didn't fall into a coma. I only woke her up once. I was too tired."

"Well, I'm glad she was okay," I said, happy to hear that Maureen didn't do every mother-related thing by the book either. I held up the sandwich. "This is great. Where did you get it?"

"My husband and I own a restaurant in town, Remoulade? It's New Orleans–style food, with a Cajun twist," she said like she was quoting an advertisement. I nodded, but my heart sank. "If I'm walking by I usually pick up some food."

"Where did you meet him? Your husband?" I asked, because I couldn't think of anything else to say. It was hard to think with Sam's voice in my head yelling, *run!*

"Do you remember that little Greek place near campus?" she asked. "I worked there after graduation, and Mike was the manager. For a while I thought I might get into managing a restaurant chain or something. But we got married; I finally got pregnant. We decided to move to Philadelphia to be closer to family. It looks like this is as close as I'm gonna get to that old crazy dream. What's your story?"

I took a bite to stall for time. The sandwich didn't taste as good as it did at first.

"Mommy, Mommy, can her come over?" Hazel yelled to me from the slide, furiously pointing at Pamela, just as I was about to get up and excuse myself.

"Maybe," I said to Hazel, settling back down. Then I said to Maureen, "I haven't worked since we moved to Philadelphia. But I did end up in hotel management, for the Addison Hotel chain." She nodded.

"Now I'm married to Sam Soto, the new restaurant critic for the *Herald*."

There. I said it. And I was not struck by lightning. Still, I was immediately sorry. What had come over me? Maybe it was being with a familiar person after feeling so alone for so long. Maybe it was my own personal game of cat and mouse—I couldn't stand to hide under the oven for one more minute.

Her hand flew to her neck, and I worried she might be choking, but she cleared her throat and smiled.

"The mysterious Mr. Food?" she asked like she just hit the lottery. "So that means my old classmate is Mrs. Food? It must be our lucky day!"

"Can her, can her?" Hazel yelled again. "Her nice. She wikes princesses, too."

"Not today," I said sternly, remembering that the first week we were here the gossip columnist for the competing newspaper wrote an item about the new critic, referring to him as the mysterious Mr. Food. Maybe that's where Sam's paranoia began.

"It was nice running into you," I said more gently, holding my hand out to Maureen and standing up. "But it probably isn't such a great idea to hang out too much. My husband is big into avoiding any and all people connected to restaurants. Actually, recently he is big into avoiding all people."

And that second, as if on cue, Hazel threw up.

"I'll get a cab," Maureen said. "Maybe that kick was worse than we thought."

Maureen had Mike come and get Pamela at the hospital. Sam was somewhere in the Delaware Valley trying to find the region's best cheesesteak. We spent three hours in the emergency room, and Maureen never once mentioned Sam or Remoulade or food again. The doctor thought Hazel was okay but gave me the same instructions Maureen had been given when Pamela fell. It was an awful night. Sam felt so bad about being out of touch he insisted on being the one to wake Hazel again and again. But I couldn't sleep anyway. The next day Maureen called. It already seemed like she had become my friend again.

"Keep it to the playground," Sam said sternly when I told him the whole story. "I'm going to have to review their place, and I don't want anyone to question whether or not they're getting preferential treatment because the kids happen to be playmates."

But Maureen was so familiar, and so different from the other women I'd encountered here that I had a hard time resisting her. Soon we were meeting regularly at the playground, or on rainy days at the Please Touch Museum. Then there was the time I rounded the southeast corner of Rittenhouse Square with Sam, and he and Maureen's husband almost walked into each other.

"This is Mike," Maureen said, glad, I know, to have them finally meet.

For a second it flashed through my mind that we could ignore them, or that I could introduce Sam by another name, but that all seemed so ridiculous. She was my friend for heaven's sake!

"And this is Sam," I said, trying to keep my voice steady.

Mike stuck out his hand eagerly. Sam took it but barely met his gaze, and then he kept walking.

"Now you've blown my entire cover, Lila," he hissed as soon as we were out of earshot. "What makes you think he isn't going to tell the restaurant community what I look like?"

"Because they're my friends," I said. "I knew Maureen before. We have a history."

"Be careful," he warned. We were, for a while. But just like last time, the sharpness of Sam's warnings faded with time. When Hazel and I got the invitation to the pre-Halloween party, I didn't think there was any chance we would go, the party being held so far after my due date. But I called Maureen and said we would try. At the time she said to bring the baby. I wish. After nine days of waiting, I had decided that all rules were off. Plus, it was the least I could do for Hazel. She loves Halloween, she loves Pamela, and we are desperately trying to pass the time until baby number two makes his entrance. I argued to Sam that at least it wasn't at the restaurant, or at their house, two of Sam's biggest no-nos.

"Just go," Sam finally said after much debate. "But don't say who you are. Try not to talk to anyone. And wear a really good costume so nobody can get a clear look at you—maybe one with a mask that covers your whole face."

"Okay," I said. I had promised him that Maureen agreed to introduce me by another name. "And I'll tell them Hazel's name is Harriet. No, I'll tell everyone she's a boy in a witch's costume. Better yet, I'll pretend I'm mute. Then I won't have to tell anyone anything."

"That's a great idea," he said. I think he was serious.

So now we are off to a private room in the Loews Hotel. Hazel skips a little as we turn up Eighteenth Street and head toward Walnut Street. On Walnut, we pass La Noix, one of the most elegant restaurants in the city. It is the second restaurant Sam reviewed here, and he gave it his highest rating—fours swans.

The *Philadelphia Herald* has the unusual system of rating restaurants with swans instead of stars. Legend has it that a former critic once dined at a restaurant where they served sorbet on ice swans between courses. He said that was the most elegant meal he ever enjoyed and forever after associated swans with fine dining. When Sam took over, he wanted to change the icon. He considered napkins folded like fans, spoons or forks, or Ben Franklin's kite, but he has since come to accept the quirkiness of the swans.

La Noix serves classic French food, the waiters wear tuxedos, plates are brought to the table under silver domes. The room is beautiful, with gilded walls, marble floors, canary-yellow tablecloths, amazing fresh-flower arrangements, and sterling silver salt and pepper shakers shaped like walnuts on every table. I peek inside. Sam and I will be dining again at La Noix tonight. It is strictly business, of course. But Sam is often able to find an excuse to go to a great restaurant on many of our important evenings: birthdays, anniversaries, visits from out-of-town friends. Tonight the official reason is a new chef. It also has to be the last Saturday night before we become parents of two; I cannot stand to be pregnant for any longer.

I'm looking forward to this meal. Not only am I already planning what I will order—I have decided on three of the seven courses—but I highly suspect that they know who Sam is here after his many visits for his review. If anybody was going to bother to find out what he looks like—maybe through a chef or restaurant owner friend in New Orleans—it would be someone at this place. Sam is in denial about that, but I have a feeling I'm right. I hope so anyway. It guarantees better service, which I, for one, can't help but like.

"Come oooooooon!" Hazel whines, dragging me away from the window. I have caught sight of the dessert cart. I quickly step closer to the window and cup one hand around my face to see if their famous walnut sour cream coffee cake is there. I'm not sure. I'll know soon enough.

"Sorry, Sweetie," I say. "Let's go."

As I turn around to face the street, I have the sense that someone is standing too close to me.

"Sorry," I mutter, trying to get around him with my huge belly.

"Lila?"

I look up into my boss's face, former boss I should say, at least for now. I take a step back and almost stumble but catch myself. Then I look frantically around for Hazel, who has let go of my hand. It takes me a few seconds to locate her behind me. By the time I turn to face Ed again, I can barely breathe and I'm sure I'm sweating. But I put on a really big smile.

"Hi!" I say.

"You look great," he says, his voice deep and familiar. Hearing it makes me long for my professional days and my suitcase, when I was always on my way to successfully solving one catastrophe or another.

I look down and laugh. Sure, I look great, a nine-and-a-half-months-pregnant squash. It flashes through my mind that he must be really glad I'm not representing the company right now.

"Well," I say, standing up straight. "I have a three-year-old and I'm pregnant."

Ed laughs. "Yeah, I know," he says warmly. Of course he knows. It would be hard to miss.

Hazel grabs my hands and pulls me with more strength than I thought she had. I pull back, holding eye contact with Ed.

"We'll go in a second, Sweetie," I say to Hazel, using my best managerial voice.

"Noooooooooooooo," Hazel wails, looking more like a witch than I meant for her to. "Nowwwwww." She tugs on the back of my pumpkin top, making me feel even bigger and more deformed.

"We better get going," I say, still trying to restrain Hazel. "She's excited about a costume party we're going to."

"Who wouldn't be excited about that?" Ed says. Then he turns to Hazel. "Hey there, Sweetie, you look really scary. I think people are going to love your costume at the party. I think you'll get extra candy."

To my total surprise, Hazel straightens up a bit and smiles. I smile at Ed.

"I cannot believe I ran into you," Ed says, turning back to face me. "You've been on my mind a lot lately. I mean, the last few months we've lost a few good people, and nobody thinks on her feet the way you do. I can't tell you how often we sit around saying, 'What would Lila do now?' I know this isn't a good time, with the baby about to be born, but maybe, at some point, we could talk about your coming back. We could really use you."

I am completely taken off guard, and for a brief second I wish Hazel would try to escape again so I won't have to answer his question. But she is mesmerized by him. Maybe she thinks he is going to give her some candy.

"Well, the baby will be here any day," I say.

"No, hey, I know that," Ed says soothingly. "I'm not talking about tomorrow."

I laugh. "That's good, because I think if you were, *I* would be your crisis," I say easily, falling back into our familiar banter. It feels good. "What are you doing here, by the way?"

"We're about to sign a contract to develop five more Addison hotels in the Philadelphia area," he says, smiling. "I'm here scouting locations."

"Wow, I had no idea," I say, trying to keep my mind from thinking too much. We're quiet for a minute.

Ed points to my pumpkin belly. "So, any day now?" he asks.

"Yeah, actually, he was supposed to be here more than a week ago," I say.

"Well, that's the thing about babies—they do their own thing," he says. "I know it's hard to plan around them. But eventually they get a little older and you can get back to a more normal life," he says, adding a tiny question mark to the end of the word *life*.

Just then Hazel twists her hand out of mine and runs straight for busy Walnut Street. I lunge toward her, grabbing the back of her black dress.

"Not so fast, wicked witch," I say, getting to her just in time. I look at Ed and raise my eyebrows. "You were saying?"

Ed shakes his head and we both start to laugh. I can't stop, wiping my eyes and pulling Hazel close. I pick her up and boost her onto my hip, around my huge belly. I laugh into her ear, just under her witch's hat. She looks from Ed to me. Moving away from the curb, I lean over and give him a quick hug.

"We have to get going," I say, still laughing, but brutally aware that I am starting to fall under his spell.

"Take care, Lila," Ed says, chuckling. "Good luck with the baby. She's beautiful, by the way. She looks just like you."

"Thanks, Ed," I say, smiling because most people think Hazel looks like Sam. The baby kicks hard, and I try to put Hazel down, but she clings to my neck, pulling my hair. When she finally stops resisting, she stands on the sidewalk pouting. She looks just like Sam.

"I'm not letting you off the hook, Lila," Ed says. "I'll give you some time, and then I'm going to get on your case. See what we can work out. You are too good to be away for too long. People have kids and come back to work; you did it. Every day people do that."

I take Hazel's hand, wondering for a minute if I would be a better mother if I worked. When I agreed to this plan, I convinced myself that I would be a better mother if I stayed home. I'm not sure whom I was fooling. Obviously, if I went back again, I'd have less time with Hazel, but I'd probably be nicer. I know I was in New Orleans.

"Okay, Ed. I promise I'll think about it," I say.

"Good, that's all I can ask," he says. "I'll call you soon."

"It was great to see you," I say, finally letting Hazel pull me down Walnut Street. I turn once to wave at Ed, but his back is to me and he is already talking on his cell phone. The baby kicks and kicks. It must be the adrenaline.

We walk a few more blocks and cross Broad Street, and my breathing gets back to normal. I squeeze Hazel's hand as I guide her into the lobby of the hotel. I try to distract myself from thinking about my conversation with Ed, trying not to give in to the familiar hotel smell, as we ride up an escalator and find the private room where the party is already in full swing.

As we open the door, we are greeted by Buzz Lightyear and Winnie the Pooh. Hazel looks from one character to the other and back again before Pooh takes her hand and leads her inside. I follow, silently cursing myself for wearing this costume. I leave the pumpkin stem hat in my pocket.

Inside the party room things are even more exciting, with decorations everywhere and life-size characters of Woody from *Toy Story*, Mickey Mouse, Tigger, Piglet, Dora the Explorer, and Blue from *Blue's Clues* milling around and dancing with the young guests. Disney must have become friendly with Nick Jr. because I can see Dora and Woody over by the bar together.

There is a cupcake-decorating table, a cookie-decorating table, a make-your-own Halloween necklace table with green and orange dried macaroni, and a crown-making table. It's over the top. But at the same time, I can't help thinking, not terribly well run. The events manager who still lives inside me thinks there should be someone directing people to the stations. Right now everyone is holding back, not sure what to do. I guess every function can't be perfect, especially if I'm not running the show.

Hazel comes back to hug my legs, banging her face into the bottom of my pumpkin, before running off to hug Pamela. I spot a wooden chair in the corner, but before I can reach it, a waiter appears out of nowhere and places an easy chair behind me. I smile but can't help noticing that it's the only soft chair around. I try to convince myself that it is because I'm so huge, and not because I'm Mrs. Food and Remoulade is up for review soon. I plop myself down. I see Maureen and wave until she sees me. She waves back and laughs as she points to my costume. Her black hair is perfectly straight and falls down her back out of a red cowgirl's hat. One of her bright-blue eyes is covered by a black pirate's patch. I try to figure out who she is supposed to be.

She puts up her finger to say she'll be over in a minute. I begin to relax and look around: I am surrounded by other little witches, firemen, princesses, Spidermen, cats, bears, and what seems to be an unusually large number of pregnant women. None have been offered comfy chairs. And none are in costume. In fact, at varying stages of pregnancy, most of them look pretty great in maternity dresses or overalls. What was I thinking? I slump lower in my seat, but it's hard to blend in when you're a bright-orange beach ball sitting in the only oversize chair in the room.

Maureen comes over holding five-month-old Brendan, who is red-faced and crying. He's dressed as Little Bear, and he looks miserable. I push myself out of the chair.

"I think he's sick again," she says. "I called the doctor but he didn't call back and there was nothing I could do because I had to get ready for the party." She always talks without punctuation when she's stressed or excited.

"Oh no," I say. "What's wrong?"

"I don't know maybe his ears," she says quickly. Before I have a chance to say anything, she is off to say hi to someone else. As she turns, I can see Brendan's cheeks are bright red and his eyes are glassy. He must have a fever. Maureen isn't letting it slow her down, and as she whisks him away, I feel the familiar relief I always do when Maureen shows me that I'm not the only one whose seemingly well-laid plans are thwarted by a child. Brendan puts his head on his oblivious mother's shoulder while she greets the manager of La Noix and her kids.

Just don't talk to any people. Sam's departing words ring in my ears as I watch them. I'm tempted to walk over and tell the manager of La Noix that we will be having dinner at her restaurant tonight, or loudly introduce myself to someone standing close to her, just to see what happens.

Instead of doing something I know I shouldn't, I look for Hazel. She is dancing in a circle of girls, moving her body to the music in her certain way—head out and then in, hips around, then a foot tap. She is tall for her age, so she stands just above everyone else. Her wavy cinnamon-colored hair is billowy under her witch's hat. She doesn't need me right now, and I don't know what to do with myself. I sit down again and fold my hands over my orange belly.

Later that night Sam and I enter the quiet elegance of La Noix. Hazel is exhausted, and at home with Sunny. I am wearing a jet-black velvet potato sack with a loosely tied satin bow—perfect to eat in. I feel good in it and stand tall as we walk to the table. At this point I don't really mind looking huge when I'm pregnant. It's *after* that isn't so good. But I will not think about that now. Tonight I have a feast ahead of me, and I am not going to ruin it with any thoughts of future weight loss.

We are unenthusiastically greeted at the front door, but, as I imagined would happen, somebody recognizes us, or rather Sam, as we walk through the crowded room. There is a sudden flurry of activity as a waiter rushes to the manager, who then rushes to the man who is leading us to our table.

"Pardon me," the manager says, and whispers to our guide.

Our destination changes as we are suddenly whirled around and seated at one of the best tables in the center of the room. We get the extra-big chairs and the extra-colorful flower arrangement, not to mention the best view of the roaring fireplace. I smile. Sam shakes his head and looks down.

"I cannot believe that," he says under his breath, once we are seated. "Do you think they know who I am?"

"No, it's a nice place. They want everyone to have a good time," I say, worried that Sam will decide we can't eat here after all.

Napkins are shaken, then spread, bread and butter are brought, menus are presented.

"A soda for you, madame?" asks a man out of nowhere.

"Yes, please. A Sprite," I answer. In a minute it is at our table with a straw. I figured they recognized Sam the last time we were here after I ordered a Sprite. It was brought to our table without a straw, and I asked for one. I saw a waiter run across the street to the Wawa to buy a box. I didn't tell Sam.

"How did they know you wanted a soda?" Sam demands quietly.

"I'm pregnant—it was a good guess," I say. Sam nods.

I pick up my silver butter knife and spread soft, sweet butter over a freshly baked olive roll. I take a bite and make a mental note to start buying unsalted butter. Then we get down to business. It's a long menu with many courses, so agreeing about what to order might take a while. On nights like this Sam begins by saying I can get whatever I want, and then he dislikes my choices. He wants to taste as much as he can, and because there is a new chef in the kitchen, he wants to try some of the new dishes. I understand that, but I still want what I want.

"How about the crab cake to begin?" I ask hopefully.

"I've had that before," says Sam. "How about the root vegetable soup with wheat berries. That's new and it sounds interesting."

I think for a minute.

"I'll get that soup as long as I can have the Dover sole," I say.

"Okay, and then why don't you try the lamb," he says slowly, his eyes still on the menu. "Medium rare."

"Fine," I say. "But I hope it isn't too rare."

Then we'll have salad, cheese, sorbets, and the dessert cart. We close our menus, and our waiter, who has been standing just off to the side, notices and rushes over as if our table is on fire and he needs to put it out. We order, and then we both sit back at the same time with a sigh. I look around and recognize many of the waiters from previous visits. One I don't recognize is heading toward us. He is handsome with broad shoulders, dark hair, and warm eyes. He smiles brightly at us. His teeth are very white. When he gets closer, I notice a small gap between his top front teeth.

"Someone in the kitchen told me you were here," he says nervously to Sam, but looks at me, too. I can feel Sam tense up—maybe I should have been more honest with him so he wouldn't be so taken off guard.

"Is it true?" the waiter asks. "Are you Sam Soto?"

Sam is silent. He just stares at the poor man.

"Never heard of him," Sam says finally.

The waiter looks confused. He starts to talk, stops, starts again.

"I thought," he says, fingering something in his pocket. "I mean, they told me. Well, it's nice to meet you whoever you are." He turns and walks quickly away.

"That wasn't good," Sam says. "How could they possibly have figured out I'm here? Do you think I threw him off?"

"Maybe," I say. "But don't forget you've been here a lot recently. That probably drew some attention. I don't know, maybe someone knows someone in New Orleans. I wouldn't worry too much. It isn't in their interest to tell anyone else what you look like. If they want to remain the best restaurant in the city, they probably won't want to give other places an advantage. Don't you think?"

Sam just shrugs, furrowing his bushy eyebrows, and I know he's trying to figure out where he went wrong.

"You shouldn't have done that, by the way," I say. "You made him feel bad. You should have pretended to be flattered, or said people often make that mistake."

Sam shrugs again.

"Now I really have to step up my game," he mumbles under his breath.

Great. I was hoping that being recognized would make him give up a little and even relax, at least a tiny bit. Now I think it is going to do the opposite. Before I have a chance to dwell on it, the first course arrives. We are quickly lost in our food, devouring everything we ordered and some things we did not.

"Compliments of the chef," we are told when, to my great pleasure, a crab cake course is added to our long meal. I wonder if someone heard us talking earlier. It happens again when linguine with white-truffle cream sauce is placed in front of us—this dish wasn't even on the menu. We also observe other diners receiving complimentary dishes, which makes Sam feel a little better, but I don't buy it. Every time they give something to another table, they make sure we can see it. It's good luck for the people sitting near us.

As it turns out, I enjoy everything more than Sam does. At first he dives in expecting the food to be as delicious as usual, but he ends up mumbling into his sleeve that the place is going downhill.

It is the confused waiter who offers dessert from the multilevel cart. By now I'm sure he knows that it is indeed Sam. I'm not sure if he feels stupid or mad or both, but after the initial awkward moment, he is nothing but professional as he goes over the delicacies. From a selection of about forty desserts, I choose only seven. That's not so bad. And they do have my favorite walnut sour cream coffee cake. We have learned that the waiter's name is Sebastian, and I'm glad to see him again. He is more focused on pleasing me than Sam, but I think that is because he's decided that my husband is a psychopath.

"I'll have the fruit tart, the mini crème brûlée, the chocolate tart, the pecan cheesecake, the banana cream tart, the opera cake, and the almond torte," I say.

"What about the coffee cake?" Sam prompts. I've been talking about it for days.

"Oh yeah," I say, trying not to bounce with excitement. "And may I please have a piece of the walnut sour cream cake."

"Of course, madame," says Sebastian, who smiles at me and cuts an extra-large slice. I guess I bounced a little.

Sam chooses only three desserts. He went crazy with the cheese course, which he prefers to the sweets. When Sam gets up to go to the bathroom, Sebastian comes over and refolds Sam's napkin.

"Sorry about what happened earlier," I say, even though I know Sam would just want me to leave it alone.

"He's a little strange," Sebastian says.

"Well," I say, feeling defensive and agreeing with him at the same time. He's a little strange himself. Who would dare call the restaurant critic strange to his own wife? But the truth is, it makes me like him even more. "Paranoid is more like it."

Sebastian smiles and walks away.

As we leave the restaurant, there is a doggy bag waiting for us—if you can call it that at a place like this. It is the shape of a small shopping bag but made out of a shimmering gold material. The handles are braided gold string. We ate everything, so we didn't ask to pack anything to go. I take it and thank the hostess. It is very heavy. When we get into the cab, I peek inside. It is an entire walnut sour cream coffee cake.

"Shit," says Sam. "This is getting out of hand."

I hold my breath for one minute, hoping he doesn't instruct the cabdriver to turn around and head back to the restaurant to return it.

Then Sam leans over and kisses my cheek. He smells like cheese and wine and Johnson's baby shampoo.

"You should get something good for putting up with me," he whispers into my ear. "Enjoy it."

I smile, pull the bag up onto my lap, and look forward to my midnight snack.

CHAPTER THREE

Inside the gumbo pot is an epic brew, steeping two centuries of culinary talent into an ever-evolving art, drawing inspiration from African-Creole cooks, Choctaw Indians, and settlers of Caribbean, French, Spanish, and German descent. The amazing complexity of its permutations is a soup-bowl homage to the talent of all Louisianans who have discovered spontaneity within the confines of tradition.

—Sam Soto

A few days after our dinner at La Noix, I am still very pregnant. And, as it has been every morning for the last two weeks, my first thought is, *Today has to be the day.* I know we can't wait much longer. Hazel was late, but not this late.

I hear Sam singing downstairs, improvising a Barney song while he gives Hazel breakfast. The words sound staticky as they are picked up on the monitor in Hazel's room and find their way to me.

I hear Hazel laughing. "Again, Daddy," she squeals.

So much has changed since Sam first sang to me in his shotgun house on Burdette Street in New Orleans. It was the first time I had made the trip from New York for the sole purpose of seeing Sam, just a month after our first meeting. It was just four months after I said good-bye to Tom, my boyfriend of two years.

The city had forgotten Mardi Gras and was already looking ahead to Jazz Fest. But Sam hadn't forgotten. In his tiny living room there were beads and masks all around, just like the week we met when the city was crazy with anticipation. Moments after we entered the house, he told me to sit and went directly to his kitchen. I heard him moving around, saw him run a lemon twist over the top of a glass, watched him shake a cocktail. He brought me an amber-colored drink, whispered, "Sazerac," as he handed it to me, and went to the piano and started singing "Mardi Gras Mambo."

"To put you in the mood," he called over his shoulder. That song had been playing everywhere we went during our first few days together. It was what we first kissed to. His singing was so corny I could barely stand it. Tom never sang to me, not once. I looked around to make sure no one could see me. But we were alone. Sam was the opposite of self-conscious then.

Sam didn't stop singing. He sang every Mardi Gras and Louisiana-themed song he could think of, including "You Are My Sunshine." And I finally relaxed; the Sazerac helped, of course. I sat back on his old purple couch and listened to his voice. And I realized, as he sang to me, that he was sparing us the potential awkwardness of reacquainting. We didn't have to talk; we didn't have to think about sex right away. We became comfortable with each other while he sang. And by the time he was finished, it was like we had always been together.

Suddenly I want to be at the breakfast table with my family. Plus, I still have a few slices of the walnut sour cream coffee cake downstairs waiting to be my breakfast.

I toss off the comforter and push my heavy body out of bed, remembering that I have to go see Dr. Berri this morning. I know we are going to have to make some sort of decision. He can't keep telling me to come back in a few days. I don't actually mind having to see him. I love Dr. Berri. It was luck that I found him. We were still in New Orleans when I learned I was pregnant for the second time. I figured it wouldn't make too much of a difference in my daily life. I imagined our babysitter, Judy Beth, would rejoin our routine as soon as I was ready, when the baby was six weeks old or so. And I imagined that having two might step up my ability to deal. At work I always did better under real pressure.

About ten months before I found out I was pregnant again, Sam had switched from being a government reporter at the *Times-Picayune* to the restaurant critic while the usual guy took a sabbatical to write a book. It was his dream come true. When the guy returned, Sam couldn't stand the idea of going back to covering the levee board. He did a countrywide search and found the job in Philadelphia. The night he told me was the night I told him I was pregnant again.

I was less than thrilled. New Orleans was vibrant and exciting. I had managed to make motherhood fit into my work life. But Philadelphia? I knew people came from all over the world to see the Liberty Bell, but how could a rusted bit of history compete with crawfish and zydeco music? Would I be able to find an arrangement that worked for all of us? And then Sam told me about his hope that I might not work when we first moved so I wouldn't be so visible. He asked that I please consider that possibility.

I was in my first trimester. I could barely walk from the living room to the kitchen without resting. The thought of finding a new job and a new babysitter was daunting. Maybe at first his request was a relief, an excuse.

When we got here, finding a new doctor seemed almost as tiring as finding a new babysitter or a new job. One day I randomly asked an obviously pregnant woman who her doctor was, and I called to make an appointment. Little did I know then that she gave me the name of the most popular ob-gyn in the city. I learned that quickly after we moved into our house. Going to Dr. Berri might be the only thing I have in common with my Colonial Court neighbors. They all go to him.

"Dr. Berri would never let that happen," the mother with the long brown ponytail said recently, after hearing the horrors of a labor gone wrong. "He's the best." They had all nodded in unison, like they were brainwashed or something.

This morning Sam offers to stay with Hazel, but I'm feeling emotional and I want her with me. After a long breakfast of coffee cake and chocolate chip pancakes—my second-favorite treat—Hazel and I get in a cab and head to Eighth and Spruce. Sam, who claims he will be taking a paternity break from his official meals, says he has to have lunch at a new Italian place. It isn't until we are getting out of our cab that I wish I'd made him come with us.

"It's hard to wait, Mommy," Hazel says, swinging her legs on the too-big chair in the windowless waiting room.

"I know, Sweetie, but it shouldn't be too much longer," I say, getting so nervous about what my fate will be that I'm having trouble projecting the calmness that Hazel needs. Maybe it wasn't such a good idea to bring her along.

"Is it my doctor?" she asks.

"No, Sweetie, it's my doctor," I say.

"Oh," she says in her tiny voice. "Good."

Thankfully my name is called, and we are ushered into an examination room. I know I'll need an internal exam, but I figure if I don't make a big deal about it, Hazel won't even notice. The problem is, I'm starting to have trouble breathing. If I'm still not dilated at all, which I wasn't as of a few days ago, and my cervix hasn't started to soften, I know there will be no choice but to have this baby forcibly removed from my body.

I hand Hazel a princess coloring book and try to take deep cleansing breaths when I hear Dr. Berri's voice in the hall. So much for calm breathing. He knocks quickly before pushing the door open. He looks at me over his eyeglasses, shakes my hand, then looks at Hazel and smiles.

"Hi, Honey," he says to her. Then he turns to me, "She's beautiful."

"Thank you."

"So, are you doing okay?" he asks. "Anything happening?"

"I don't think so," I answer.

"Let's have a look," he says and scoots his stool to the bottom of the table. Hazel watches him but doesn't seem upset as he feels around.

"Lila," he says. "You're still tight. I'm sorry, I know you were hoping to avoid this, but we're going to have to schedule a C-section. I'm thinking it should be today."

I can't help it; I start to cry. Hazel looks at me. I should never have brought her.

"What, Mama?" she asks.

"Nothing, Sweetie, I just wanted to spend Halloween with you, that's all," I say as I try to pull myself together.

"Tell you what, let's do a quick scan and if everything looks okay, we'll put it off until tomorrow," Dr. Berri says.

"Okay," I say. I quickly get dressed and we walk to the ultrasound room. Dr. Berri is waiting. I lie down, and Hazel sits quietly on the edge of the cot by my head. Dr. Berri swirls the wand around my huge belly. Hazel stares at the screen.

"There's the face," he says. "Everything looks fine. There's plenty of fluid. But he's a big baby, and he isn't showing any signs of coming on his own. We're doing the right thing, Lila." He wipes off the gel with a white sheet, flicks on the lights, and says he will be right back.

"Eight o'clock tomorrow morning," he says matter-of-factly a few minutes later. "Be here by six. And don't eat or drink anything after midnight. Any questions?"

"Is there any way to get out of this?" I ask, only half kidding.

"None that I can think of," he says. "There is always the chance you'll go into labor later today, but I doubt it, and with such a big baby and knowing how hard it was last time, I'm not sure you wouldn't need a C-section anyway. I'll be there. Everything will be fine."

Hazel moves down and wedges herself between my legs with such force it's like she wants to plant herself there and prevent the doctor from doing what he has to do. I hug her and ease her away so I can stand up.

"Okay. See you tomorrow," I say as cheerfully as I can.

"See you tomorrow."

As we start looking for a cab my phone rings.

"It's closed," Sam says.

"What is?"

"Enzo's," he says like I should know what he's talking about. "I have to eat there today or I'll get completely off schedule."

"I'm going to have a C-section tomorrow morning at eight," I say, leaving the *thanks for asking* in my head. I don't want to fight.

"Great, then we can go out to dinner tonight."

"What? No, we can't. It's Halloween. And it's our last night alone with Hazel. And I don't think I can eat after a certain time," I say. I stop and pull the instructions out of my purse. They say I shouldn't eat after midnight.

"Lila, please, your mother just got here, so she can stay with Hazel. We can have a late dinner, after Hazel goes to sleep. The place is right on Twentieth Street," he says. "Please."

I think for a minute. When am I going to have a chance to eat out again?

"Fine," I say. "But I'm not going to eat too much."

"Good," Sam says. "And there's one more thing. Can you find two people to join us? I've spent the last hour trying to get someone from the paper to come, but absolutely nobody is available."

"Wait," I say. "You mean you were planning to eat out tonight? Before you even asked me? You didn't know if—"

"No, of course not," Sam says soothingly. "It was just in case. I would have canceled if I had to, obviously."

"Well, okay," I say, still holding on to the hope of not fighting.

"Should I ask one of the neighbors?" I say.

"Oh, no," Sam says quickly. "We still haven't vetted them."

"Then who?" I ask.

"How about someone from the Octavia? Maybe the doorman?" he suggests, referring to the building we lived in just before we moved to Colonial Court. "He was nice."

"Fine," I say.

When Hazel and I get home, I call the doorman.

"Calvin, it's Lila Soto," I say. "We used to live in 11B. I wanted to ask you—"

"Eleven B? Yeah, that's the Steiners. I'll connect you," he says, interrupting me.

"No, Calvin, wait," I say, but the phone is already ringing. I hang up.

I try to think of what other nonthreatening people we knew in the building. There was a really nice Indian couple who lived down the hall from us at the Octavia. I call Calvin back, disguising my voice a little.

"Can you please connect me to the Maliks?" I ask. He hesitates, but then I hear him punch in the numbers. He must think I'm crazy.

"Hello?" a voice with a slight Indian accent says.

"Gita?" I ask. "It's Lila Soto; we used to live down the hall. How are you guys?"

"We are good, Lila," she says. "It is nice to hear from you."

"Yeah, it's nice to talk to you," I say, thinking this might work out. Maybe we can actually become friends. "Are you and Deep available tonight for dinner? This might sound like a strange invitation, but Sam writes about restaurants for the newspaper here, and he is planning a last-minute visit to a restaurant. Would you like to come?"

"We thought you'd never ask," she says. "We'd love to."

The rest of the day passes in a daze of Hazel tantrums, Halloween costumes, and too much candy. People talk to me, but I'm not sure what I say in response or if I'm even polite—just like at my wedding. I put Hazel to sleep and am surprised to feel tears well up after I pull her door shut. The last night I will be just her mother.

I wait for Sam in the kitchen. He disappeared a long time ago, and when he comes into the room, my mouth drops open. He has on a fake full beard that covers his entire neck, and a strange mustache. His eyes look different, and for a minute I think he has colored contacts, but then I realize he has on eye makeup. I wonder if he is trying to look like Alice Cooper.

"Did you use my makeup?" I ask.

"A little," Sam says. "I need to get more supplies. But I did buy some new glue. It seems to work great. What do you think?"

"I think you look like you're wearing a Halloween costume," I say, not so nicely.

"Good, 'cause it's Halloween," he says.

We say good-bye to my mother and start our short walk. Gita and Deep are waiting for us, and there is a lot of oohing and aahing over the size of my belly, but when they try to talk to Sam, he barely responds. I see them looking at him. I desperately want to tell them what's going on with him, but I can't figure out a way to do it. I can't mention Sam's name, and I can't talk about the disguise in public. We were never really friends, and now I'm wondering if they thought Sam was someone else to begin with. It isn't until we get settled at the table that I realize why, in addition to his new look, they seem so put off by Sam. He can't move his face. The glue has dried and his mustache is stretching his skin so tight that he can't form words. He mutters as best he can, without moving the top of his mouth, and when it comes time to discuss the menu, he does a lot of pointing and nodding. My husband now looks crazy, sounds crazy, and acts crazy. Gita and Deep are clearly confused. They keep looking from the menu to Sam, then back at the menu. I am never going to make any new friends.

When the waitress comes over, she looks at Sam's face a little too long, and I know she is trying to figure out what's wrong with him. When it's his turn to order, she kneels down by his place and talks very slowly, then waits for him to get the words out, nodding sympathetically.

"Would you like pasta, like spaghetti, you know, long noodles, or a vegetable?" she asks, as though he may never have been in a restaurant before.

First Sam tries to say *pasta*, but there is too much upper lip involved; *spaghetti* is even worse, so he finally says *noodles*.

"Oh, you'll like the noodles," the waitress says, pushing herself up to standing. She looks back at Sam. "For you, I'm going to ask the chef to put a meatball on top."

We manage to talk a little, and things aren't too bad until Sam's soup arrives and the steam from the bowl melts away the glue he used to put the mustache on. The peeling away is subtle at first, only the tips of the two ends, but after a few bites the whole thing falls into his tomato bisque. We all just stare at the bowl as the mustache sinks to the bottom before rising to the top like a hairy caterpillar. Sam snatches it up with his napkin. Red soup drips on the table and on his pants. This almost couldn't get any worse. I wish I had never agreed to come out tonight. Sam gives me a sideways smile. I think he is wishing the same thing.

Another waiter rushes over, since something is so obviously wrong at our table, but luckily there is no evidence of the mustache, and it is the first time he sees Sam, so he doesn't know anything is missing. At least Sam can talk now.

"We're fine," Sam says, and I'm glad to hear him sound normal. "Just admiring the color of the bisque."

The waiter nods and walks away.

For the rest of the night Sam covers his upper lip with two fingers whenever our waitress comes over. She talks more and more slowly to him, having, I think, decided he definitely has some sort of problem. Gita and Deep are polite enough, but I think they can't wait to go home. I am so distracted by my upcoming surgery that after the initial shock I stop caring about what is happening at our table.

The food isn't so great. Gita's salad is overdressed. Deep's sautéed shrimp are fishy. If I had any energy, I would worry that our potential friends are not enjoying the company or the food.

My veal medallions are terrible; they look more like thin, messy hamburgers, which is fine because I shouldn't be eating much now anyway. But in a rare moment of concession, Sam suggests that I should send them back. I know he feels sorry for me. When the waitress asks what I want in their place, I ask if I can have meatballs. She gives me a knowing smile, like she thinks I'm trying to make Sam feel better by ordering the same thing he had. I smile back, shrugging a little to indicate I have to do what I have to do. She nods.

When we finally leave, the waitress comes running after us. Sam puts his fingers to his lip just in time.

"You forgot this," she says to Sam, handing him the flag that was stuck in his meatball. One side is the normal American flag, and the other side is the same but meatballs are the stars and spaghetti noodles are the stripes. Sam mumbles a thank you and heads out the door. She hands me a second one. "Just in case," she says.

Deep is already hailing a cab before I make it down the stairs of the restaurant to the sidewalk. As we wave and watch their cab drive north on Twentieth Street, all I can think is that I am so grateful Sam didn't want me to ask the neighbors.

"That was awful," I say, thinking that the few blocks home at this point seem like miles. I look at my watch. That was the fastest dinner on record.

"No, it was okay," Sam says, putting his arm around me. "Nobody suspected a thing."

"I guess you're right," I say, leaning into his arm. "But you're not planning on wearing that to the hospital, are you?"

"Lila, I wouldn't embarrass you like that," he says.

At three o'clock in the morning my eyes shoot open. I am wide awake. Sam is sleeping peacefully next to me. He didn't come to bed until close to midnight, because it took him a good hour to get all the glue off of his face. Hazel is sleeping even though she wasn't thrilled when I told her we wouldn't be here when she woke up. My mother is sleeping in the guest room at the ready to take care of Hazel. I can't sleep. I can't watch TV, because I don't want to wake anyone. I'm not allowed to eat. I don't want to read. I wait. Three more hours until we have to be there. Two hours and forty-five minutes until we have to leave. Two more hours until we have to officially wake up. I have nothing to do but think.

I can't get the image of the knife cutting me open out of my mind. How do they manage to slice me but miss the baby? Why didn't I ask that question when I had the chance? I glance around the room in the near darkness and try desperately to think about something else. I look over at my snoring husband.

If I hadn't met Sam on that cold pre–Mardi Gras day almost five years ago, two whole people wouldn't exist, and I would probably be eating room service in Hawaii right now. The day we met was an unusual one for me to begin with. When I was working in a city, I almost never left the hotel to explore. But I woke up that morning thinking about Tom and couldn't stop.

Until then, I had convinced myself that I had done the right thing when we broke up three months before. Our entire relationship was based on not slowing down and not settling down. We both traveled a lot for our jobs, and that was always okay. Neither of us whined that the other was away too much; neither of us pressured the other to be around more. That was our deal, until it wasn't. When I looked back over our years together, it became clear that spending so much time apart is what allowed us to stay together as long as we did.

But that dark morning in New Orleans I couldn't help but wonder if I had made a mistake. I was lonely. I missed calling him from the road. I missed the way he always brought me flowers when I returned from a trip, his welcome-home hugs, his bad attempts at home-cooked meals in our microwave oven. If only that oven could have continued to be enough for him, we would probably have still been together. But I could see he wanted more; I knew it and I pretended I didn't. Being away from each other more than half the time still worked for me, but it didn't work for him anymore.

In New Orleans that morning, I worried that I had acted rashly. Nothing better had come along. I wasn't much happier without him, at least not yet. Maybe we both could have changed some of our habits and rearranged some of our hopes. Maybe we could have compromised.

It was foggy and gray, and the Crescent City seemed mysterious. I ended up at a corner café on Magazine Street. Through the glass door, I could see red-checked tablecloths and a shiny wood floor. Purple, green, and gold streamers fell from the ceiling. When I walked in, I noticed it was empty except for a man wearing a silver-and-black feather mask around his eyes and a black satin cape over what looked like regular clothes. He was sitting alone at a table with five bowls of something in front of him. He would take a spoonful from one, ponder it, then take a spoonful from another. I remember thinking how strange he looked and was about to walk out when a smiling woman appeared, called me *chère*, and seated me before I had a chance to say anything. I was hungry, and I wanted gumbo. But there were so many kinds I couldn't decide: duck, seafood, chicken and andouille. I asked the woman which was best.

"Get the duck," the masked man said, his voice much younger and warmer than I expected. "It's delicious."

I wasn't sure what to do. Who did he think he was, the Phantom of the Opera? I didn't realize at the time that there were Mardi Gras parades that day and I would see other people in costume. I was afraid to take his advice, and afraid not to take it.

"I'll try the duck gumbo, please," I said after the man went back to his bowls. It arrived steaming hot, I ate it, and as promised, it was delicious.

The next morning I was eating my usual breakfast of black coffee and half a grapefruit in the large, impersonal hotel dining room when a man came over to my table. He was vaguely familiar, but I couldn't place him. I figured he must be one of the hotel employees I had dealt with during the past few days.

"Hello," he said. "Nice to see you again."

"Hi," I said back. "Thanks. Nice to see you, too."

"Mind if I sit down?" he asked.

"No," I said, moving some newspapers over. "Sit."

I was ready for him to ask me about an upcoming conference, or about dealing with crises on a local level. But he just sat there. I started to get nervous.

"So do you like working here?" I asked.

"Here?" he asked. I looked around to see if there was anyone I could signal if things got strange. The dining room was bustling so I figured I could probably get help quickly if I needed it.

"Here, at the hotel," I said.

"I don't work at the hotel," he said, looking just as confused as I felt. Then something clicked and he smiled. "Oh, I had the mask on yesterday. I'm the duck-gumbo guy. I saw you at Joey K's. It was good, wasn't it?"

"Yeah, it was good," I said, not sure how to handle the conversation. What were the chances of running into this guy twice? Was he following me? But for some reason, I was curious, not afraid. "Why were you eating so much?" I asked.

He raised his bushy eyebrows as though to say, *Was I eating a lot?* I noticed he was handsome, with big brown eyes and a red tint to his thick hair. He was tall, but he let his shoulders sag a little.

"I'm working on a story about gumbo for the magazine *American Food*," he said. "That's how I knew the duck was the best. I had tasted them all. I'm Sam, by the way."

"Lila," I said, shaking his outstretched hand.

We ended up sitting at that table for two hours, and I had to reschedule a conference call. I learned that he was single, originally from California, lived in New Orleans, wrote about local government for the *Times-Picayune*, but dreamed of writing about food full-time. He was at the hotel to cover a meeting and was just grabbing something to eat when he saw me. He seemed a little surprised that I was in hotel management, and somewhat deflated when I told him I was from out of town and that I would be leaving in a few days for Burlington, Vermont, to tackle another hotel event.

"So, where do you live?" Sam asked.

"Well, technically in New York," I said. "But I travel a lot. I haven't been home in a while."

"I guess you don't have any pets, then," he said. "What about plants?"

"Not even plants," I said.

I didn't tell him that my ex-boyfriend had taken over the apartment, so even if I did go to New York, I would stay at one of our hotels.

I might even pick the one in Westchester so that there would be no chance of running into Tom.

I was surprised to find myself a little sad when Sam said he had to leave to get ready for a levee-board meeting. But I got over it, and after we said good-bye, I didn't expect to see him again.

The next morning when I came down for breakfast to have my coffee and fruit, Sam was waiting at the entrance to the restaurant. He jumped a little when I turned the corner, then grinned at me. He was wearing a plaid button-down shirt and khaki pants.

"Where's your cape?" I asked.

"Very funny," he said. "Listen, I couldn't help but notice the food wasn't so great here yesterday. Do you want to have the best chili omelet, waffles, and pecan pie of your life?" I wasn't sure. For years I'd barely had anything more than my grapefruit before noon. I was sure chili would give me indigestion.

"Come with me," he said when I didn't answer.

"Where?" I asked, more unsure. "Do we have to go in a car?"

"Nope," he said warmly. "The streetcar will take us there."

Looking back, I think if the meal had involved a car ride I would have said no thank you. But public transportation seemed safe enough. Should I credit my children's existence to the streetcar? I know the answer is no. The credit for making me feel comfortable enough to go along that day goes to Sam.

By four o'clock in the morning I can't stand it anymore. The image of the knife has pushed all other thoughts away. What if something goes wrong? Would Sam be able to take care of two children alone? I get up quietly and go to the bathroom. I turn on the light and stand there, blinking under the glare. I have the strong feeling that I am setting something in motion.

I brush my teeth for a good ten minutes, spitting and reloading the toothpaste. Then I run the shower hot. I climb in and take the longest shower of my life. I figure I won't have another one for a few days. When can someone take a shower again after major surgery? When will I be able to stand up? I think Mrs. Blueberry Buckle had a C-section. I wish I'd ignored Sam's rules and spent more time with her when I had the chance; I could have asked her about it.

When I'm finished, I towel off and tiptoe back to the bedroom. It is 5:03. Sam sits up.

"How long were you in there?" he asks.

"I think about forty-five minutes."

"Are you okay?"

"No, but I'm very clean," I say, and we both laugh. I let the towel fall to the floor and climb into bed over Sam. He touches my naked belly. There is an entire baby in there. It is full and whole and ready to come out.

"I'll miss your pregnant body," Sam says.

"You will?" I ask, surprised. I rub my hand on his cheek, which is still red from the effort of getting the disguise off.

"Want to have sex?" he asks, half-serious.

"No," I say. "Now get up." We untangle our bodies, mine huge for a few more hours, his strong and muscular, except for a tiny ring around his middle—too much foie gras, we always say. The last time we will lie like this, our baby contained inside me.

Sam senses my melancholy mood. He lies down again and hugs me, then gets up for real.

"Come on, Lila—everything is going to be great," he says. He pretends to push imaginary glasses down his nose and, looking over his imaginary lenses, does his best Dr. Berri impression. "Let's go meet this kid."

Just before we head downstairs, we tiptoe into Hazel's room. She is sleeping, and I want to scoop her up, but I don't dare. I turn and walk out the door. When Sam doesn't follow me, I walk back in and find him holding Hazel and nuzzling her face. I watch as he smells her cheek and gently places her back into her crib. She doesn't wake up. He puts his arm around me, and we walk out of her room.

The cab comes; we get in, hold hands. It is still dark outside. The cabdriver doesn't even say hello—he just keeps talking into his cell phone. Who is he talking to so early in the morning? I want everything to be perfect, so it bothers me more than it usually would.

We get out at the hospital, take the elevator to the third floor. I had wanted to wear my favorite striped maternity shirt, but it was just too dirty, smelly even, to wear one more time. So instead I chose the ugly green blouse I wore to dinner with my mother and Elaine. It isn't until we get off the elevator that I notice it has tomato sauce on it.

We walk up to the desk, and it takes a few minutes for anyone to acknowledge us.

"Yes?" a tired-looking nurse asks.

"We're here for my scheduled C-section at 8:00 a.m.," I offer hopefully.

"Doctor?" she asks as though everyone has a scheduled C-section every day. No big deal.

"Berri," I say, trying not to cry.

We are told to sit on a tiny bench behind us. I wiggle on; the hard seat digs into my thighs. Sam takes my hand, and his eyes say everything will be okay.

"What if I don't get a private room?" I whisper to Sam.

"You probably will," he says. "It doesn't seem too busy."

We are taken to a room to prepare me for the surgery. The tired nurse has trouble with my IV but eventually gets it in. Dr. Berri stops by, and as usual, I am glad to see him. Then it is time for me to go to the operating room—Sam will meet me there in a little while. I am given flimsy slippers. Somehow I had pictured a long good-bye with Sam as

I was wheeled through the halls, waving as I was pushed through the doors. But instead, I just walk there.

"I'll be right behind you," Sam says, grabbing my hand before I'm out of reach. He doesn't let go. I walk the few feet back to him. He puts his arms around me. "You make me very happy. Marrying you is the best thing I ever did."

"Me, too," I mumble. Twenty other things run through my mind, like *What if this doesn't go well?* and *What if there's something wrong with the baby?*, but I don't say any of them. I tug my hand away gently and start my walk toward the operating room.

"Right behind you," Sam calls after me.

Then I am leaning over the operating table, trying to bend my spine into a circle, and I am clinging to the nurse's hand. The swirling diamonds on my hospital gown are jumping up from my lap and making me dizzy. I shift my focus to the green linoleum floor and notice streaks of dirt. I hope the surgical equipment has been cleaned more recently than the floor.

It is hard to find a good place on my back for the needle, and I feel an extremely uncomfortable jolt as the sharp metal is pushed in. Now I am lying flat, can't feel my legs, my arms are tied down. The anesthesiologist settles in somewhere behind me.

"Tell your husband to try the new Italian restaurant on Broad Street," he says. "My wife and I loved the pasta. The sauce is out of this world."

"Okay," I mumble, seeing Sam's point about not telling people what he does. I told Dr. Berri during our first visit, and he must have told other people. If I weren't about to be sliced open, I might tell the anesthesiologist that the sauce is canned.

Dr. Berri comes in and pours rubbing alcohol on my belly. I feel moisture, but nothing cold. Then they are starting. Sam comes in and has to walk by my already pried-open abdomen. He doesn't look but comes to the other side of the sheet barrier and sits by my head, a little too close to the anesthesiologist for my liking. I feel pulling, pushing, tugging. Then I think I am going to throw up. I start retching but can barely move at all.

"Give her something," Dr. Berri tells the anesthesiologist, and I feel like Dr. Berri is taking care of me. The drugs kick in as the anesthesiologist and Sam are discussing the best place to have an anniversary dinner. I'm grateful that Sam isn't being rude. At least he realizes this is not the time to pretend he doesn't know what someone is talking about.

"Don't leave me," I hear myself saying to Dr. Berri. I'm pretty sure he's more concerned about my baby than about the next restaurant he will go to.

Dr. Berri glances at me. "I won't," he says.

Then there is Henry, whom we name after my father. He comes out crying quietly, looking around. His sister came out screaming, mad. But she had been through much more than he has. Sam has abandoned his conversation and is looking at the baby.

Now Henry is crying louder. He looks great, they tell me. He weighs eight pounds, fourteen ounces. Big. Then he is brought close to my face. My arms are still tied down so I can't touch him yet. He is covered with slime.

"Who does he look like?" one of the nurses singsongs.

"My husband," I mumble. They each have a penis. But for a minute I wonder if he will have any of my father in him. I try to conjure up my father's boyish face, his light-brown eyes and his crinkling nose. All I see is a picture my mother has on her piano.

Then we are in the recovery room, waiting for my spinal to wear off, and I can hold him. I feel good, though I'm self-conscious while the nurses work around me. I wish they would leave. I try to breast-feed but Henry is uninterested. The nurses are not concerned. Then he is taken to the nursery for a bath, and Sam goes for a cup of coffee, mumbling something about a new shop two blocks away that roasts its own beans. All I have to do is lie here. It's nice. Someone just gave me morphine.

The first time Sam touched me was on the streetcar on our way to breakfast. We settled onto the wood benches, and he patted my leg and smiled. At the time it seemed so intimate I wasn't sure if I liked it. What had I gotten myself into? As promised, the food was amazing, especially the pecan pie, which was put facedown on the griddle before it was served. I have no idea what we talked about; I was determined to keep it casual. After the meal, we walked along the cracked sidewalks to Audubon Park, and Sam pointed out the live oak trees. I had been to New Orleans a few times in the past, but I had never noticed them since I'd barely left the hotel. The more time we spent together, the more I wanted to touch him. Soon we were holding hands.

In my attempt to keep the conversation safe, I asked about his family.

"Both my parents are alive," he said slowly. "But it was really just my father and me when I was growing up." He looked me right in the face, and I got the sense he was used to saying that.

"Did your parents get divorced?" I asked.

"Yes, eventually," he said. "But it wasn't that simple."

I had to admit that I was intrigued.

"But you lived with your father?" I asked. He nodded, then took a deep breath. It was the first time he seemed hesitant since I met him.

"My mom basically took off," he finally said. "She had some issues with being a wife and mother. Anyway, we think she lives in Florida. I haven't seen her or spoken to her since I was ten. My dad was great, though. He pretty much gave up everything to raise me. Not that we don't have issues of our own, but that's another story."

So much for keeping the conversation light. I didn't know what to say.

"Sorry," Sam said. "Maybe that was a little too much information. You probably thought I would just say my parents are fine and retired recently to Pensacola."

"No, I'm sorry if I asked a personal question," I said, realizing that I didn't know the man sitting next to me any better than I knew the jogger stretching over by the fountain. I moved a quarter of an inch away from him.

"We got used to it," he said. "But sometimes I wish I could just ask my mother what went wrong. Maybe that would help me understand. Right now I can't help thinking marriage must be pretty bad if it drove her away like that. I'm not sure I want to get married."

My heart was beating fast. Could I really be this lucky twice? Another man who didn't want to settle down? I let my body relax into the park bench and took in the yellow and pink flowers. We listened to the soft sound of the fountain, and I could hear ducks quacking in a nearby pond.

"What's that smell?" I asked, breathing it in.

"The sweet olive trees," he said proudly, like they were his own creation. He moved a little closer to me.

"What about you?" Sam asked. "What is your dark story?"

"What makes you think I have one?" I asked, laughing.

"Everyone does," he said.

"Well, my father died when I was twelve, so I grew up in a two-person family, too," I said.

"Oh, I'm sorry," Sam said gently.

"And my mother, who always focused on me anyway, focused on me even more when it became just the two of us," I continued, surprising myself with my own words. I didn't talk about this very much. "My father died suddenly. He had a heart attack after his usual Saturday morning tennis game. Looking back I now realize that he hadn't been feeling well for a while, but we just thought it was a lingering flu. So, after the initial shock, my mother stepped up and got a job. She had been a teacher before I was born, but she went back to school part-time and got into guidance counseling. She has always pushed me to think about my career. When I was in high school, I was always telling her to leave her counseling at work and leave me alone." I stopped talking for a minute. "But eventually I went off to college and then graduate school, and then I started working for the hotel company." I wasn't used to talking about my personal life with near-strangers, and suddenly I felt exhausted.

"Wow," Sam said, and I could tell he had been listening very closely. He let a minute go by. "And, are you dating anyone now?"

"Oh that," I said. I was on a roll, so I figured I might as well just tell him everything. "Three months ago I broke up with my boyfriend of more than two years. We had . . . issues. I know it was the right thing, but it's been a little hard."

Sam nodded.

"Breakups usually are," Sam said. "What was the final straw?"

The final straw? It was that stupid real oven he started talking about, which I knew was as close as I was going to let him get to a proposal.

Suddenly, sitting next to Sam, I was breathing heavier than I would have liked.

"Sorry," Sam said. "I shouldn't have asked."

We sat in silence for a few minutes. And then I was surprised by the sound of my voice.

"Do you have an oven?" I asked.

"Yeah, I love my oven," Sam said. "I splurged and bought a top-of-the-line Viking last year. I love to cook."

I could have walked away while I still had the chance.

Henry is one hour old when we are taken to a room that is not private. Sam looks in as the door opens, and he tells me there is someone in there. When I look, I see her grabbing greasy pizza boxes off what will be my bed. It looks like she has been here for a long time and she has spread out. I'm still feeling good from not being pregnant anymore, and I'm flying on the drugs, so I don't care that much. When I'm settled, Sam leaves to take over with Hazel so my mother can come see the baby. I close my eyes.

Suddenly I hear a grinding noise and I'm moving. I open my eyes as the mattress tilts sharply up to see a little boy playing with the buttons on my bed. Someone rushes over and grabs him, and I see the new mother next to me has a crowd. Now I care.

Hazel refuses to come to the hospital. At first I want Sam to push her, even if she is reluctant. But then he tells me that whenever he asks if she wants to see the baby, she insists that there is no baby. When Sam tries to convince her otherwise, he says she throws herself on the floor and pretends she is asleep, or in a coma, or dead. And it takes a good hour and lots of promises of candy and ice cream to pull her out of it. I decide to steal the chance to rest and deal with that when I get home. I'm not sure the Colonial Court mommies would approve.

But it isn't very restful anyway, because the nurses are driving me insane.

"My mother is lactose intolerant; do you know of any restaurants that cater to that type of patron?" an older nurse wearing scrubs with pink-and-blue teddy bears on them asks me on my second day. She has just hoisted me out of bed for the first time since my surgery, and I feel dizzy and nauseated. She doesn't seem to notice.

"Everything has dairy in it, even the things you don't expect to have dairy in them," she continues. I think I am going to pass out. "I mean, there are places with no meat, places with no carbs. There must be a place with no dairy."

I take a deep breath. "Maybe a vegan restaurant would work for her," I say weakly. "I think they don't use dairy."

I would be rude, but I still want a private room.

That same day I am taken off my liquid diet, which is good news because I am surprisingly hungry. I imagine that even the hospital-issued lasagna or pot roast will taste great after more than a day of broth and Jell-O. But when my tray arrives, it holds a plate of pureed chicken and carrots: a disturbing yellow, orange, goopy mess.

The same nurse comes and takes a look, then studies the card.

"Hmmm," she says. "That's a tray for people who are having trouble with solid food. Wonder how it got sent up here."

Despite my attempt to find her mother a dairy-free place to eat, she is unable to straighten out the confusion by dinner, when I am served pureed broccoli and beef. In fact, for the rest of my stay I am given the digestion-challenged diet. Sam surprises me with a Domino's pizza and a pan of homemade Pillsbury cinnamon rolls that are still warm. Both things fall into Sam's category of "not real food," but he knows they are among my favorites. We sit together on my bed, Henry sleeping in his plastic bassinet, and Sam feeds me.

On Saturday another doctor fills in for Dr. Berri. He barely smiles, looks at my chart, glances at my name.

"Is your husband Sam Soto?" he asks after examining my incision.

"Yes," I say, expecting him to ask for a recommendation or tell me he enjoys Sam's reviews.

"It wasn't nice of him to criticize our hospital food," he says, frowning at me over my chart. "It's a hospital for heaven's sake."

Suddenly I understand everything: the much-visited roommate, the strange food. When Sam first arrived in Philadelphia, he thought it would be funny to do a roundup of the hospital cafeterias. There are so many hospitals in the city, and he figured it would be a good way to get to know his way around. A few surprised him with fresh, tasty food, and others, like this one, were awful. The joke is that they have since changed their food vendor. But I guess people don't forget. The only problem is, Sam hasn't suffered at all. I have. I can see there are other reasons to keep Sam's profession a secret.

We leave the hospital on a Monday morning. We decide not to take most of the flowers that came from various relatives and friends, but I want the cards. The one from Cece reads: *To my best friend, I miss you, I love you, and someday I want to be you. Just kidding, but having babies sounds pretty great! I'll come visit you and you come visit me (I'll be at the office). Love to Sam and Hazel, too.* And the one from Ed reads: *Congratulations! You are no longer a pumpkin! Probably too soon to call but it's on my calendar. All the best from Ed and the gang.* I show them both to Sam and he laughs, but he doesn't ask what they mean. Maybe they don't really mean anything. Maybe they do.

Sam insists on taking the flower arrangement from his great aunt that came with a card reading, *Love to the baby. Please come visit, Lila. I'm lonely.* People write very strange things on cards welcoming babies.

But the way Sam responded, it was like his Aunt Gladys sent a script along. He called her immediately from the phone next to my hospital bed.

"It's Sammy," he said. "The flowers are beautiful. Aunt Gladys, you are too generous."

Sam nodded and smiled to whatever she said. I had never seen him act that way.

"Let's see. Some are pink, and purple, there's a little yellow," he said. I rolled my eyes. "Yes, of course. We'll come soon."

More nodding, then a look of confusion crossed Sam's face.

"Oh, okay, I'll tell her," he said. "We send our love."

"What was that all about?" I asked him when he hung up, worrying that my continuously agitated state would further delay the arrival of my milk.

"She's a sweet old lady, and the only one in my family who tried to help when my mother left," Sam said sheepishly. How could I give him a hard time about that?

"You'll tell me what?" I asked.

"Oh, she wants you to come visit alone with the kids," he said, looking at the floor. "Something about a lady's tea and her offering some practical baby advice."

"She's eighty-seven!" I said. "I think things have changed a lot since she had babies."

"Well, she had five of them—maybe she remembers something," Sam said. "Just think about it."

"Okay," I agreed.

Sam slides the flowers from Aunt Gladys into the trunk, while I snap Henry's infant carrier into the car seat base in the backseat.

Sam starts the car and heads down Eighth Street.

"Hey," he says. "We aren't far from this new hoagie place everyone is talking about. It's just a few blocks south of here. Why don't I swing by, and we can pick up some sandwiches?"

"Sam, we are taking our baby home from the hospital! And I haven't seen Hazel in four days! Can you stop thinking about food for one minute?"

"We have to eat," he says, unfazed by my comment. "Come on. It'll only take a second."

Of course it's not a second. The place is many blocks south of where we started, and not actually on Eighth Street. We end up driving around for a while before we spot the tiny storefront. Sam leaves me in the car with a quiet Henry who quickly becomes loud after the car stops. It's lunchtime, so a good twenty minutes go by before Sam appears again with three bags stuffed with sandwiches. It looks like he got enough to feed our whole block. By now Henry is screaming. I have him in the front seat with me, but he is too upset to nurse. I can't believe Sam did this now.

"Sorry," he says when he gets into the car. "Let's go home."

Home. It is something I never realized I wanted. I was happy in hotel rooms. I liked the idea of moving around the world. I loved going from one adventure to another. I loved not having anything that really needed tending to. And I knew my mother's house was there if I wanted to go, always waiting for me with open arms and the smell of my childhood.

Before I knew it, I could pack my bag in a matter of minutes. After years of doing it, I broke down and had a suitcase custom made. I was able to live out of that bag for months. It helped that I could send anything to the hotel laundry and have it back the next morning.

I deeply miss that bag. It is just the right size to hold five days' worth of clothes, with an inside hanger to keep things on the top from wrinkling. My matching cosmetic case holds three lipsticks, blush, moisturizer, and all my eye makeup, with room for jewelry and any extras I come across. It fits perfectly in the upper right corner. The whole thing is made out of a dark, shimmering-purple waterproof material. When I had to check it, it blended in with all the dark bags, but the special fabric made it easy to see when it turned the corner toward me on the baggage carousel. That suitcase is under my bed now, empty and collecting dust. Sometimes I pull it out and unzip it. If I get really close, I can still catch the scent of jet fuel. I breathe it in, and it takes me back.

After that first full day with Sam, we ended up back at my hotel. He didn't leave until we had to go to the airport the next afternoon. He drove me—I trusted him enough by then to get into his car—and afterward he went to work. I got on the plane and wondered how I could create a situation that would bring me back to New Orleans soon. I considered calling in repeated bomb threats to the Oak Addison Hotel, or paying someone to stage an incident in the lobby. But as luck would have it, two weeks later a barge lost control on the Mississippi River and crashed into the hotel. No one was killed, but there were injuries. And there was a need for crisis management. As usual, I couldn't wait to get on that plane. For the first time in a long time my wish wasn't to escape, but to arrive.

The next morning I found myself at Sam's little house. It was gray with purple trim and a purple door. When he told me he was taking me to his place, I hadn't expected a real house. A house needed tending to. A house was far more settled than I had expected him to be. I reluctantly followed him into the first room and stood still, immediately feeling the walls close in a little, when an old lady from next door knocked.

"Oh, Sammy, I didn't know you had company, dear," she said, smiling at me. "I have a little problem in my dining room."

"Hi, Mrs. Boudreaux, this is Lila," Sam said proudly. "Lila, this is Mrs. Boudreaux."

"Hi," I said, taking her soft, wrinkled hand in mine.

"What can I do for you?" Sam asked, not seeming put out at all.

"Those nasty palmetto bugs are back," she said, looking a little embarrassed. "I don't know what has happened to me in my old age. I used to scoop them up and take them outside. But I just can't stomach it anymore. Won't you please come and kill it? It looks like it has been around since the Dark Ages, and it's flying."

Sam grinned at me, then took Mrs. Boudreaux by the arm and led her out.

"I'll be right back," he called over his shoulder.

And just like that I was alone in his house.

At first I didn't move. Then I thought about waiting for him on the porch. But I had to go the bathroom, and I was thirsty. I wandered through the sparsely decorated front room, glad to see that Sam didn't seem to care too much about his surroundings, and headed up the stairs to the small bathroom. It was clean, with white fixtures, a white tile floor, and a navy-blue shower curtain, but there were no personal touches. I poked my head into his bedroom. It was painted light blue, with a cluttered dresser, a neatly made double bed, and a rocking chair with clothes hanging over the top. Okay, so Sam had a house, but he hadn't taken any time to decorate it. And I hadn't noticed any pets or plants. I felt lighter as I went back down the stairs.

When I stepped over the threshold of the kitchen, I stopped short. My first thought was that his kitchen was more sacred and more personal than his bedroom. I moved in slowly, noticing the yellow walls that reflected the morning sun. I looked up at the pot racks. Sam must have had a pot or pan for every occasion, and they were all lovingly arranged. My eyes drifted to his Viking oven, beautifully polished. I observed the different types of salt—sea salt, salt with thyme, kosher salt—all in small labeled glass jars. I brushed my fingers over them and found myself wondering if I would ever really be a part of his world.

There were pots of fresh herbs covering the windowsill. There were spices arranged in a cherrywood rack. There were recipes clipped from magazines that were held on the refrigerator with magnets in the shape of plates of red beans and rice. Suddenly I wanted Sam to use his pots and salt and spices to cook one of those recipes for me. I stood at the refrigerator, leaning against the door, and tried to decide if I should request lemon chicken or jambalaya. I actually felt an urge to water his fresh herbs.

The next thing I knew I felt like I couldn't breathe. I backed out of the kitchen, found the sofa in the living room, sat down, and put my head between my legs.

"Squashed, dead, and buried," Sam said as he entered the house; then he saw me. He rushed over, put his arm around my back. "Are you okay? What happened?"

What could I say? That for the first time in my life I thought I understood the appeal of standing still? That I wanted him to cook for me and kill bugs for me and maybe, just maybe, if I had all those things I wouldn't want to leave him, and I might be able to sleep in the same bed for more than a week? Instead, I told him that I thought I was dehydrated. He went into his lovely kitchen and brought me a tall glass of chilled fresh lemonade that he poured from a glass pitcher. It was sweet and tart, and I asked for two more glasses. Then we went on with our weekend. But I was never the same. I haven't been the same since.

CHAPTER FOUR

The genius of a great hoagie is its ability to harness an abbondanza of flavors into the simple harmony of a single sandwich. A mouthful of perfection that is greater than the sum of its parts. But Carmine's Corner Deli fails in its attempt. The Carmine's Constellation is a perfect example of what the deli is doing wrong. It's a full Italian hoagie plus a chicken cutlet and sautéed greens. Simplify, simplify, simplify! The ingredients may be fresh and delicious, but piled into this towering Hoagie of Babel, the beauty of each ingredient is easily missed.

—Sam Soto

I can see Hazel through the window as we drive up. She is wearing navy-blue corduroy overalls; her hair is brushed and shiny. As soon as Sam stops the car, I jump out as fast as my incision will let me and run up the stoop, leaving Sam to deal with Henry. My mother pulls open the door and lets me in. Hazel is in my arms in an instant. I had Sam go to the gift shop to buy a stuffed kitten that I wanted to present to her right away, but I think this is enough. I'll save that for later. I take her to the couch and hug her on my lap, aware that she is closer than she has been in a long time because my belly is no longer protruding. It's still fat, but Hazel can mush herself into that. Then Sam comes in with the car seat and Hazel tenses up. I keep hugging Hazel even though Henry is crying and I can feel my milk start to let down. But I can almost feel the air change. The first time Hazel is not the only baby in this house. She pulls away, and we all sit and stare at each other.

My mother jumps in, hands me the Boppy pillow, and takes Hazel onto her lap. I pull a squirming baby out of his car seat and offer him my breast. I notice that my mother's bags are packed and waiting by the door.

"Are you leaving today?" I ask, realizing that I have been completely in my own world and have no idea what her plan is.

"I've been away from work for five days now. I have to get back," she says. "I figured that once you were all home, you wouldn't need me anymore."

As with so many of these statements that she has uttered throughout my life, I take this as a challenge.

"Well, okay," I say. But I want to say that I don't know that I am ready to take care of two children and worry about dinner and laundry and everything else that needs to be done.

"I think you four need time to become a family. Plus, in addition to work, I have to get the garden ready for the winter while the ground is still soft enough," she says. Her tone is gentle, and I think that if I really wanted to, I could convince her to stay. I consider telling her that we *are* a family, and we could use a little help being one. But maybe she's right. If she stays one more day, would that make any difference?

"Eunice, we brought sandwiches," Sam says from the door, his arms loaded with bags and the flowers from Aunt Gladys. "At least stay for lunch."

"Okay," she says, moving into the kitchen and setting the table. The sandwiches are the best things I have ever tasted after the pureed hospital food, and I am actually grateful that Sam had enough sense to think about lunch. After we eat, Hazel begs my mother to play Candy Land. I fall asleep on the couch with the baby, and before we know it, we are thinking about dinner. My mother moves her bags away from the door, and I know that she will stay one more night. I'm glad I didn't have to directly ask her. She makes my favorite spaghetti and meat sauce.

The next morning I am ready for her to go. Henry was up much of the night, and I worried about his waking her.

Sam is supposed to take two weeks off to be with Hazel and help me get used to having a new baby again. But after a few days he gets antsy and starts coming up with excuses about dishes that need to be tasted immediately, or chefs who have to be interviewed right away because they will be out of the country for months.

It is on the fourth day that I'm home that he tells me he has to go to a meeting at the office.

"Why?" I ask, only half interested in his answer. "Don't they know you're taking two weeks off?"

Sam pauses and takes a very noisy deep breath. Now he has my attention.

"Lila, I haven't mentioned this because I didn't want you to worry," he says. "But there might be a strike."

"What?" I say too loudly, startling Henry. "I didn't even know that was a possibility."

"Well, I told you the contract was up next month, and apparently the union is not happy with the negotiations. There are a bunch of sticking points and . . ."

"What sticking points?" I ask, wishing we could move back to New Orleans where the paper was not unionized and there were no threats of strikes.

"Well, our pension, for one, and health care and sick days."

I don't know what to say, but I do know from my experience at Addison that those are not good sticking points to have.

"What's the meeting about today?"

"We're going to take a strike vote so we're ready if it comes to that," he says.

While Sam is at the office, Willa, our neighbor who lives across the street with three kids, brings meatballs and fresh bread and takes a peek at Henry. It seems silly and mean to refuse her food, so I take it and thank her. It smells good. She tells me that Janie, who has no kids but seems to be a member of the mommy group anyway, is planning to bring quiche and a bowl of carrot sticks tomorrow, and that someone else—I don't catch her name—will bring us brisket the next day. I don't even want to admit to myself that I kind of like this aspect of the block. At least until I wonder if I'll have to cook for someone else one day. I would have to order in for them, or go to a prepared-foods place and transfer it to another plate to take credit for it. I am trying to decide what would be a better bet—brisket or salmon—when Sam walks through the door.

Right away I know it isn't good. I have put the meatballs in one of our pots, and they are simmering on the stove. Sam doesn't ask how I managed to pull this together and I don't tell him.

"What happened?" I ask.

"Only two people voted against a strike," he says.

"So do you think there will definitely be one?"

"I don't know," Sam says quietly. "It looks like it."

"What does that mean?" I ask. "Will you still get paid?"

"I'll know more in a day or two," Sam says. "I promise I'll tell you everything as soon as I hear it. Can we eat now?"

It isn't until we sit down to eat the brisket two nights later that a question moves across Sam's face.

"Did you make this?" he asks, holding a forkful of juicy brisket just waiting to be eaten.

I consider saying yes, that I have become superhuman over the course of the last week, but I'm too tired to even joke.

"No, one of the neighbors brought it," I say, picking up a carrot and popping it into my mouth.

"What? Who?"

"Calm down," I say. "They do this for everyone. You know that—I heard you tell Elaine about all the crazy traditions of the block. I promise, I barely talked to any of the people who dropped off the food."

"Did they come inside?"

"Sam, you are being ridiculous," I say. "Just eat the brisket."

Sam puts his forkful in his mouth and chews slowly.

"When they came in, did they look around? Did they see our mail or anything?"

"Sam, I am not even going to answer that," I say. "There is no way we can live here without our neighbors finding out who we are. No way."

"Did you at least ask if any of these people own restaurants, or cook in one?"

"I haven't heard of anybody like that," I say. "But I'll try to find out, I promise."

A few days later, when I am certain that whatever we eat for dinner will be up to me, our doorbell rings around five o'clock. Henry is sleeping, and Hazel is watching *Sesame Street*. I am leaning on my elbow at the kitchen table, moments from actually falling asleep.

I jog groggily to the door, pull it open, and find Mrs. Blueberry Buckle holding a casserole dish in the palm of one hand and a salad bowl in the palm of the other. She smiles, steps inside, and marches into what I am sure is the messiest kitchen on the street. The red-and-white linen towel, which protected the blueberry buckle she brought us on move-in day, is hanging from the oven door. It is a very nice towel and has come to be the first one I choose after the rare occasions that I do the laundry. I see her do a double take, and I imagine her thinking, *So that's where my towel is*, but I decide not to say anything. Instead, I make a mental note to send the question in to *Martha Stewart Living*.

"It's still warm," she says, having a hard time looking away from the towel. If I had thought she'd be in my kitchen, I certainly would have put it away. "But heat it quickly at 350 for about ten minutes or so, then blast the broiler to melt the cheese."

Before I have a chance to ask her about blasting the broiler—I'm not so good with ovens—or question her about whether she or anyone in her family owns a restaurant, she turns and is gone so fast that I'm left standing at the pass-through window of the kitchen, watching her pull the front door shut. I wonder if she is going to tell everyone on Colonial Court that I stole her towel.

Maureen keeps calling to ask if she can bring us food. Ironically enough, she is the only one whom I feel comfortable accepting food from, and obviously the one Sam is most uncomfortable taking it from. I have to admit she did say something about bringing us food from the restaurant. That night, while we're eating the delicious chicken divan from The Blueberry Buckle Lady, I get up the nerve to talk to Sam about it. He had come in, sat down, and just started to eat—no questions asked. So I think it might be a good time.

"Maureen wants to bring us dinner, too," I say casually.

"Lila, you know how I feel about that," he says, clearly enjoying this meal.

"Please, Sam, I don't know how to say no to her."

"I will not let her bring free food into this house that may or may not have been cooked by people I am going to review in a few months," Sam says. I know he's exasperated that I will even consider it.

"But we've run out of neighbors," I say pathetically. "Plus, I want my friend to be able to do something nice for us."

"Maybe that's why it isn't such a good idea to be her friend," Sam says, squinting his eyes.

My other friends don't live around here, I want to say, but don't because I'm afraid I'm going to cry. I also refrain from telling Sam that I've known her longer than I've known him.

"Listen, Sam isn't comfortable accepting free food from the restaurant," I say when I call her back later that night.

"Why?" she asks. "It has nothing to do with anything."

"Well, it does, sort of," I say. "He doesn't want anyone to think his opinion was swayed by your kindness."

"Okay okay I'll send dinner over on Wednesday and it won't be from the restaurant," she says quickly.

"But where will it be from?" I ask.

"Trust me," she says.

I try, but I'm a little nervous, hoping she doesn't send the chef from Remoulade over anyway to whip something up in our kitchen. I can just picture him wheeling his flambé cart up Colonial Court. I don't mention anything to Sam. I figure if someone inappropriate shows up, I won't let him in. I think we have some Swedish meatballs from Ikea in the freezer. But at six o'clock that night the doorbell rings, and it's pizza and salad and Sprite from Lazaro's, our favorite place a few blocks away. I breathe a sigh of relief, enjoy the delicious pizza, and then call Maureen to thank her.

The weather is pretty warm for November, so I take a few walks up and down the block by myself. Suddenly everyone is glad to see me. By having just had a baby, I seem to have made some strange inroad into the secret society of the block. On a few occasions someone spots me through her front window and comes running out with questions about my delivery or what foods I'm avoiding while breast-feeding. Each time, I think I might ask if anyone on the block is associated with a local restaurant in any way, but I always chicken out, worried that my question will bring questions I am unable to answer. Eventually, I stop going outside. I start to ignore the telephone, the doorbell, and the voices of neighbors out front.

With the possible strike looming and Ed's having planted the seed in my head, I can't stop thinking about the idea of going back to work. I sit and nurse Henry. I smell his little ear, or play with his tiny fingers, and I picture myself the way I used to be: professional, well groomed, fast on my feet. I can't help but wonder if this is going to be it for me: former hotel executive, reluctant mother of two, and the restaurant critic's wife.

Hazel is also having trouble defining her job description, which has, without her consent, changed from baby to big sister. Unfortunately for her, there's no wiggle room there. Twice she has asked to "suck mommy there," pointing to my breasts. When I tell her that she did nurse when she was the baby's size, she just says, "There is no baby."

One night I decide Hazel needs a boost, so I plan a big-sister party. I send Sam out to buy Pooh plates and napkins, a piñata, presents, streamers. I wrap the stuffed kitten from the hospital gift shop. We order a cake with a bright-pink flamingo per Hazel's request. But I'm way too lazy to ask anyone to come. It seemed like a fine plan, until I hear Sam running up the stairs. He practically trips over a Lego beach house Hazel has been working on in the den. He looks pale.

"Are you okay?" I ask.

"Yeah, I'm fine, but we have a problem," he says, catching his breath.

"What's going on?" I ask, getting alarmed.

"Hazel is down there setting up all the party stuff," he says. "And she just asked when everyone is coming. You know, all those friends who have no idea there's a party."

"Oh no," I say, putting Henry down in the bouncy seat and standing up.

"Oh no is right," he says.

"What should we do?"

"You're the crisis manager here," he says. "We have a crisis."

I swallow my pride and call Willa, because her name is the only one I recognize on the block list. After she files away the knowledge that I am a thoughtless mother—no other Colonial Court mother would let this happen—she agrees to send her three-year-old son Russell over. And despite the fact that I have barely spoken to her, or that in addition to Russell she has twins at home, or that the invitation was last minute, he arrives with a beautifully drawn homemade card. On the front is a picture of a little girl hugging a baby wrapped in a blue blanket. Inside it reads, *Congratulations, Big Sister.* I know Willa made it. Hazel immediately finds a crayon and scribbles out the baby on the card. Then she and Russell dance, eat cake, and blow whistles.

Henry starts to cry when the whistles get too loud, and Sam says he'll take him upstairs. I grab a whistle and join the action.

"No, Mommy," Hazel whines. "Just kids."

"But it's fun," I whine back. "I want to come to your party."

I reluctantly put the whistle down and go sit halfway up the stairs overlooking the living room so I can keep an eye on them. Henry is surprisingly quiet. I glance upstairs and see the door to the den is closed. Sam opens it, comes out with a wide-eyed Henry in his arms, and goes down to the basement. Then he comes back up with some tools. He has a sheet of sandpaper balanced on Henry's stomach.

"What are you doing?" I ask.

"Nothing," Sam says.

"Don't let him get those tools," I say.

"He can't get anything. He's too little."

Sam goes back in the den and closes the door. I'm torn between bursting into the den and wanting to watch the kids—they are having such a good time. A minute later the phone rings. It's Willa.

"Can you meet me in the middle of the street with Russell?" she asks nicely. "The twins are asleep and Jake's out playing basketball."

"Sure," I say, not wanting to break up the party. "Give me two minutes."

"Two more minutes," I yell down to the kids. They both groan in protest. Then I go up and push open the den door. Henry is lying on the floor surrounded by tools and loose screws, and Sam is screwing something into the back of an unusually big pair of glasses.

"What are you doing?" I ask again, walking over and pushing the screws away from Henry.

Sam thrusts the glasses behind his back, then pulls them forward again.

"Something broke," he says casually. "I'm trying to fix it."

"Can't your eye doctor fix it?" I ask. "And those aren't your normal glasses."

"I got some new ones," Sam says, screwing some more.

Before I have a chance to question him again, I remember Willa. "I'm taking Russell across the street. I just wanted you to know."

"Okay," he says. "Close the door on your way out."

It is hard not to mutter *weirdo* as I pull the door shut behind me.

The next morning I decide to call Ed. I'm nursing Henry, Hazel is watching *Baby Mozart*, and the minute the idea pops into my head I feel my heart beat faster and my breath come in spurts. I never thanked him for the flowers; it's a perfect excuse.

When Henry is finished nursing, I put him in the wooden cradle and go look for my address book. I know Ed's number by heart, but I'm not quite ready, and this will give me a few extra minutes. I find it, look for his name. Then, without even looking at the number, I pick up the phone and dial. A voice I don't recognize answers, and for a second I think about hanging up. But I don't. I clear my throat.

"Hi. Ed Chambers, please. This is Lila Lippencott Soto," I say as professionally as I can.

There is a pause and I imagine she thinks I am some crackpot—or worse, a nobody.

"*The* Lila Lippencott?" she asks. "The one who turned a blimp disaster into an opportunity to market toy blimps? The one who calmed Jane Pauley when all the gold-plated balloons deflated because they were too heavy at her daughter's graduation party? The one who got President Bill Clinton to come to the opening of the new Addison in Little Rock, Arkansas?"

"Yes," I say, laughing. "All of the above."

"Well, it's great to meet you—on the phone that is—I'm Sandra Johns, Ed's newish assistant. I've been here for about eight months," she says. "They cite your accomplishments around here regularly."

"That's very nice to know; thanks for telling me. And it's nice to meet you, too," I say. "Is Ed in?"

"Oh," she says. "Sorry. Yes, he's here, but he's on a conference call. Can I have him call you right back?"

"Sure," I say, trying to keep up my enthusiasm, but a tiny bit of me loses steam. I hate putting the ball in his court. What if he was just being nice? What if he didn't mean what he said? What if he never calls? "That will be fine."

I have about three minutes of feeling great before Henry spits up and Hazel screams that it's gross. I am cleaning up when the phone rings. I take a soaking-wet baby to the phone, answer, and try to hear the response over Hazel's cries. Of course, it's Ed.

"Lila," he says, acting like there isn't a tremendous amount of noise in the background. "I was glad to hear you called."

"Hi, Ed," I say. "Believe it or not, when I called ten minutes ago all was quiet here."

"I believe it," he says warmly. "I hear things went well with the baby's arrival. What did you name him?"

"Henry, after my father," I say. "I'm calling to thank you and everyone there for those beautiful flowers. That meant a lot."

"You are very welcome," he says, then says to someone else, "Okay, I'll call him back. Sorry about that, Lila. Have you thought any more about our conversation?" I have to strain to hear him.

I open the cabinet and search desperately for something to distract Hazel, whose cries have reached the pitch of an ambulance siren. I look at my watch; it's ten in the morning. Is that too early for a Hershey bar? No. I take it out and show it to her. She sucks in her breath and is immediately quiet. Crisis defused.

"Well, yes," I say. "I mean, I don't have a plan or a timeline in my head, but the thought of coming back is hard to shake."

"We have a few events coming up, could really use your help," he says. "One is—"

But before he can tell me, Henry spits up again. He starts to whimper and then really cry.

"Oh, I guess the little one needs you," Ed says kindly, not finishing his thought. "I'll call you in what, a few weeks? A month? You tell me, Lila. I want to work with you."

"How about I call you, Ed; would that be okay?" I ask. "It might be a little while. I want to think this through, talk to Sam about it. And Henry is still so little."

"That will be fine," he says. "I'll look forward to it."

A few days later, Sam's father, Edgar, comes to visit. He is a strange, quiet man who hates to leave home but wants to see his new grandson. Even though Edgar lives in California, he comes for only two nights. I try to concentrate on getting ready for him and decide not to tell Sam about my conversations with Ed until after Edgar leaves. Sam has been completely distracted anyway, spending the last three nights scouring the sports pages and stocking up on spylike gadget ideas so he and Edgar will have things to talk about. He hasn't been able to sit still all day.

Whenever we see Edgar, I think about how Sam's mother left them. It seems crazy to me now that she made it through about ten years with a baby, toddler, and then child but left when he was able to do so much for himself.

When Sam first told me the story and expressed his own fears about settling down and having children, I saw it as a ticket to get involved without ever being needed or expected to change my lifestyle. I mean, this was even better than Tom. No children *and* no marriage.

Then one day when I was leaving Sam's house on my way to a situation in Idaho, I was so distraught I could barely say good-bye. A cab was waiting for me out on the street; we had been so casual about our good-byes that Sam rarely drove me to the airport anymore, unless I had a very late flight. I had had breakfast—homemade blueberry pancakes and cappuccino instead of black coffee and grapefruit—and I had kissed the top of his fluffy head as he sat at the small table in the bright kitchen. He reached around to hug me. I grabbed the handle of my beloved suitcase that was by the door, I walked onto the porch, and I could not go any farther. I tried, but the empty feeling I already had from knowing how much I was going to miss him was unbearable. For the first time, the Bear Lake Addison seemed far away and not quite so important. The cabdriver honked, and I put up my finger to tell him to wait.

Five minutes later, when he honked again repeatedly, Sam came to the front window, saw me sitting on the top step, and came out in his bathrobe. He put his arm around me, looked into my eyes, then motioned for the cab to leave. I didn't protest.

"What's going on?" he asked, his voice soft.

"I don't know," I said, feeling my muscles relax and letting the tears come. "I just don't want to go away anymore."

He eased me back into the house. A few minutes later I called Ed and said I was sick and wouldn't be able to go to Idaho, and somebody else would have to deal with the aftermath of the tornado. He didn't even question me; I hadn't called in sick in five years.

"I don't really want to be alone either," Sam said a little later, after he had suggested for the first time that I try to put my brain in park. The image had made me laugh. I could picture my overactive brain pulling into a parking spot, and then I envisioned myself turning off the motor and walking away from it. We had finally started to relax and were settled on his couch in his living room. I found myself wondering what I could do to spruce up the place.

"What I really don't want is to be away from you," he said, turning my face to his.

"I didn't expect this," I said. "What will happen to me?"

"You'll have a great meal, some great sex, and you'll leave for Idaho tomorrow."

"Okay," I said. I didn't mention that by then it would be too late—the bulk of the crisis would be over, and plans would already be in place—or that I wasn't talking about just that one day. I simply never went. I flew to New York a few days later to talk to Ed. I told him that I wanted to spend some time in one place.

"Who's the guy?" he asked.

"Sam Soto," I told him. "A guy with an oven and herbs and a tiny gray house with a purple door."

"It happens to most of us at some point," he said reassuringly. "Whatever you need, I'll do my best to help you."

And he did. I came back to New Orleans with my little suitcase and a full-time job at the Oak Addison, went to Sam's like I always did, and never left. The only person I told the full story to was Cece, who was by then rising to the position of food and beverage manager for the hotel chain, traveling all over the world. In her usual way she listened kindly, and never ever pointed out the fact that this was exactly what I thought I didn't want.

Very slowly I started to buy extra shirts and underwear. A new pair of jeans, a few pairs of socks. One rainy afternoon we adopted Desire from an animal shelter on Magazine Street, not too far from the café where we met eating gumbo, telling ourselves that Sam was perfectly capable of taking care of her when I was out of town.

At first I made it sound like I was working on a long-term project at the local Addison. Before we knew it, six months went by. They were wonderful months. We didn't talk much about the future, but when we were together, I didn't want to be anyplace else, and I didn't think Sam did either.

And then I found out I was pregnant. One morning I woke up feeling dizzy and sick, and when it didn't go away for five days, I walked to the local Rite Aid, still purple from when it used to be a K&B drugstore, and bought a test. It was positive.

That night I told Sam.

Sam looked at me, then got up and went into the kitchen. I figured he needed a minute to decide how to tell me to leave. Then I heard him open and close the refrigerator, take pots down from the rack, rinse herbs. I sat on our new leather couch and listened. The sound of something frying in a pan came just before the amazing smell of garlic and tomato. I realized I was starving. When Sam called me to the table, I couldn't get there fast enough.

"The way I see it we have a fifty-fifty shot at getting this right," he said as we ate the pasta he had made. "Your mother was loving and giving and present, and mine was not."

I smiled at him, so relieved and so hungry and sick at the same time.

"This is either my chance to make right what my mother made wrong, or it's my chance to understand why she did what she did," he told me. "Either way, it's a chance I can't pass up."

We ate in silence for a while.

"We might as well get married," he said, surprising me. "We might as well go all the way."

I was too nauseated to disagree.

As I attempt to make my house presentable for Edgar, I wonder what kept him going after Sam's mother left. Edgar managed to maintain a somewhat normal life for Sam through high school. They lived in San Francisco, and Edgar was a high-powered banker until Sam went off to college. Then Edgar sold his house, quit his job, and moved to a hut with no electricity or running water at the base of Mount Shasta. Who does that?

When I had pointed out how wacky that was, Sam said he wasn't shocked by Edgar's change of lifestyle; he was just surprised that he didn't move deeper into the woods, away from all civilization. Once a week Edgar rents a motel room to shower, shave, and watch *Jeopardy!*, the one part of the civilized world he just can't seem to let go.

An early clue to Edgar's current lifestyle was that he'd always been obsessed with camping. Sam said they would go every weekend. While Edgar planned hikes and fishing trips, Sam planned the meals they would cook over the open fire or camp stove. While Edgar packed gear and warm clothes, Sam carefully poured home-dried herbs like basil and thyme into empty plastic film canisters. Apparently Sam's mother was a great cook, and it was something that Sam held on to.

Edgar wanted Sam to work in a national park. He took Sam to every single one in the continental United States, trying to find the best fit for him. All Sam wanted to do was find each area's best restaurant or write about the scenery.

In college, Sam grudgingly majored in forestry but took writing courses, too. Edgar couldn't imagine his son as a writer; it was too dainty. He wanted him to wander with the bison, build bridges over creeks, and enforce national park rules. When Sam started writing about food, it was more than Edgar could take. He didn't even ask about Sam's job here for the first few months. Instead, they would talk about sports or plan hypothetical camping trips that they both knew they would never take.

When Sam started telling Edgar about the challenge of keeping his identity a secret, he became more interested. And when Sam started buying gadgets, like his recording device and a machine that measures the noise level in restaurants, Edgar wanted to hear about it. I guess the spy angle made it a little more manly.

Edgar should be here in fifteen minutes, and the house is a wreck. I remind myself that I have a ten-day-old baby and a three-year-old, and that Sam's father lives in a hut with no electricity or running water. This should seem like the Ritz compared to that. I sit back, nurse Henry, and wait for Edgar to arrive. I'm a little concerned that he'll show up with a newborn-size sleeping bag and try to talk Sam into taking the baby camping.

The doorbell rings and I tense up. I hear Sam start to run down from the third floor, but I reach the door first. As soon as I pull it open, I'm sorry for all the recent thoughts I've had about Edgar. He already has the storm door open and can't wait to get inside. He steps in and has eyes only for Henry. He takes him from me tenderly and kisses his baby cheek. Then he sniffs his forehead, and I know he is breathing in his baby scent. At that moment Hazel runs in from the kitchen. Edgar quickly hands the baby back to me and kneels down to catch her as she opens her arms and jumps at him.

"I thought about hugging you during my entire trip here on the plane," Edgar tells Hazel. "I kept knocking on the pilot's door and telling him to hurry up because I had to get to my beautiful granddaughter." Hazel laughs and hops around in a little circle.

"Rewy, Grandpa?" she asks. "Who is the powit?"

"The pilot, bear cub; he's the one who drives the plane," Edgar says. Then he stands up and hugs me.

"Sorry, Lila. If your children weren't so mesmerizing, it wouldn't take me so long to notice you," he says. "You look terrific. Did you really just have a baby?"

"Thanks, Edgar," I say. And then Sam pushes past everyone to get to his father. They are exactly the same height, not quite six feet, with slight shoulders, long, straight backs, and exceptionally big feet. They have the same thick hair. Sam's is the same cinnamon color as Hazel's; Edgar's has turned a bright white. They both have small bumps at the bridge of their noses, and bushy eyebrows. But their eyes are different. Sam says it is the one physical trait he took from his mother. Where Edgar's are small and the color of a murky, slightly greenish river, Sam's are huge and round and dark, with fluffy, long eyelashes. I watch as my husband first takes his father's hand, then hugs him. Edgar settles into the hug, and it occurs to me that he probably doesn't get to touch many people.

He's wearing an old gray suit that's fraying around the sleeves and the pant cuffs. I think it's the same suit he wore to our wedding, and I'm touched that he thinks this is such a special occasion.

"Grandpa, Grandpa," Hazel screeches, tugging on his pants. "What did the powit say when you said that to him?"

Edgar pulls away from Sam and goes to Hazel.

"He said he would push through the clouds, quickly pass the moon, cancel afternoon tea with the sun, and get me to you as soon as he could," Edgar says. Hazel squeals.

Why was I dreading his visit? I have an urge to reach out to him, to tell him to move to the woods outside of Philadelphia so we can see him more. I want to thank him for raising Sam. I want to tell him that even though Sam didn't particularly love camping, it was very nice of him to spend every weekend with his son. I don't say any of those things. Instead, I tell myself to remember this feeling should the other judgmental ones creep back in.

The next morning we're still in bed when Sam tells me we're going out to dinner that night.

"I can't," I say. "I can't leave Henry yet."

"Then we'll bring him," Sam says. "I'll incorporate him into my disguise."

"Can we bring Hazel?" I ask. "I don't have a babysitter. Would she fit into your disguise?"

He thinks for a minute.

"No, I'd be too afraid that she'd give me away," he says seriously. "Can you call Sunny?"

"Why do I have to go?" I ask.

"Because I don't want to be alone with my father," he says. "We won't have enough to talk about."

I get out of bed and find Sunny's number. She's glad to come tonight and sit with Hazel. This is the first time Sam wants to take his dad out for a review meal, and I'm a little intrigued. In the past, Edgar said he wasn't interested. He said he didn't come to see Sam work, and he didn't care much about food anyway. But I know Sam's talk about disguises and spylike gadgets has captured his interest.

Sam informs me that we are going to a classic French restaurant that has been around for years. Sounds good to me. In fact, I'm surprised to find myself looking forward to it all day. I don't start to get nervous until I think about the reality of having Henry at the restaurant. About twenty minutes before we're set to leave I take him into his room to nurse him. He falls into a deep sleep. I try to rouse him, but when I lift his arm, it drops like tiny baby lead. He's out. I put him in his bassinet, figuring if he wakes up we'll take him. He doesn't even move.

"Sunny, Henry is fast asleep so I'm going to leave him with you," I say as I enter the kitchen. I hand her the baby monitor. "We'll be back in two hours, but if he wakes up, please call me. I can be home in ten minutes."

"No problem," she says, turning on the monitor and putting it on the window ledge behind her. She goes back to finding hidden pictures in a book with Hazel.

"What?" Sam says. It's the first time I've looked at him and I cannot believe it. At any moment I expect him to start playing his air guitar. He has on a wild, long-haired, highlighted wig, some sort of cheek lifters that are put on with putty, a little eye makeup, and big Elton John–like glasses.

"You aren't taking Henry?" Sam asks.

"No," I say, still staring at him. "He fell asleep. It is so much easier to leave him."

"Who am I going to say you are now?" Sam asks, pushing some of his rock-star hair out of the way of his rock-star glasses.

"Who was I going to be?" I ask.

"The nanny," Sam says.

I glare at him, not wanting Sunny to think that I think there is anything wrong with being a nanny. But why should I pretend I am the nanny to my own child?

"I know," Sam says. "I'll say you're my publicist. If Sunny calls during dinner, we'll pretend there is some public relations crisis. Perfect."

Edgar comes into the kitchen and looks at Sam. Then he smiles and reaches out his hand for a manly shake. It occurs to me that Sam missed his chance here; he should have dressed as a park ranger.

Le Shack is clear across the city, but Sam insists on walking. I know he wants to show his father that he is rugged and outdoorsy. The wind is blowing crazily, escorting in a nor'easter. Edgar doesn't seem to notice. He saunters along, hands in the pockets of his old gray suit. He looks up at the stars—or the rain clouds, as the case may be. He takes a deep breath.

I am still a good eight blocks from the restaurant, walking between my rock-star husband and my Grizzly Adams father-in-law, when the rain starts to fall. Big, huge Henry tears at first, then steadier, smaller drops. Without a word, Edgar walks to the curb, puts out his hand, stops a cab, and helps me in. When we are all settled, I lean over and hug him. Maybe he isn't as crazy as I thought.

"Le Shack, please," Sam says in a vaguely British accent. I think he's practicing.

The cabdriver looks at him through the rearview mirror a few times.

"Hey, do I know you?" he finally asks.

"I don't think so," Sam says, getting antsy. Six blocks to go.

"No, really, I think I have some of your records," the cabdriver says. "Yeah, I recognize you from the album cover. What is your name? Wait, don't tell me. You're . . ."

"No," Sam says quietly. Edgar seems amazed by the exchange. "I'm not." Three more blocks.

"Oh, I get it," the cabdriver says. "Keeping a low profile, huh? I won't tell anyone." How ironic.

The cabdriver smiles for the rest of the drive. He acts like he has Elton John himself in the back of his cab. When we get there, he tells Sam the fare is on him; it's been a pleasure to drive him.

"No, I insist," Sam says, handing him a twenty-dollar bill and getting out of the cab fast.

"It really *is* you," the cabdriver says as we hustle through the rain toward Le Shack. Edgar and I look back to see the driver pick up his cell phone and dial furiously. He must be eager to tell someone he had a star in his backseat.

We walk up a grand stone staircase and enter an extremely elegant room with a fireplace and stained-glass windows. I am so glad I didn't bring Henry. The hostess greets us nicely, but already I can tell that Sam is not going to be the star he was in our taxicab. She looks him up and down, glances at Edgar's fraying sleeves. Then she leads us through a series of rooms with long, burning candles and beautiful china on each table, to a room in the back. I think they call it the library. It is still a fine table, but I guess the hostess thinks we will offend fewer people here.

"Interesting," Sam says in a voice that does not sound anything like his own. "So that's how they treat people who don't buy their clothes at Brooks Brothers."

"This suit is from Brooks Brothers," Edgar says seriously.

"I wasn't talking about you, Dad," he says quickly. "I was talking about me."

We take a few minutes to look at the menus. Sam fiddles with his microphone. When the room is clear of waiters, he makes a big show of describing the room into his sleeve. Then he fiddles with his huge glasses, looking down, then up, then down again.

We go through the menu and order. Edgar sticks to the basics but is an easier dining companion than Sam imagined he would be. Le Shack is famous for its soups, which come to the table in big tureens that are ladled into each bowl by tuxedo-clad waiters. I have the creamy crabmeat soup with a splash of sherry, Sam has a delicate vegetable soup served with fresh pesto, and Edgar orders the vichyssoise. He says he is used to having his soup cold. Once the soups are served and the waiters have gone, Sam starts to fiddle with his glasses again. I hear a click. He focuses on each of the soup bowls and clicks again. Edgar and I watch him.

"It's a digital camera," Sam says proudly when Edgar raises his eyebrows. "It helps me remember what everything looked like when I sit down to write, and a cell phone would be too obvious."

So that's what he was putting together during Hazel's big-sister party. Where did he get the idea for that thing? From a James Bond catalog? He's never used a camera before. His audiotape is more than enough description. I have an urge to rip off his glasses and scream in his face, but I don't. I take six very deep breaths and turn to Edgar.

"So tell me about your property, Edgar. What's going on now that the weather's getting really cold? Do you have to do anything to prepare?" I ask. The truth is I really don't care so much. But Sam is drowning under a desperate need to impress his father. Usually this sort of question will elicit a twenty-minute response.

"It's still autumn, Lila—let's enjoy it while we can," he says. And then he is all Sam's. They talk about gadgets Sam might buy. They talk about Sam's cooking. They come up with some imaginary restaurant that you have to hike many miles to reach. I am very bored and my breasts are starting to hurt.

A young waiter brings our main courses: mine is a Cornish game hen covered in a mixed-berry sauce. I try to wipe the smear marks off of the strange black plate, when my phone rings.

"Hello," I say, trying to sound official for Sam's sake. I immediately hear Henry crying.

"He's up," Sunny says. "Sorry."

"No problem," I say. "I'll be right there to take care of it."

I look at the men.

"I've got to go," I say, trying not to laugh. "Some problem with the photo shoot that's going on right now with the band. Not enough milk or something. I've got to get back to the office."

"No problem," Sam says in a thick English accent. "I'll have them pack up your food, and I'll get it to you. Thanks."

I wave as I grab my sweater off the back of the chair, then walk to the front of the restaurant. The hostess asks if I need a cab, and I'm home taking care of that milk problem in minutes.

We barely leave the house again during Edgar's visit, and he does not suggest that we take Henry camping. He does play with Hazel and hold Henry as much as they'll let him. And he continues to be interested in Sam's job.

"Life is funny in the city," Edgar says on his last morning with us, and I immediately know what's coming. I guess he's been holding it in. "Sam, don't you miss the sound of raindrops on the trees?"

"Dad, we have trees," Sam says as gently as he can. "When it rains, and we're lying in bed, we hear it."

"It's not the same," Edgar says grumpily, shaking his head and looking at us with a know-it-all smirk that I have seen on Sam many times. He's quiet for a minute, and I think that might be all he has to say. I'm wrong. "You know, they've been having trouble with the bears and wolves in some of the parks out west. Of course, the animals come to where the garbage is, but I just don't see why the parks don't handle it better, maybe have underground receptacles that the animals can't smell, line them with concrete or something. Sam, you'd be good at working that sort of problem out. Lila told me you spent some time in a restaurant Dumpster recently. Or what about marketing those camera glasses for bird watching? That might be a good idea."

"I'm happy, Dad," is all Sam says. We both know Edgar has been out of the wilderness for too long.

Hazel cries when Edgar has to go and begs him to come back soon. Edgar gives Henry a long cuddle, tells Hazel he'll have a talk with the pilot about when he can bring him back, and kisses my cheek.

"Thanks for making Sam such an incredible family," he whispers in my ear just before he heads out the door. It is the first time anyone has said anything like that to me. I turn to see Sam smiling, and Hazel trying to cover Henry with pieces of newspaper. Sam gently takes them away. Have I made an incredible family? I never would have thought myself capable of that.

"Thanks for making Sam," I whisper back. I want to say more, making Sam what? But it is enough for Edgar. He holds my hands tight, and then he is gone.

WINTER

CHAPTER FIVE

It's hard to stand out among the new hot spots in Old City, but Decadence has managed to do just that. On a recent visit we ordered the whole lobe of foie gras. It was presented at the table in eight thick, charred slices of oozing pink richness placed atop a proscenium of diced mango and pineapple glazed in sweet sauternes wine and rendered fat. I placed a jiggly slice on butter-soaked brioche toast and hummed as this epic ode to indulgence melted away against the roof of my mouth.

—Sam Soto

As the holiday season approaches, so does the strike. One night in late December, Sam comes home with a huge overflowing box. I see files, a few cookbooks, an adorable picture of Sam and Hazel sharing an ice cream cone.

"Did you quit?" I ask.

"Ha-ha," he says, as if it's the least funny thing he has ever heard. "We were told to leave tonight like we were leaving for a long time. The strike is probably going to begin at midnight. If it does, I won't be able to get back into the building."

I decide not to pepper him with my usual questions. I believe he doesn't know what to expect. We eat dinner. He plays with the kids. If there is no work, then maybe Sam can just be here with us. It is so nice I find myself hoping for a strike.

Later in the night he can't sleep so neither can I. He is up and down. At about twelve thirty he comes back to bed.

"Are you awake?" he whispers. Henry is sleeping next to me.

"Yes," I whisper back.

"It's definite," he says. "The union is on strike. I'm going to have to walk the picket line at a certain time each day if I want to get my strike pay," Sam says from his side of the bed.

"Okay," I say groggily.

"Tomorrow I have to be there at ten," he says.

"Okay," I say again, keeping my eyes closed.

"Last night I was eating the biggest plate of foie gras I have ever seen, and now I'm on strike," Sam says, getting up and walking to the closet. "Go figure. This totally sucks."

He starts to look through his side of the closet, then goes over to mine.

"Do you have any wigs?" he asks.

"Wigs?"

"I'm going to be standing out on the street in broad daylight; I need a disguise," he says. "I can't worry about a beard or mustache falling off, and I don't think my rock-star getup would be appropriate."

I push myself up on my elbows and watch him search through my side of the closet. I can't imagine what he expects to find there.

"Sam, you don't have to wear a name tag," I say. "People who see you out there are not going to know it's you."

"I can't take that chance," he says. "What if someone who knows me drives by and stops to take a picture or notifies other people and then they drive by and look at me?"

I throw the covers off, get out of bed, and walk to Hazel's room. She's fast asleep. I come back holding an Ariel wig in one hand and Cinderella in the other.

"These are the only wigs I can find," I tell him.

He looks at me, comes over and considers both, then takes the Cinderella wig out of my hand and tries it on. He goes to the mirror and pulls it as tight as he can.

"I don't know," he says. "It's a little small."

I don't even answer him. I get into bed and try to fall asleep.

At first, there is lots of talk about the end of the strike, but it seeps into January. Sam gets to try out one disguise after another. He wears all of Hazel's wigs, including Jasmine from *Aladdin* and Jessie from *Toy Story*. He also buys a bunch. There are days when his supervisor actually calls me to say Sam never showed up. When that happens, I tell him to look for the cowboy or the princess, or whomever Sam is impersonating that day.

We spent a lot of money on our move, so our lack of savings, and the lack of my income, is becoming a concern. Each day I think about calling Ed. This morning, after Sam leaves wearing overalls, a huge straw hat, and a fake scar on his chin, I decide I am going to do it. But before I have a chance to, the phone rings.

"Hello?" I say, feeling like I've somehow been caught doing something I shouldn't be doing.

"Lila, dear?" a creaky old voice asks. "When will you be here?"

"Here?" I say, trying to figure out how someone who has the wrong number could possibly know my name.

"For our tea party, dear?" the voice says. And then I remember. Weeks ago I agreed to visit Sam's lonely great aunt. I don't think I even wrote it down. Excuses clog my head—I could say Hazel is sick; I could say our car is in the shop.

"I've been cooking all night, dear," she says. "Sammy told me you like tarts."

"We'll be there around noon."

When I hang up, I decide she's done me a favor. I shouldn't call Ed on an impulse. I have to think it through first.

When it is time to leave, I put Henry in the BabyBjörn for the first time by myself, almost dropping him on the floor twice while I try to get the snap shut. Once he's secure, I drag the stroller down the stoop, and I try to lift Hazel in. She won't bend.

"No, Mommy, no," she screeches, kicking and shoving Henry's head away from her. I try to protect the baby's head while holding on to Hazel.

Willa, Mrs. Arts and Crafts, walks by with Russell somehow quietly nestled on the back of a double stroller and the twins sleeping in it. She looks at me with what I'm sure is pity.

"Do you need some help?" she asks, wheeling her brood over toward me. Hazel pushes back, and her head smacks the infant car seat that I balanced on top of the stroller. She starts to wail.

"Mommyyyy!" she screams.

"No," I say to Willa, trying to be heard over Hazel's distress cries. "We're fine."

"Okay," she says with a tone that tells me she doesn't believe me. "Just holler if you need anything."

I hear her humming to herself as she steers her heavy load toward her own stoop. Did she say *holler*? I cannot stand the thought of her watching me. So I balance the empty infant seat in the part of the stroller where Hazel should be, push the stroller with one hand, grab her hand with the other, and we walk the few blocks to where Sam last parked the car. When we finally get there, I leave the stroller and its contents on the sidewalk and shove Hazel into her car seat. But when

I lean over to buckle the straps, I still have Henry in the Björn, and I smack his head into hers. They both start to cry.

"Mommy," she says with a hiccup. "You hurt me. You so mean."

"Sorry, Sweetie," I say. I want to kiss the top of her head but I don't—what if I hit her with another baby part?

I check to make sure no one is bleeding and then continue. I notice an old lady on the sidewalk has stopped and is standing near my stroller.

Once Hazel is in, still whimpering, I walk over to the woman. She smiles. I know I know her from somewhere, but I can't place her. Then I realize she is Carol, one of my baking neighbors. I decide not to say anything; maybe she doesn't recognize me.

"I'm guarding it for you," she says in her raspy voice. I can't imagine why this poor lady feels she has to stop to help. I should be helping her cross the street or carrying her groceries or something.

"Thanks," I say. "We're fine." Maybe if I keep saying it, it will become true.

I pick up the infant seat, walk around, and snap it in. Hazel is still crying. I get Henry out of the front carrier, set him in his seat, and now *he* won't bend. I use some gentle strength and finally manage to snap the buckles. Carol is still standing there. Henry is screaming, Hazel is pounding on her window, and I'm sweating in my winter coat. As I walk around to my side of the car, my neighbor pulls a plastic bag of greenish cookies out of her big purse and holds it out to me.

"A snack for your kids," she says. "I made them myself."

"Thanks," I say, taking the bag. A strange smell seeps through the plastic. I don't tell her the cookies look moldy, or that Henry is too young for solid food. I get into the car and take deep breaths.

"Mommy!" Hazel whimpers from the backseat. "You mean."

"No, Honey, I'm not mean," I say, though I'm not so sure. "We're going to have fun. Really. If this all works out, I'll get you some candy, soon. Okay? Now we're ready to go."

As I am about to pull away from the curb, I look behind the car and notice that the stroller is on the sidewalk, next to my neighbor, who is still staring at us. Without a word, I turn off the car and retrieve it.

"Thank you," I say again to Carol.

"See you back on the Court," she says, finally getting on her way. Did I really think she didn't recognize us? I wonder if she had a hidden camera in that purse and will show the video to the others. Maybe they have a weekly screening of real-life bloopers and blunders.

By the time I finally pull away, Henry is crying so hard I'm afraid he is having trouble catching his breath. I drive to our house, park in front, load the heavy diaper bag and a booster seat for Hazel as quickly as I can before Carol makes it home, and get settled again in my seat.

"I hafta go potty, Mommy," Hazel says.

"Okay," I say as kindly as I can, stopping myself from pounding my fists on the steering wheel. I get out of the car, unbuckle Hazel, walk her up our front steps, get Henry out, and we all go inside and up to the bathroom, where Hazel decides she doesn't really have to go.

"Honey, why don't you let me put a diaper on for the car ride?" I ask hopefully.

"No, I wrike my Pigwet underwear," she says sternly.

"But then you can relax; there might not be a bathroom on the way," I offer.

"Mommy, there is batroom on way, I know," she says.

I sigh, thinking that perhaps she is smarter than I am.

"You're right," I say. "I'm sure there is a bathroom on the way." She smiles Sam's know-it-all smile.

I get us all back in the car. The whole process takes about an hour. I could direct a team of employees on how to handle the reopening of a resort hotel after a hurricane killed six tourists, demolished the main building, and closed it down for two years in less time. I start to wonder why we only hear of rock stars being hospitalized for exhaustion and never mothers. Then I call Aunt Gladys from my cell phone and tell her we are going to be late.

I keep hoping Henry will quiet down, but he just gets louder and louder. I glance at the clock on the dashboard—11:45. He hasn't eaten since a little after eight o'clock. He's hungry. I pull over just on the other side of Twenty-Second Street and stop the car. We've gone four blocks.

"Sorry about this, Sweetie," I say to Hazel. "I'm just going to feed Henry quick."

"Nooooooooooooooo," she wails.

"I have to, he's hungry. He's crying."

"He is not hungry," she says louder, kicking the back of my seat.

I am somewhat encouraged by the fact that she acknowledged his existence, possibly for the first time. That's progress, right? Never mind that she wants him to starve. I unhook Henry from his seat, take him into the front with me, and nurse him. He is very hungry.

"I want to go," Hazel yells over the newfound peace in our small car. "Put it away." I think she means my breast. Or maybe she means the baby.

"We'll go very soon," I say quietly, trying not to disturb Henry. "Just a few more minutes."

And it isn't long before Henry is sound asleep. I feel the tightness in my shoulders start to loosen. The pain in the muscle I think I pulled while trying to get Hazel into the stroller eases a little, too. I put Henry back in his seat. Then I call Aunt Gladys to tell her we are going to be later.

For the rest of the drive Henry sleeps and Hazel lets me listen to Van Morrison. I find my way to Aunt Gladys's neighborhood but get lost on the small Swarthmore streets. I am starting to worry that Hazel will ask about a potty any minute, or that she'll arrive with urine-soaked pants, when I pull up to the house. It is shingled, with a huge wrap-around front porch.

Aunt Gladys, whom I have met only a few times, teeters onto the porch to greet us, and the first thing that comes to my mind is that she is way too frail to help me with the unloading process. The minute we get inside, I want to turn around and go home.

"This no candy store, Mommy," Hazel protests. "I thought we were going to get candy."

My face flushes red.

"No, Sweetie," I say. "Today we are visiting. Maybe tomorrow we'll get candy."

"Nooooooo," she wails. "Candy, now."

"I think I might have a little something sweet," Aunt Gladys says. She is wearing what looks like an old evening gown, shimmery gold, with white stockings and red shoes. She has on lots of jewelry and too much perfume. I feel very lonely.

She teeters away and returns with something that she hands to Hazel. I look around, but instead of seeing antique china and unusual sculptures, I see all the things that Hazel can break. I glance over at Hazel just as she is about to put an extra-large yellow sour ball into her mouth. I grab it away. She screams. So much for Aunt Gladys's offering *me* advice—she almost choked my three-year-old.

I tell myself we'll stay for less than an hour.

"I thought we could enjoy some tea together, dear," Aunt Gladys says, pointing to a table set for two with fine china. Didn't she specifically ask that I bring my children?

"Thank you," I say, taking my place with Hazel on my lap and Henry in his carrier on the floor at my feet.

"I thought iced tea would be better around the little ones," she says, pointing to a pitcher. "And I baked some cookies for the little princess."

Okay, maybe I got the wrong first impression. Maybe this can still be fun. Hazel takes her cookies and sits on the floor. I begin to relax.

"I miss having company in my house," she says. "Sammy has always been so nice to me, but my own children almost never come around. They're spread out all over the world."

"Where is everyone?" I ask, trying to make conversation. She launches into a long explanation about her five children. I look at my watch; twenty minutes have gone by. Then I look at the floor. I see a big pile of crumbs, but I don't see Hazel. She must have slipped away while we were talking. When I get up to look for her, I spot her in the next room gripping a snow globe. My first impulse is to scream, and I am proud of myself for holding back. I don't want to scare her. As I get closer, I see it is a big glass snow globe that houses a snowman holding three colorful balloons—red, green, and blue. It barely fits in the palm of her hand. Henry starts to cry; Hazel turns at the sound and knocks the glass ball into a table, cracking the globe in half. Water pours out along with the plastic snow. Thin glass crinkles to the floor. Then there is a louder crash as Hazel drops what is in her hands.

"Is everything okay in there?" Aunt Gladys calls.

I check Hazel for bleeding, glad to see she didn't cut herself.

"Well, one of your snow globes broke," I say as Hazel starts to cry. "I'm very sorry."

Aunt Gladys shuffles into the room. Then she goes to get a broom and dustpan and slowly cleans up the mess.

"I can do that," I offer, feeling mad at and sorry for Hazel at the same time.

"No, I'll do it," she says. "I should have put that away. It's my fault. I've had that snowman since my first granddaughter was born. That's more than ten years."

"I'm so sorry," I say. "Maybe we can replace it."

"It is irreplaceable," she says nicely, but is she being a little mean under the surface? I can't tell. "Come, let's go back to our tea."

I smile weakly at Aunt Gladys and take my seat again, patting the floor for Hazel, who is whimpering. Henry is still crying, and I try to soothe him by rubbing his foot. Something smells awful. I wonder if it is Aunt Gladys. I try to ignore it, but soon Aunt Gladys is sniffing around. I look at Henry and see brownish moisture seeping through his clothes. I consciously stop myself from saying *shit* out loud.

I scoop him up, trying not to let anything get on me. I force Hazel to come upstairs with me. I put the diaper mat on top of the bathroom rug, but the runny poop exceeds the borders of the mat and gets everywhere, changing the creamy-colored rug to one with mustard-yellow spots. Hazel refuses to try to pee, and I worry about her getting a bladder infection. I can't remember the last time she peed. When I try to encourage her to, she tries to unfasten the door. Henry is crying on the floor, and I am furiously trying to scrub out the stains. I use a little Dove soap, I try shampoo. Nothing works. Aunt Gladys keeps calling up to see if we are okay. Finally I scrunch up the rug and jam it in the diaper bag, hoping Aunt Gladys is confused enough that she won't notice it's gone.

We go downstairs, and I try again to resume our tea party. But Hazel becomes clingy and wants to be on my lap, and when I try to put Henry down he screams, so I end up holding both of them for most of the time.

"I don't want him here," she says. "Move him."

"Sweetie, there is plenty of room," I say to her. I turn to Gladys. "Did your children have trouble accepting new siblings?"

"Not that I recall," she says, looking past me. "Can you and Sam come back to visit this weekend?"

"Maybe," I say. "But I think we really have to go now."

I gather our things, put Henry back in his seat, and grab Hazel's hand.

"Thanks so much for the tea," I say.

I get us into the car, and this time everyone complies. Aunt Gladys comes out to the porch and waves. I reluctantly get out, praying that she didn't spot the missing bathroom rug. Between this and Mrs. Blueberry

Buckle's towel, I am clearly challenged when it comes to textile etiquette. I leave the car door open and walk over to her.

"It was such a lovely visit, dear," she says, reaching out her hand. There are rings on three of her fingers, and her bracelets are clanging. I can't help but wonder why she bothered with all the jewelry. "It gets easier, really it does. And then, just when you want them around, they get their own lives and don't need you anymore."

I just look at her. I cannot imagine that.

"Well, thanks," I say.

"And here is something for you." She hands me a package shaped like a shoe box.

"Thanks," I say again. Aunt Gladys turns and teeters back into the house. I put the box in the car and pull Henry out of his seat and try to relax and nurse him. He eats but is not as hungry as usual, which surprises me because I keep forgetting to feed him today.

We make it about one hundred yards before Henry starts to howl. I don't think he's hungry. I pray that the motion will mesmerize him. Just as Hazel dozes off about ten minutes into our thirty-minute ride, I hear a horrible sound. I turn to see vomit everywhere—all over what I can see of Henry from the front of the car, all over his blanket, even on the window. I pull over, take everything off him, dig through the diaper bag, and find one last pair of too-small pajamas that I force on him. I throw away the stained bath mat and the vomit-covered clothes in a nearby garbage can. I'm sure most mothers actually wash these things, but I have an overwhelming urge to get rid of them, and it seems like a good short-term solution to me. I wonder all the way home if maybe he's sick and I somehow missed the signs. I bet humming Willa never misses the signs.

Just as we hit the city line, it starts to sleet. Henry is whimpering, and I'm cringing, expecting him to throw up again. Now I can barely see the road, and I think it is getting more slippery every minute. I slow down, try to tune everything out, and we make it home. I pull up in front of our house just as Henry falls asleep. Now I have two sleeping children, sleet, and no place to park since there is no parking on our street. When we first moved here, that seemed like a good thing. Now I'm not so sure. I decide that I will just wait here until something happens: someone wakes up; the sleet stops; my children grow up. Something. There's a big meeting about the strike tonight—the two sides are getting closer to an agreement—and Sam said he could be very late. I wonder if we'll have to wait here until he gets home.

I listen to more Van Morrison. I pluck my eyebrows. I wipe the dusty dashboard with a baby wipe. Out of the corner of my eye I notice movement in a window across the street. When I look, it stops. After a few minutes I catch the lady with the dark ponytail—I have to start learning people's names—watching me through her window. I feel like I'm being watched by the nosy neighbor in *Bewitched*. I'm afraid that she doesn't recognize me, and that she will call the police to report a suspicious vehicle. I roll down the passenger-side window and try to stick my face out. She sees that it's me and waves.

The next thing I know she is knocking on my window. I roll it down, and without a word she hands me a mug of steaming hot cocoa.

"Thanks," I whisper.

"You've been out here a long time; are you guys okay?" she asks. She seems nice. Maybe now is a good time to ask if she owns a restaurant.

"Oh yeah, we're fine," I say. I can't help thinking that if I were Pinocchio, my nose would be really long by now, and getting longer by the minute. "Lots of times I put the kids in the car so they can nap and I can get stuff done," I say. She smiles an unsteady smile. "I can read, balance the checkbook, plan my meals for the week. You know, the usual."

"You do that, too?" she says a little too loudly. Then she adds more quietly, "Plan your meals, I mean. But I try to avoid letting my kids sleep in the car. You know what they say about junk food and junk naps. But that's just me."

I put my finger to my lips, then point at my sleeping children in the backseat. I'm glad I didn't engage her in a longer conversation. I just want her to leave us alone.

"Thanks for this," I say finally, holding up the mug.

She gets the hint and waves. I'm sure the cocoa is imported from Belgium, but I can't bring myself to drink it. *Junk food, junk naps.* I want to scream. But I can still see her looking at me. I imagine her calling all the other mothers and having all eyes peering in my direction. I try to look busy.

I open the present Aunt Gladys handed me, even though I had intended to wait for Sam. It is wrapped in gold-and-red striped paper, about as unbaby as I can imagine. Under the paper I find an actual shoe box and open the lid to find actual shoes. They are lacy black flats that look a little like slippers, with big bows on the front. They are an adult size and look well worn. A note inside reads, *For your little girl to play dress-up.* How strange is that? Maybe Sam can wear them on the picket line tomorrow. I put my head down on the steering wheel and cry quietly. When I look up, I see the sleet has changed to snow.

Suddenly I am starving. I haven't eaten much, and I have the feeling that if I don't eat soon I am going to pass out. I scoot down in the seat so my neighbor won't see me, and I drink the cocoa. It is a little cold by now, but delicious, and I finish the entire mug. It's a pretty nice mug; maybe I'll add it to my collection. I sit back up and try to think of what to do next. I pull a pile of maps out of the glove compartment.

I'm trying to find the best way to get home from Detroit when I see someone walking toward me. As the hooded figure gets closer, he bends down and looks into the car, then starts waving and smiling. At first I worry it's another neighbor, but then I realize it's that nice waiter from La Noix. The one Sam was mean to.

"Hi!" he says as I put down the window. "How are you?"

"Oh, fine," I say, brushing icy snow off the window ledge.

"Have you been crying?" he asks. I'm shocked that he would notice. I'm definitely frustrated by the highway system surrounding Detroit, but I haven't cried in a good ten minutes.

"Well," I begin, but don't know what to say. He seems nice and I'm glad to see him. I'm glad to see anyone who doesn't live on this street and who hopefully isn't judging me. And I already know his restaurant-affiliation status. But I don't want to get too personal. "Just a little. Your name is Sebastian, right?"

"Right," he says.

"Where are you headed in this weather?" I ask.

"I'm just going in to work early," Sebastian says, shaking snow off of his sleeves. He is wearing a parka, but a tuxedo shirt and black bow tie peek over the zipper. I look down and notice he is wearing tuxedo pants, which he has neatly tucked into his boots.

"I don't have to be there for an hour, but I figured they would need extra help tonight," he continues, zipping up his parka as far as it will go. "With this weather I'm sure we'll be shorthanded. Any excuse to get out of my empty house. What are you guys doing?"

"We went to visit a great aunt in Swarthmore. It was a strange visit, definitely not what I expected, and judging from our drive home, I am clearly not equipped to take two children out of the house at the same time," I say, with what sounds strangely like a nervous giggle. I clear my throat. I want to keep the conversation going. I don't want him to leave—I was so lonely a minute ago—but I worry he is getting cold and wet. I peer out the window and see the tops of his boots are filling with snow.

"What happened?" he asks, acting like it is a bright sunny day and we're chatting on a street corner. I take a deep breath.

"Do you want to get in for a minute? You must be freezing," I say, not quite believing my own words. Sam would kill me. Divorce me at least. And what might my neighbors think?

Sebastian walks around the front of the car and pulls open the door. Snow blows in around him. He smiles, pushes his hood off his head, and takes a seat on the passenger side, gently moving the shoe box out of the way. I feel relieved, having felt so stranded just a few minutes ago. I'll worry about what to tell Sam later.

"So, tell me about your day," he says.

I tell him the whole story with too much detail, just like Sam always says I do. And Sebastian listens and doesn't seem to mind. While I talk, I look straight ahead, pretending to be interested in the worsening weather. Turning to face him seems way too intimate.

When I finish my dark tale, we just keep talking. He tells me how he came to La Noix after spending a few years in Greece, where his parents were born. He talks about how proud he is to work there, despite the crazy chef. He tells me that his dream is to one day open an upscale cheese shop of his own. And then for the first time since he walked up to my car, he looks sad.

"Is something wrong?" I ask.

"Oh, sorry, it sounds like you had a hard enough day without hearing about my problems," he says with a sigh that sounds vaguely like a heave. He isn't going to cry, is he? *That* would be way too intimate. But I kind of want to know about what's bothering him. I want to hear about someone else's problems.

"Oh, that's okay, you can tell me," I say. "I'm tired of talking about myself anyway."

"I just went through a really bad breakup," he says slowly. "A little more than three weeks ago we were living together, seeing his kids every other weekend, talking a little bit about maybe, someday, adopting a baby of our own, and then he was out the door, took his stuff, said I couldn't see his kids anymore. I mean, of course now that I look back I can see things weren't perfect. But he didn't have to . . ." His voice trails off.

I don't know what to say. I had guessed he was gay, but I'm glad to know it's true. I couldn't help but notice how handsome he is. His homosexuality removes one of the threads of inappropriateness from whatever we are doing. I think. I stop looking out the window and turn to face him.

"I'm sorry," I say finally. "That's awful."

"Well, yeah," Sebastian says. "Anyway, I didn't mean to dump that on you. But for some reason today has been hard. Maybe it's the weather, the idea that it's the first big snow of the season. I think one of the hardest things is not seeing his kids. He has two kids from a marriage when he was really young, before he . . . Well, sometimes I think I miss them more than I miss him. I would have loved to take them sledding today."

We're quiet for a minute.

"Of all my regrets, and I have many, my biggest one is that I will probably never have kids of my own. My sister has kids. I love kids," he says, perking up a little.

"Huh," I say, because nothing else comes to my mind.

"And I wasn't entirely truthful a minute ago. Stuart and I talked a little about adoption, but the truth is he wasn't at all sure he wanted to take on such a big responsibility again. I mean, he already did it," he says. "I crave being around kids. There is something about a tiny little person just starting out in life. I love to watch kids try to understand what they see around them. These last three weeks I have spent so much time with my sister's kids that she finally had to tell me to leave, to just go home. I was driving her crazy."

"Maybe Stuart knew what he was talking about, since he already raised his children," I say. Sebastian looks at me. "The family and baby thing sort of took me by surprise."

"You're lucky," Sebastian says.

"Yeah, well," I stall. "I love them and I wouldn't change them. But I feel pretty overwhelmed a lot of the time lately. I don't have time to do the things you just talked about, notice how their minds are working and stuff. That doesn't even occur to me. My neighbor just came out and basically told me that letting them sleep in the car is like giving them junk food for dinner. Or something like that. Sometimes lately I look at a really old person on the street, doddering along, and I think that person is so lucky because she gets to go home and rest."

Sebastian laughs. "Yeah, for another year or two maybe," he says.

"What I mean is that Stuart probably felt like he'd been through it, and now he is ready to rest a little, or do something else, something for himself maybe. How old are his kids?"

"Nine and twelve," Sebastian says wistfully. I worry that I made a mistake asking about them. "Hudson and Rachel."

"Is that why you broke up? I mean, because Stuart wasn't sure about adopting a baby?" Okay, what is my problem? This is none of my business. But at the same time I can't help myself. I haven't thought about my own problems in a good ten minutes.

"No. I mean yes. I mean no," he says, and I can tell he doesn't mind that I asked. "The truth is he has always liked men and women. With me, for a while anyway, I think he really thought it would be different. But it wasn't. He met a woman and they're dating. And he was totally honest with her about me, his ex-wife, everything. And she was open to trying. So, I know I should wish him well. I just thought I would be enough. I had convinced myself . . ."

"Yeah I had convinced myself of a lot of things, too," I say.

We're quiet for a few seconds, and I wonder if we've run out of things to talk about. I consider asking if he wants to study the maps from the glove compartment with me. I've been in this car way too long.

"Why don't you tell me more about you?" he asks, saving us from the maps. "What, may I ask, did you do before all this?" He gestures toward the backseat.

"Oh, I worked for a big hotel and resort company. The Addison Hotel and Resorts? I worked my way up to being their head of publicity, but I earned the reputation of being their top crisis-management guru," I say proudly. "I would fly all over the world dealing with situations facing the different hotels."

"That sounds great," he says. "Do you work now?"

I look down at my stained shirt and ratty pants, rub my makeupless swollen eyes, touch my messy hair. How could he possibly think I am a working person?

"Actually, yes," I say, lowering my voice. "I work undercover, going to different hotels and pretending to be a guest. This is a disguise."

Sebastian looks at me for a minute before he breaks out into a grin. I grin back.

"Well, I just thought I'd ask," he says. "So you didn't want to go back?"

I take a really deep breath. I have not even talked to Sam about this yet.

"Actually, I'm seriously considering going back—for a number of different reasons," I say. "But there are also a number of reasons why Sam and I have decided that I shouldn't right now."

"Like what?" Sebastian asks.

"Like the fact that Sam is desperate to remain unknown, and he thinks the fewer people I come into contact with the better. Also, at least when I worked before, I was in the newspaper a lot. And he wants to avoid that completely."

"I understand that," Sebastian says. "But you can't put your life on hold, can you? Not that having babies and taking care of them is putting your life on hold. I didn't mean to imply that."

"That's the thing," I say, shifting in my seat so I can sit up straighter. I take another deep breath. Then another one. "I think I am totally losing it being home all the time. I mean, you could throw me into anything at work and I could make some sense of it, but leave me alone with the kids for the day and I am lost in a dark forest. I ran into my boss recently. He said I could come back anytime. Adding my income to the pot again would be nice."

At that moment I notice that Hazel is watching us. I hope she didn't hear me say that. I don't want her to think I don't want to be with her, or that I'm going to abandon her.

"It's okay, Sweetie," I say. "We're home."

She stares at Sebastian with wide dark eyes.

"Hi," he says to her quietly with a wave. "I'm Sebastian."

She continues to stare. Of course, I have no idea what the next move should be, but Sebastian comes up with a plan. I'm grateful someone is capable of devising a plan. He helps me get everyone and everything in. I put the still-sleeping Henry into the Pack 'n Play in the living room. Sebastian carries our bags through what has turned into heavy snow. And then he takes our car and parks it. It was a choice between trusting him with my children and trusting him with my car, and I picked the latter.

While I stand at the door waiting for him to return with the keys, I realize I haven't felt this light or this good in a long time. But in the fifteen minutes it takes him to park and get back, most of those good feelings drain away. What am I thinking, befriending a waiter? And one who works at one of Sam's favorite restaurants. If the word gets out, people might think Sam gave La Noix such a high rating because we are friends with an employee. But the word can never get out, because fraternizing with restaurant staff is breaking Sam's golden rule. On the other hand, if Sam isn't going to let me be friends with other people, what does he expect me to do? I feel like a teenager whose parents have told her not to drink, so instead she has gotten into drugs, creating a worse scenario than they ever thought possible. Maureen is bad enough. Sebastian and I can't be friends.

When I see Sebastian trudging up the street, I can barely crack a smile.

"I parked on Eighteenth just below South," he says, pushing down his hood. "It's all locked up."

"Thanks for doing this," I say, trying to sound friendly.

We stand at the door for a minute, Sebastian's hood filling up with snow. I know he's waiting for me to invite him in, but I can't; I know I can't.

I can see it register on his face. He looks behind me and notices Hazel across the room, whispering to the cat. He leans in.

"I was thinking," he says in a conspiratorial voice, keeping his eyes on Hazel, "and I might not have another chance to say this, that you should call your boss. My mother worked for my entire childhood. She's a dressmaker, has her own shop. It's her passion. There are pictures of all of us at the shop when we are tiny. But mostly my aunt took care of us during the day. It was fine with us. My mother has always been very happy."

"Oh," I say, because this is exactly what I've been looking for, exactly what I want to talk about, and I can't have it. "Thanks for that, and for parking the car, but . . ."

"I know, I have to be off," he says, trying to punch the snow out of his hood before pulling it on again. He winces for a second as the remaining snow touches his neck. "Bye Hazel, nice to meet you," he calls quietly. She looks up from the cat and waves.

Through the window, I watch him pull his hood on tighter and start his walk to the restaurant through the snow.

CHAPTER SIX

The Hot Bowl has an imposter oozing inside its fondue pot. The cheese was supposed to be from Switzerland and France. But I detected some good ole American cheddar. I was right. The chef confessed that they add some for body but don't feel they need to claim it. Can't anybody step up to the plate these days and take responsibility for the integrity of their ingredients? Why is everyone always trying to be something other than what they are?

—Sam Soto

Henry is ten weeks old when Cece calls and says she needs me. Needs me right now, cannot wait, I must come. It is Tuesday morning. Hazel is in school and Henry is sleeping. Sam is walking the picket line. I am watching some morning talk show and eating Pillsbury croissants that I baked because I was bored.

"Where are you?" I whisper into the phone. We have not spoken much since Henry was born. We've left messages back and forth,

and I've e-mailed baby and three-year-old pictures, which Cece coun-
tered with pictures of her and Simon, her boyfriend, on a bridge in
Amsterdam, and then at a winery somewhere in France. She spends
half the year in Europe and half the year here, flying back and forth and
everywhere else as she is needed.

"I'm here," she whispers back. "In Philadelphia."

"What? Why didn't you tell me? When did you get here?" I am
having a hard time keeping my voice down.

"About three o'clock this morning," she says. "I wasn't going to
come. I've been at the Paris Addison for three weeks. I love it there—it's
hard to leave. Plus, I had to leave Simon in Europe. But you know it's
time for the US version of the Addison Celebrity Guest Weekend, and
I couldn't resist the chance to see you."

"You're here?" I ask. "I can't believe it. Can you come over?"

"No, actually, now that I'm here they're putting me to work, and I
could really use your help," she says. "As always, this one is going south."

"Who is it?" I ask. I always hated the celebrity guest weekends—
one of Ed's ideas. First, we had to come up with a bunch of celebrities,
then we had to get each of them to agree to come to one of the hotels,
and finally we had to build events around them. It was a way of bringing
people and publicity to the hotels. At first, Ed came up with the idea
in an effort to bring attention to the less-traveled hotels. But only a few
celebrities would ever agree to go to Alaska or Kansas City. So, usually
they go to the bigger cities anyway.

"It's Chef Luke Landry from . . ."

"I know, I know, from Chez Landry in Lafayette, Louisiana," I say
excitedly. "How did they get him to come? I've heard he rarely leaves
his kitchen and almost never leaves Louisiana."

"Rumor has it that his wife made him come," she says, giggling.
"Their oldest daughter lives in Bucks County and they are tying it in
with some family event. But he's supposed to have a big master class
and cooking demonstration tomorrow, leading into a much-publicized

dinner. We're sold out. But everything has gone wrong. The crayfish, which were supposed to be shipped fresh, are actually just frozen tails from China. The sausage is not what he asked for, although I'm really not sure what he asked for. The kitchen is too big and noisy, he said. Oh, and the red beans are canned."

"Okay, okay, I can see there are a lot of problems," I say, laughing. "But what can I do about it?"

"Fix it!" Cece says.

"How? Henry's sleeping. I have to pick up Hazel in three hours and . . ."

"Please!"

"You're at the Bell Addison?" I ask.

"Yeah," she says like I already said yes.

Twenty minutes later I am getting out of a cab at the elegant Bell Addison Hotel, just a few blocks away from the Liberty Bell. Henry is miraculously still sleeping in the BabyBjörn that he let me put him in without even opening his eyes. I push through the revolving door and breathe in the hotel smell like I am breathing in ocean air. Cece practically jumps me. We stand and look at each other for a minute. She looks so beautiful, and sure enough she has a light-blue and canary-yellow silk scarf perfectly tied around her neck. Her hair is short and perky and blond. Her eyes are bright.

"Thank you, thank you, thank you," she says. Then she stops, looks at Henry's sleeping head. "Wow. Look at that tiny little boy. Can I hold him?"

"Let's get as much done as we can before he wakes up," I say, all business, but I am so glad to be standing next to her. "Then you can hold him."

"Fine," she says, hugging me gently without touching Henry. I put my head on her shoulder for a second and then straighten up.

"Okay," I say. "First of all, it's *crawfish* to Chef Landry, not *crayfish*. Tell everyone who will be working with him. I'm sure hearing the word *crayfish* over and over adds to his agitation. What time is it? Do you think it's too early for a drink?"

"For you?" Cece asks.

"No, for the chef," I say.

"Oh, no, I don't think it's too early. I think he's been up all night. He's a weird guy. Maybe a drink would calm him, let him sleep a little," she says. "He has his family event tonight, so we wanted to have everything in place for tomorrow before he leaves."

"I thought you weren't doing the celebrity weekends anymore," I say as we walk toward the bar. "Didn't you and Ed decide they were more trouble than they're worth?"

"Yes, but, believe it or not, he missed them," she says. "So we're doing seven this year and then we'll make a decision . . ."

"Hey, did Ed tell you I saw him just before Henry was born?"

"Yes," she says.

"What did he say?" I ask, just as we reach the bar, and Cece doesn't have a chance to answer.

"Lila, this is Chad. Chad, this is Lila," she says to the young man behind the bar pouring orange juice into champagne glasses. "Let her have the run of the place." She turns to me. "I'm going to make some calls. I really only came here to see you. This event was supposed to run itself. But somehow, that hasn't happened so far. I guess it never does. I should know better. I have to check in about a bunch of other things. He's in room 314. Call up before you go."

"I know," I say to her. "I've done this before."

"I'll come find you soon," she says.

"I'm not promising anything," I say, gently rubbing my hand over Henry's fuzzy head. "And I have to go in a little over an hour."

"I know, I know," she says, backing away. "Do what you can."

"What is that all about?" Chad asks, wiping a splatter of orange juice off of his shirt.

"Oh, Cece called me in to do some cleanup work," I say. "I used to work here."

"Well, good luck," he says, hoisting the tray of glasses up to shoulder level. "Let me know if you need anything."

"Thanks," I say. When he is out of earshot I take out my phone and dial Sam's cell phone number.

"Hello?" he says after the first ring. It sounds like he is putting on a Spanish accent. Who does he think is calling him? I can hear the chanting of the picket line in the background.

"Hi, it's me," I say, glad he's in a noisy place so my background sounds won't give me away. "I have a quick question."

"Sure," he says. "Shoot."

"How do you make a Sazerac?"

"A Sazerac?" he asks. "Are you boozing it up already?"

"No, but my mother is planning a Mardi Gras party and wants to know," I say, feeling only slightly bad about how easily the lie falls from my mouth.

"Really?" Sam says, not quite believing me, but not sure why he shouldn't believe me either, I think. "Okay, wait a minute; it's my turn at the mike." I hear him yell, "José say no way! José say no way!" A pause. "Okay, I'm back. First—"

"Who is José?" I interrupt. "And why are you not using proper grammar?"

"Oh, I'm José today, and *José*, *say*, and *way* rhyme. I thought it was catchy. Okay back to the Sazerac," he says, yelling over the crowd. "First you need a chilled glass, preferably a rocks glass or an old-fashioned glass. Take about a teaspoon of Herbsaint—do you have a pen?"

"Yes, right here," I say, rolling the Addison Hotel and Resorts pen between my fingers.

He gives me detailed instructions, which include coating a glass with one spirit that isn't even part of the drink, using a shaker, finding simple syrup, straining it, and doing something with a strip of lemon zest. I'm glad I'm writing it down.

"Okay?" he asks. I can tell he's getting impatient.

"Okay," I say, still writing furiously. Somehow I didn't think this would be so complicated. It looked so easy when Sam made it for me all those years ago.

"Are you sure your mom's friends are up to a Sazerac?" Sam asks just as Chad comes back toward the bar, covered in more orange juice than before.

"Yeah, pretty sure," I say. "Thank you. I'll see you at home later."

"Okay, have a nice morning. It's almost my turn at the mike again."

"Okay, bye," I say, hanging up before I have to hear him say his line again.

"How's the cleanup work going?" Chad asks as he approaches.

"I'm just getting started," I say. "Do you mind if I make a drink?"

"Not at all," he says.

First, I look for a house phone and call room 314. I'm a little worried that the chef may have fallen asleep and I am going to wake him, but I might as well try.

"Yes?" a male voice asks, wide awake but clearly unhappy.

"Chef Landry?" I ask, in as professional a voice as I can find.

"Yes?" he says again.

"My name is Lila Soto, and I'm, I'm downstairs in the hotel and I'd like to speak with you. I know I can help get you on track for tomorrow's events. Can I come up or would you like to meet me in the bar?" I say, hoping he didn't notice my hesitation. I almost said I was an employee of the hotel, but I'm not, of course.

"What can you do for me?" he asks, and I can hear the Cajun in his words.

"I can get you better crawfish, for one thing," I say.

"What else?" he asks.

"Better beans," I say.

"Anything else?" he asks, cheering up a tiny bit, I think.

"I'll make you a Sazerac," I say.

"I'll be down in about fifteen minutes," he says.

I glance at my watch. Time is ticking away, and Henry isn't going to sleep forever. I get to work making the Sazerac, following Sam's instructions exactly. Chad helps me find all the ingredients. I am thoroughly relieved when he hands me a pitcher of simple syrup and finds me the right glass. Then I ask if he has a computer I can borrow. He points to a laptop under the bar. I pull it out and start looking up crawfish. I know there is one place in Lafayette that everyone loves. What is it . . . ? That's it, Chez Francois. I write down the number. What is that sausage place? I type in *andouille, boudin, Cajun country*. Finally it comes up: Best Stop in Scott, Louisiana. I write down that number, too.

Ten minutes later, just as I see the rotund chef get off the elevator, I have everything set. Seventy-five pounds of live crawfish will be shipped overnight via UPS. The andouille, boudin, and six bags of Camellia red beans will be taken to the crawfish place for us before the shipment leaves. Everything will be charged to the hotel. The chef approaches me, looking confused. I know Henry has thrown him off. But I motion for him to come over just as I'm hanging up.

"Chef Landry, I'm Lila," I say, reaching out my hand. "Please, sit down."

As he sits, I hand him the drink. He accepts it, looks at it, sniffs it, takes a long swallow. Finally he smiles, easing back into his chair.

"Who did you say you are?" he asks, giving me a crooked smile.

"I'm freelancing at the moment," I say. "Cece Reynolds asked me to help get things straightened out for tomorrow. I think I have." I tell him what I've done and he nods.

"I hate it here," he says quietly. "I want to go home."

"It's just a couple of days, right?" I say. "I'm going to try to make them as painless as possible."

"My wife made me come," he says. "I don't like to travel."

"I heard," I say. "But people are very excited that you're here. You might as well try to enjoy it."

He takes another long drink, looks in the glass, then finishes it off and raises his eyebrows, holding up the glass. I take it, go to the bar, and make another, but as I am getting the ice into the glass, a small piece of cold ice falls on Henry's head and he squirms. I finish making the drink and take it over to Chef Landry, hoping Cece will appear and take this opportunity to hold my baby boy. But Chef Landry reaches for the drink, thanks me, and puts it down. Then he reaches for the baby. I hesitate, knowing Henry is hungry and also not sure how much this man has already had to drink. He may have been drinking all night. But I untangle Henry from the Björn and hand him over. Chef Landry's big hands envelop the baby and make him look so tiny. Then he starts to hum in Henry's ear, a Cajun lullaby, I think. Another idea comes to my mind. Music. If we fill the kitchen with his favorite music, it won't seem so noisy and strange. I let him hold Henry and jot down some names on a napkin: Rosie Ledet, Boozoo Chavis, Buckwheat Zydeco, Beau Jocque. I'm guessing, but he might like them. At the very least they will be familiar.

Cece comes around the corner and I stand, reaching for Henry. Chef Landry hands him back and smiles, like holding him was better than the Sazerac. Funny.

"We're all set," I say, suddenly worried about getting to Hazel in time, and a little desperate to find a place to feed Henry. "Everything will arrive first thing in the morning—here's the tracking number. Also, here is a list of music that will cozy up the kitchen, I hope. I'm sure you can get it all on iTunes. Gotta go."

"Where did you find her?" Chef Landry asks. "She's something."

"We know," Cece says. "She's been out of the game, but we're trying to get her back in."

"I'll call you later," Cece says as I move toward the lobby. Just before the main room I notice the staff room off to the side. I've spent time in there before, getting away from things for a minute. I peek in—empty. I go in, lock the door, and sit on a big couch and nurse Henry. He eats eagerly.

When Henry is finished, I glance at my watch. I have enough time to walk to Hazel's school. I put him in the Björn. On the way out I stop in the gift shop and buy a toy blimp for Hazel, a remnant of one of my unexpected public relations twists so long ago. We arrive at her school ten minutes early.

I feel so good for the rest of the day that I decide I am ready to have sex again. It has been more than a month since I got the go-ahead from Dr. Berri to resume normal sexual activity—or whatever it might be considered at this stage in the game.

Sam and I used to have incredible sex. On hot days in New Orleans we used to prefer to turn off the air conditioner, open the windows, and let our sweat add to the pleasure of slippery sex. I could not get enough of him. With Tom, everything had been very basic and reserved. I didn't know it could be the way it was with Sam.

It hasn't been that way for a while now, though we have had some good moments and we have certainly tried. After Hazel, we rented a few porno movies. I was surprised by how much I enjoyed them, watching for just a few minutes until Sam and I were excited enough, and I wanted to climb on top of him. I would, letting him continue to face the movie, and we would let go. After we were finished, we would quickly turn off the video, embarrassed suddenly by the images on the screen, not wanting to see any more. But when Sam suggested trying those movies again recently, I said no. We literally share walls with people. I worry they can hear our televisions and computers. I envisioned Sam walking down Colonial Court and running into one of our nosy neighbors who would of course ask if we've watched anything good lately.

"The last one was called *Licking Lola*," I imagined Sam saying.

Not to mention my concern that Hazel might come across it thinking she was about to see *The Many Adventures of Winnie the Pooh*.

Sam has been very patient. Maybe a little too patient. I've been starting to worry he doesn't miss sex any more than I do. But when I whisper in his ear after dinner that it seems like a good time, his eyes light up.

"Have you been drinking those Sazeracs?" he jokes. "Oh, I have an idea. Give me a minute."

I'm in bed, waiting for Sam and trying not to worry about the kids waking up or the crawfish arriving in the morning. A hand appears through the door and pushes the light dimmer. The lights go down to a glowing near-darkness.

Sam walks in and I am startled for a moment. Who is that? It takes me a few seconds to realize that he is wearing a disguise from his stash that he uses to walk the picket line.

He turns and shakes his butt, clad in a leopard-print thong. I look down at my body, try to smooth it out a little. Impossible. It occurs to me that Sam missed the boat on this one; he should have put me in a disguise, maybe a flesh-colored girdle with a removable crotch. But I resist the urge to hide under the covers. I am naked. I lie here, waiting for my mystery man.

He comes toward me, and I notice that he is also acting a little. His movements are changed; his whole being has taken on a new aura. As he approaches the bed, I can see he has put on a small brown mustache and slicked his hair back with his dark-brown brush-in dye. He is wearing cologne that I don't recognize.

"I've been waiting a long time for you," he says quietly with a hint of an accent. Is it French? Italian? Greek? Whatever it is, I like it and I pull him closer. I can still smell Sam through the new cologne, which makes me smile.

The sex is good. For the first time in a long time I'm able to relax. Instead of rushing through it to the end so that we can get on with the next activity, we make it last. We take a long time to touch each other, moving around to different positions before we find the one that will take us where we want to go. I forget about my body. No, that's not really true. I stop being conscious of my changed body, and instead of closing up I stretch out, exposing everything, feeling everything. I am in my body, not hiding from it. And Sam, or Milo, or Pierre, whoever he is, is clearly enjoying himself.

When we are finished, I settle my head on his chest and allow myself to relax into the motion: up, down, up, down. After a few minutes I prop myself up on my elbow and look at him.

"I've been thinking about some things lately," I say hopefully.

"Uh-huh," Sam says.

"I'm really thinking about work a lot. I think I have to get back," I say, remembering how good it felt this morning. "And the strike makes it pretty clear that we don't have a lot of extra money lying around."

"Oh, Lila, I've been afraid of that," Sam says quietly. "But the kids need you, and, you know, I'm still very concerned about your being too visible. When the time comes, we'll have to come up with another plan. We'll figure it out. I promise. We still have a lot of time, though. Don't we?"

"A lot of time for what?" I ask. "Isn't this a possibly good time to think about it? What if the strike goes on for months?"

"It won't. Do you mind if I turn out my light? I can barely keep my eyes open," Sam says, pulling most of the pillows out from behind him and settling on the chosen one. "But keep talking, I'm listening."

"No, that's okay, we can talk tomorrow," I say, moving over to my side and away from Sam. The last thing I want is to let Sam make me agree to something that I'm sorry about. I have to think this through. "Or not," I mumble.

Sam turns his light back on and bunches the pillows up behind him again.

"Okay, let's talk," he says. "I'm sorry."

I look at him, surprised, wanting to tell him to just forget it and keep my back to him. But I know that won't get me anywhere.

"I miss working so much," I say, and before I know it I'm crying. "I can't explain it, but I can think so much faster when it's about other people. It's really hard to be home. I miss our old babysitter, Judy Beth. I miss feeling in control."

Sam nods. I take a deep breath.

"And I am going to need more friends. It's been quiet on the street because it's winter, but when the spring comes, we're going to need a better plan. I keep meaning to ask people if they own a restaurant, but it never seems like the right time." I'm crying hard now and, despite my drama, Sam is still having a hard time keeping his eyes open.

"But besides all of that we have so little money coming in!" I continue. "The strike is going on for longer than we thought. I could be making money!"

He reaches his arm across my stomach and lets it rest there. He puts his head back and closes his eyes. For a minute I think he has already fallen asleep.

"I'm really worried about that, Lila," he says, his eyes still closed. "I'm worried about not having control. Once you go back to work and start to make friends like a normal person, we're going to lose any control we might have had."

"No, that's not true," I say, jumping at the tiny open door I hear in his voice. "What if I promise that I'll always be very careful? I won't do anything crazy and I'll take tiny, tiny steps. I won't make any rash decisions or jump into anything too fast."

He looks at me out of the corner of his eye. He is actually smiling.

"You? Not make any rash decisions or jump into anything?" he says sarcastically but nicely. He takes my hand. "I want you to be happy, Lila. I didn't marry you to make you unhappy. I know we have to work something out. I want to help you fix this. Now, can we get some sleep?"

"Yes," I say, feeling more relieved than I've felt possibly since we got here. "Let's go to sleep."

Sam turns out the light and settles into his side of the bed. He reaches out and grabs my hand, the way he used to every single night we were together until things got so crazy. That was how we always fell asleep. I can hear his breathing slow. I spend most of the rest of the night with my eyes wide open, smiling.

The next morning Sam wakes up to a pillow covered in hair dye. His mustache is askew, and he looks embarrassed or annoyed, I don't know which. He gets up and goes to shower. I am stripping his pillowcase when I hear Henry, then Hazel. And it's like our romantic evening never happened.

As soon as he's out the door, I call Cece. I wanted her to come over for dinner last night, but at the last minute she had to go to New York—something about a sommelier at the Apple Addison having a fit and threatening to break some crazily expensive bottles of wine. But she had to be back here this morning for Chef Landry's big day. That was always one of Ed's rules: never abandon a project or crisis until it is over or resolved.

"Hey," I say. "Did the crawfish arrive?"

"Fifteen minutes ago," she says. "Everything is perfect. We have Boozoo Chavis playing in the kitchen, and I think I actually saw Chef

Landry smile and do a little dance step when he thought nobody was looking."

"Good. Listen, what's your plan for the rest of the day? I could really use a good talk," I say.

"Well, I'm pretty much stuck here for the day, and I miss Simon so much I'm going to try to get back to France on the first flight after the dinner," she says. I can tell she's distracted. People keep asking her questions. "Can you try to stop by here?"

"I'll try," I say, thinking I might be able to. "But I'll have both kids with me."

"I'd love to see Hazel," she says. "It's getting really busy over here. People are going to be arriving any minute. Thank you so much for yesterday. We couldn't have done it without you."

"It was fun," I say. "I'll try to come by."

"Oh, I almost forgot. I have another favor to ask," she says. "Ed just hired a new general manager for the region. She's young and perky and eager, but a little green. Ed wanted me to ask if she can call you with questions? If anything comes up?"

"That should be okay," I say. Sam seems to be coming around. "Sure, give her my number."

"No, not there, not there," she yells at someone. "I have to go. I hope I'll see you."

But Henry is especially fussy, and when Hazel wakes up from her nap she has a fever. So I don't go see Cece, and before Hazel's fever breaks, Cece is back in France.

Two days later the phone rings. It's Maureen.

"You're in trouble," she says right away, and there are so many ways that could be true I don't know what to say.

"Did you see the *Philadelphia Busybody* today?" she asks when I don't say anything.

"No, we just get the *Herald*, and I barely have time to read that," I say. "Why?"

"Here, let me read it to you," she says. I hear papers flipping. "It's in Sy Silver's column—you know, the gossip guy? Under a subhead that reads 'Table for One' it says, 'It is no wonder that the restaurant critic's wife was dining alone recently, considering she was eating at Trifle, which her husband gave the undistinguished award of no swans. My sources tell me she enjoyed a hot bowl of tomato soup and a BLT on a brioche bun. For dessert she had the coconut cream pie, of which, I am told, she didn't leave a crumb. Isn't she embarrassed to ignore her husband's words so openly? Is she trying to give us a message?' That's it."

I can't believe it. It's true that I went to Trifle for an early lunch after I ran into Sunny and she said she'd be happy to come over for a few hours. I guess I wanted to see how having her around during the day might work.

The restaurant is close to our house and, to be perfectly honest, I like it there. The sandwiches are great, and I love their tomato basil soup. Also, it's very comfortable and, probably thanks to Sam, not very crowded. Sam thought the dinner menu was terrible and the food poorly cooked. A roasted chicken was raw at the bone, a steak was charred, the carrot soup was sickeningly sweet, he wrote. And to make things worse everything was overpriced. Sam went back a few extra times to give it a chance, but it was bad every time he was there. Does that mean I can never go there again? Besides, he did say in his review that lunch was slightly better.

"Well that's no good," I say.

"No, I didn't think it would be," she says.

"And I think I almost had Sam convinced that it would be a good idea for me to go back to work."

"How'd you do that?" she asks.

"I don't know. I think he just finally listened to me. Plus the strike and the fact that we have no cash flow. Even he knows we can't go on like this," I say. "But it's pretty creepy not only that they knew who I was, but that someone paid attention to what and how much I ate."

"Was he right?" she asks.

"Yes—that is exactly right,"

"Hey, do you want to meet at the playground later? Pamela would love to see Hazel," she says.

"I don't know. Maybe someone will see me talking to you," I say, only half kidding.

"I doubt it at the playground," she says seriously.

"Fine, let's meet around four after Henry wakes up."

"Good, I'll see you then, and Lila?"

"What?"

"Maybe Sam won't see it," she says.

"Maybe."

When Sam comes home that night, he's even more distracted than usual, which I hope will work in my favor. He comes right to the kitchen and pulls open the refrigerator door.

"Can you hand me the cucumber?" I say. I might as well be talking to a cucumber. He reaches in and pulls out a slab of cheddar cheese. He holds it in his hand, staring at it for so long I finally yell at him. He jumps.

"I had fondue the other night at that new place, The Hot Bowl," he says, still in a daze. "My cheese fondue was supposed to be an elegant blend of Swiss and French cheeses. But it dawns on me now, standing here, that there was cheddar in it. I know I tasted cheddar."

I just stare at him.

"I wish I had taken a sample," he says, finally closing the refrigerator door. "Maybe I'll have to go back." He looks at his watch.

I want to yell, *Did it taste good? Because nobody really cares about what was in it!* But I don't. Sam puts the cheese back on the shelf, reaches for the cucumber, and looks at me.

"Trifle, huh?" he asks.

My heart sinks. I take the cucumber from his hand and busy myself with it: peeling, seeding, chopping.

"In a way I'm glad," he says. "We were starting to let down our guard. I'm sure you can see now why we have to be so rigid."

"Can you call him? This Sy Silver guy?" I ask. "Maybe if you talk to him as one reporter to another he'll leave us alone."

"Lila, that's like a restaurant owner calling to say it's inconvenient that I am planning to review his restaurant," Sam says, clearly disgusted. "It's his job! And it is our job to make his job impossible."

"I get that, I really do, and I promise to be careful; I promise to do everything in my power to make his job impossible."

"Lila, I hear you, but I don't know if you can do it. I'm starting to think that letting you out there is like setting a wild animal free in a city—you just can't help yourself," Sam says.

"You know, Sam, I don't need your permission to be *let out* there, as you say. I can do anything I want to do. But I'm trying, for the sake of our marriage, to find a middle ground, a place where we will both be happy and comfortable. Can you just work with me here?"

Sam looks at me. He seems tired and defeated. His eyes are puffier than usual. I actually feel a little sorry for him.

"I need to see how this settles, how it affects my daily life," Sam says. He comes over to me. Puts his arms around me. If I had more energy, I would tell him that his daily life will definitely be affected—by a very unhappy wife. But I don't feel like fighting anymore, at least not tonight.

"This isn't over," I warn. "Not by a long shot."

He isn't listening anymore. He is back in the refrigerator, rummaging through the cheese drawer.

A few days later Sam comes home and tells me that the strike is over. To celebrate, he decides to take us all out to dinner. He thinks the people at this restaurant may be on to him, and that taking two kids along will throw them off. He messes up his hair, throws some ketchup on his shirt, and wears two different shoes. When he suggests that I put my shirt on backward I refuse.

"Parents with babies are supposed to be a mess," he says.

"I am a mess," I say. "I don't need to make it any worse."

The evening is surprisingly warm, so we walk the six blocks to a new place called Noodles of the Nations. As its name implies, the menu is full of noodle dishes from every place imaginable. We settle Hazel into a high chair, and I keep Henry on my lap. I watch as huge steaming bowls of rigatoni tossed with garlic, oil, oven-dried tomatoes, and broccoli rabe are brought to almost every customer there. That must be the specialty of the house. It looks so good. I try not to stare as people pierce the greens flecked with red pepper flakes and place them in their mouths.

"I'll have that," I say to Sam as another bowl goes by.

"That?" he asks, not even trying to hide his annoyance. "We might as well go to an Italian bistro. That is the most boring thing on the menu. How about the stir-fried duck bowl with glass noodles? That will be better for my story."

"Really? It looks awful."

"I know," Sam says. "It will give me something to write about."

I don't answer but focus on getting Henry comfortable in my arms with the hope that he'll fall asleep and I'll be able to put him back in the stroller. When the waitress arrives, I am about to angrily order the stupid duck dish when Sam clears his throat.

"She would like the rigatoni," Sam says. "And I'll have the stir-fried duck bowl." We also order Hazel buttered penne with parsley.

"Thanks," I mumble when the waitress walks away.

"Anything for my queen," Sam says in a ridiculous voice, and we both start laughing and can't stop. When my huge, delicious-looking bowl arrives, I dig in and love every bite. Sam looks disdainfully at his messy bowl of gnarly duck, overcooked, brownish vegetables, and wet noodles. He ends up eating as much of mine as I'll give him and finishes Hazel's penne.

"That place sucked," he says as we leave, Henry in the stroller and Hazel skipping out the door.

I don't say anything, even though that was one of the best pasta dishes I've had in a long time. I wonder when I can come back.

As we are walking home, my cell phone rings. The noise surprises me because it so rarely rings anymore.

"Hello?" I say, not recognizing the number. Sam is ahead of me with Hazel on his shoulders. I have stopped walking and have one hand on the stroller.

"Is this Lila Soto?" a timid female voice asks.

"Yes," I say.

"This is Jeannie Riddle; Ed gave me your number," she says, sounding more panicked by the second. "Do you have a minute?"

"Sure," I say, wondering how long it is going to take Sam to realize that I've stopped walking. "What can I do for you?"

"Okay," she says like she is trying to calm herself down. "I'm at the Horse and Buggy Addison in Lancaster, and the indoor water park opened yesterday, and last night the fire alarm went off for hours, and today we ran out of propane to heat the water in the park, and I've been fielding complaints all day, but I don't think anyone is satisfied." She stops talking and takes a breath.

"Did you order more propane?" I ask.

"Uh, no, we just shut down the water park," she says.

"The second we hang up you should order the propane—it could be there first thing in the morning," I say. "But for now you should offer everyone a free night's stay anytime this year. If people have left, mail them a nice letter telling them. If people are still there, push a note under their doors. And give everyone a free breakfast tomorrow."

Silence.

"Hello?" I ask.

"Can I do that?" she asks incredulously.

"Yes," I say, exasperated. "Now go order the propane."

I hang up just as Sam notices I'm not behind him. He is three full blocks ahead.

"Who was that?" he asks when I catch up.

"Some new regional manager who is having a water park crisis," I say.

"Why was she calling you?" he asks.

"Ed asked me to be a sort of mentor to her," I say.

Sam gives me a questioning look, then starts walking again.

"The strike is over, Lila; you don't need to go back to work anymore," Sam says. "Besides, with everything that's happened, I thought you understood that working right now is not a good idea," he says, looking straight ahead.

"Sam, that was the phone—nobody can see me," I say.

"Well, keep it that way," he says. "Could you help her?" he asks after a few more blocks.

"Yeah, I could," I say. "It was easy."

The next day we go to Maureen's house to play. I definitely feel like I'm pushing my luck with Sam, but we made these plans last week, and I don't want to disappoint anyone, especially Hazel. Plus, I tell myself, there certainly won't be any Sy Silver spies at Maureen's house.

Maureen lives across Broad Street on one of the tiny, alleylike streets that are common in Center City. It's so narrow you can barely drive a car down it. Logistically it seems like a hard place to live, but it's quaint and makes it easy to imagine what the city looked like two hundred years ago. As we turn down their street, I can see Maureen waiting at the door.

She opens it wide as we approach, and Pamela sticks her head out. Her long black hair is braided down her back and tied with a red ribbon. Her blue eyes look just like Maureen's.

"Hi, Hazel," she says, but it sounds like *Hi, Hawel.* "I want to show you my new Bawbie dawl. She has long haiw and a lellow dwess. Come in! Come in!"

"Hi, Pamela," I say. "We missed you."

Maureen has already gently gotten Hazel out of the stroller and into the house, and is folding it up. I'm grateful for the help. Henry is fast asleep, so when I get inside I take off my coat but leave him in the BabyBjörn. Hazel has her coat off and is jumping up and down with Pamela.

"Welcome," Maureen says. "Let's go into the sunroom so the girls can play Pamela can't wait to show Hazel her Barbie dolls Brendan is still sleeping and lunch will be here in a little while." Her familiar lack of punctuation makes me relax.

"Great," I say. "What are we having? Pizza?"

Maureen just raises her eyebrows. If I had to guess, I would say she looks a little nervous. And with that my relaxed feeling is replaced with an uneasy one. I'm sure she ordered food from the restaurant.

My phone rings, making me jump as it always does these days. My first reaction is to shove it deeper into my purse. What will I say if it's Sam? I glance at the number. It's Jeannie Riddle.

"Hi, Jeannie," I say, rolling my eyes at Maureen.

"The propane isn't here!" she wails into the phone. "People are banging on the door to the water park. I'm afraid there is going to be a stampede."

"Jeannie, take a deep breath," I say. "Can I speak with the head of maintenance? Oh, but before you do that, there's an arcade there, right? Give unlimited free tokens all day at the arcade, and give out the good prizes. Try to keep people busy. Hopefully we'll have the propane there soon."

After thanking me, she finds the maintenance man and hands him the phone. It turns out she didn't even consult him about ordering the propane. In five minutes we have it sorted out and, though the price will be more than double a usual shipment, the propane is on its way.

"What was that all about?" Maureen asks when I hang up.

"Oh, that was a new employee for the hotel chain, a regional manager if you can believe it. My old boss asked me to help her out," I say. "She seems to be clueless."

The girls come running in to get us for their "Barbie play." Pamela lets Hazel play with her new Barbie, the one with the "lellow dwess," while she plays with an older one. The play consists of the dolls going to a restaurant. One doll is the customer and the other is the waitress. Hazel has never played this before, but she jumps in like an old pro, ordering wine and pigeon. Then she complains that the wine is hot. Maureen and I laugh. I have to remember to tell Sam about that— though I'll have to fib a little about the circumstances of the game.

The boys wake up at the same time, and after I nurse Henry and Maureen retrieves Brendan, she says she has a surprise for the kids. We go into her big bathroom, where she has taken up the mats and spread a shower liner on the floor. She tells the girls to take off their clothes, then sprays shaving cream on the liner and puts tiny dabs of finger paint on each white mountain.

"Go ahead," she tells them. "Mush around."

The girls squeal and start rolling in the cream and making all sorts of colors. Then Brendan wants to join in. I even let Henry lie on his stomach in the far corner and watch. They play for almost an hour. When they're finished, Maureen rolls up the plastic liner and throws it away. We rinse the girls in the tub and get them dressed.

Maureen goes to the next room to change Brendan's diaper, and the doorbell rings.

"Can you get that, please?" Maureen asks. I hear her push a diaper into the Diaper Genie.

"Sure," I call.

I walk to the door, wearing Henry, and pull it open. There is Maureen's husband, Mike, with two guys and lots of big trays.

"Hi," I say.

"Hi," he says back, smiling.

"What is all this?" I ask, hoping Sy Silver isn't lurking around the corner. "I shouldn't be eating this."

"Lila," he says. "Don't worry about it. I bring food home all the time. This is nothing out of the ordinary. Some of it's for our dinner."

I find that hard to believe. There is a tray of delicious-looking shrimp remoulade on top of crispy fried green tomatoes; there is fried chicken and mashed potatoes; there is spicy chicken gumbo; there are mini po'boy sandwiches for the girls; and there is pecan pie for dessert. Then I see Mike tell one of the guys to go back out to the pickup truck that has its wheels on the sidewalk, literally straddling the street. He comes back with a silver cooler full of ice and small glass bottles of Coke, my favorite. Sure, this is nothing out of the ordinary; they do this every day. Mike gives his family kisses and then leaves, saying it's a busy lunch hour and he has to get back.

Maureen already has the table set, so I put Henry on a blanket on the floor, and he doesn't protest. Then I sit down. Hazel loves her sandwich. I take a bite of the shrimp and immediately know it isn't going to be great. The remoulade sauce is all mustard, no balance or softness to it. Not a good sign considering it is the restaurant's namesake. And the chicken is bland. The gumbo is pretty good, and the pecan pie and Coke are delicious. I eat a lot, despite the fact that I'm distracted by how much I want the restaurant to get a good review, while I worry that this incredible playdate is more about Sam than Hazel. I tell Maureen that I love the food, and I tell myself that nothing travels well, and it would all be better at Remoulade. And I tell the tiny voice in my head to be quiet, trying to believe this isn't because we are the Food Family.

Finally it's time to go. I start to bundle everyone up.

"Here, take this," Maureen says, thrusting a beautifully packed bag of the leftovers at me. I glance inside the bag and realize it isn't the leftovers. It's something that Mike must have packed specially at the restaurant. I hesitate.

"Thanks," I say, taking the package and setting it under the stroller.

I wait until we are on the other side of Broad Street before I throw it away.

CHAPTER SEVEN

Waiting for a table at Igloo can be like running the Iditarod sled race—it's a test of endurance, and it might even involve sledding, not to mention encounters with bear noses and free-range venison. But once you settle beneath the fur in your igloo and start in on some good old Inuit bison-marrow dumplings, you'll realize it was worth the wait to find the Eskimo's house.

—Sam Soto

The doorbell rings. It's Sunny five minutes early. I rush downstairs, fling open the door, and practically pull her inside. She laughs.

"I think I smell like sour milk," I say, a little out of breath. "We have to leave in twenty minutes, and I'm not even a little ready."

"It's okay. I'm here," she says, and I immediately feel my blood pressure begin to drop. I have to get ready. We're going to Igloo, the most talked about new restaurant in the city, owned by Philadelphia's renowned restaurateur Kasper Kite. To add a little more to my anxiety level, we are meeting Ed and his wife there.

"Give me Henry." Sunny reaches out her arms. "Come here, little boy. We're going to be friends, just like me and your sister."

"Sunny!" Hazel yells as she bumps down the stairs on her tush. She runs over to Sunny and hugs her legs. Then she looks up and sees Henry in her arms. She is quiet for a second, and then she starts to cry.

"Noooooo!" she whines. "Put him down! I don't want you to hold him!"

I reach out my arms for him, trying to think of where the bouncy seat is so I can take him into the bathroom with me while I shower.

"Sweetie, it's going to be okay," Sunny tells Hazel, holding firmly on to Henry. "We'll have fun all three of us tonight. I promise."

"We can *not*," Hazel says adamantly through her tears. "I don't want him at this family!"

But Sunny is already slipping him into the BabyBjörn, and he doesn't protest. Then she reaches for Hazel's hand and starts to lead her to the playroom. I watch for a few minutes, thinking that if I am able to find my way back to work, Sunny would be great with the kids. Then I sprint upstairs, brush my teeth, and jump into a hot shower. Sam comes up and starts to get ready just as I'm heading down.

I find Hazel and Sunny in the kitchen eating dinner.

"I put Henry down," Sunny tells me. She is incredible.

I glance at the clock, worried that we are going to keep Ed and Tanya waiting. Sam comes into the kitchen. I do a double take; then I give him a dirty look. How could he do this to me?

He has done something to his ears that makes him look vaguely like Spock, but it is his beard that draws my attention. It is brown and thick and covers almost his entire face. He looks like the Wolf Man.

"There is no way I'm going out to dinner with you looking like that. Did you learn nothing from our experience at Enzo's?" I say. Hazel and Sunny look up from their plates. Sunny starts to laugh, but Hazel whimpers. She's afraid of him.

"It's okay, Sweetie," I say. "It's only Daddy wearing a silly costume, like on Halloween."

"I don't wrike it," she says. Then she starts to cry.

"Neither do I," I say.

"Take it off, Daddy," she says.

"Yeah," I say. "Take it off."

Sam sighs. "I thought I did a pretty good job," he says. "I switched to a different glue that is used a lot by theater people, and I think it looks real."

"Who has hairy cheeks?" I ask. "It looks fake."

"Fine, fine," he says, frustrated. "But I have to wear something. People at the paper told me that Kasper Kite has hired people whose sole job is to figure out what I look like. I'll be right back."

A few seconds later Sam is back. His ears are still Vulcan-like, but the beard is gone. He kept only the mustache.

"It's a disguise," I say immediately when we find Ed and Tanya waiting for us outside the busy restaurant. "Sam doesn't want the people at the restaurant to know it's him."

Ed smiles, giving us each a hug. Tanya winks at me, then hugs me tight. I haven't seen her since our wedding. Sam is preoccupied with his mustache and won't take his finger away from the center of it. It's pretty funny because he looks like he's pointing to himself, which is the opposite of what he hopes to achieve with his disguise. Ed and Tanya don't seem to mind. They came all the way from New York for this, and I think they are just glad to have a chance to try this restaurant that's been written up in all the food magazines.

Kasper Kite opened his first restaurant a little over five years ago, and it is still very popular. It's called Grass, and eating there is like being in a huge field with tables. The restaurant is on the first floor of a loft building in Old City, so the ceilings are high. The floor is hilly and covered with AstroTurf. It sounds weird and tacky, but it works. The walls and ceiling are painted varying shades of blue, and there are colorful kites hanging everywhere. The tables are covered in red-and-white checked cloths. All the food is delivered in picnic baskets. Sam has never officially reviewed it, but we've eaten there a few times anyway.

After that, Kite opened Shell, also in Old City. It has an ocean theme, fresh fish and seafood, and a small beach toward the back where you can hunt for shells. The staff buries new ones every day. Sam liked this one, despite the fact that he found it a bit gimmicky. He gave it three swans, saying the food was consistently delicious and that being there made him feel like he was on vacation.

Next came River with—you guessed it—a river running through the restaurant. Then Mountain, complete with Tibetan food, prayer flags billowing with the help of wind machines, and a mountain-climbing wall to enjoy while you're waiting for a table. It was at that point that Sam started referring to Kite's restaurant empire as the Universal Studios of the Philadelphia eating culture.

His newest creation is Igloo. We open the heavy door, and cold air rushes out. I can see what looks like snow and ice everywhere. I heard that you're supposed to feel like you're dining in a Canadian winter, and from what I can see, we will.

The restaurant has been open for about two months and it's packed—no reservations accepted. We wind our way through the throngs of people—young and hip and holding blue drinks in martini glasses just above their chests so they don't spill. The drinks are supposed to look like glaciers. I wonder what they taste like.

I find the hostess stand and stop short. Tanya bumps into me, and Ed bumps into her. Sam has his head down and is trying to remain unnoticed.

"Hi," I say to the tall woman who greets us. "There are four of us."

She glances at her very long sign-in sheet, looks at us, decides we aren't anyone important, and says, "It's going to be a little over two hours tonight."

"Okay," I say reluctantly. I would never willingly wait that long for a table. But this is Sam's first visit, and not only do I know that his tight work schedule means we have to eat here tonight, but I also know he wants to have the whole experience.

"Name?" she asks, barely looking at me.

I am tempted to say *Soto*, but I refrain. "Tanya," I say instead.

"You can have a drink at the bar, if you like," she says, seemingly oblivious to the fact that there is no room within five feet of the bar. Whatever.

"Thanks," I say.

We wiggle farther in and stand in a tiny circle so we can talk. Sam is still keeping his head down. I want him to pick it up. I want someone to see him and recognize him. Here's hoping Kasper Kite really did hire people to figure out what Sam looks like. I do not want to wait over two hours for my dinner. I'm hungry.

"This better be the hottest place in the city right now," Ed says jokingly to Sam. "The hottest, coldest place, that is." Sam just nods. He still can't talk, and I wonder how he is going to eat.

"If we wait two hours, I worry you'll miss the train back to New York," I say.

"No problem," Ed says. "Then we'll just stay at the Bell Addison and take the first train out in the morning."

"I want one of those blue drinks," Tanya says, raising her eyebrows at me.

"Yeah, I'm curious, too," I say.

"Ed?"

"No, I'll wait until we sit down," he says.

"Sam?" she asks.

He shakes his head, then nods, keeping his finger on the mustache, and mumbles something that sounds like *me* or *tea*.

"Okay," Tanya says enthusiastically, and gracefully eases her model-like figure up to the bar. She comes back about five minutes later with three drinks. Two blue martinis and one steaming mug of tea.

"It's all about eye contact," she says proudly. "The bartender looked at me right away. You said *tea*, right?" she says, handing Sam his mug. Sam shakes his head and tries to say something; then he shrugs and accepts the tea.

"They had some special brew with Canadian foliage or something," she tells him, and Sam tries to smile. He finally raises his head to take a sip and looks around. It's amazing. The walls look like they are made of ice bricks, there is the faintest mist in the air, and it smells like snow. How does Kite do that?

Sam is having trouble drinking his tea and making sure his mustache stays in place. I have an urge to rip it off, but before I have a chance to, Tanya reaches up gently and pulls it out from behind his finger. She slips it into her purse. Sam glances around to see if anyone noticed. Then he smiles at Tanya.

"Thanks," he says. "That was annoying."

I look at my watch. We've been here for ten minutes. We have over a hundred minutes to go. What else is going to come off of him, I wonder, as the tall hostess snakes through the crowd looking for someone. Fifty someones straighten up and turn to face her, hoping she will end their waiting period.

"Tonic?" she says, looking at me. It's too good to be true.

"Tanya?" I ask hopefully.

"It's *your* name," the hostess says snottily. But I forgive her because clearly she means us.

I can't believe it. Ten minutes. Someone definitely recognized Sam. Yay for Kasper Kite. I'm so relieved I giggle. I look at Sam; he is scowling. *Did you really want to wait two hours?* I want to yell at him, but I don't. I'm hoping to have a peaceful night in the Canadian woods.

"Follow me," the hostess says loudly. For a minute I worry that people are going to protest, demanding they be seated in proper order. But the place is so crowded that nobody has any idea of who came first. She leads us to what looks like one of the four best tables in the room— a booth enclosed in an igloo. It's bright and somewhat chilly inside. I look down and see we're sitting on a banquette that looks very much like smooth ice covered with a furry animal skin. On second glance, the seat seems to be made of refrigerated glass. I have the sensation of cold covered with warm.

The hostess hands us our menus, which are printed on various sizes and shapes of thin wooden slabs.

"The Eskimos eat a lot of things raw," she says, and I'm sure it's at least the thirtieth time she's given this speech tonight. "The chef will be more than happy to give you an authentic experience. Everything is very fresh. But he will also be happy to cook your meat any way you like."

We thank her, and when she's gone we start to laugh.

"This place is crazy," Tanya says. "I feel like I'm in Disney World."

"He does seem to have taken this a step too far," Sam says slowly. "But let's not make any judgments until we taste the food."

"I don't want anything raw," I say.

"I know," Sam says, clearly annoyed. "Nobody has to eat anything raw. I might, but you don't have to. Can we just look at the menu?"

We're quiet while we look. Among the appetizers are dumplings made of bison bone marrow, skull soup, sliced bear nose *en gelée*, goose liver pâté, rabbit stew, and short ribs of free-range venison. The entrées look a little more normal: elk fillet, fresh trout with lemon and butter, Canadian pheasant with bacon and mushrooms, musk ox chops, broiled salmon, and onion-smothered walrus liver. The list of side dishes simply reads: berries, roots, and stems. We look up from our menu. I want steak. I want pasta. I do not want walrus liver. Why is this place so crowded?

"Okay, let's start with the entrées and move backward. Tanya?" Sam says.

She bites her bottom lip. "Can I have the salmon?" she asks.

"Okay, salmon for you," Sam says, pointing to her.

"Lila?"

"The trout?" I ask timidly. Sam rolls his eyes.

"Fine," he says. "Plus, I'll be back again, hopefully with more adventurous eaters."

"Ed?" Sam says.

"How about the ox chops?"

"Good choice," Sam says, smiling. "Now for the appetizers. Who wants the bear nose?"

We are all quiet and pretend to be concentrating on our menus.

"Fine," says Sam. "I'll get it for the table. I've never had bear nose before. Ed?"

"The pâté?"

"Okay. Tanya?"

"The short ribs, I guess."

"Lila?"

"The rabbit stew," I say proudly. Sam looks at me for a second, then smiles. It's not so hard to make him happy, I guess.

"Perfect," he says. "And I'll have the skull soup."

The waitress appears and takes our order. She seems truly surprised that we don't have any questions. Sam always orders last, so when we are all finished he says he'll have the walrus liver—raw. She looks at him for a second, then shakes her head.

"I have to tell you," she says, and I am hoping beyond hope that she will save him from eating raw liver. "The pheasant is the best thing on the menu. I suggest you get that—cooked."

"Sounds good," Sam says, clearly relieved. He doesn't even pretend to be disappointed. "Oh, and can we try one order of berries, one of roots, and one of stems, please?"

"Sure," she says.

While we wait for our first course, I look out our igloo window. There are still tons of people waiting. I glance at my watch. An hour hasn't passed since we got here. If someone hadn't recognized Sam we would still have more than an hour to go. The place is unbelievable. There are kayaks and harpoons up on the walls. A big soapstone sculpture of a polar bear dominates the middle of the room. All the way in the back of the restaurant there is a crowd, and people are cheering.

"What's going on over there?" I ask, pointing.

"I don't know," Sam says. "Go see."

I walk through the big room, missing our cozy igloo, and come to stand in a line of about twenty people.

"What are people waiting for?" I ask a woman in a very short skirt.

"Sledding," she says.

I can't see anything from where I am so I walk forward. Amazingly enough I find myself at the top of a small, snow-covered hill, and people are taking turns sledding down. A guy climbs onto an old-fashioned sled. First he lies on his stomach. Then he shifts to sit up.

"I'm ready," he yells, to warn people below. "Wahoo!" he shouts as he descends the tiny slope. Before he reaches the bottom, a woman in high heels settles sidesaddle onto a sled at the top of the hill, raises her arms into the air, and closes her eyes for the ride. The first guy scrambles out of her way at the bottom. I think about waiting for a turn, but the line is pretty long. I head back to our table.

"They're sledding," I tell everyone.

"No way," Tanya says. "I want to sled."

"Come on," Sam says to her. They disappear into the crowd. A few minutes later our appetizers arrive, but we can't touch them. Sam always wants to describe everything into his microphone before anything is touched. So we wait. But they look and smell delicious. I start picking at my food and then try to cover up the place I picked at so Sam won't know.

"Lila," Ed says, looking toward the sledding hill. "I've been wanting to talk to you. I hear Jeannie called you a few times."

"Oh, yeah, she did," I say. "She was having a hard time."

"Yeah, I hired her because she seemed so eager, and she had a great background, but she doesn't have the stamina for the job, I guess. She quit last week," he says.

"Sorry to hear that," I say.

"So, we're down a regional manager," Ed says slowly. "And we have two hotel openings, one celebrity wedding, and who knows what else in the next month. What can I say to talk you into stepping in until we can find someone permanent? Or maybe you want the job. It's close, wouldn't involve too much travel . . ."

"Wow, Ed, I don't know what to say," I say. "I've really been thinking about it, and getting my feet wet this last month has just made me want it more. But Sam and I haven't worked out the details, and—"

"Please, Lila—we're stuck. We have a boutique hotel opening up in Ephrata next week, one in Princeton the week after, and the governor's youngest daughter is getting married right here in Philadelphia on the twelfth," he says.

"I don't have any child care lined up, but I have found this great babysitter. It would be nice to have the money again, nice to be back. But there are other issues," I say, wanting nothing more than to just shout *YES!* I see Sam and Tanya start their walk back to the table, laughing.

"Okay, then just be available to field calls, do a lot of the work from home, and plan on working for, say, two days around each event. What do you say? I'll send over the paperwork on Monday. I'll put you down as an independent contractor, for now," he says, leaning in, waiting for my answer. Sam and Tanya are two tables away.

"Fine," I say, just as they sweep up to our igloo, their clothes a little wet from melted snow and sweat on their brows.

When I'm officially allowed to eat my rabbit stew, it is tender and peppery. I love it. I immediately ask Sam if he can ask Kasper for the recipe. Sam gives me a stern look. He hates when I try to influence him, particularly so early in a meal.

Sam's skull soup looks like thick, luscious beef-barley soup. He takes a bite and closes his eyes.

"That's incredible," he says.

"Is it really made with skulls?" Tanya asks.

"Think of it as bones," Sam says.

The pâté is smooth and creamy, served with cornichons, mustard, crisp garlic toasts, and some small red berries that I don't recognize. The minute I taste it I'm sorry I didn't order it. We keep taking a little off Ed's plate. We consider ordering another portion, but Sam reminds us that there will be plenty of food.

I don't want anything to do with the bear nose, but Sam eats it and says we have to try it. He says it reminds him of beef cheeks he had once at an extremely fancy restaurant in New York. We each take a tiny bite. The meat is juicy and tangy. But I pretend to hate it.

Our entrées are at least as good. My trout is lemony and moist. The salmon is smoky and spicy at the same time. The ox chops are moist and herby. And Sam's Canadian pheasant looks like a crisp roasted chicken. Sam says it is one of the best birds he has ever tasted. I don't remind him that he almost ate raw liver for dinner. The side dishes are succulent: the sautéed berries are a perfect mixture of tart and sweet, the stems are bright green and salty and crunchy, and the roots are roasted cubes of carrots and turnips that are lightly caramelized.

We finish our meal with delicious desserts, including cinnamon spice pudding, chocolate cake, and a berry tart. Kite must have a sense of humor, because the last item on the dessert menu is an Eskimo Pie, which I remember from my childhood. It's a brick of vanilla ice cream surrounded by a frozen chocolate shell. We order one of those to share.

As we are paying the check, there is some commotion over by the bar. We can't hear the words, but we see someone standing on top of the bar point to his watch and then punch his arm into the air. I guess he's tired of waiting.

We get up from the table, and Ed gently grabs my wrist. When I look up at him he smiles, then nods with a question in his eyes. I nod back. As we wind our way through the arctic landscape of Igloo, toward the familiar Philadelphia streets, I notice a group of people who were waiting next to us when we arrived. I glance at my watch—almost three hours have gone by. No wonder that man lost his mind. He probably thought he was going to die of starvation in the Canadian wilderness. These people haven't protested yet, though. They are waiting their turn, and they are so drunk now that they aren't even trying to keep their blue glacier drinks from spilling. I feel sorry for them. I want to tell them to hang in there; it's worth the wait. But I don't. One vocal, opinionated diner in the family is enough.

On Monday morning at 9:35 the doorbell rings. It's the FedEx man with the papers Ed promised. I am still in my pajamas, Hazel is watching television, and Henry is already taking his morning nap. The young, tan-even-though-it's-been-a-long-winter man thrusts the thin envelope at me. Without thinking, I put my hands behind my back. He looks surprised, then smiles.

"Something you don't want, huh?" he asks. "Or do you want to play rock, paper, scissors with me?"

"Neither, I think," I say, smiling at him. He seems nice, like Sebastian. "It's just that it might be more than I can handle."

"I know that feeling," he says, pushing the envelope toward me again. This time I take it.

"Thanks," I say.

"Don't mention it," he says, turning to go down the stoop. "Good luck," he calls over his shoulder.

I close the door and sit on the couch with the sealed envelope. I look at the front. It is addressed to me. The image of my suitcase comes to mind. I go upstairs and pull it out from under my bed, trying not to wake Henry, who is sleeping in the bassinet next to the bed. Then I sit on the floor, using the suitcase as a table. I open the envelope, read through the papers. Everything is in order, just as Ed promised. I'm not committing myself to more than a few weeks of freelance work. I am not signing on to be a full-fledged employee. This is a short-term contract. I'll stay away from the media. As I look at the space on the first form that asks for my full name, I get a great idea. I should change my name! I could go back to my maiden name! Maybe Sam wasn't so crazy when he suggested that before we moved to Colonial Court. If I had known this was going to be such a big obstacle, I would never have changed it in the first place. No, that's not true. I want to have the same last name as Hazel and Henry. I don't know what to do. Which is the bigger sacrifice? I am thinking this all through when the doorbell rings again.

I run back down and open the door. It's the FedEx guy again.

"I didn't realize," he says, smiling. "That was a round-trip."

"What?" I ask.

"It means that if the addressee answers, I'm supposed to wait and take it back to the sender," he says.

"Oh," I say, thinking how smart Ed is. "No, I know what a round-trip is. I'm just surprised—that's all." I am about to tell him that I'm not ready, that I have to decide about changing my name first, when it sinks in that it really isn't going to make any difference. Even if I change my name back to Lippencott, Sam still isn't going to want me to work. On the flip side, if he comes around, it isn't going to be because I changed my name. It is going to be because he understands that having me stay home full-time is asking too much of me.

"So?" the FedEx guy prompts me.

"Wait here," I say. I sprint up the stairs. Henry is cooing in the bassinet. I pick up the papers on the suitcase, scoop up Henry, and run back down. I put Henry on the floor and sit down next to him. I write my name, sign the bottom, scan the information one last time, stuff it in the envelope, stand up, and hand it to him. "Here."

"Thanks," he says with a grin, and I wonder if he flirts with all the women he encounters.

I watch him go down the stoop for a second time. Then I close the door and lean against it, waiting. Nothing happens. The phone doesn't ring. Sam doesn't appear in front of me, mad. There are no claps of thunder.

When the phone does ring a few hours later, and I hear Ed's voice on the other end, I am actually surprised. My heart starts to speed up. I imagine someone swinging his arm in wide circles, letting it finally point toward me, and saying, "You're on."

And I am, suddenly. Ed and I talk like we used to during our once-a-week this-is-what's-happening call. I write down the information about the upcoming events: What's in place and what still needs to be done. Where I have to be, who will be working with me. I used to have these perfect pads of paper that fit right in the front pocket of my suitcase. Now I use a pad of Hazel's construction paper.

When we hang up, I call Sunny. She is available all but one of the days I need to be away from home, assuming there aren't any unplanned events—the very things I used to crave. As long as there isn't a major storm or a fire, I'm pretty confident that I'll be able to handle anything that pops up over the phone. Despite my overflowing excitement, I do not discuss any of this with Sam.

The first hotel opening in Ephrata is easy and smooth as banana cream pie. I take both the kids there the day before, meet the people, check everything out. The next day, the day of the opening, Hazel has school. Sunny will pick her up when school's over, and because there was someone at the hotel the day before who offered to take care of Henry, I take him with me. He sleeps in a hotel room most of the time and, smart boy that he is, wants to nurse only at the most convenient times. The opening goes off without a hitch; I pat myself on the back, thinking that I am finally back in my bailiwick, and I am home before six. Sam doesn't even know I left town.

The second opening in Princeton is a little trickier. The place is not as kid friendly. But Sunny comes through, taking great care of both kids and successfully giving Henry a bottle, and I am home before five both days.

It is the governor's daughter's wedding that tosses me into the real world. Sunny can come the day before, a Friday, but is totally unavailable on Saturday. I consider asking my mother, but that would force me to tell Sam what I'm doing anyway. Plus, it would tip her off to the fact that I do not have this work thing as under control as I led her to believe.

On Wednesday night Sam doesn't have to go out to dinner. When he gets home, I've made a pot roast, a potato and leek casserole, and a surprisingly tasty-looking spinach salad—never mind that the spinach was from a bag and the turkey bacon was microwaved.

"Hi," I say when he opens the door. Henry is sleeping in the Pack 'n Play, and Hazel is watching television in the kitchen. "I was tired of takeout."

"Smells great," he says, coming in and washing his hands. He looks around, pushes the roast with his finger and nods, gets out the salad dressing, and helps get everything to the table.

"What's Hazel having?" he asks.

"Fish sticks and corn," I say, pointing to the toaster oven.

Henry wakes up just as we are about to sit down, so I sit on the couch in the living room and nurse him.

"You guys go ahead," I call. "We'll be right in."

When I join them in the kitchen, I can see Sam is struggling to cut through the meat, but he's eating it anyway. I sit down to a plate that Sam has assembled for me. I take two bites.

"How was your day?" I ask.

"Good; busy but good. I had a few interviews with chefs, and I started my next review," he says, sticking his fork into a piece of brown meat. "So, you just felt like cooking, for the first time in a year?"

"I've cooked this year!" I say, trying to keep my tone light.

"Well, yeah, frozen ravioli and stuff, but a pot roast?"

"I've been feeling a little more . . . I don't know, balanced maybe, these last few weeks," I say. "I've been doing a little work for Ed."

"Yeah, you told me you were mentoring someone?" he asks. "How's that going?"

"It's turned out to be a little more than mentoring," I say. "In fact, that person quit, and I've been filling in a little."

"Lila, what are you talking about? Have you left the kids? Who's been with them?" he asks, exasperated. "How long has this been going on? How could you not tell me? Have you met any people?"

"Not long," I say. "A few weeks. And the kids have been great. I took them once, and Sunny has been with them. And I've met a few people, but my work has mostly been outside of the city."

Sam shakes his head.

"And that's exactly why I didn't tell you," I say. "You are so negative."

"You know how I feel," he says. "I think it's important to be with the kids when they are so small."

"No, you just don't want me to get any publicity," I say, mad, but trying not to raise my voice for Hazel's sake.

"Yes, and that, too," he says with a sigh. "There's no question that some people know who you are—Sy Silver's column proved that. If you start getting your picture in the paper, then you really can't come out with me anymore. And I don't want people to know so much about us anyway—any more than they have to."

"What do you want me to do?" I ask, suddenly near tears. "Since I've been working, I feel like myself again. I can't help but think I was really thrown off by not working, and now I'm back a little. Plus, it seems that no matter what we do, people are figuring out who you are. I bet Sy Silver won't write about me again anyway."

"Don't bet any of our money," Sam says, taking more potato casserole. "And this is a big city. There are still hundreds, maybe thousands, of restaurant employees who wouldn't be able to pick me out of a lineup. By the way, the potatoes are really good."

"Thanks," I say, softening a little. "The reason I'm telling you now, in addition to not wanting to live a secret life, is that I need your help. I have to work this weekend. The governor's daughter is getting married at the Bell Addison. Sunny can come on Friday, but I have to be there on Saturday. I give you my absolute word that I will remain in the background."

"Do they know your name?" he asks.

"Well, yes, they do," I say. "But I won't talk to any of the press, I promise. I'll have someone else do that if necessary. I won't allow my picture to be taken."

"So you've gone back to work?" he asks after a minute.

"No, not really. I signed on for a month. In fact, I'm on standby, but this is the last event I have to work. Ed is looking to hire a permanent regional manager. But I want to go back. I was thinking after the summer. I'll try to hire Sunny full-time."

Hazel wants more corn and there isn't any, so she starts to cry, and Henry is getting fussy.

"I'll take them up. Okay?" I say.

"Fine, I'll clean up down here."

On Saturday morning I get up and get dressed for work. I put on a navy-blue suit with a very light-yellow blouse. I choose it because the skirt has an elastic waist. Sam doesn't say anything.

We go about the morning as usual, acting like I'm wearing my pajamas and I don't have makeup or earrings on. Finally it is time for me to go. Henry is taking his nap; Hazel is happily painting.

I start to gather my bag. I considered taking the suitcase for good luck but decided that would be crazy. I put in some papers, phone numbers that I'll need, pictures of the kids. Sam comes up behind me.

"You look good," he says.

"Thanks," I say, realizing that I am totally counting on the fact that he will do this for me. We haven't mentioned it since Wednesday.

"You look like your old self," he says.

"I feel like her, too," I say, leaning in to hug him.

"We'll try this," he says. "I mean, we'll be fine today. I haven't seen you looking this happy in a long time, Lila. I want that for you. I wish I were enough to make you this happy."

"Sam, that's ridiculous. You are, but nobody is happy if they're cut off from other things they love. You get that, right?"

"I get that," he says, and I wonder if he's thinking about his mother. Was there anything that might have made her happy? He rarely talks about her, so I don't really know. I do know one thing: he doesn't want me to end up like that.

I want to say, *Thanks for letting me go today*, but that isn't what I mean. "Thanks for supporting me," I say.

"I guess that's part of my job description, too," he says. "The whole work thing, we can try it, but we have to make sure the kids are happy. And we have to make sure it doesn't conflict with my actual job—the one I get paid for."

"I know," I say, realizing Sam would never let me leave without one of his usual caveats. "I promise."

"The governor called me himself," Ed says when I pick up the phone on Monday. "He was very happy with the whole event—smooth from beginning to end, he said. Lila, only you could keep the chaos behind closed doors. I heard about how the band leader slipped in the bathroom and broke his knee, how you had the ambulance come to a back hallway, how you had someone else there to take his place before the end of the break. I'm telling you, nobody thinks on her feet like Lila Lippencott—sorry, I mean Lila Soto."

"I'm glad the governor was happy," I say, wanting so much to be back there right now, in the halls of the hotel, smelling that hotel smell.

"Okay, so, I'm going to ask one more time: Do you want this job?" Ed says. "Because . . . we have someone we are about to hire, but I'm thinking this might be a good way for you to get back in. You'd be close to home. You could do a lot by phone, going in only when absolutely necessary."

I close my eyes. Breathe in through my nose.

"No, thank you very much, but it is a little too soon," I say. "If you're really in a bind, you can call me, but I'm thinking the end of the summer would be a better time for me to start. Is that too long from now?"

"Well, yes, but if I have your word, and if you're willing to fill in here and there, I think we can make it work," Ed says. "You'd outgrow this job in a matter of months anyway. I know that. But can I sign you on for another few weeks? I don't have any events coming up, so it should be pretty quiet. But it would help with the transition."

"Sure, I'd be happy to," I say.

The same FedEx guy comes the next morning with another short-term contract. This time I don't even take it inside. Standing on the stoop, I fill it out, sign it, and hand it back, smiling.

CHAPTER EIGHT

During my second meal at the Hearth Stone, one guest almost set our table on fire with oil from the votive lamp. He was that frustrated. But who could blame him? His entrée, a grilled veal T-bone sitting on a bed of mashed potatoes, had been yanked out from under his nose just moments after it was placed there. The T-bone, as well as a Dover sole removed from the clutches of my other companion, disappeared into the kitchen, only to reemerge one minute later and be placed on our neighbors' table as we watched hungrily.

—*Sam Soto*

I pick up the phone, and it's someone named Suzanne calling from the Valley Forge Addison. Her voice, which I imagine is probably always a little high pitched, sounds like she's been inhaling helium. And she is having trouble breathing. I catch words like *lost* and *four-year-old* and *a half hour ago*. Then *Ed said* and *help find* and *don't panic*.

"Suzanne!" I yell, trying to startle her and stop her river of crazy words. "Please calm down."

"But they say that the more time goes by the less likely you are to find him," she says. She starts sobbing.

"Okay, quickly, try to tell me what happened. And who you are," I say, realizing I have no idea. I ease Henry into the baby swing so I'll have my hands free if I need to write anything down.

"I'm Suzanne Ebon, manager of the Valley Forge site," she says, regaining some composure. "About thirty minutes ago we got the report that a four-year-old boy is missing from the hotel. The father reported it. The mother is hysterical. We've called the police. Already there are reporters here, and the mother won't leave the hallway because she thinks he will be able to find her there. It's on the ground level, leading to the dining room, so the reporters are trying to get to her. She's right there! Ed said to call you," she says.

I've dealt with missing children before. Every time, the child was found within an hour, on the hotel grounds, and because it was resolved so quickly, I almost never had to go to the location. Once I did, because there was a strange custody situation, and the media became interested. I can hear Suzanne breathing. I glance over at Hazel, who is sitting on the floor in her Hello Kitty nightgown playing with her My Little Pony.

"Dogs," I squeak out. I clear my throat. "Have the police brought in dogs?"

"Yes, just now," she says. "But there is no sign of the boy so far. Can you come? To deal with the questions from the media? We're planning a news conference at noon."

"Um, yes, I'll come. But I can't head the news conference. I can advise, though," I say, getting myself together.

"Okay," she says. "I have a four-year-old boy."

"I'll be there as soon as I can," I say, not wanting to think about the fact that I have kids now, too.

First I consider taking Hazel and Henry. Then I realize how crazy that would be. I can't come in to help, maybe comfort the parents, with my kids along. I call Sunny, but I can't find her. Then I call Sam. He is not happy to be bothered at work. But when he hears the tone of my voice, he says he'll be right home.

Sam is in the door in twenty minutes, saying he'll work from home today. I kiss him, then kiss Hazel, then lean over Henry's sleeping body and try to catch a whiff of his baby scent.

I drive to the Valley Forge Addison. There are local news vans out front, cars with press stickers on them. I go inside to find Suzanne. I spot the boy's mother immediately. There is no question about it. She is standing at the far end of the lobby, at the beginning of a long hallway, begging everyone to help. She walks one way, then the other. She is as distraught a person as I have ever seen. *Come on*, I tell myself; *I've seen way worse than this.* Way worse. But no matter how hard I try to recall where that may have been, my mind is blank.

I step farther into the lobby. And that's when I feel something click in my brain.

"Where's Suzanne?" I bark to the nearest employee. He points to a woman wearing a yellow suit, sitting on one of the chairs in the lobby. She looks almost as distraught as the missing boy's mother.

"I'm Lila Soto," I say as I approach her. She looks at me blankly. Ed is going to have to do something about the people he's been hiring lately. He seems to have lost his touch. "Ed told you to call me for help. We just talked a little while ago?"

"Oh, yes! Thanks for getting here so fast," she says, snapping out of her stupor. She looks at her watch. "It's been over an hour."

From my calculations it has been way over an hour, but I don't say that.

"Let's walk around, and tell me everything. Where he was last seen. Any quirks about the hotel, everything," I say.

Suzanne gets up and seems unsure of which way to go. I walk in the direction away from the mother. She follows.

"They were eating breakfast," Suzanne says. "There was a buffet. His mother said he loved the cinnamon buns and kept wanting to go back for more. Finally she let him walk up alone. She can't even remember that moment between when she saw him and when she didn't. He was just gone."

"Did you—"

"I will never let my child go to a buffet alone," she says. "Never."

"Let's worry about what's going on here, okay?" I say. "Has this entire floor been searched?"

"As far as I know," she says.

"Have you confirmed that with anyone?"

"I assume—"

"Don't assume." I say. "Can you show me the dining room?"

We walk down the hall. The dining room is now a crime scene. Police are milling around. Hotel guests are being told of nearby restaurants where they can get lunch. I wander around. The buffet table is still set up, and the fruit is just starting to smell. I look at the baked goods. There are muffins and cheese and berry pastries, but I don't see any cinnamon buns. I walk into the kitchen. I don't see a single police officer, so I keep wandering. Food preparation has stopped and it is quiet. I open the door to the walk-in refrigerator. Except for the food, it is empty. I know I'm missing something. He wanted cinnamon buns, but there weren't any when I looked. Were they there when he went back for more? I see the remnants of a life-size gingerbread house that must have been part of the hotel's holiday display. It is against the far wall of the kitchen, near the trash cans, and the roof is starting to cave in. But there is still candy sticking to it. I walk over slowly, holding my breath, and peek inside the window. And there is a sleeping boy.

"Over here!" I yell.

In seconds there are twenty people by my side.

"Is that him?" I say, just as the boy wakes up and starts to cry. "Someone get his mother."

She is there in an instant and he is in her arms. The mood goes from bleak to euphoric. Apparently he went looking for more buns, slipped into the kitchen, and found the edible house. He was too scared to come back out. He thought he would get into trouble.

I stay around for the press conference, being careful to remain out of the way of all cameras. Not much advice is needed. It was an unfortunate situation, not the hotel's fault at all. I feel good as I drive back to the city.

When I get home, Sam is on the floor playing Candy Land with Hazel. Henry is in the Pack 'n Play just waking up. I am about as happy to see them as I've ever been.

"Hey," Sam says, moving his green plastic figure three spaces. He lands on an undesirable space, and Hazel squeals. "I can't believe it," Sam says, like he means it. Hazel bounces as she picks her next card. She is very close to winning, and I wonder if Sam rigged it that way. I would like to think he did. As they finish the game, I go over to Henry, pick him up, sniff behind his right ear.

"I saw some of it on the news," Sam says. "When they were sleeping."

"Oh," I say. "It was a madhouse."

"Who found him?" he asks.

"I did, actually. But I asked them to keep that quiet. I didn't want to be part of it; I just wanted to help fix it."

"Well, thanks for staying behind the scenes. I didn't see you once, not even in the background."

"Sure. I told you I would," I say.

"Was it awful?" Sam asks.

"Yes."

"Well, I'm proud of you," he says. "But, you know, I can't come home every time you have to take care of something like this. We need to come up with a better system."

"I know," I say. "We will."

My euphoria lasts for about nineteen hours. That's when Sam calls to tell me I can't do this anymore.

"This isn't working," he says, clearly angry.

"What?"

"It's worse than I thought, but at least nobody got a picture of you."

"What are you talking about?"

"There is another lovely little item about you in the *Philadelphia Busybody*'s gossip column. Do you want me to read it to you?" he asks in a harsh voice. My heart sinks.

"Do you?" he asks, sounding even harsher if that's possible.

"No. I'll read it myself," I say. I can't listen to him read it. "Sam, I'm really sorry."

"So am I," he says, surprising me. "I thought I could stand it. I know how important this is to you. But I can't. I can't stand the idea that our name could be in the paper at any time. I can't stand the idea that people are paying attention to the things you're doing. It has to stop."

I try to stay calm as I pull the story up on the website, but it won't load no matter what I do. Our Internet has been wonky lately, but it always kicks in eventually. I wait; nothing happens. The kids are getting antsy. I consider knocking on a neighbor's door to ask if I can use their computer, but I don't. Instead, I get the kids ready and head to the grocery store two blocks away, where they always have a pile of newspapers. I am standing at the entrance, furiously leafing through the paper to find the column, when I get a creepy feeling. I look up to see an old man taking his time choosing green apples. He picks one up, studies it, puts it back, looks at us. The more I look at him, the more I think it is possible that he is a woman dressed as an old man. Or maybe an effeminate young man dressed as an old man. Maybe it's Sy Silver himself!

"I'm soakshooed," Hazel yells, her word for soaked through. She peed in her pants. Are my child's potty training issues going to end up in tomorrow's paper? Could this day get any worse?

I take the newspaper to the checkout, where we have to wait behind a very slow woman who has suspicious-looking facial hair. We finally pay for the paper and go home. But I have to clean Hazel up and change her before I can get to the paper again. I finally find the column on page nine:

> Follow the Crumbs . . . The restaurant critic's wife saved the day yesterday when she resumed her job as crisis manager and found a missing four-year-old boy at the Addison Hotel in Valley Forge. Apparently the youngster wandered off and ended up in a gingerbread house, where no one else thought to look. I guess her husband isn't the only one who is drawn to the kitchen.

I read through it again and put down the paper. That isn't too bad. But I'm back to square one as far as convincing Sam that my going back to work is a good idea. I could argue that this doesn't do any harm, since there is no description of me, no picture. None of Sam's secrets are being given away. But I know it's the fact that people are paying attention to us and the idea that somebody knows who I am that bothers Sam.

I am suddenly not sure what to do with this day that I expected to be free and easy. I wish I could call a neighbor and ask to get together, but I fear my behavior this fall was interpreted as aloofness. All winter

I saw the neighbors traipsing down the street with their kids in tow, heading into one house or another, probably to do crafts or to celebrate the winter solstice or something. We were never invited. Calling them now is not an option.

I consider the various museums, the library, the square. And then I have an idea. I might not be working anytime soon, but I want to be in a hotel. I go upstairs, pull my special suitcase out from under my bed, and bring it downstairs. Hazel watches me as I take everything out of our bright-blue quilted diaper bag, spread it on the floor, and neatly pack it into my suitcase. There is plenty of room for diapers, wipes, changes of clothes, a blanket. I put the diaper cream into the now-empty cosmetics case. Just being in the presence of this bag makes me feel better. When Henry wakes up from his nap, I calmly get him dressed, put him in the Björn, and get Hazel in the stroller. I push the stroller with one hand and drag my suitcase / diaper bag behind me with the other, and we set out.

As soon as we get away from our block, I imagine that we just look like a family on a trip. The idea that we could be that free soothes me. We walk across the city toward Independence Hall. We go to a big, beautiful hotel that is not an Addison—I assume nobody will be looking for me here. I direct us through the sliding glass doors. The doorman points to the reception desk. Instead of heading there, though, I walk through the lobby to the elevator. Nobody stops me. I've been here before; I know where I'm going. I press "M" for mezzanine, and moments later we step out of the elevator into a huge grand hall with ballrooms branching off on all sides.

The smell of newly vacuumed rugs mingles with the more powerful smell of lilies. I get Hazel out of the stroller. At first she just looks at me. The place is empty.

"It's okay," I tell her. "You can run around."

She is hesitant at first, but soon begins to run around the geometric shapes that are part of the carpet's design. I find a small couch, pull the suitcase over, get Henry out of the front carrier, and sit and nurse him while I watch Hazel play. After an hour, Hazel starts to get bored and tries to leave the immediate area. I keep calling her back.

"Can we go in there, Mommy?" she asks, pointing to the grand ballroom.

I peek through the crack in the door to see if there is anything set up for a meeting. The room is empty. I pull the door open. *If they didn't want people in here, they would lock it,* I tell myself.

"I think it's okay," I say to Hazel, holding the door open for her to run through, then following with my suitcase. The heavy door closes behind us. At the far end of the ballroom is a big stage. Hazel immediately runs to it and starts putting on a show. Henry is fast asleep. I unzip my bag, find the blanket, spread it on the floor of a tiny alcove by the door, and place Henry on top of it. Then I head over to Hazel and join in her singing and dancing.

The next thing I know, Henry screams, and I turn to see a startled woman with a clipboard jump back. She is with a young couple, and before I have a chance to figure out what just happened, I decide they are searching for a place to hold their wedding, and the woman is the events planner.

The grown-ups stand like they were just tagged in a game of freeze tag. Hazel keeps dancing like nothing happened. I jump off the stage, sprint to Henry, and scoop him up.

"I stepped on the baby!" the events planner tells me, clearly stunned. "What are you doing in here? This room is off-limits to hotel guests unless there is a function."

I don't tell her that we aren't even hotel guests.

"What part of him did you step on?" I ask, cursing myself for leaving him so far away from where we were playing. But in my mind I'd imagined he'd be out of reach of Hazel's jumps and twirls. "Did you step on his body? His hand?" He is still screaming, and I know he is in pain.

"His hand, I think," she says. I look at his tiny hand, and it is very red. Her high heel pierced his palm, which was face up while he was sleeping. He's bleeding a little, but I don't think anything is broken.

I gather our things and call to Hazel. I'm surprised when she comes right away. I struggle to pull my suitcase through the door while holding Hazel's hand and shoving the stroller with my knee. The stern lady doesn't even offer to help.

When we get home, I clean Henry's wound with alcohol and Neosporin and settle both kids in the den. I have an overwhelming desire to talk to somebody. I can't call Sam; he'll just worry that the story of Henry's hand will end up in the newspaper tomorrow. He would probably scold me for leaving the house at all. I consider calling Cece in France, but she seems so far away. I dial Maureen's number, but no one answers, and it goes to voice mail.

So I call my mother, and as soon as I dial the first few numbers, I feel desperate to talk to her. The phone rings four times before she answers, out of breath.

"Hi, Mom. Are you busy?" I ask, trying not to cry.

"Hi, Honey," she says. "Oh, I was just outside thinking about what I'll do with the garden this spring. March is just around the corner. Are you okay?"

"No, not really," I tell her. "It's a long story—and let me begin by saying that I have not been completely honest with you about my work. I was not working at all for a while, and honestly I had no plans to. I know that disappoints you, but that is what Sam and I, mostly Sam, decided was right for the kids and his new job and everything."

I stop talking. I'm just relieved to have that off my chest.

"That's okay, Honey," my mother says soothingly. "Having a new baby is a big deal. Being married is a big deal. To say there is a lot of compromise involved in both would be an understatement. Is that why you're so upset?"

"Yes. No. I don't know," I say. "Even though it wasn't the plan, I have been working a little lately. It was so great, and I had Sam almost convinced that it wasn't going to jeopardize his job in any way—you know how paranoid he is—and then I ended up in the gossip column one time too many. Sam is so mad, and I didn't know what to do with the kids, so I took them to a hotel, where I always feel better, and it was really fun for a while, but then someone stepped on Henry's hand. I mean, he was lying on the floor; they could have crushed his entire body." I can barely talk; I'm crying hard now.

"Is he okay?" my mother asks with concern. "Did you have to take him to the doctor?"

"No. I put Neosporin on, and I think he's fine," I say. "I'm the one who isn't so fine."

"Do you want me to come?" she asks. "I can get the 4:10 train. I'd be there by dinnertime. I'll make spaghetti with meat sauce. Do you need me to pick up some Coca-Cola?"

"What? Oh, Mom, you don't have to do that, really. I'm not that bad. Just talking to you makes me feel better."

"Are you sure?" she asks. "I could be there in less than three hours."

"No, really; I'll figure this out," I say.

"Okay, but call me tomorrow and let me know about Henry's hand."

After we hang up, I sit for a minute, then wipe my face with my hands. I walk into the den. Hazel has dozed off in front of her video. I was so distracted that I forgot about her nap. I pick her up, and she wraps her little arms around my neck. I pull her small pink shoes off of her feet and let them drop to the floor. I carry her up to her bed and cover her with the Disney princess fleece throw. *She is perfect, as perfect and as important as one of my crazy hotel projects.* Everything would be so much easier if I could convince myself that that was enough for me.

I check on Henry, who is sleeping in his little wooden cradle. Then I go down to the basement and find two giant black garbage bags. They look a little like body bags. I take the bags to the living room, and I empty my suitcase. I put everything back in the diaper bag where it belongs. Then I cut the plastic bags into sheets and double wrap my suitcase like a present, carefully folding and taping the corners on each end, smoothing the plastic as I go.

When I'm finished, I carry the suitcase upstairs and gently push it under our bed until it is in the middle, as far away from my reach as it will go. I lie down on my bed and am struck by the thought that I am going to figure this out—that somehow, I will. The tiny nugget of an idea creeps into my mind. I yawn, position myself on the mattress so that I am lying directly over my suitcase, and we all sleep the afternoon away.

A few days later we are in Rittenhouse Square. Henry is happy in the front carrier, facing out, and Hazel is drawing with chalk. I am trying to not think about my future and just be in the moment. I kneel down next to Hazel and help her draw a dinosaur with green chalk. Henry giggles and tries to grab the chalk. Hazel lifts it away from him, and he starts to wail, loud, sirenlike screams. I feel like all the other mothers are looking at me. I'm honestly not sure what to do to make everyone happy again. If I grab the chalk from Hazel, I can't give it to Henry, because he wants to eat it. Besides, then she'll cry. I try to hoist myself up to standing, thinking I might be able to distract Henry, but I fall back, and something sharp cuts into the palm of my hand.

"Ouch," I say, so urgently that Henry stops crying and Hazel starts.

"Are you okay?" a familiar voice asks. I turn to see Sebastian sitting on the rounded concrete bench that surrounds the popular goat statue. How long has he been there?

"Hi," he calls with a sheepish smile. "Long time no see." He stands up and walks over to us, then takes Henry's hands and jiggles them. Henry smiles.

"Hi," I say back. I'm a little embarrassed because I haven't seen him since he walked off into the snowstorm after he helped us so much. My cheeks flush red, and I have to look away. "We haven't been out much. But it is such a beautiful day I had to try. How are you?"

"I'm fine. How's your hand?" he asks, taking his wallet out of his back pocket and fishing around. He pulls out a Band-Aid and hands it to me.

"You're kidding," I say, taking it from him. "*I* don't even have Band-Aids."

I unwrap it to find a *Blue's Clues* picture on it. I show it to Hazel, who jumps up and down, and then I give Sebastian a questioning look.

"I take care of one of my nieces once a week," he says with a proud smile. "You never know when you're going to need one."

"That's for sure," I say, wiping the blood away and covering the small cut with the festive Band-Aid. "Thanks. Were you watching us?"

"Not really; I was sitting here reading," he says, holding up a *New Yorker* magazine. "But I looked up when I heard your kids crying."

"Oh," I say, not sure how I missed him sitting there. "How's work?"

"Busy. Chef's hired extra guys to take the pressure off, make sure we can concentrate more on the customers."

"Oh, that's good," I say, immediately sorry that I asked, and not sure if he is saying this to me or hoping I'll repeat it to Sam.

"It was hard for a while," he continues. "Chef would scream at us if anyone had to wait a second for more water or bread. Once he threw a basket full of bread at my face because a customer had to ask twice for more. One of the baguettes scratched my cheek."

"That's terrible," I say, relaxing. I guess it wouldn't be so good for the restaurant if Sam knew that.

"And how's everything else?" I ask.

"Well, with all the new hiring, I've been promoted," he says. "You're looking at La Noix's newest cheesemonger."

"Congratulations," I say. "What will that entail?"

But Sebastian is ignoring me. He sees Hazel trying to draw something, and he goes over to help. She looks up at him and grins.

"I'm trying to draw Greg from the Wiggews," she tells him. The Wiggles are her most recent obsession.

"The what?" he asks.

"The Wiggles, those Australian guys who sing children's songs," I offer. "Greg is her favorite."

"He has brown hair," Hazel says. "And he wears a yewow shirt."

"And he's tall," I add.

When Hazel goes back to drawing, I turn to Sebastian and whisper, "Greg isn't even a Wiggle anymore, but don't tell her that. We inherited a bunch of old videos from my mother's neighbor."

"Your secret's safe with me," Sebastian says. Then he says to Hazel, "I think I can handle this." And we watch with delight as Sebastian draws a tall man with dark hair wearing a yellow shirt. It actually looks like Greg.

"You have to write *Wiggews* here," she says, pointing to the place on Greg's chalk shirt where the logo appears. Sebastian writes it. Then he looks up.

"Want to have lunch?" he asks. "It's almost noon."

We don't have any plans, but taking both kids out to lunch is hard. I have the stroller, so Henry could sit in that, and Hazel could sit in a high chair or booth somewhere. We have absolutely no food at home.

"Come on," he says. "I could take you to the restaurant. They let us bring friends if we're early enough. The kids would like Dover sole, don't you think?"

"Oh," I say. "We have tons of food at home. We just went shopping, and I don't want to waste it."

"Lila," he says, laughing. "I was just kidding about the restaurant. How about McDonald's?"

"Yes!" Hazel shouts. Her absolute favorite.

"That sounds great," I say.

"Good."

Sebastian helps me pick up all the chalk. He takes Hazel over to the drawing of Greg and says a proper good-bye. It's cute. On the way back to us I hear her tell him that now, because I have a boo-boo, too, Henry and I have matching hands. I hope I don't have to get into that whole story, but I am surprised and happy to hear her mention her brother.

We walk through the square to the McDonald's on Walnut Street. It is getting crowded, so Sebastian grabs a booth with Hazel, who is more than happy to sit with him and talk about the Wiggles. I take Henry and go order the food.

"Leave it up there after you order it," Sebastian yells to me. "Come back here and I'll go get the tray."

"Thanks," I shout back. But I'm more than capable of doing this myself. I order our food, and I can feel Henry getting fussy. I know he's hungry.

"It's okay, baby boy," I tell him. "I'll feed you soon."

I jiggle Henry up and down while our food is placed on the tray. I lean over slightly to lift the tray. I turn carefully so I don't topple anything. As I head toward the table, Hazel sees me, and her eyes light up. Just then Henry kicks and knocks Hazel's Coke to the ground. It splashes everywhere, and she lets out a shriek. I don't know what to do. I stand still and try to balance what is left on the tray. Hazel is pouting, and Henry is crying because cold soda dripped down his leg. I look over and see a man dressed in a business suit glare at us and shake his head. And suddenly I see myself, five years ago, at a diner in California. I was heading from one hotel to another and stopped for lunch in my business attire. A woman came in with three little kids and sat in the booth behind me. I can't even remember if her children were boys or girls—it meant so little to me then. But I do remember that they were noisy, and she could barely control them. I kept looking at her over my shoulder, wondering why she didn't do something to stop them. And then one of them spilled a chocolate milkshake over the side of the booth and down my back. I was livid. I jumped up and turned to glare at the woman, who was practically in tears. A waitress ran over and helped me sop up my back.

"Thanks," I said, with great hostility in my voice. I know I looked at that poor woman and her children exactly like the businessman just looked at us. Then I made a huge show of cleaning up, huffing and sighing and turning in my seat to look at them.

What if she never dared leave the house with her kids after that? I, on the other hand, walked leisurely to my car, changed my jacket, and didn't think about it again. Until now. I wish I could write that lady a letter.

Sebastian has managed to quiet Hazel, and he comes running over, grabs the tray, and leads me to the table. The mean businessman is still shaking his head. Either he doesn't have kids, or he has never taken them out alone. I am trying so hard not to cry, when Sebastian comes back to the table with a fresh tray and a fresh Coke for Hazel. In the meantime, a nice employee has cleaned up our mess.

"I used to be mean," I whisper to Sebastian. He looks up from pushing the straw into Hazel's drink.

"You were?" he asks so sincerely that it makes me laugh.

"Once I made a woman feel really bad because her kids were so noisy and one of them spilled a milkshake on me," I say. "I had no idea how hard this is."

"That's okay," he says. "I'm sure she got over it."

Hazel is completely content again, but Henry is not. I get him out of the carrier and hold him on my lap. It doesn't help. He's never had solid food, but in my desperation I pull a French fry out of its holder, blow on it, and hand it to him. Maybe he can suck on it. He bats it away.

"Are you nursing?" Sebastian asks, as if on cue.

"Yes," I say.

"Go ahead," Sebastian says. When he sees my questioning look he adds, "My sister nursed my three nieces until they were all two. I'm used to it. I promise."

So I take a deep breath and, as subtly as I can, offer Henry my breast. He relaxes and eats heartily. Now that we are settled, I know Sebastian can't see anything but the baby's head, and even that is obscured by the table. I just hope the mean businessman doesn't walk by and accuse me of indecent exposure.

Sebastian helps Hazel unwrap her hamburger, finds her pickles upon request, and hands them to her. I struggle with the dressing and my salad. Sebastian helps me.

"Thank you," I say.

Henry nurses for a long time before falling asleep. Hazel is much more sedate than usual, talking to Sebastian and eating chocolate chip cookies. Sebastian tells me that he had lunch with Stuart and his kids a few weeks ago, and it confirmed his suspicion that he missed the kids more than he missed Stuart.

"So does that make you feel better or worse?" I ask.

"Both," he says, but I can tell from the way he's talking that it is getting a little easier.

"And," he says, drawn out like a drum roll.

"And what?"

"I haven't told anybody this yet, but I went on a date," he says, then covers his face with his hands. I feel myself smiling. I hold Henry tight with one arm and lean over the table to pull Sebastian's hands down. I'm able to grasp the top of one of his fingers. He laughs.

"Nothing serious; I'm not even sure I liked him, but it's progress," he says, sitting back.

"Sounds like it," I say.

"What's going on with you?" he asks.

"With me?" I reply. "I actually went back to work. Slowly and hesitantly, but one thing led to another, and I spent the last six weeks filling in as regional manager until they found someone permanent. It was great. But then, well, something happened, and I'm not sure it's going to work out. But when I was there, it was amazing. I felt like my old self."

"Checkup, pwease," Hazel says, interrupting me. Sebastian doesn't even ask what she means; he finds a ketchup packet, rips off the corner, and squeezes some onto her fries. Then he looks at me.

"Is that a good thing? You just got finished telling me that your old self was mean," he says. "You seemed rather disturbed by it, actually."

I hesitate for a minute.

"Well, yes, I certainly didn't understand how hard it can be to handle kids, and I hope that woman wasn't doing a test run of going out alone with them and then I ruined it," I say. "But I did a lot of great things, too. Believe me, none of this is about me." I move my eyes from Hazel to Henry. "Plus, Sam is so wacky these days."

"How?" he asks. For a minute I think about telling him everything, about Sam's wanting to keep me out of the public eye, about his obsessive separation of professional and personal, and about my fear that I can't do what he wants, that I'm not doing it right now. I have the urge to run; what if I'm being watched?

"You know, I really should be going," I say, jostling Henry. I look toward the door. On the sidewalk outside someone catches my eye. I think I see Tom, my ex-boyfriend, walk by, going toward Eighteenth Street. He is moving fast, but I see his curly brown hair, his broad shoulders that make him look taller than he is, his uneven gait. I can't seem to focus on anything. I just stare out the glass door.

"What?" Sebastian finally asks.

"Oh nothing," I say. "I just thought I saw someone I used to know walk by."

"It must have been an important someone," Sebastian says. "You looked like you saw a ghost."

I glance up just in time to see Tom's lumpy gait go the other way. There is a bank a few doors down; maybe he went to take out some money. But what would he be doing in Philadelphia? That's a dumb question. He travels as much as I used to. A better question would be if he knows I'm here.

Now I'm afraid to leave. What if it really is Tom? I didn't even shower today. I settle back down, wishing I had some dark sunglasses.

"Maybe we'll stay a minute longer," I say. "I wanted to ask your opinion about something anyway."

"Great," Sebastian says.

"Well, this follows what I was just telling you about my going or not going back to work," I say. "I know I can't give up working altogether. I don't want to. I think I do better all the way around when I'm working . . ."

"What's your idea?" Sebastian practically yells at me, smiling.

"My idea is to start some kind of program, preferably at Addison hotels, where, say, once a month there is some sort of daylong event in the conference rooms, for mothers with young children. It would be open to guests of the hotel as well as local families. There could be activities for the kids and the mothers, or fathers, and food. Just basically a big, safe place where lonely, possibly desperate parents can talk and kids can crawl around, or dance around, or whatever," I say, sitting back.

Sebastian smiles.

"What?" I say, letting a smile creep onto my face.

"I think you have a good idea," he says.

"Thanks."

Henry starts to cry. I put him up on my shoulder, and he eventually burps, but he is still fussy.

"Time to go," I say. Sebastian nods and helps me collect our things, including Hazel's Happy Meal toy that fell on the floor. He offers to walk me home, but I say no. He insists on holding the door open while I push the stroller out.

"Thanks," I say. "And thanks for listening to all that."

"Anytime," Sebastian says. "By the way, I take care of my niece one morning a week, usually Thursdays. I think she and Hazel would get along great. Do you want to meet us so the girls can play? We could play in the square and come here for lunch. What do you think?"

"I don't know. Let me think about it," I say, still uncomfortable with my mutiny, and thinking a regular, scheduled playdate might be too much. "Give me your number. I'll call you."

Sebastian seems satisfied with that plan, jots his number down on a piece of paper, and says good-bye.

Sam is in the door only five minutes when Hazel blows my secret. He is folding up the empty pizza box he used as a prop so people would think he was delivering our dinner as he walked to the door.

"Daddy," she whines, to get his attention. "Sebastian hewped me draw a picture of Greg. With chawk."

I freeze mid-stir in front of the stove, where I am making spaghetti. Then I jump back when the scalding water splashes onto my wrist.

"That's nice, Sweetie," Sam answers, taking off a bright-red baseball cap. Ten seconds later he says, "Sebastian who?"

"You know, Daddy," Hazel answers. "Sebastian from the snowstorm."

"Can we talk about this after dinner?" I ask hopefully. "The pasta is ready, and the meatballs were ready hours ago."

"Did you run into him today?" Sam asks, pulling a Pizza to Go T-shirt over his head.

"Yeah, and we go to McDonawd's," my bigmouthed three-year-old says. "It fun. He sing 'Hot Potato.' Oh, and Mommy saw a ghost at the door." Does she have to tell him everything?

Sam turns to me, apparently not willing to wait until later.

"Why did you have lunch with that guy?" he asks me. "I assume you're talking about the strange waiter from La Noix."

"Yes," I say, as I spoon meatballs into a glass bowl. "That's the one. We've run into him a few times, and today, at the last minute, he asked if we wanted to grab a quick lunch with him. He's very nice. He helps a lot with the kids."

"Lila," Sam says like he's talking to Hazel. "You know I don't think it's a good idea to socialize with people so closely associated with a restaurant. Maureen and Pamela are bad enough, but this Sebastian guy? What if someone saw you? They might think you were trading secrets or doing favors or something. And when you know that people are interested in what you're doing!"

"He already knows who we are," I offer.

"What are you thinking?" he asks. "Please, Lila, can you try to make some normal friends?"

"But you don't want me to make those either," I say, trying not to cry. "It's hard to ask every person I meet if he or she owns a restaurant."

Sam just looks at me.

"He's gay, you know."

Sam looks up, shakes his head. "That isn't what I'm worried about."

We sit down at the table and eat in silence. I bought the meatballs at one of our favorite restaurants in the Italian Market, and they are delicious. I just wish I had an appetite.

I watch as Sam twirls a huge forkful of spaghetti and spears a piece of meatball. He separates his smirking lips and shoves in the food.

"Don't forget da ghost, Daddy," Hazel says.

"There's no such thing as a ghost," he says nicely to Hazel after he swallows his big mouthful. Then he turns to me. "What ghost?"

"I thought I saw Tom," I say, but it doesn't register on Sam's face. "My old boyfriend? The man I dated for two years before I met you?"

"Yeah, I know who Tom is," Sam says, already bored. "What did he say?"

"I didn't talk to him. I just thought I saw him through the window," I tell him.

Sam has tuned out, but I want to yell, *Hey, do you know how strange it is that you are so upset that I spent a little time with my homosexual friend, but you couldn't care less that I saw the man I slept with for years?* Then I remember the mean businessman, and for a minute I want to tell Sam about my realization that I had done the same thing so many years ago, but when I look at him, I know he won't care about that either. I go back to my spaghetti, and we are quiet for the rest of the meal.

CHAPTER NINE

I slice into a flaky purse of crunchy phyllo dough that is resting in a deep pool of black-truffle sauce, revealing the sweet, pale meat of herb-infused lobster inside. Tender medallions of lamb stuffed with earthy black trumpet mushrooms ride a delicious slick of garlicky syrup. By this time, I am long under the spell of chef Kevin Stein's food at the Golden Horse. I sit back, the wooden chair beneath me creaking, a bit too stiff. After hours of eating here, I could use a cushion. But I'll get over it.

—Sam Soto

"I hungry," Hazel announces. I haven't even thought about our dinner. Sam is out for the third night in a row. "I want pepperoni pizza."

"Good idea," I say, getting the phone and ordering.

About thirty minutes later we sit down to eat. As I dab grease off my slice with a Care Bears napkin, I picture Sam digging into his filet mignon.

Both kids go to sleep easily, and I turn on the television and settle in to binge watch *Lost*. At first I think Sam left on the surround sound, because it sounds like someone is talking in my den. I push the mute button, and I can still hear the voices. I look around until I see the light bar on one of the baby monitors going crazy. I pick it up and put it to my ear. I can clearly make out a man's voice. I sprint into Henry's room to make sure he's okay. He is. It's just a phone conversation the monitor picked up. Then I go back and listen. It's Jake, Willa's husband.

"Yeah, he's feeling better, but he's still gonna be home for a day or two until the antibiotics kick in." Jake must be talking about Russell. "But I'll be in a little after two tomorrow, as soon as Willa gets home. She has to take the twins to music class or something in the morning."

"Great, see you then," I hear another male voice say. I wait for more, but the line goes dead. It is so strange to hear a conversation you aren't supposed to hear. I'm surprised I didn't enjoy it more. It just makes me crave a friend.

I'm tired of being by myself at night. I try to focus on what's happening on the island in *Lost*, but I can't. Instead, I keep wondering what my life could have been like if I had stayed with Tom. Right now, if I wasn't traveling, we might be walking somewhere on the Upper West Side, deciding if we wanted to see a movie or listen to music. We could do anything; nobody was depending on us at home. We could stay out all night if we wanted to. Maybe I would be heading out in the morning to one exciting work adventure or another. I would be able to walk away guilt free.

I get up and search for the one photo album I have in this house that predates Sam, and I spend the next forty-five minutes looking at pictures of me and Tom. I study the one of our apartment. It was so uncluttered I can't believe it. I remember the couch we're sitting on, the coffee mug on the empty table. If I could have one wish, and I could blink my eyes and be back there, would I do it? I don't know. It looks a little dreary, or maybe *lonely* is the better word. I hear Sam open the door. I close the book and stuff it back on the shelf; then I go downstairs and find Sam piling things on the dining room table.

"What is all that?" I ask.

"Hi," he says. "Some leftovers. And I took samples of some things."

"Samples?" I ask.

"Yeah," he says, taking full test tubes out of a plastic bag. He holds them up. "This is the decaf coffee, to make sure it's really decaf. And this is the hollandaise sauce, to make sure it's really from scratch." He takes them into the kitchen, and I hear him put the glass tubes in the refrigerator.

I start to go through the other bags.

"I don't even know what you had for dinner, but I brought you some leftover steak and a great pasta dish," he says.

"Good, thanks," I say, realizing how hungry I am.

Sam goes up to the bathroom, and I open the bags. There is the steak, the pasta, and a pretty red box with a card. *For your daughter,* the note reads.

I look inside and see an assortment of miniature pastries. They are adorable and smell great. I quickly close the box and jam it under the sink just as Sam comes into the kitchen. My guess is that he didn't realize he was recognized tonight, and I would like to keep it that way. I can't stand another conversation about the importance of Sam's remaining unknown.

"Did you find everything?" Sam asks, sitting down next to me.

"I did," I say. *And more,* I think, but instead of saying it, I dig into the pasta.

At least I'm not hungry when I get up every hour during the night to nurse Henry. And then we wake up to a blanket of snow. When Hazel gets up, I'm ready for a nap. But she wants to go outside to build a snowman immediately. I tell her we have to eat breakfast and let more snow fall so we can make a better, bigger snowman. She agrees once I get a carrot out for its nose and let her hold it while she takes a few bites of her cinnamon toast.

It takes us about an hour to get dressed for the snow. I had already put a lot of the winter clothes away since we are nearing the end of March. I spend half an hour searching for the right gear. I layer Henry, dress and boot Hazel. Then I put him in the front carrier, and we finally step out.

Just as I open the door for Hazel and tell her to be careful, she pushes by me and slips on the stoop. She lands hard on her tush and bounces down the three stairs to the sidewalk. She's fine but a little surprised. She looks up to see all the neighborhood kids playing outside. Nobody else is wearing snow pants. She looks down at her own bulky teal pants and gets up, comes up the steps, pushes her way back inside, and stands on the carpet, crying.

"I hate my pants," she yells. "Nobody ewse wear pants."

I dart a look at the neighbors from the top of our stoop. I keep hoping to have an opportunity to show them I'm interested in becoming their friend, but I know this looks like we are being antisocial again.

Henry is mesmerized by the falling snow, opening and closing his mouth like a little frog trying to catch flies, and he screeches when I go inside.

"But you need the pants so you won't get wet and cold," I say, trying to reason with her. "Come on, you couldn't wait to build a snowman."

"Noooooooooooooooooo," she whines, ripping off the layers I just carefully put on her. Henry is kicking and grunting as he strains in the direction of the door. Then he starts opening and closing his mouth, looking up at the ceiling. It's pretty sad.

"No, Sweetie," I say as gently as I can. "There isn't any snow in here."

I take a deep breath.

"Okay," I say to Hazel. "You don't have to wear the snow pants. We'll just change you when we come back in." I bend down to help her get dressed again. She pushes me away and keeps peeling off the layers. I remember that she didn't have much for breakfast and she's probably hungry. The box of miniature pastries pops into my mind.

"I just wanna be inside, Mommy," she says, sitting in only her underwear at the table and eating crackers.

What's so wrong with that? I lean under the sink to retrieve the bright-red box. I place it in front of her, and her eyes light up.

"What is it, Mommy?" she asks.

"Treats," I say. "From the nice men at the restaurant."

I watch as Hazel, thrilled, picks the tiny muffins (blueberry, cranberry, banana), the miniature croissants (plain, almond, chocolate), and the tiny Danish pastries (cinnamon, berry, walnut) out of the box and arranges them in the order in which she plans to eat them. I stand at the stove and make hot chocolate with mini-marshmallows. She loves it.

But by four o'clock our snow day seems like the longest day of the year. I call Sam.

"We've been inside all day," I say.

"I'll try to come home a little early, but I still have to transcribe two tapes of my meals at SoHo, and I have to call the chef at the Hilltop, and I have to set up a photo assignment. What are we doing for dinner?"

"I don't know, mini-marshmallows?" I say.

"Ha-ha. Okay, I have to taste some food from Satsumaya; it's Japanese-French. Why don't I do takeout?" he asks. It's another perk of Sam's job that we can bring in food that he needs to try, and the newspaper pays.

"Great," I say, relieved that he can take care of this. "That sounds really good. And order something that Hazel likes, too."

"She likes dumplings and tempura, right?"

"Yeah," I say, hungry already. "Get a lot. And bring home some Sprite; we don't have any."

A few minutes after I hang up with Sam, my neighbor Willa calls. I can tell she's trying to keep her voice down, and I can barely hear her. I can't believe how happy I am that she is calling me. Maybe she'll invite us over to do some crafts. I didn't even know she had my phone number.

"What?" I ask. I think she says something about needing to borrow eggs and that she'll be right over. I'm thrilled; this is my chance to make a friend. I quickly put on more water to boil so I can offer her hot chocolate. I don't even worry that she probably makes her hot chocolate with milk.

I have the door open in the time it takes for her to cross the street, and she's talking before she's even in the door.

"The stupid thing," she says, as though we've been carrying on a conversation for a while, as though I have had many intimate conversations with her in the past, "is that Jake won't even realize that I'm not going to cook anything, so why do I need eggs?"

"Are you okay?" I ask, so happy to have adult company. But I wonder why she called me. She always looks thin, but now her clothes are hanging off her. And her wavy brown hair is crazy looking. Her messy hair makes me feel a little better about the state of my physical appearance.

"Well," she says, looking me right in the face. "I feel like everything is turned upside down. I realized about an hour ago that Jake and I haven't said a single word to each other all day that didn't involve the kids. So I decided I want to get pregnant again."

I look around to see if there is someone standing behind me whom she might be talking to. Could she possibly have called the wrong person and entered the wrong house without noticing? I'm not sure whether to answer her, or try to guide her to one of her real friends' houses.

"Would you like some hot chocolate?" I ask, not sure what else to say.

"Oh, no, thanks. We had some earlier. And I'm sorry to dump this on you. I know you are very busy, but I don't feel like I can tell Janie or anyone else; they will just talk about me when I'm not there. They seem to think having twins means you can't have any more babies. Period.

And I tried to call my sister, but she wasn't home. I saw your light on. I hope you don't mind. I was desperate to say this out loud, and I needed a minute away from them," she says, looking out my window in the direction of her house. I almost want to dance in a little Hazel circle because I'm so relieved that not everyone on Colonial Court is perfect. I assumed the other mothers talked about me, but I didn't think they talked about each other. Maybe this place isn't so boring after all.

"Plus," Willa continues. "You seem different from the other people on the street."

I have no idea if she means good different or bad different. I don't dare ask.

"No, I don't mind," I say. "I've been wanting to talk to you. And I'm not really all that busy." I glance over at Hazel and Henry, who don't even seem to notice Willa's presence, despite the fact that we have had so few casual visitors since we moved here. Hazel is putting all the Fisher-Price Little People in a yellow plastic school bus and driving them to school. Henry is chewing on a huge plastic orange frog and seems to be enjoying himself. On occasion he gags if one of the legs gets too far down his throat, but he just coughs and repositions it. I look back at Willa and do some quick calculations. Russell is three; the twins are almost a year old. It wouldn't be impossible. But why?

"I haven't told anybody this," she says, lowering her voice. I don't dare move; I want to be in on her secret. "But once a week I skip taking the pill. I just toss it into the toilet. I don't know if that will even make a difference, if it lowers the hormone level enough to get me pregnant, but I'm doing it. And I don't even feel guilty—well, maybe a little. But if I do get pregnant, nobody would believe it was an accident. Who gets pregnant by accident these days?"

It takes me a minute to catch my breath. I'm trying, because I don't want Willa to think I'm judging what she is doing. I'm not; this has nothing to do with her. And I don't want her to be sorry that she told me. I think I like her. It's just that . . .

"Well, maybe that was a little too much to share," she says nicely. I don't think I've lost her yet. "Sorry."

"No, no," I finally blurt out. "We all do some sort of version of that. Right? Some sort of deception. It wasn't what you told me. I mean, it isn't like you went off the pill altogether. You could do that, right? But you haven't. And even if you did, I wouldn't—"

"No, I would never do that," she says quickly. And I can't help but burst out laughing. It feels really good, and both the kids look at me. Then Willa starts to laugh, too.

When we finally calm down and I wipe the tears away from my eyes, I tell her.

"I got pregnant by accident," I say, keeping my eyes on hers. "Twice."

"Really?" she asks, her eyes wide.

"Well, that's the story anyway," I say. "With Hazel definitely. With Henry I was a little more involved than I let on."

Willa likes that, I can tell. She smiles at me. I know now is the time.

"Hey," I say. "Do you or Jake own a restaurant?"

"What? No. Why do you ask?"

"Does anyone on the street?"

"Not that I know of," she says. "Why?"

"No reason. Being new in town, I was just wondering about places to eat," I say, sounding totally lame.

"Why would you need to ask about places to eat?" she asks. "Aren't you married to the expert?"

I'm stunned. And then it takes me only a second to realize how silly it is that I'm stunned. It's as silly as Sam's thinking we can wander through the world without uttering our names.

"How long have you known?" I ask.

"That your husband is the restaurant critic? Since before you moved in. The realtor told us."

"Huh," I say. "That's pretty funny."

I see her glance out the window toward her house, and I know she has to go soon.

"Okay, back to you. It seems to me that if you want to talk to Jake about something other than babies, getting pregnant is not the answer," I say. And she looks at me like I just struck oil in the middle of our block.

"You're right," she says. "I feel like I don't know him anymore. Maybe more distractions aren't the answer." I can't get over her openness—she barely knows me. Maybe it's like calling in to a talk show or something. Before I have a chance to respond, she says, "But I'm so happy and focused when I'm pregnant. I know exactly what's important. It reminds me of the way I used to feel, when I was doing my art. Besides, another baby . . . Maybe I would have a girl this time."

"Maybe," I say, not sure what she wants to hear. "Your boys seem great; Jake seems great, even though I've only met him a few times. You seem to have a nice family just the way it is. What do you mean your art?" I ask, suddenly realizing what she said.

"Oh, I thought you knew. I was—am—an artist; I just don't ever get to do it anymore," she says with a wry smile. Then she twists her arms above her head and twirls around, like she is presenting herself. "A sculptor," she says.

"Oh, wow, that explains so much—your creativity and everything," I say.

She smiles, and for a minute I think she is going to hug me, but she doesn't. My kids are getting restless. Hazel keeps taking the frog away from Henry and trying to jam it in the bus. He screeches, she gives it back to him, he chews for a minute, and then she grabs it away again.

"All right, well, they're probably killing each other over there, and Jake is probably looking out the window," she says. "Thank you."

I have an urge to ask her not to leave. There could be so much more to talk about. It was interesting that she feels estranged from Jake. Do all parents of young children feel that way? And I would love to hear more about her pre-baby work. Maybe she would even be interested in hearing about my work, or lack of it, too. But Willa is heading toward the door. Just before she turns the knob she stops, and I think she might want to talk some more. I'm getting my answers ready, continuing the conversation in my head, but "Can I have a few eggs?" is all she says.

The thing I didn't have a chance to tell Willa is that the month we conceived Henry, I ran out of the sperm-killing gel that I use with my diaphragm. I always meant to get more but never got around to it. We were still in New Orleans. I didn't think I'd get pregnant, but I figured it would be okay if I did. I had things under control.

So on the few occasions when we wanted to make love, I used plain Vaseline to allow me to push the diaphragm in. And then I was pregnant and telling Sam it was a complete surprise again, which it was, but not in the same way.

And Sam didn't mind; he seemed happy even. But since we've been here, and everything has taken so much more effort, I sometimes wake up dreaming about putting that gel on the counter at our pharmacy on Carrollton Avenue in New Orleans, paying for it, and bringing it home.

Later that night, I toss and turn as Sam snores beside me, mumbling about Chilean sea bass, and I know for sure that I am not going to have that dream anymore.

SPRING

CHAPTER TEN

*Eating within the intimate confines of the Red Rose, I felt like
I was dining in someone's home while being treated to the private performance of award-winning chef Leo Line. This chef
could easily be working somewhere larger, somewhere fancier,
somewhere more profitable, somewhere far less personal. But
if intimacy has its appeal for diners, it also has its draw for
Line, who says he wants to master every detail of his cuisine.
The results are often exciting.*

—Sam Soto

After a crazy night with the kids that included barely getting to the door
when the delivery guy rang with our Mexican takeout, and spending
hours trying to get Hazel into the bath only to put it off once again
and spin her in a cloud of baby powder instead, I am relieved they are
finally, finally asleep.

I tiptoe downstairs with the monitors and snuggle under my blanket, reading a few pages before I feel my eyes getting heavy. I'm startled

when Desire suddenly dashes into the room. It takes me a minute to realize she has a long tail coming out of her mouth. I stand up on my chair just as she drops the mouse, and it scurries under the chair. My heart is racing, and I am surprised to find myself absolutely terrified. Where has my toughness gone? I don't remember being bothered by the giant-size rats at the hotel in Brazil.

I am mentally walking through the pros and cons of calling Sebastian—he lives in the neighborhood, he is always willing to help, I miss him, Sam would kill me—when the doorbell rings. I jump off the chair and run out of the room, pulling the door closed behind me. I run down, look through the peephole. I can't see anyone.

"Hello?" I call, trying to sound normal.

"Lila," I hear Carol's raspy voice say. "Are you there?"

I am so relieved that I pull open the door and smile at the sight of my crazy neighbor wearing a ratty green terry-cloth robe and holding a tray full of what look like brown biscuits.

"I had to get these out of my house," she says when I push open the storm door and feel the cool spring air on my face. "They're almond cakes, and I already had one today. I keep going down to the kitchen and looking at them. I know it's late, but I saw your lights on."

"Come in," I say.

"No, I have to get to bed; just take them," she says, pushing the tray toward me.

"Carol, I hate to bother you, but are you good at getting mice?" I ask, taking the tray out of her hands.

"Why, do you have a little sucker?" she asks, pushing past me and tightening the belt on her bathrobe.

"I'm afraid I do," I say.

"I need a bag and a brush," she demands.

"I think it might still be alive," I say, putting down the tray and running to get a paper bag and the sweeper. I hand them to her, then lead her up the stairs and point to the closed door of the den.

She opens it without hesitation. I peer in behind her. Fortunately, Desire has captured it again, and this time it isn't running away.

"Pick up the cat," Carol barks at me.

I can barely stand to get that close to the semidead mouse, but I do as she says. Then she uses the sweeper to push the mouse into the bag, turns down the top, and walks to the stairs. I put down the cat, who sniffs furiously where the mouse just was. I follow Carol down the stairs. She opens the door and takes the brown bag with her.

"Thanks," I say. "Really."

"Don't mention it," she says, already walking down the stoop. I watch as she slowly crosses the street and goes into her house. I wonder what she is going to do with that mouse. Bake with it maybe? But I take comfort in the fact that a person I know is awake and only a few feet away. I realize, though, that I don't have her phone number. I close the door and tell myself to work on getting some of the neighbors' phone numbers. No need to pretend anymore; they know who we are.

The next week, just days after the last of the snow melts, the cherry tree blooms. It sits on the sidewalk in front of our house, and I can see the pink, billowy clouds of flower puffs. Ever since we moved onto this block, I have heard people talking about the magic of the cherry tree.

I walk outside and look up at the tiny pink petals, guessing they will be at their splendor only a short time before everyone will be tracking them into their houses on stroller and tricycle wheels. Why does everyone look forward to this so much?

It doesn't take long for me to begin to understand. Most of my neighbors are outside, playing with their kids. Today Willa is on her stoop with the twins. She waves when she sees me. I feel such relief that people know who we are and, as far as I can tell, don't care so much, that I decide we'll join everyone.

I hear a smacking sound and turn to see Hazel with her face up against our storm door. Then she grabs the door handle and frantically tries to open it.

"Wait a minute," I say, noticing that she is still in her pajamas and is barefoot. I see the lady with the long ponytail open her door and look out, and Janie is heading up the street. She doesn't have kids, but for some reason she doesn't work, so she is part of the crowd. From what I can tell, she likes to hang out with the kids and is a member of the babysitting club even though she doesn't get anything back.

I pull the door open and shimmy inside so Hazel can't escape.

"Let's get dressed and find your shoes," I say, spotting a pile of clothes under the dining room table. I bend down and pick it up. It's a pair of very dirty pants and a not-so-bad shirt that Hazel wore a few days ago. It was bunched up to take down to the laundry room but must have fallen under the table somehow. Good. I just hope these clothes didn't involve a leaky diaper or one of those rare, and still often unsuccessful, underwear days.

No socks. I find some of Henry's tiny socks and force them on her feet. The cuff barely makes it around her heel, but she's so eager to get outside she doesn't notice. Her shoes hold the socks in place.

Hazel has gathered her new Wiggles sidewalk chalk, her favorite red 76ers basketball, and her Hula-Hoop.

"Are you sure you need all of that stuff?" I ask.

"Yes," she says, without a doubt. She's been dying to show everyone her toys.

When we get outside, Hazel takes off to join the other kids. The women are standing in a circle talking. I inch over, listening for a chance to break in, but I keep hearing words like *foxglove*, *primrose*, and *wild thyme*. The woman with the ponytail, who I finally now know is Lynn, mentions something about finding acorns for a tea set. How do you break into this sort of conversation? Are they talking about planting a garden on the street? How would the acorns fit into that? Then someone mentions Saint-John's-wort.

"I tried that once," I say, and everyone turns to look at me. "It's supposed to make you feel better, moodwise. That's what you're talking about, right?"

Before I even have a chance to feel stupid, Willa opens up the circle a little so I am not so clearly standing on the outside.

"Actually, I'm planning a fairy and goblin party to celebrate spring," Willa says. "Saint-John's-wort is supposed to protect people from fairy spells or something. But I did take it once; it didn't work. I called and got a prescription for Wellbutrin instead."

"You did?" I ask.

"You have twins," Lynn says. "What's my excuse?"

"What's my excuse?" Janie says. Everyone turns to look at her, and it gets really quiet. I sense an awkward moment. I wonder why. "But, I can't take anything anymore," she adds, smiling.

"I have an announcement to make," she says. "Some of you may already have guessed, but I couldn't bring myself to tell until now. We've had all the tests, and everything looks good, and I can't hold it in anymore. I'm pregnant. Sixteen weeks." Everyone starts to cheer; then people rush to her and hug her. I just stand there. I don't know her well enough to hug her, but I'm happy for her.

"What did I miss?" Carol shouts in her raspy voice from her stoop.

"Janie is pregnant," Lynn answers.

"Not another one," she answers. "We have enough kids on this block already." She turns and goes back inside. Everyone looks nervous for a minute, but then it passes. I wonder what I'm missing. I find myself sneaking peeks at Janie's stomach, wondering about the baby inside and thinking how amazing that is. Then I scold myself for being so sentimental.

I hear a loud thud and then Hazel's cry. I was so distracted that I didn't notice that Russell climbed up behind her on the stoop across the street and pushed her off. I run over.

"He push me!" she is screaming through her tears. "He push me!"

"I did not push!" Russell says, looking at his feet. "She fall."

Willa, who apparently saw it happen, takes Russell by the arm and leads him to their stoop for a time-out. I look Hazel over. She has a scratch on her forehead and her hands are scraped up, but she's fine. That's all I care about. I pick her up and hold her for a minute. Right away she squirms to get down and goes over to Russell to play with him again. A minute later they are drawing lines with chalk and jumping over them. Willa and I look at each other. If only all conflicts were resolved that easily.

The next morning I call Sebastian. I wasn't going to, but the truth is, I can't help myself.

Right away he is glad to hear from me. He says he will be taking care of his niece on Friday morning, and he would love to meet us. We agree to meet at Sal's Pizza for lunch and let the girls play in the square after.

When we get to the restaurant on Friday, Sebastian is alone. He's sitting in a booth and jumps up when he sees me, taking the stroller out of my hands. I haven't been feeling well since I woke up—my left breast is really bothering me—so I am happier than ever to see a friendly, helpful face.

"Thanks," I say, plunking down on the red plastic booth.

"You don't look so good," Sebastian says, always so observant.

"I'm okay," I say, brushing it off. "Where's your niece?"

"Ear infection," he says. "I would have called you, but I don't have your number since it's blocked and obviously you aren't listed."

"Oh, sorry," I say.

"No, I'm glad to see you anyway. I hope you don't mind," he says, smiling.

I suddenly feel sick. My left breast is incredibly sore, and I don't think I'll be able to stand it when Henry wants to nurse. As usual, Sebastian takes over and orders the pizza, pays, and brings everything to the table. He also helps Hazel with her pizza. Following her instructions, he peels off the pepperoni and puts it into a pile, then takes off the cheese and cuts the slice into strips. She is thrilled.

"I was hoping you'd call sooner," Sebastian says. "I told Charlotte, my niece, all about Hazel."

"Actually, I thought about calling a few times," I say. "There were a few things that held me back."

"For instance?" he asks, letting some of the grease from his pizza drip onto the white paper plate.

"Well, to begin with, Sam doesn't condone this friendship," I say.

"You're a big girl," says Sebastian. "I think you're old enough to choose your own friends and decide whom you can trust."

"And," I continue, "there are people watching me."

Sebastian looks over his shoulder in an overly dramatic way, and it makes me laugh.

"I've been in the *Philadelphia Busybody*'s gossip column twice," I say.

"Oh yeah, I saw those," he says. "They were great."

"Well, Sam didn't think so," I say.

"What did you think?" he asks.

I smile, then look from side to side to make sure nobody is listening to us.

"I kind of liked it," I say.

We both laugh. My head pounds. With that, Sebastian turns to Hazel, who has been completely mesmerized by the pepperoni.

"So, Greg, or is it Murray?" he asks, knowing she wants to be called by one of the Wiggles' names.

"Greg," she says through a big smile.

"Well, Greg, what is your favorite flavor of ice cream?"

"Mint," she yells. Sebastian looks at me and I smile. We don't have anything to do, and it is a long day ahead. Even longer, since Sam won't have a chance to come home before his dinner tonight. He is reviewing a restaurant in the suburbs and could get only a seven o'clock reservation. Ice cream will be good. But as we stand in line, I feel worse and worse. I push the stroller over to a chair and sit down.

"Are you okay?" Sebastian asks. "You look really pale."

"Actually I haven't been feeling great all day, but now I feel awful. I think I better just go home."

"Give me a second and I'll help you," he says. I sit there shivering and dreaming about putting my head on a pillow. Sebastian whispers to Hazel. He runs up and orders a quart of ice cream to go. I can see from the color that it's mint chocolate chip, Hazel's favorite. Sebastian helps me up, takes hold of the stroller, and pushes it while I walk slowly beside him. He helps me inside, where I immediately sit on the couch. Then he gets Hazel out of the stroller, up the stairs, and in the door, and drags the huge stroller with the sleeping Henry up the stoop and inside so he can continue to sleep. I start to tell him thank you, but I think I say, "I love you" instead. He just smiles and tells me to call the doctor. If this is a breast problem, as I suspect, then I better call Dr. Berri. At that thought I perk up. Then I sigh. My life has become more pitiful than I realized if this is what passes for excitement.

I go to the bathroom and look at my breasts. The left one is full of red streaks, the telltale sign of a breast infection. Sebastian has taken Hazel into the kitchen and is dishing out ice cream for her, so I grab the phone and call. I know the number by heart. A nurse answers, and I tell her my trouble. She says she'll have the doctor call me. I lie down on the couch near the stroller, where Henry is still sleeping soundly, and drift off to the sound of Hazel laughing. The phone jolts me awake.

"Hello?" I say groggily.

"Hi, you." It's Sam. "You sound funny. Are you okay?"

"Oh," I say, wanting to wave to Sebastian and Hazel in the kitchen and tell them to shut up. What if he hears them? "Actually, I'm sick. I think I have mastitis. I just called Dr. Berri, and I'm waiting for him to call back. Can I call you after that?"

"Sure," he says. "Call me as soon as you hear from him. I can pick up a prescription if you need me to."

"Okay, thanks."

Two minutes later the phone rings again.

"It's Dr. Berri," he says when I answer. I love his voice. "What's going on?"

I tell him, but I talk too fast because I'm nervous. He tells me to take a deep breath, gives me a prescription for antibiotics, and says to nurse Henry through it.

"Take care of yourself, Lila," he says warmly. "Call me if you need anything else."

After a peaceful afternoon thanks to Sebastian, he finally says he has to get going because he has to work later.

"How about next Thursday?" Sebastian asks after I've thanked him fifteen times. "Same time, same place, one addition? I'm sure Charlotte will be fine by then."

I consider telling him that I'll think about it and call him, but I'm tired of that.

"Sounds great," I say.

Sam does pick up my prescription but does not offer to cancel his dinner out. At least he leaves work early enough to come home before going out again. To him, that is a big change in plans, one worthy of appreciation. And he does help feed Hazel. But then he is gone. I use all my energy to pull out the sofa bed in the den. I put Henry between me and Hazel, turn on a Barney video—another hand-me-down from my mother's neighbor—and drift in and out of restless sleep. In my dreams I am sitting down to a meeting with Ed, telling him I want the circus to come to the Addison. He just stares at me. I keep trying to tell him that the elephants won't be too smelly. He just shakes his head. Finally, I am pulled out of my groggy state and realize that it isn't elephants that smell, it's Henry. I get up, change his diaper, and we all go back to sleep until Sam comes home.

Two doses of antibiotics later, I call Ed. He answers the phone himself.

"What are you doing answering the phone?" I say. "I didn't realize you were that short staffed over there."

"No, we're not, but I gave Sandra the afternoon off because she wasn't feeling well," he says. "I'm glad to hear from you, Lila. Have I thanked you enough for helping us out these last few months? Finding that kid was just incredible. And have I told you how much we look forward to having you officially on board again?"

"Yes, Ed, plenty of times for both," I say, laughing.

"So, what will it be, can you do twenty-five hours a week? Some travel? I'm thinking we'll keep you close to home for the first six months. Hopefully you won't have to go too far. Maybe a few nights in Pittsburgh or Hartford, but nothing across the country or overseas. Then we'll see how you're doing. Does that sound about right?"

I hesitate. I had every intention of being honest and telling Ed about Sam's problems with my working, and that he and I were still working through them. I planned to tell him about the gossip column. I even, in my most confident moments, thought I might be able to tell him that I have a whole new idea for a project: something that would help other mothers, something that would keep me closer to home.

"That sounds about right," I say, feeling like I just said it sounded like a great idea that I go work on the moon.

"Good, good, good," he says. "I'll get the ball rolling. Let's set up a meeting for . . . Let me see here . . . Can you come in to the New York office, say, August first? I know you said end of summer, but that's pretty close. What do you say?"

"That's a little too soon, Ed," I say finally, hating the words as they leave my mouth. But I owe this to Sam. "I can't tell you how much I want this, but I need more time. Could we push it back a few weeks? At least until Hazel starts school?"

"Oh, Lila, I hate to," he says. "Fall is such a busy time. But yes, as long as I can call you if anything comes up."

"Fine," I say, knowing Sam would hate that. Hopefully nothing will come up.

CHAPTER ELEVEN

The true measure of a great restaurant is its willingness to please its guests, even if they're three years old and the task involves the ego blow of setting aside the house specials to cook from a box. Hence the Mac and Cheese Test. Not only did it reveal the true colors of the restaurants down the Shore, but those that succeeded best also had the most peaceful dining rooms as my finicky daughter happily settled into her meal.

—Sam Soto

A week later, Sam announces that we are taking a spring trip to the New Jersey Shore with the kids. He wants to do a feature about summer restaurants.

"Does it mean we would be eating out with you all the time, or staying in the hotel room? Because I would rather be here than—"

"No, we'd eat out together," Sam says before I can finish. "Things are more casual at the Shore."

"Okay," I say. "I could use a change of scenery."

"Good," Sam says. "It'll be fun."

By the time we're driving down Route 55 toward Cape May, I tell myself to try to leave my worries in Philadelphia.

"Where are we eating tonight?" I ask Sam.

"We have a few choices," he says. "We can either go to an extremely fancy new seafood place that will be the most formal place we have to go, or a bistro-type place in Atlantic City."

"Where's the fancy seafood place?" I ask.

"I think it's right in Cape May; I have to check."

"Let's go there, then. We can get the fancy place over with before the kids get too tired of it, and we won't have to drive far, considering we'll have been in the car a lot by that point."

Once we get to Cape May, we settle into our motel and change our clothes. Just before we leave, I nurse Henry, who is in very good spirits, and Sam calls the seafood place to get directions and make sure they have a high chair.

"Were they nice?" I ask when he hangs up.

"Pretty nice," he says. "They have a high chair. We're going early anyway; don't worry."

When we get there, I worry. It is a beautiful, big room facing the ocean, with huge windows all around. The tables are close together and set with china, silver, and pristine white tablecloths that I know will be multicolored on our table in a matter of minutes. There are two other parties already seated, and I give Sam a concerned look. He just shrugs.

The hostess smiles and leads us to a table with two fancy place settings, two removed, and a nice little high chair pulled up to one side. Maybe this won't be so bad; they seem ready for us. But it takes all our energy to jam Henry into the seat. He is new to high chairs, and he would rather be on my lap. Hazel decides she wants a high chair, too, even though she certainly doesn't need one anymore.

"I need a high chair," she squeals, and I imagine the other diners glaring at us. "I cannot sit in a seat," she says, staccato. "I need a high chair."

Sam flags down the hostess; do they have another high chair? They do, and it is carried to our table. It's hard to wiggle Hazel in because it is an old-fashioned kind, and she is pretty big now, but she is determined, and we manage. We open the menus, and Henry starts to fuss. He's a little young for Cheerios, but I have decided it is a good time for him to try. I pull out a miniature box and place three on his tray. He pokes and pokes and tries to pick one up.

"I want some of dose," Hazel whines. I put a small handful in front of her. She crams them into her mouth and asks for more.

"We'll get bread and butter soon," I tell her. "Just wait one minute."

"I want Coke," she announces. Sam glares at me. He is mad that I have introduced her to soda at such a young age.

"It's too late for Coke," I tell her. "It would keep you up."

"I want Sprite," she announces. Fine.

We look at the menu. Everything looks so good. There are the usual crab cakes and broiled flounder, but they also have a curried shrimp dish with chickpeas, a seafood marinara pasta dish that I am eyeing, and a tempting grilled duck breast with red wine jus and honey mashed sweet potatoes. Sam looks at me. He knows what I'm thinking.

"Definitely not the seafood marinara," he says. "But I would like to stick with fish and seafood—so no duck. I'm not so interested in the shrimp. The sauce sounds interesting. Well, maybe the shrimp. Or the halibut. The Asian bouillabaisse sounds great. What do you want?"

"I'll have the shrimp," I say quickly. "And can I have the crab and vegetable spring rolls to begin? They sound so good."

"Sure, and I'll have the bouillabaisse and the mussels."

Just then I look at Henry. He managed to get a Cheerio into his mouth, and he is gagging. I jump up, prepared to do something—I'm not sure what—and a stream of milk with one Cheerio comes shooting out of his mouth. I think he is too young for Cheerios. I take the other two away, and he starts to whimper. Just as we are wiping up his spit-up with the white linen napkin, the waitress comes over.

"I want a Sprite," Hazel tells her immediately.

"She can have one," I say, when the waitress looks at me. "And I wanted to ask, do you have anything on the menu for kids?"

"Not really, but there are a few things the chef is happy to do," she says nicely. "He will panfry a fillet of fresh flounder and cut it into sticks, he will grill a chicken breast, or he will toss pasta with butter and cheese." They all sound good to me. I look at Hazel. She is frowning.

"Sprite, pwease!" she says.

"Hazel, I said you can have a Sprite, but you have to have dinner, too. Which of those things sounds good?"

She doesn't answer. I look at Sam. Just then a group of six arrives. As they are led to their table, I see that they are dressed perfectly. The men are wearing different-colored striped shirts with blue blazers and crisp floral ties; the women are wearing bright sundresses. This is probably some important night. I look away when one of the women smiles. *Don't smile*, I want to say to her. *This is not going to be pretty.*

"Why don't we order," Sam says. "Then we'll figure this out." We order and the waitress smiles and walks away. She is back in a minute with bread and butter, and Hazel's Sprite. Hazel expertly pulls the paper off the top of the straw and takes a long sip. She sits back and smiles like she just had a swig of a really good Scotch.

"That is *one* good drink," Hazels says. Out of the corner of my eye, I see Sam wince.

When the waitress walks away again, Sam leans down and digs around in the diaper bag. He pulls out a box of Kraft Macaroni & Cheese and holds it up. Hazel cheers. I am horrified.

"What are you going to do?" I ask. "Demand a bowl and fill it with hot water from the bathroom?"

"No," he says. "I'm going to ask them to make it. It requires butter and milk, water, and a saucepan. Any good kitchen has those things. And any good restaurant should want to make its customers happy. I'll call it the Mac and Cheese Test and see how each restaurant deals with the request. As far as I know, it's never been done before." He clears his throat in a way that tells me he's getting choked up. Is he kidding?

"It's macaroni and cheese," I say. "Not a peace treaty."

"For some families it might be," Sam says.

I want to slide under the table. Suddenly I am so mad that I want to spit. Sam had this planned all along and didn't bother to tell me. I knew our week at the Shore was a work vacation, but now I feel like he brought us along just so he could do this. He's using us, especially Hazel. I don't even look at Sam. I keep hoping that the waitress will refuse and kick us out.

But when she returns with our appetizers and Sam holds up the box, she takes it and says she'll ask the chef. I can't believe it. About fifteen minutes later she comes back with a china bowl full of beautifully prepared macaroni and cheese. It looks creamier than I have ever seen it, and it is sitting on a doily on top of a china plate. Hazel is thrilled.

"Thank you," Sam says. "And please thank the chef." The waitress smiles.

Just as our entrées arrive, Henry gets very upset. Maybe he senses my anger. Sam, on the other hand, hasn't even noticed that I haven't said a word since he announced his great idea.

It becomes clear that Henry will no longer sit. I have already fed him his chicken with apples baby food. I unhook him from the chair, pull him onto my lap, and offer him my breast. He takes it, and soon falls asleep and stays asleep while I one-handedly eat my shrimp. Hazel is happy. She eats the entire bowl of macaroni and moves on to a beautiful ice cream sundae complete with whipped cream and a cherry. I soften a little. If Sam is using her, she certainly isn't suffering.

I eat big forkfuls of a summer-berry napoleon. The berries are bright and crisp, and the flaky pastry is lined with a delicious sweet cream. I make a face when Sam reaches over with his fork for a bite.

"I have to try it," he says.

"I know," I say. "Just don't take too much."

Sam takes my hand under the table, and I decide that maybe he didn't do such a terrible thing. Then he speaks.

"Listen, I've been thinking," he says. "I want Hazel to be hungry for dinner so she'll eat the macaroni and cheese and tell me how it is. So let's make sure she doesn't eat anything after two in the afternoon, okay?"

"I don't think that will work," I say, mad again. Why did I think we were making progress? Sam is acting exactly the way he has acted since he got this stupid job, like anything can be sacrificed for the sake of his calling. And apparently this idea contains an element of deprivation for my poor little girl. "We're on vacation! Plus, she'll want stuff on the boardwalk."

"We'll go early," he says.

The next night we try the bistro in Atlantic City. It doesn't look familiar when we drive up and park, but the minute we step inside, I know I have been here with Tom. His cousin got married about five years ago in Atlantic City. We had a great weekend, stayed at one of the big casino hotels in a high-roller room. After the wedding festivities, we decided to stay an extra night. The family had cleared out, so it was just the two of us, and we came to this restaurant.

As the waitress leads us to our table, I remember that back then I was wearing a light-yellow summer dress and brown sandals. At the moment I'm wearing a big green nursing shirt over large khaki shorts, and sneakers. Back then, we sat down at a table in the corner, and I remember saying how nice it was to dine by candlelight. Now we quickly whisk the silverware away and blow out the tapered candle. Back then, once we were settled, Tom reached across the table and said there was nobody he would rather be sitting across from. Now we cram into the banquette and have to rearrange ourselves a few times because Hazel keeps changing her mind about whom she wants to sit next to.

When Sam pulls out the box of macaroni and cheese, I excuse myself and go to the bathroom. As soon as I walk in, I remember the flowered wallpaper and the pink couch. I remember that after dinner Tom said he wanted to drive south a little, to a special spot on the beach, and I came into this very bathroom and put my diaphragm in so that I would be ready if his spot proved to be as special as he promised. Now I sit on the pink couch and try not to cry.

I have the strongest urge to speak to Tom. I search in my purse for my cell phone. I pull it out, and without even thinking I dial his cell phone number. It takes a few moments to start ringing, longer than usual, but I don't even consider hanging up. It finally rings, and my heart jumps, and then it goes right to voice mail. "Hi, this is Tom. Leave a message."

The sound of the beep brings me out of my trance. I quickly hang up. I can't quite process the sound of his voice, which continues to ring in my ear. It makes me feel so many things: sad, nostalgic, curious, annoyed. And what was I thinking? I don't want to call him when I'm down.

It isn't until I have put my phone away that I realize how crazy it is that I remember his number, just as though I had dialed it yesterday. Aren't things like that supposed to leave your mind when you have children with someone else? *Here comes the baby; oh, and there goes your old boyfriend's phone number; it's floating away.*

As I rejoin my family, the waitress emerges with a small casserole that is still bubbling. At first I think that they made their own, and I want to tell Sam, *I told you so*, but when I look closer, it is definitely Kraft. I see the thin, small elbows that have become so familiar. They just put it under the broiler.

"That looks great," Sam says. "This is going better than I planned. The places so far are right on target with how they should be."

A few nights later we go to a new American fusion place in Margate, where the waiter is not happy with our request. He tells us they have fabulous food—why would we bring our own? I am so relieved for a minute that I want to kiss the waiter, who, I can't help but notice, looks a little like Tom. Sam explains that we want their fabulous food, but our three-year-old daughter is picky. Somehow he gets them to do it. When it comes back to us, it looks as if someone put all the ingredients in a bowl and microwaved it without even stirring it. Hazel stares, then starts to cry. I glare at Sam, but he is thrilled. He doesn't like our food any better than Hazel likes this version of the macaroni. It fits perfectly into his plan.

The night before we head home, I can't sleep. What would I have said if Tom had answered his phone? When Henry wakes up to nurse, I don't mind; in fact, I'm glad to have something to do. When he lets me put him back down again, I try to settle into bed, and I glance over at my snoring husband, the strange restaurant critic. I finally fall asleep.

It seems like just minutes later when Sam nudges me and tells me we have to get going. He wants to pack up, drive north a little, and have lunch at a grand old inn before we head back to Philadelphia. It is much too fancy to take children to for dinner, but maybe lunch will work. I want to ask if he is over his stupid test, but I know I won't like the answer.

When we arrive for our early lunch, I look around the inn with growing concern. The rooms are full of overflowing flower arrangements, the walls are a crisp white, the chairs are covered in beautiful prints. The hostess has to dig the high chair out of a closet because it is so rarely used. As soon as we sit down, Hazel starts demanding her lollipop. We've gotten into the habit this week of giving her one because we've been eating out so much. At home we usually don't pull that trick out until we become desperate. Are we already desperate?

"There is going to be a lot of good food, Sweetie," I tell her. "Then you can have it."

"I want my wowy," she says, a little too loud. The couple behind us turns to see who is inconsiderate enough to have brought children here.

"Hazel, we'll get your macaroni and cheese," Sam says.

"I don't want macaroni," she wails. "Too much macaroni."

I give Sam an evil look. He just shrugs and pulls out the box anyway.

"Noooooooooo," Hazel cries.

Her piercing shriek jolts Henry awake, and he tries frantically to find my breast. As I start to lift my shirt in desperation, the couple behind us asks if they can move to another table. I pull down my shirt, hand Hazel her treat, and get up with Henry to find a place to nurse.

About twenty-five minutes later Sam finds me sitting on a folding chair in the basement, nursing Henry. Hazel is trailing behind him.

"She didn't eat much," he says. I just look at him.

"Why don't you go eat something," he says. "I'll take them outside."

I hand him the baby and skulk up the stairs to our table. When I sit down, I look outside through the huge windows circling the dining room and see Sam holding Henry and chasing Hazel around the lawn. Henry is smiling and Hazel is clearly happy. Most of the people in the restaurant can see them, and I'm aware of their glances and shaking heads. I'm embarrassed and eat as fast as I can with my head down. When I'm almost finished with my crab cake, an elegantly dressed woman walks over to me. I quickly swallow and wonder if I can leave the table before she gets here. She is probably going to say that watching Hazel through the window has ruined her meal.

"You have a lovely little girl," she says. I look at her, waiting for her to say *but*. She doesn't.

"We have a grandson, about her age, who isn't healthy. He's sick with . . . Well, what I wanted to say to you is how much I have enjoyed watching her today. She is a joy. It's a gift to have a healthy child." She smiles sadly and turns to walk away.

"Thank you," I call a little too loudly. She turns back to face me. "I thought you were going to complain. What you said means a lot to me. I'm really sorry about your grandson."

"Yes, well, so are we," she says, and walks away. I sit for a minute, wondering what is wrong with her grandson. Then I look out the window and see Hazel jump off the third step of the porch onto the grass and roll around. Sam cheers her on, holding Henry over his head, then bringing him close for a belly kiss. I hold my head up higher and enjoy the rest of my crab cake. Then I go outside to take over so Sam can come in and order dessert.

After lunch, we begin our drive back to Philadelphia. I fall asleep almost immediately, and we are close to home when I wake up. Hazel and Henry are both sound asleep in the back, and we are listening to Dan Zanes because we want to. I turn to look at Sam as Dan sings about the sunny side of the street.

"I've been mad at you," I say.

"You're kidding," he says sarcastically.

"If you knew, why didn't you say something?" I ask, trying to cast off my groggy feeling. I dig into my purse and pull out one of Hazel's lollipops. I open it, suck on it.

"Sometimes you're very hard to talk to," Sam says gently. "I figured it would pass, or you'd bring it up when you wanted to."

I don't know what to say. His tone calms me, but I feel like I am on a roller coaster, one minute thinking, *This is good*, the next thinking, *This is bad; how did I get here and how do I get off?* Are all marriages like this? There has to be some more even ground somewhere.

"Then at the restaurant today a lady told me she liked watching Hazel. She said her grandson is about Hazel's age and sick—she didn't say with what. But she said how nice it is to see a healthy child. It sort of put things in perspective. I mean, you drive me crazy. Your stupid macaroni test almost sent me over the edge. But then I see you playing with them, and that lady says that. And I think, yeah, it is so lucky to have healthy children. And even though I miss working, at that moment I thought, I did something great. My body made two healthy babies."

Sam looks over and smiles at me. His face is warm and open.

"Maybe that will be enough for you," he offers tentatively.

"Oh no you don't," I say, but my tone isn't harsh. "Don't use my words against me. I'm going back to work at some point, and we have to figure out a way that you'll be comfortable with that."

"Do we have to figure that out now?"

"No, I'm too tired."

Sam smiles a little and concentrates on the road.

"Oh, wait—before I forget, I wanted to tell you I have another idea," he says, looking straight ahead. "Next time we do this, let's bring along cans of Campbell's soup for Hazel. I was thinking either tomato or cream of chicken. I'll call it the Soup Test."

CHAPTER TWELVE

I might have enjoyed the veal chop more had it not been nearly three inches thick, which is a height of pure carnivore hubris. If I hadn't needed to lean over just to see the other side of the plate, I wouldn't have dirtied my blazer.

—Sam Soto

Sam returns to the office and to a rumor that a picture of him is circulating in local restaurant kitchens. He calls to tell me. He is completely distraught.

"How could they get my picture?" he whines. "I'm so careful. Why would anyone do that to me?"

"Maybe it's just a rumor," I say, trying to reassure him. "Maybe people think that if you think they have your picture, you won't bother to be so careful anymore."

I don't really mean it. After all this time it isn't such a surprise that someone got a picture of Sam. All the restaurants are desperate to know what he looks like. As the day goes on, Sam is increasingly tortured trying to figure out what sort of picture they might have and who might have gotten hold of it. At three o'clock Sam calls to say he's coming home. We're playing outside when he rides his bike toward us. He is wearing huge dark sunglasses that I've never seen before. They practically cover the entire upper half of his face.

"There's Daddy," I say to Hazel. She looks at him for a second before she decides it really is Sam. Then she runs down the street to meet him.

"Play hopscotch with me and Russell," she says, practically pulling him off his bike. At first he resists. He gives me a questioning look. I know he wonders what we're doing out here. But then he takes a deep breath and lets Hazel lead him to the game.

"Nice glasses," I say. "Did you get them at a stand on the street?"

"No, I bought them at the little store in the lobby," he says. "I couldn't just ride home in broad daylight." I nod slightly and keep my mouth shut.

"Daddy, Daddy, I get invited to Pamewa's birthday," Hazel says, jumping up and down. "Mommy, you say."

Actually, I was sort of hoping not to say, at least not right now. While we were away, a very fancy invitation had arrived, inviting Hazel to Pamela's third birthday party at an indoor gym called Banana Boat. Hazel has already put the bright purple-and-yellow invitation in her bed so she can sleep with it tonight.

"Hazel was invited to Pamela's party," I say casually. "It's next Saturday."

"She can't go," Sam says. "Not when there's a picture of me out there. It's too risky. You and Hazel could get into pictures. What about the gossip column? No way. This is all too much."

"Sam," I say quietly, making a face at him to indicate we'll talk about this later. But it's too late. Hazel crumples to the ground and lies on the hopscotch game.

"Get up," Russell shouts at her, nudging her with his foot. It is his turn. Hazel just lies there.

"Yes," she says finally, pushing up on her elbow. "I can go to the party. I want to go to the party. I can go."

"Hazel, we'll work this out. Daddy is upset about something else right now," I say.

"Okay," she says, sniffling. "But I do go to the party. I do."

"I'm sorry, Sweetie, but because of Daddy's work there are going to be some things you can't—"

"Sam," I say loudly. "She's three!"

"But Mommy, I want to go to party. I can go to party," Hazel says, trying to be brave. It breaks my heart.

"Yes, Sweetie, you can probably go to the party," I say, glaring at Sam. "We just have to work out a few details."

I tell myself to not get too mad at Sam; he'll come around. But how could he possibly stand the thought of breaking Hazel's heart like that?

I find him looking relatively relaxed in our bedroom that night after the kids are both asleep, and it seems like a good time to have a talk about it.

"Hi," I say.

"Hi," he says.

"I want to talk to you about Pamela's birthday party," I say. Sam tenses up. "I just think Hazel should be able to have a normal—"

It is at that moment that we hear Carol, our nutty across-the-street baking neighbor, utter Sam's name over the baby monitor. We both stop and listen.

"Did you see his review last week?" she is asking someone in her raspy voice.

"Turn it up," Sam yells at me, stiffening. I try, but the louder it gets the more static it picks up. I try to adjust it so we can hear.

"I did," we hear Jake, Willa's husband, say. "I always read Sam's reviews."

"Every time he writes about an Italian restaurant it makes my blood boil," Carol says. "I used to think he was good, but I don't anymore. His column is full of errors, full of them."

Sam and I look at each other.

"It's a great restaurant," Carol says, referring to Sam's recent review of a new Italian place on East Passyunk Avenue. "I've known those people for years, and let me tell you, they're great cooks. Their veal is out of this world. Sam Soto does not know his stuff."

Static blurs out Jake's response.

"Yeah, well, if he doesn't want to spend so much money, then he should go for lunch," we hear Carol say.

"I said that in my review," Sam protests to the monitor. "I said that it isn't worth the cost of dinner, but lunch is a better deal. Did she even read it?"

"Shhhhhhh," I say, pointing to the monitor.

"You know," she continues, "I hear a lot of people complain about him. Some people can't stand him."

The static increases, and we miss what Jake says again. Then Carol starts talking about another neighbor. She's complaining about how Ben and Janie always leave their car parked out front.

"The nerve!" she says. "Someone ought to give them a talking to."

She moves on to complain about how another neighbor, Jeremy, never shovels snow.

"You have to shovel. Six hours after the snow stops falling, you have to start shoveling!" she says. "This year I'm gonna call the police if he doesn't. I'll time him. One of these days I'm gonna slip and break a bone."

I click off the monitor and it's quiet.

"What if she says something else?" he asks.

"I don't think she will; she's on to someone else."

"We've been so careful," Sam says. "How do they all know who we are?"

"Oh, well, I meant to tell you that they've known since before we moved in," I say, not looking him in the eyes. "Willa told me that the realtor mentioned it. But the good news is that nobody on the street owns a restaurant."

Sam lets his head flop down on his pillow. We just lie there for a minute. Then I push myself up to sitting.

"If I were you, I would go over there right now, knock on the door, and tell her she makes your blood boil," I say, grabbing his wrist to get him moving.

"No," Sam says, sounding drained. "I can't do that." He stares up at the ceiling. "I wonder who can't stand me."

I won't be able to if you don't let me take Hazel to her friend's birthday party, I think.

But I say, "Sam, can we get back to what we were talking about?"

"Not now," he says.

I am exasperated as I follow him downstairs and watch him search for his review from last weekend. I know where it is, but I don't offer any help. When he finds it, he sits down and reads through it for a long time. I know he is trying to see if Carol could have been right in any way. He wants to understand what she saw in it. But I want to scream at him. Isn't his family more important?

"Come on," I say finally, thinking I might still have a chance to connect with him. "She's a wacky lady. Besides, she was talking about everyone on the block, not just you."

"Yeah but she wasn't talking about their profession or their charac-ter. Just about some annoying things they do," he says, barely looking up from the newspaper.

"I guess," I say coldly. "Well, I'll see you up there."

"Okay," he says.

I don't fall asleep for a long time, and Sam doesn't join me in bed. When Henry wakes up to nurse, I realize Sam hasn't come to bed at all. I look at the clock: 5:03. That's pretty good for Henry, but where the hell is Sam? I go downstairs before I rescue Henry from his torment, and I find Sam asleep with his head on the dining room table. He has bunched up the newspaper section under his head like a bad pillow, and he is snoring loudly. I gently shake him and he jumps.

"Hi," I say.

"What time is it?" he asks, looking down at his crumpled review and trying to smooth it out.

"After five," I say. "You never came to bed."

"Sorry," he says, getting up. "I'll go now. Is Henry crying?"

"Yeah," I say, realizing I forgot about Henry for a minute. "I'll go get him."

I follow Sam up the stairs. I turn off at Henry's room, and Sam continues up the next flight. When I push open the door, Henry's cries turn into giggles.

"Hi, little boy," I say quietly, hoping to keep him in the sleep zone. But I think he is wide awake. "You're my little man."

I pick him up and hug him. Then I settle him onto my lap. He nurses and we both doze off. The next thing I know, Hazel is standing in front of us. It takes me a minute to figure out where we are.

"Mommy?" Hazel says.

"Hi, Sweetie," I say, trying not to wake Henry.

"Daddy won't wake up," she says. "His eyes won't stay opening."

"He's tired," I say. "Let's go have breakfast."

I try to put Henry in his crib, but he tenses and starts to whine. It was too much to hope for. I decide to let Sam sleep for a little while, partly because I know how annoyed he'll be by it. We have breakfast, I get the kids dressed, and we go out for a walk.

Two hours later we get home. Still no sign of Sam. Henry is dozing, so I take him upstairs, hold my breath, and put him in his crib. One. Two. I exhale and tiptoe out.

Sam is coming down the stairs as I pull Henry's door shut. I put my finger to my lips to tell him to be quiet, and he follows me downstairs.

"I'm so late," he says, raking his hands through his hair. "Why did you let me sleep so long?"

"Hazel said she tried to wake you and you went back to sleep. I decided you needed it. Besides, we were out," I say. "Aren't you going to take a shower? Or change?"

"No," Sam says. His hair is still sticking up, he is wearing the T-shirt and jeans he slept in, and there is a smudge of newsprint on his cheek. I think how funny it would be if someone got a picture of him now. He bends over and furiously tries to rub a spot off his shirt. "I'm just going."

It is at that moment that I decide without a doubt that I will take Hazel to Pamela's birthday party.

Two hours later we arrive in Rittenhouse Square for our playdate with Charlotte and Sebastian. We get there first, so I trail Hazel as she runs around a big tree. Henry giggles. Out of the corner of my eye I can see Sebastian and a little blond girl approaching. When I catch sight of his dark head and his bright-white teeth, I wait for the comfort I usually feel when I see him to kick in, but instead I feel like I've been punched in the stomach. Sebastian bends down and whispers something to the little girl. She shakes her head. He points toward Hazel, and this time she nods. I don't say anything as she picks up speed and runs right at Hazel until she is just a few inches away from her face. Hazel cracks up.

"Hey there," he calls, waving.

I wave halfheartedly, then turn back to watch my daughter and her new friend chase each other around the tree. Henry kicks and squeals, and I know he wants me to bring him closer. But I can't move. Sebastian was in our house not too long ago. Sebastian followed Hazel up to the third floor, passing stacks of pictures I was trying to sort through. Pictures of me, and the kids, and Sam. While I was lying on the couch, thinking how wonderful it was to have some peace and time to rest, there may have been a rat traipsing through my home.

"Hey," Sebastian says again once he has reached me. He puts his hand on my shoulder and squeezes. "How are you?"

I turn to look at him. His eyes are warm, and I think I must be wrong. Sebastian would never do that to me. They know who Sam is at La Noix; why would he steal a picture? Lots of reasons, actually—for a friend at another restaurant, or to impress the crazy chef. No, he wouldn't do that. He doesn't care enough about the restaurant to do that.

"Hello?" he calls, coming close to my face like Charlotte did to Hazel. "Is anybody home?"

"I just remembered," I say to Sebastian, knowing Hazel is going to fight me on this. "The termite guy is coming. I have to go back now or I'll miss him."

"Okay," he says, not at all suspicious of me. Why do I have to be so suspicious of him? "Why don't you leave Hazel here with us?"

"No, that's okay," I say. Hazel is eyeing me. I expect her to start yelling, or run the other way, but I think she is so surprised she doesn't have a fight in her. When she gets up, her lip is already trembling.

"We'll do this again soon," I say, turning toward home. Thank goodness she still has the birthday party to look forward to.

On the morning of Pamela's party Sam literally gasps when he sees us at the door with a big pink present. We haven't mentioned it since my attempt to discuss it. I know he thinks I decided to concede and not go. Too bad. I'm prepared to take Henry with me if Sam gets really mad and storms out. But he just stares at us. He'll get over it. He has to, doesn't he?

"Come on, Mommy," Hazel calls. "I want to go to Danana Boat."

I give up on Sam and take Hazel to the car. We get on I-95 South, and I try to relax. I'm sure Sam will speak to me when we get home. When we arrive, I tell myself we are here now, so I shouldn't worry. I will do my absolute best to avoid being in any pictures. As soon as the door opens, I can sense the chaos, and I feel a rush of humid air that smells like kid sweat. I tell the woman at the desk we are here for the birthday party.

"Which one?" she asks. I didn't know there would be more than one.

At the mention of Pamela's name, we are given bright-green wristbands. Apparently the parties are color coded so you can figure out whom you are supposed to play with. As we head into the actual banana boat, I see a mother I recognize from Hazel's preschool. She smiles at me.

"Welcome to hell," she yells over the noise.

I smile back, and as soon as we step over the threshold, I understand what she means. It is a huge warehouselike room with interconnected tunnels and slides and rope ladders all leading to a huge banana boat in the middle that is filled with hundreds, maybe thousands, of colorful plastic pieces of fruit. Swarming all over every surface are screaming, overexcited children, some much older and bigger than Hazel and Pamela. There might be as many children as there are pieces of fruit in the banana boat.

I follow Hazel into the maze, where we are for about ten minutes before I turn my head and feel the muscles spasm painfully. I know I'll be stuck looking left for the rest of the afternoon. I have no choice but to continue on, hoping that Hazel is not heading for the dreaded banana boat. My head is turned completely to the left when we enter a long, dark tunnel and I run face-to-side-of-face into Mike, Pamela's dad. He is pointing a camera at me. Before I have a chance to say anything, he snaps. Now I can't move my neck or see—I'm blinded by the flash. My only consolation is that I'm sure you can't really see my face because I'm so twisted.

There is no way that Mike and I can get by each other without one of us backing out and letting the other one through.

"Hi, Lila," he says with a tone of *sorry about this, but now we are all in it together*. "I'm glad to see you and Hazel made it. I'm taking lots of pictures of the adults. I think it's really funny to see them trying to keep up with the kids." And with that, he jams his body up against the side of the tunnel so I can get through.

"Hi, Mike," I say as I pass him. My face is a little too close to his, but I can't manage to turn it. "Please don't show anyone that picture," I say, wanting to add that the foundation of my marriage might depend on it. But I leave that part out.

"I've got your back," he says cheerily. My mind is suddenly occupied with the image of arrows racing toward my back and no Mike in sight, and a miniature Sam dressed in a devil's costume flying around and laughing. I try to think of something else.

Finally, we are called away for pizza and cake. We walk through a tunnel, which leads to a rainbow arch, which leads us into the party room. It is a huge space that has been broken up into about eight sections for different parties. I look for the green bands, but that doesn't help; there are too many people milling around. After about five minutes of looking, we find Pamela's princess cake. It is bright pink with a castle standing tall in the center. There are flags, a moat, sprinkles and candy everywhere, and all the Disney princesses are scattered around. It is one of the most beautiful cakes I have ever seen, and I wonder if Mike's pastry chef had this assignment.

I get Hazel settled in a chair next to one of her friends, and I head up to the table to get some pizza. Mike is standing next to the tower of boxes, handing out the slices.

"Hi," I say when it is my turn. He just stands there and looks at me. Then a huge smile breaks out across his face, and I want to run. But I know Hazel is hungry.

"Could we have one piece of pepperoni, please?" I say, because I just want to get away from him. Probably Sam was right about coming. This is a little too public.

"Let me find you a perfect slice. Bubbles or no bubbles?" he asks, looking intently at the pizza in front of him.

"Any piece will be great, thanks."

"Okeydokey," he says nicely. He studies the pie for the best piece and pulls it out.

"Thanks," I say, turning before he has a chance to say anything else.

I walk back to Hazel and sit next to her, eating the crust that she doesn't want.

When it is finally time to leave, I find Maureen. She has been so busy during the party that we haven't had a chance to talk. She gives me a hug.

"I'm sorry I couldn't talk more can we get together next week?" she asks.

"That would be great," I say.

"What a strange party," Maureen whispers to me, and I can't help but laugh.

I take Hazel's hand and we head through the other parties, under the rainbow, into the tunnel, back into the real world, and home to my angry husband.

CHAPTER THIRTEEN

The chef told me that this rustic method of cooking was popularized by mountain hunters in his grandfather's region of Italy. One hunter on the expedition would carry the oil, another the garlic, another the rosemary, and a fourth the frying pan. All of them carried wine, and upon making their kill, they would cook a feast on the spot.

—Sam Soto

Sam stays mad. When Hazel and I return from Pamela's party, he tells me Henry is sleeping and then barely talks to me for the rest of the day. He hugs Hazel and halfheartedly watches as she proudly shows him the contents of her loot bag. When she is done, he mumbles some excuse about having to try a deli in the suburbs and is gone before I have a chance to ask if we can come, too.

We manage to put on a show for Hazel the next day but don't say one single thing to each other that doesn't involve the kids. Finally he tells me that the reason he's been so mad is because he worries that his editor—and the whole city if Sy Silver catches wind of it—will hear that I took Hazel to Pamela's birthday party just before he reviews Remoulade. Will people believe Sam can still be objective?

"I can't win," he says through clenched teeth. "If I give it a good review, people will think it's because you are all such great friends, and if I pan it, people will think I'm bending over backward to not give them a good review for that reason, and if I take the middle road, people will think I'm a wimp. How could you put me in this position?"

One minute I feel sorry that we went, and the next I feel glad that we did. I am mad at Sam for taking so much away from us for the sake of his job, but at the same time I can see some of his concerns. One minute I am lonely and wondering how I'll ease my way back to Sam. Then this morning I can't even remember what it feels like to be close to him. Hazel is in school, so I put Henry in the BabyBjörn and decide to go for a long walk. I need to keep moving, and it's the only short-term solution I can think of right now.

We walk east on Pine Street, cross Broad, and at Tenth Street I cut down to South. Henry is slumped over, fast asleep. I decide to get an early lunch at a cheesesteak place. As I approach it, I remember that Sam once said the rolls were like mattress stuffing. I can smell the onions and hear the meat sizzle on the griddle. There's a pretty long line. Sam must have been wrong; obviously people like it here. I walk in, get in line, order. When I'm served, I decide to stand at a counter that faces a mirrored wall because it is hard to sit with Henry strapped on. I take a big bite. I try to chew, but I feel like I have cotton in my mouth. Damn it—the rolls are like mattress stuffing. I am deciding between swallowing and spitting out my food when my cell phone rings. I chew as fast as I can, trying not to choke. I swallow, then answer.

"Hello?" a familiar voice asks in response to my garbled greeting. "Um, I'm sorry to bother you, but someone called me from this number, and my phone was down for a few weeks—well, actually, I was out of the country and using another phone, but I saw this number on the list of missed calls and I didn't recognize it. This is Tom Hardy."

I know. I think it was the um, or the long explanation, but there was no doubt in my mind that it was Tom. I hesitate and actually consider hanging up. I have a new cell phone with a Philadelphia number, so of course he didn't recognize it. And it's just like him to go back through all the calls he missed and try to put everything in order.

"Hello? Is anyone there?" Tom asks politely.

"Tom, it's Lila," I say. "I called you."

"Lila?" he says. I wait, but he doesn't say anything else.

"Yeah, sorry, I was trying to call another 212 number, and strangely enough your number was still etched in my brain. I dialed it by mistake. Sorry."

"Oh, that's okay—I've been wondering about you. It's been strange not knowing where you are. Last I heard, I think it was New Orleans," Tom says.

"Yeah, then we moved to Philadelphia. We've been here for almost a year now," I say.

"Are you still with the same guy?" Tom asks.

"Oh, yeah, we got married," I say.

"Married?" Tom says. "I never thought . . . Well, congratulations."

Henry squirms and wakes up and, as though he is expressing my feelings, starts to whimper, then kick and cry. I glance up, and the image of myself in the wall mirror makes me lose my appetite, if the phone call or the terrible roll hasn't already. Still holding my phone, I wrap up the rest of the cheesesteak and throw it away. Then I walk outside.

"Is that a baby?" Tom asks.

"Yup, that's Henry. And his big sister is in preschool right now. In fact, we have to go get her soon," I say.

"Wow, two kids," Tom says. "I guess I thought, well, so you aren't working? I mean, I haven't seen you or heard your name in a while. I just assumed you were doing something else."

"No, I've been working a little lately. A celebrity weekend here, an opening there. Did you hear about the missing kid in Valley Forge?" I ask. What is wrong with me?

"Um, no," he says.

"Anyway, I'm toying with the idea of going back on a more full-time basis," I say. Toying? I don't think I've ever used that word.

"Yeah, I can't imagine you as a nonworking person," he says.

It is such a relief to speak to someone who doesn't know Sam, who doesn't care what Sam thought of the buffalo burger at the place around the corner, who hasn't seen me fumbling with my kids, who still pictures me as a professional person.

"Well, I did decide to take some time off to get settled into our new city," I say, making it sound like it was what I wanted. "But Ed's really pushing me to come back now."

"That's exciting," Tom says.

"What about you?" I ask.

"Same old, same old," he says.

"Huh, well, I really should go," I say.

"What? No, I just found you," he says. "Don't go yet."

"Well," I say, turning toward home and starting to walk.

"Philadelphia, huh? I've been there a few times this year for a project with a bunch of hospitals."

"I knew I saw you." I'm surprised by how excited I feel. Is it Tom? Or am I just glad I'm not going crazy?

"You did?" he asks. "Why didn't you talk to me?"

"Oh, you were far away," I say. "I wasn't sure it was you."

Despite my walking and my attempts at jiggling him, Henry is getting louder. He wants to nurse, and I don't think he likes the way I have to keep my arm up to talk on the phone. He's used to playing with my hands.

"Listen," he says. "I would love to talk a little more. I think I'll be in Philly again in July, maybe August. Can I call you?"

"I don't know," I say.

"Oh, that's my other line. I'll call you, Lila," he says, and hangs up.

For the first two blocks of my walk home I don't think anything. Henry quiets down once I really get walking and give him both my hands, and I decide to try to get home to nurse him if he'll let me. I'm a little afraid to stop.

Would I have told Tom not to call me if he'd given me the chance? How strange it was to talk to him. I make it home fast, half jogging, and I sit on the couch and start to nurse Henry when I realize I forgot all about Hazel. I look at my watch. I am ten minutes late. So much for short-term solutions.

I curse myself and pull a contented baby off my breast. He screams and desperately tries to latch back on. I pull my shirt down, pick him up. He cries so hard he sounds like he's choking. I feel like I'm torturing him. When I get to Hazel's classroom, she is the only kid there. She's curled up in a ball, whimpering, her teacher by her side.

"Here's Mommy," her teacher says cheerfully. Hazel looks up, uncurls herself, and runs to me.

"I thought you forget me, Mommy," she says, sniffling.

"Oh, no, Sweetie, I would never forget you," I say, leaning down to hug her. Henry is still beside himself. I take Hazel's hand and lead her over to the pillow area where the books are. The teacher nods and smiles at us, telling me it's okay. I sit down, offer my breast to Henry, who is beyond frantic, and tell Hazel to choose a book. It is the first responsible thing I have done all day. *Focus,* I tell myself. *This is what can happen when you get distracted.*

It seems like I spend the entire day apologizing to Hazel, and again at night when I put her to sleep. But when we come downstairs the next morning, Hazel immediately spots something on the rug below our mail slot that makes her forget about my slipup. She runs over and picks it up, then brings it to me. It is a light-purple envelope with flower vines twisting all over, and it is addressed to Hazel. As soon as I open it, I see it is an invitation from Willa to the fairy and goblin party that is set for three o'clock tomorrow afternoon.

Come fairies and goblins, both short and tall

We want to celebrate with one and all

Wear costumes and shoes, but nothing on your head

Hats will be provided, and you will be fed.

Hazel makes me read it to her three times, and she squeals whenever I get to the end.

"Are goblins scary?" she asks very seriously.

"No, they're nice, but full of mischief," I say.

"What will I be fed?"

"I don't know," I say. "Probably something good."

"What costume will I wear?"

"We'll have to find you one," I say.

There is even a note at the bottom saying that a baby goblin hat will be provided for Henry. I have to say I am pretty happy to get an official invitation—for Hazel's sake, of course.

We spend the next day and a half turning one of Hazel's princess dresses into a fairy costume complete with sparkly wings and pointy flower shoes. She loves it, and once it is ready, she refuses to wear anything else. I even find myself an old purple T-shirt, pull out the hot-glue gun my mother gave me when we bought this house, take it out of its packaging, and glue sparkles on the shirt.

By the time 3:00 rolls around, we are both so excited we're wrecks. I wait until 3:07, with Hazel banging rather loudly on the inside of our front door, before we head out to join the party.

I have Henry in the backpack. I take Hazel's hand and we step out onto the stoop, and then we stop. The street is blocked off by big barriers at both ends. There is colorful crepe paper strung overhead, from one tree, then across the street, and to the next tree, giving the feeling of being in a forest. There are miniature flowers everywhere. Bright paper butterflies hang from the tree trunks.

Willa motions for me to come over to a table. She hands Hazel a beautiful floral headpiece with ribbons gliding down the back. Henry gets a tall black hat, which he bats off immediately. And before we leave the table, Hazel is handed a small jar full of glitter and dried flower petals.

"Fairy dust," Willa whispers to her.

It is possible that I have never seen my daughter happier.

Once everyone is outside, Willa organizes a few games with the fairies versus the goblins, and there is an arts-and-crafts table where children can paint acorn tea sets. The food table is full of pastel-colored cupcakes with flowers and butterflies, as well as chocolate cupcakes with tiny black licorice hats and walking sticks, and there is pink lemonade with edible flowers. After a little while, Willa brings out a CD player and puts on some new-age music; then she gives the kids ribbons, and they dance and run around, spreading fairy dust wherever they go. Henry falls asleep on my back. The women settle onto stoops or sit on the curb.

I see an ever-growing Janie. She's wearing an adorable floral dress that makes her belly look like a small beach ball, and strappy sandals. People come up and pat her stomach, then hug her. I have to pull my eyes away from her. I don't want to be caught staring.

I am managing to make small talk with Janie and Mrs. Blueberry Buckle, who I now know is Daisy, a former admissions officer at Penn. I am not wishing I could be somewhere else. I am amazed by the details of the party, the care that Willa put into it. I am not thinking that I could do a better job if I were in charge of this event.

At some point someone suggests ordering pizza for dinner, and everyone agrees. We order six large pies and drag out tables, folding chairs and high chairs, soda from our refrigerators, and desserts from our pantries. Jeremy, the neighbor who apparently never shovels snow, brings out teething biscuits, and people look at him like he's crazy.

"The babies can eat them," he says. "We had a lot left over." I take a few for Henry.

When Sam rides up on his bike, the party is in full swing. Hazel is sitting next to Russell on our stoop, and they are eating black-olive pizza off of someone's leftover second-birthday plates. Henry is still dozing.

"What's going on?" Sam says—shocked, I know, to see me in the center of the action.

"We were all too lazy to cook," I say.

"I only have a few minutes," he says, and goes over to Hazel. He picks her up and twirls her over his head, and her fairy costume makes her look like she's flying.

"I shouldn't be too late," he says to me. Then he goes inside to get ready. When he comes back out, he has his blazer on, and I can see him fishing with one hand for his microphone wire in the opposite sleeve.

"Have a good time," he says. "Hey, are there any nonblock people here?"

"No," I say.

He nods, and leans over to kiss Henry on the top of his head. Then he hugs Hazel.

"Who are you meeting?" I ask, realizing I have no idea, though it is almost always someone from work. I guess he figures they know who he is anyway.

"Josh Freed from the copy desk," he says, leaning over and kissing me lightly on the top of my head. It feels good. "I'll try to be home early."

"Okay, good," I say, meaning it.

I watch him walk down the street, and I feel happy that he seems to be easing up. That was the most normal exchange we've had in days.

Around 7:45, Hazel and Russell start to fight over which Wiggle is better. Hazel prefers Greg, and Russell says Anthony is the best one. In fact, Russell says in his little-boy way that he doesn't even know Greg. Uh-oh.

"You do know him, everyone know him," she says, her face scrunching up in a pre-cry position.

"Do not," Russell screams in her face. "He isn't on my video."

Willa and I look at each other and go over and grab our respective children.

"Let's get them settled and then come out and clean up," she says. "I'll bring out some Malibu Rum."

"Great," I say. "I have pineapple juice."

Henry is just starting to stir. He doesn't complain too much, so I keep him on my back while I get Hazel washed and brushed. She insists on sleeping in her fairy costume, and I let her. But I take her headpiece off and hang it on her closet door.

"That was fun, Mommy," she says, as I turn out her overhead light and adjust her sleeping lights. "Can we have another fairy party tomorrow?"

"Probably not tomorrow, but soon." I kiss her on the forehead.

"This is a fun place, Mommy," she says. I can't help but smile. At least I'm finally doing something right for her.

"Yeah, it is a fun place," I say.

When she's asleep, I take Henry downstairs, put him in his high chair, and feed him some baby food. I know he won't go to sleep yet, having taken such a long, late nap, so I put a light sweater on him, grab Hazel's monitor and the pineapple juice, and go back outside. The party is almost entirely cleaned up, except the crepe paper is still strung across the street, illuminated by the white lights on the trees. It has cooled off a lot since this afternoon, and there is a refreshing breeze. I sit on the top step of our stoop, lean against our door, and put Henry on my lap. Willa comes out with the white bottle of coconut rum and two glasses. She crosses the street and sits on the step below me.

"I didn't think of glasses," I say. "Thanks."

"Don't mention it," she says. She opens the bottle and starts to pour. I hear the crinkle of liquor hitting ice cubes. She leaves space in each cup for the juice, and I pour it in, trying not to spill any on Henry. Then I notice the glasses are hand painted. Mine has pink circles and squares and hers has yellow circles and triangles. They are adorable.

"Did you do this?" I ask, holding up my glass.

"I did," she says. "Yesterday, when the kids were napping."

"I can't believe the things you find time to do!" I say. "You still do your art, you know."

"Well," she says, looking at me sideways with her eyebrows raised. "You know what I mean."

"I definitely know what you mean," I say. "Is Russell asleep?"

"Yup," she says. "His last words were, 'Tell Hazel, Anthony is the best.'"

"No, they weren't," I say. "Were they?" And we both laugh.

Willa settles onto the step below me, and we take long sips of our drinks that are much more rum than juice. We are quiet for a minute.

"Listen," she says suddenly. "I've been meaning to talk to everyone about this. I really want to do something great for Janie after the baby comes."

"That sounds nice," I say. "But why after? Aren't showers usually before?"

"She doesn't want to do anything to celebrate this baby until it arrives," Willa says. "With everything that's happened."

"What happened? I mean, it seemed like something was going on, but I don't know anything about it," I say.

"Oh, you weren't here then," Willa says, and winces a little. Then she is quiet. I wait. I am dying to know what the deal is, but I don't want to pry and push Willa away. She glances up and down the street. Her eyebrows are raised, and her mouth is pursed to the side. Once she determines that we're alone, she looks at me.

"Two years ago, Janie was pregnant. Everything was fine; she knew it was a girl. Then, when she was twenty-two weeks, she was in a car accident and lost the baby," Willa says. She takes a long sip of her drink.

"I had no idea," I say. "How awful."

"It was," Willa says. "She was in the hospital for a few weeks. She had a lot of internal injuries. And at the time the doctors told her she might not ever be able to have a baby. But she healed. That's why she waited so long to tell us. I mean, we all knew she was pregnant. Didn't you guess?"

"Well, no," I say carefully, still not sure what might kick me out of the group. "I guess I wasn't paying attention."

Soon Lynn and Daisy come out, and I listen as they plan the grandest baby party they can imagine. And more often than not, they ask me my opinion before they settle on something.

"I better get this little guy to bed," I say after a while, hoping that when I come outside tomorrow I will still feel as comfortable around these people as I do right now.

"Yeah, I better head in, too. The twins went to sleep so early tonight I'm afraid they'll be up before I even get to bed," Willa says.

I walk upstairs to Henry's room and settle onto the rocking chair, thinking he might want to nurse some more. But he is out cold. I debate whether or not to change his clothes and decide against it. I kiss his warm baby cheek and nuzzle his ear. It smells a little from all the milk that gets stuck back there, and I kind of like it.

I reluctantly stand up and lay him in his crib. I go to Hazel's room, where she is sleeping soundly, clutching her fairy headpiece. She got out of bed at some point and took it off the door. She looks so sweet. I kiss her cheek. Then I quietly close her door and get myself ready for bed.

CHAPTER FOURTEEN

An otherwise sublime filet mignon was ruined by a revolting sauce of sweet amaretto liqueur. And the strangely shaped crawfish ravioli tasted nothing like crawfish at all. That's after we found them—the little pillows were so disguised in a soup of dark broth beneath melted cheese that they recalled a creation scene from the dawn of time.

—Sam Soto

"Just so you know, the review of Remoulade will be in the paper this weekend," Sam says.

"Oh," I say. I have a feeling he didn't like the food any more than I did when I tasted it at Maureen's house. But I've been afraid to ask for details.

"So, overall, how was it?" I ask casually. Soon his words are going to be out there for everyone to read.

"The catfish was fishy and dry; the crawfish were chewy and too small; the filet mignon was overcooked and the sauce was too sweet; the chicory coffee wasn't authentic tasting," he says coldly. I know his anger isn't directed toward the restaurant; he wanted to like it as much as he wants to like any new place. His anger is directed toward me for putting him in a position where he might hurt people we know.

"The red velvet cake was a fake," he continues.

"Stop!" I say, putting up my hand. I can't stand to hear it. I pretend to be busy, spreading strawberry jam on Hazel's toast, which is the only thing she wants for dinner tonight. I don't think I could even eat the toast; I have completely lost my appetite. But I have to ask . . .

"What did you give them?"

"What?" he asks.

"Mike and Maureen? What did you give them?" I ask, my heart pounding.

"I didn't give Mike and Maureen anything," he says sternly. "I gave Remoulade one swan."

"Oh," I say. One swan means it's "worth a try, but nothing special." It is definitely not what any restaurateur wants. Even though it is what I dreaded, I try not to think about it. I tell myself that what Maureen and I have is bigger than one restaurant. I just hope she thinks so, too.

I hear the phone ringing as I pull Hazel's door shut after a longer-than-usual nighttime ritual.

"Hey just thought I'd call to say hello and see what you and the kids are up to," Maureen says. Her voice is not as warm as usual, and her lack of punctuation seems exaggerated. But I'm so glad to hear from her.

"Not much," I say, trying to sound normal. She can't possibly know about the rating yet, but Sam had called the restaurant to say he was reviewing Remoulade and to ask questions about the menu, as he does before he settles in to write any review. I don't think she would call to find out about that. Would she? "What about you guys?"

"Brendan has another ear infection so we didn't do much today," she says, and I realize she isn't being cold. She sounds nervous.

"Well, I hope he feels better."

She is quiet, and *I* start to feel nervous.

"Thanks for calling," I offer.

"Yeah okay talk to you soon," she says, and hangs up.

When I wake up on Saturday, Sam is already in the shower. Just as well, since there is nothing I want to say to him right now. I go downstairs, turn off the alarm, and open the door. I bring the newspaper in from the stoop, thumb through the sections the way anyone would, the way Maureen and Mike probably are doing, find the section with Sam's review, and look at it. I could have asked Sam to show me earlier this week. But the truth is, I didn't want to know until I had to. I take a deep breath.

"The Good Food Doesn't Roll at Remoulade," reads the headline, with a subhead that says, "Don't expect too much from this new Cajun bistro on Walnut Street, except for authentic Louisiana beer and good zydeco music." Right next to the review is one single swan, neck out in an elegant pose. But looking very lonely. What are Mike and Maureen thinking right now?

I read on.

There are two types of restaurants in New Orleans. Those that cook their gumbo from the heart, that understand that spices are a tool of seduction, intended to deepen the meaning and power of their stews. And then there are the others: those that cook solely for the tourists, that wear the label *Cajun* as a license to scorch everything they touch. I went to Remoulade hoping for a taste of the true Big Easy, but unfortunately, it wasn't there.

He continues, saying that the menu made his mouth water, but the kitchen didn't come through. Still, he says, the roasted duck with pepper jelly is worth trying, as is the trout *almondine*, and the crab cakes are good—the best thing he tasted there. The room is pleasant and bright. But, but, but . . . I go back up to the top and take one last look for something good. Maybe I missed it. But I didn't. I feel profoundly sad because I have a feeling they won't understand, that it will never be the same with Maureen again. I don't even let myself think about what this might mean for Hazel.

I put down the newspaper and think about calling them, but what would I say? *I really like you, and I'm sorry that my husband just panned your restaurant and probably made you lose thousands of dollars' worth of business that you would not lose if he didn't exist?* Or, *Don't worry, no one reads his reviews anyway?* So I don't call. I don't do anything.

I do not talk to Maureen at all the week following the review. I leave her a message on Monday, just saying hello and that I hope everything is okay. On Thursday I call again, saying I know it's hard but could she please call me?

Today, a full week after the review appeared, I try Maureen again. The phone rings twice and she picks up. If she hadn't been answering in an effort to avoid me, I guess I threw her off by calling on a Saturday.

"Hi, it's Lila," I say quickly. "Don't hang up." As soon as I say it I'm sorry. I don't want to give her any ideas.

"I won't," she says, sounding pretty normal. "But Mike doesn't want me to talk to you."

"Really?" I'm a little surprised. He always seemed easygoing to me. Not, I guess, when it involves his livelihood. "I didn't write the review."

"Yeah, but you're sleeping with the guy who did."

"Very rarely," I say. But she doesn't laugh. I try again. "I was hoping, well, Hazel keeps asking about Pamela. Would you guys be able to come over to play? Maybe have a little lunch?"

Maureen hesitates, then sighs, and I have no idea what she is going to say. My heart is pounding because if she says no, that will be it—I won't be able to call again.

"Okay," she says quietly. "We'll come Monday morning and let the girls play a little."

"Good," I say. "Come at ten o'clock."

I feel much better after we first hang up, but a feeling of dread slowly creeps over me during the course of the rest of the weekend. Was I crazy? Why did I think we could be friends in the first place? But I like her so much, and Hazel loves Pamela. Maybe some friendships are worth fighting for.

At ten o'clock on Monday I have Hazel dressed, Henry asleep, and cookies cooling on the counter. Nothing like fear to get me organized. But the doorbell doesn't ring, and time goes by.

"When are they coming?" Hazel whines. She has already decided what she wants to play with Pamela and in what order. And she told me that she is going to let Pamela wear her favorite Ariel costume, and she is going to wear Cinderella.

"Don't worry," I tell her, very worried. "Maybe they can't find a place to park."

At 10:45 they arrive. No apology, no smile from Maureen. Pamela is her usual self, happy to see us. I offer them a snack and juice, which Maureen refuses for both of them, and we head down to the playroom. The girls immediately go to the dress-up chest and dive in, but I can see Maureen is uncomfortable. Usually we would plunk down on the floor and watch the babies and talk about everything. This time she continues to stand, holding Brendan close to her. She looks mildly crazed.

"Sit down," I say.

"Oh, that's okay," she says. "We're not staying."

"You're not?" I ask. "I thought the girls were going to play for a while and then we'd eat lunch."

"Pamela, keep your clothes on," she says sharply as the girls start wiggling into their respective princess dresses.

Pamela looks at her. She leaves her shirt on, but with her eyes on Maureen, slowly pulls her leggings down. As soon as they are off, Maureen walks briskly over to her.

"I told you to keep everything on," she says.

We just stand there for a few minutes. Pamela pulls her pants back on and manages to get into the costume anyway. As soon as the girls start to have a tea party "under the sea," Maureen walks over to me. She will not look me in the eyes.

"This isn't going to work," she says. Then she looks at me.

I know. I know this isn't going to work. I just wish it could.

"Look," I start, but I don't know what to say. To say there are a lot of critics and some like places and others don't just devalues Sam's opinion. To say a review isn't important is a lie. Sam has had people call to tell him that they wished his reviews didn't come out on a Saturday because that's their busiest day, and if it's a bad review, they lose a lot of reservations. I look over at Maureen and see she's crying, but mad at the same time, and is trying to hide her face from Brendan and Pamela, and me.

"Mike's talking about moving," she says a little too loudly, and the girls look up from their princess teacups for a second. Then, more quietly, she says, "He says there's no way we'll be able to afford private school around here if the restaurant fails. He's already thinking about giving up, or trying someplace else. More than that, Mike believes in the restaurant and the food. But he says with a new restaurant everyone listens to the critic in town. Even if a few people liked it and come back, we've lost so many new customers it's impossible to count . . . And he really thought he had you," she says. Then she quickly adds, "We have to go."

At first I don't know if she means they have to leave town or leave my house. But then she picks up her stuff and grabs Pamela's arm.

"No, wait," I say, wanting to take something back, but I'm not sure what or how. I have always known Sam's work has a huge impact, positive or negative, on a restaurant, but I can't believe it would make a whole family uproot itself. How could someone give up based on one person's opinion? I want to challenge her, tell her I don't believe her, that I think she is just trying to make me feel bad. I feel adrenaline start to move through my veins. I open my mouth, but nothing comes out. Then suddenly I feel very tired.

"I'm sorry, Maureen," I finally say, knowing for sure now that we will never have one of our playdates again, never compare stories about the kids, go over memories of our days in graduate school, or talk about going back to work.

My defensive feelings have already started to cancel out my friendly ones. Maureen didn't know whom I was married to when we first started talking, but she did shortly afterward. Is that why she was so eager to be my friend? What did she mean when she said Mike really thought he had us?

Maureen has to pry the teacup out of Pamela's hand. She pulls off her slippers and dress. Both girls are crying. But it is a sad cry, not the usual three-year-old demanding cry. I'm trying not to cry myself.

At the door I can't stand it anymore. She is almost gone, almost out of my house. I touch her arm.

"Were we friends?" I ask, making it as simple as I can. She has both kids in the stroller, and she takes one step toward them, then back toward me.

"At first," she says thoughtfully. "Then maybe not. And then I couldn't help myself."

All I can do is nod. Hazel and I watch them walk down Colonial Court and turn right onto Eighteenth Street. When they are out of sight, I wonder for a minute when each phase she described ended and began. I wonder if we will talk to each other if we run into each other at the playground. I squeeze Hazel's hand. We just stand there, looking out.

It's a beautiful day. Hazel is being so brave, and Henry is just waking up. I decide we need something nice, so I get everyone organized and take us to McDonald's. I think about calling Sebastian, but I still haven't resolved the picture issue, and, in light of what just happened with Maureen, I'm not sure I can trust anyone. So I don't.

I'm surprised when Hazel cheers up quickly, and we have a nice day just the three of us. She doesn't mention the morning again until she is about to go to sleep. She is all tucked in, with her giraffe nightlight turned on and her teddy bear lights dancing on the ceiling. I'm sitting in the rocking chair next to her bed, waiting for the right moment to tiptoe out. I think she has dozed off.

"Mommy?" she asks, surprising me.

"What, Sweetie?"

"Why was Pamewa's mommy so mad?"

I don't know what to say. I don't want to tell her that her father's job can sometimes ruin lives and friendships and maybe even marriages. Hazel knows that Sam eats out a lot, and he always tells her that he is going to work when he doesn't eat dinner with us. But I don't think she knows much more than that.

"Well," I begin. "You know how Daddy goes to restaurants all the time for his work?"

"Ye-ah," she says, in two syllables.

"Well, when he eats out, he's deciding if the food and everything that goes with that are good or bad." I stop for a minute. "Say a new McDonald's opens on our street, and all the kids want to go there and spend their money. Daddy would go a few times and taste everything, see if it's clean, and then he would write an article telling you and Russell if the French fries are good and worth your money, or if the hamburger is better than the chicken nuggets."

"Is McDonawd's coming to our street?" she asks, perking up.

"Oh, no, Sweetie—maybe that was a bad example," I say. "But Daddy might do that with the McDonald's where we had lunch today. Does that make any sense?"

"Ye-ah."

"So, Pamela's dad has his own restaurant—not McDonald's, but another place."

"Ye-ah."

"One time when we were at Pamela's, our lunch came from his restaurant. Do you remember those tiny sandwiches that you girls loved?"

"Ye-ah," she says. I think I'm boring her.

"Anyway," I say. "Running that restaurant is Pamela's dad's job, just like writing about restaurants is your dad's job. Daddy didn't think the restaurant was so good. He wanted to tell people that some of the food might not be worth their money. It had nothing to do with Pamela or her family—he really likes them—but the restaurant just wasn't that good. At least Daddy didn't think it was. He wrote that down, it was printed in the newspaper, and it made Pamela's mother a little mad, because she thinks it is a good restaurant. And they want lots of people to come eat there and spend their money. Basically, we just didn't agree." I'm quiet for a minute. I can't tell her that it might make Pamela's family lose a lot of money, or even possibly lose their business. I try to decide what to say next, and I realize Hazel is fast asleep. I sit for another minute, then tiptoe out.

SUMMER

CHAPTER FIFTEEN

The mood in the dining room was fit for a fairy tale. Unfortunately, the fairy tale ended in a nightmare at the kitchen doors. Over the course of two dinners, a menu of grand ambitions and beautifully presented plates rarely stood up in taste to the promise of the setting. Sauces were oversweetened. Meats were overcooked. Our striped bass was undercooked. The signature veal came to the table lukewarm. Shrimp were chewy in both the soup broth and salad.

—Sam Soto

We are at the outdoor area behind the Franklin Institute looking at a giant tire, when my cell phone rings. I look at the number and I know it is Tom. I shift Henry to my other hip and lift the phone to my ear; he tries to bat it away.

"Hi," I say. Why bother with the pretense?

"Lila?" Tom asks.

"Who else would it be?" I say, remembering how he always wants everything to be analyzed or spelled out for him. Sam is so different from him in that way.

"Oh, hi," he says, clearly a little flustered. "Hey, I'm so sorry I didn't call sooner. I haven't been to Philadelphia yet this summer. But I'm coming tomorrow night. I was wondering if we might be able to get together for coffee or something on Friday?"

While I think about it, Henry succeeds in batting the phone out of my hand, and it goes tumbling down the three steps leading to the tire and lands in dirty sand. I carry Henry down the stairs, pick up the phone, and put it to my ear, dirt and all.

"Are you still there?" I ask.

"What happened?"

"Oh, Henry knocked the phone out of my hand. Sorry."

"So, what do you think about coffee? Friday?" he asks. "I'll be at the Bell Addison, so if you know of any restaurants or anything, we could meet there, anytime you say. I guess morning might be better for me."

"Yeah, I might know of a few restaurants," I say, thinking he has no idea how much I know about restaurants in this city. "Let me think about it. I'll call you tomorrow."

Tom hesitates, but then I hear a click, and I know it's his other line and that he'll let me go.

"Okay, great," he says. "I'll talk to you tomorrow."

I look up, and I don't see Hazel. I climb the stairs and look inside the tire, and there she is, trying to hide from me.

"Hi," she says, smiling and waving. Henry squeals.

"Hi," I say.

"Who that, Mommy?" she asks. "That Daddy?"

"No, Sweetie, that was an old friend," I say.

"Let's go in that tube, Mommy," Hazel says, pointing, not interested if it isn't her father. Three-year-olds are so much smarter than I ever would have thought. Why can't I follow her lead?

I'm not sure what is going to make me decide whether to see Tom or not. For almost a year now he has been this thing I think about, this specter of my old life. But do I really think that being in his presence is going to transform me into the in-control, professional person I used to be? At the very least I'm curious, and it would be nice to spend some time with someone who thinks of me in a business suit free of spit-up.

All day I try not to think about it. After the kids are asleep, I find Sam organizing his reviews at the kitchen table. The newspaper is going to publish a book of his favorites, and he is obsessed with getting his list together.

"Hey," I say.

"Hi." He glances up for a second, then goes right back to his pile of reviews.

"How was your day?" I ask.

He glances up at me again like I just asked him if he spent the day on Mars, and then he looks down again.

"We haven't had a chance to talk about my going back to work," I say, resorting to that to get his attention.

"Yes we did," he says, looking up and spreading his hand over the pile of papers he already went through. "I thought we decided that you will go back at some point, but we just need a little more time to figure it out."

He's right. That's what we said.

He is so distracted by the reviews it would be funny if I didn't feel so desperate. He slowly lowers his eyes back to the pile of papers he hasn't gone through yet. I just stand and stare at him.

"Tom called me today. He's doing a project in Philadelphia and wants to meet for coffee on Friday," I say. It hadn't occurred to me until now to use Tom's visit to my advantage, but it's worth a shot—maybe that will seem more important to him than his newspaper clips.

"Uh-huh," he says, flipping through his pile.

"Tom, my old boyfriend," I say sternly.

Sam puts down his pile and looks at me again.

"Okay," he says more deliberately.

"You don't care?" I ask.

"Should I?" Sam asks.

"You're a smart guy," I say. "Why don't you figure that out."

I can feel him watching me as I go toward the stairs, but I don't look back.

The next day Hazel begins her second year of preschool. Her school offers a two-week get-up-to-speed program that begins in mid-August. She is so excited she doesn't even fight me about what she is wearing: a bright-pink shirt with red flowers and a red cotton skirt. She has socks on and her best playing sneakers.

At first Henry and I say good-bye to Hazel and Sam from behind the screen door. I hold Henry's wrist in my hand, and we wave together. But as Hazel jumps off the bottom step to the sidewalk, Henry starts to wiggle with all his might, peering around to see where she is. I push open the door, and we step out into the late summer morning.

"We'll miss you," I say to Hazel. "Have a great morning."

I stand on the stoop holding Henry until Hazel and Sam turn up Eighteenth Street toward her school. Then Henry begins to cry. It is so sad. He's used to going everywhere with her lately.

"It's okay, little boy," I say. "We'll have a nice time."

But the morning drags. We play inside; we have lunch. I am just finishing the dishes when I see Sam's neatly stacked reviews on the counter. I dry my hands on Daisy's towel, walk to my purse, pull out my phone, and dial Tom's phone number.

"Hi, Lila," Tom says. It's noisy wherever he is.

"Hi, where are you?"

"Just about to get on the train," he says. "What do you think about Friday?"

"I'd love to," I say. "I'll meet you in the lobby at ten o'clock. I'll get a babysitter. We can go somewhere for coffee."

"Great, I'll see you then."

I glance at the clock and realize that it's finally time to pick up Hazel.

"Come on, sweet boy," I say, nuzzling Henry's cheek that is warm and always smells vaguely of saliva. "Let's go get Hazel."

His eyes widen, and he smiles when he hears his sister's name. "Ha-ho," he says. "Ha-ho."

I kiss the top of his head and scoop him up. With the other hand I drag out the double stroller and settle him in.

It is a beautiful day. Bright-blue sky with puffy white clouds, not muggy and hazy like the last few days. We get to Hazel's classroom just seconds before the door opens, and she comes leaping out to hug me. Her teacher tells me Hazel did great, jumping right back into the swing of school.

"This calls for a celebration," I say. "What do you say to a big chocolate ice cream cone?"

"Yay!" Hazel yells. Then she goes over to Henry in his stroller and says, "Mommy is taking us for ice cream, baby Henry!" He wiggles with delight, not because of the upcoming treat, I know, but because it is the first time Hazel has ever addressed him directly. I hold my breath for a few seconds, then let it go.

We head north to the Cone, everyone's favorite ice cream store. We decide to get it to go. Hazel chooses mint chocolate chip in a cup with chocolate sprinkles. I order lemon water ice in a lame attempt to watch what I'm eating, and I get a small cup of vanilla ice cream for Henry.

We go to the square, which is packed, but we find a nice bench in the sun and settle there. Hazel sits with her ice cream on her lap, and at first I try to cover her with napkins, but then I decide I can just wash her clothes later. I get out a spoon and start to feed Henry tiny bites of vanilla. He is shocked by the cold at first, but then he loves it, opening his mouth again and again like a little bird. In between bites he smiles

Elizabeth LaBan

wide, his eyes little slits, and jostles his head back and forth. He looks at that instant like he is soaking up the best jazz music in the world.

Hazel's ice cream is beginning to melt all over her, and she doesn't like that, and I'm not giving ice cream to Henry fast enough, and he is getting mad. I try to clean Hazel's hands and arms, ignoring Henry for a second, and when I look up, I see Sebastian.

"Hi," he says. Then he goes over to Henry and tickles his belly. Henry stops screeching and looks at Sebastian with wide, dark eyes. Hazel bounces up and down excitedly.

"I started schoow today, Sebajin," she says proudly. "I did a good job so my mommy said we get ice cream. But it's messy."

"I see that," he says, turning his attention to her. "I bet it still tastes good."

"Yeah, it does," she says.

My heart is pounding. I don't know what my problem is. I knew I would run into him sometime. But I'm completely taken off guard.

"I've been meaning to call you," I say. "The summer was so busy. You don't have any wipes, do you?"

Sebastian laughs.

"Sorry, none on me," he says. I can't tell if he knows I've been avoiding him. "Actually, after those few times you canceled, I haven't really been taking care of Charlotte much this summer anyway. I was in Greece for a while. I just got back last week."

"Oh," I say, not sure how much of a conversation I want to start. Sebastian looks great with a deep Mediterranean tan. He's wearing a bright-yellow T-shirt that seems to radiate sunshine. Just having him near us makes the melting ice cream seem not so bad. I want to tell him about how I have started to make friends on our street, about how Hazel talked directly to Henry, about my work dilemma, and more about my project idea. But something is stopping me. It's that stupid picture of Sam.

"I have to get them home. Henry needs a nap," I say more coldly than I mean to.

"Lila," he says. "I haven't seen you in a while, and now you're rushing away? Can we go for a walk? Or can I walk you home?"

I should say no, but I say yes. I watch as he takes a napkin and wipes Hazel's face, hands, and arms up to her elbows, as I do the same for Henry. Then we fall into step as we walk south through the square. I am starting to relax, but I keep thinking of the picture. I remember how Sam came home that day wearing those huge sunglasses and feeling so defeated. If Sebastian is involved, then I don't want to let down my guard around him. I don't want to waste any more time with people who aren't really my friends.

The picture circulated for a while, and then we stopped hearing about it. I'm sure it still hangs in a bunch of restaurants, but I don't think it is being passed along anymore. At least I hope it isn't. Sam has even let up a little with his disguises. Still, I can't help but wonder.

"Sebastian," I say, and he looks right at me. "There's this picture of Sam that a few restaurants have. We heard about it a few months ago. I was wondering, do you know anything about it?" There. I said it. And I didn't actually accuse him. I realize that I'm holding my breath. I can't bring myself to look at him. I'm going to miss him, maybe as much as I miss Maureen. The only good thing is that I nipped Hazel's friendship with Charlotte before it got too intense. She hasn't asked about her in a long time.

I feel Sebastian's strong hands on my wrists. He turns me away from the stroller and looks at me until I am forced to look him in the eyes. I can smell his toothpaste.

"What do you think, Lila? That I rifled through your personal items while you were sick on the couch? Or maybe I ransacked your diaper bag while you were in the bathroom at McDonald's. I'm sorry, Lila, but clearly you don't understand me at all. Do you really think I would sell out my friend for a pat on the back from Chef?"

I feel myself shaking my head, and I know I have made a terrible mistake, but at the same time I am so completely relieved. Of course Sebastian didn't do it. He doesn't care enough about the restaurant. He cares about me and the kids. What was I thinking?

"I'm sorry," I mutter, having a feeling from the look in his eyes that there is nothing I am going to be able to say to make this better. Sebastian gently drops my wrists. I want to say more; I want to grab his wrists and shout in his face that I am being driven crazy by Sam's paranoia, and that I have no idea whom I can trust anymore.

I watch as Sebastian walks around to the front of the stroller and kneels in front of the kids. He takes Henry's hands and makes him laugh. Then he turns to Hazel and whispers something in her ear. Then he stands up and starts to walk away.

"Sebastian, please," I say, crying now. "I made a mistake."

But he keeps going, past the goat statue, out of the park, and down Nineteenth Street.

I watch him go. He is a tiny speck when I look down at Hazel, who has turned around in the stroller and is staring at me.

"What did Sebastian say to you?" I ask as calmly as I can.

"He say thank you for teaching him about the Wiggews," she says, smiling, and I am amazed by his ability to keep the sadness away from her. "He say I a good teacher."

"You are that," I say, brushing tears out of my eyes. "Let's go home."

I move forward a few feet, trying to decide which way to go; it feels funny to follow Sebastian's exact path. Instead, I turn toward Eighteenth Street and walk home that way.

The next day is just as beautiful, and I take the kids to the park hoping I'll run into Sebastian again. He's reasonable; if he has some time to think about it, I know he'll understand where I was coming from. We get ice cream and sit on the same bench. It melts, just like yesterday, but this time Hazel cries and Henry spits up. He probably shouldn't have so much dairy yet. I am furiously trying to wipe them both while repeatedly looking over my shoulder so I won't miss Sebastian if he walks by, when my phone rings.

"Lila," Sam says, and I know he is mad.

"Hi. We're at the square, there's ice cream everywhere, and Henry just spit up. Can I call you when we get home?" I ask hopefully. I am in no condition to deal with my angry husband. Maybe he found out that I am going to go through with meeting Tom. Maybe he didn't really believe that I was going to do it.

I hear him sigh on the other end.

"Yeah, of course," he says, his voice a little softer. "But call me soon."

We hang up, and I gather everyone and get us home. I think about not calling Sam, but I know I can't do that. I actually miss him, and making this space between us bigger is not the answer—but I know it takes two to close that gap. Right now it seems so wide.

"Hey," he says when I call back.

"Hey," I say.

"Are they okay? How's Henry?"

"They're okay. I think I'm giving him too much dairy. I'll tone it down. What's up?"

I hear that sigh again.

"Someone just put a copy of the *Philadelphia Busybody* on my desk. Do you want to know what it says?" he asks.

"No, not really," I say, wishing I hadn't reminded him about why he called in the first place.

"Well you should know," he says. "Lila, this is getting out of control. If you won't let me read it to you, please go read it yourself. This has to stop."

I turn the computer back on and pull up the website for the *Philadelphia Busybody*, clicking on Sy Silver's column. With a heavy chest, I watch as it fills the screen.

Under the subhead "Schmoozing in the Square," the column reads:

> The Restaurant Critic's Wife was seen yesterday in Rittenhouse Square having a heated discussion with La Noix's cheese man. Was she complaining about the cheese cart or her Sprite? Was he trying to find out if Mr. Food prefers Époisses over Taleggio? Sam, do you know where your wife is?

I don't even try to stop the tears anymore. I glance over at the kids and am happy they are mesmerized by the video they are watching. I try to call Sam back. This isn't my fault. It was a bad sequence of events. I hadn't even planned on meeting Sebastian. I dial Sam's number at work, but the call won't go through. When it finally does, it goes right to voice mail.

I suddenly feel trapped. I need fresh air. I walk to the front door, pull it open, and step outside. I see Willa coming down the street. Russell is holding her hand, and the twins are in the double stroller. She is speaking sternly to Russell, who suddenly pulls his hand away and starts to run toward Nineteenth Street. She looks at me, leaves the stroller in the street, and bolts after Russell, catching him about twenty feet before he gets to Nineteenth and all the speeding cars. I, meanwhile, run down the steps to retrieve Willa's stroller from the middle of the street and push it onto the sidewalk. The twins sleep through all the commotion. I run back up the stoop and peek inside. The kids are still sitting where they are supposed to, watching the screen. Willa carries Russell down the street like he is a football tucked under her elbow.

He kicks and tries to spit, and I think I see her smack his bottom, but I can't be sure.

When she gets to her house, she unlocks it, pushes Russell inside the vestibule, and pulls the door closed. He presses his face against the glass, screaming and crying, pounding on the door. She locks the door and walks calmly over to me.

"Thanks," she says, breathing hard. "We had a little trouble at the store."

"No problem," I say, cringing every time Russell bangs the glass with his fist. I hope he doesn't put his arm through it. But Willa seems unconcerned.

"How are you guys?" she asks, glancing over her shoulder at Russell, who sees her and quiets a little.

"Not great," I say. "Sam and I are having a fight."

Willa is just about to say something when Russell makes such a loud noise against the door we both jump.

"You go," I say. "I'll tell you about it later."

She smiles weakly and reaches out for my arm. I'm not sure if she is trying to steady herself or offer me support. Maybe it doesn't matter.

I go back inside, grateful for the peace in my house, take a deep breath, and dial Sam's number again.

"*Herald*, this is Sam."

"Hi," I say.

"Lila," he says coldly. "I'm so mad that I don't think it's a good idea to talk in front of the kids. It is clear to me now that you have no intention of working with me to keep my job and my identity safe. Why don't you understand how much we have at stake?" I hear a click, and I guess that he hung up, but then I hear his voice again. "There's a new pub on Thirteenth Street I have to try, so I'm going to go there for an early dinner. I'll be home later. Maybe we can talk then. Kiss Henry and Hazel for me." He hangs up.

I feel a little sick. I glance over at the kids playing nicely on the floor in the living room, and I walk back into the kitchen where they can't see me. I burst into tears, trying to cry quietly. I take deep breaths and wipe my eyes quickly, but I can't stop crying. I take a quick look at the kids again; they are still doing okay. Then I duck back into the kitchen and dial Sam's number.

"It's me," I say when he answers. I'm not so worried anymore about masking my emotions or playing a game with him. "Wait there. I'm going to see if Sunny can come tonight."

"What did I just say to you, Lila?" Sam asks. From the sound of his words I think he is clenching his teeth. "I said that you cannot come out to dinner with me anymore. I mean it. We'll talk when I get home."

"No!" I yell. "Just wait there."

"Sorry, Lila," he says. "You did this to yourself."

He hangs up. I think about calling him back, but I don't think there is any way I am going to get through to him. I call Sunny. She doesn't pick up her cell phone, so I start dialing around. I find her taking care of a family on the next block.

"I know this is extremely short notice," I say, a little out of breath. "But Sam and I had a big fight and . . ." I am trying not to cry. "Can you come tonight and take care of the kids for a few hours? I just want to have a chance to talk things through with Sam."

"Sure," she says. "Tonight is fine. I'm finished here at six o'clock. I'll come right over."

"Thank you, Sunny," I say. We hang up, and I realize I haven't checked on the kids in a while. I run into the living room, and there are pillows everywhere. Hazel is arranging them, but I can't see Henry.

"Where is he?" I demand.

"There," Hazel says innocently, pointing to a smiling Henry, sitting in his sister's pillow playhouse. He tries to wave in his awkward sort of way. I wave back wearily.

"Oh," I say. "Well, thank you for taking such good care of him."

When Sunny arrives, I head upstairs to take a quick shower. Then I take time to put on jewelry: a red-beans-and-rice bracelet with silver beans and pearl rice grains that Sam gave me when Hazel was born, and a silver locket my mother gave me. I start to put on a pair of pearl earrings, and then I remember that Tom gave them to me for a birthday years ago. I stuff them back in the box and choose a pair that I bought for myself in Hong Kong. I put on some makeup. I look for my favorite lipstick instead of just putting on the first one I pull out no matter what the color is.

"You look good," Sunny says when I come downstairs. "Is everything okay?"

"I think so," I say. "I'll tell you the whole story tomorrow. Thank you so much for coming."

Just before I walk out the door, I remember something.

"Sunny, are you available tomorrow morning from about nine thirty to noon? An old friend is going to be in town and—"

"Not really, but I think I can rearrange some things. You seem to be having a hard time, Lila; maybe talking to an old friend will help. I'll be here," she says.

"Thanks," I say.

I decide to walk to the restaurant in case there are other pubs I don't know about.

As I near the one where I think Sam is, I tell myself to try to be nice, not defensive. I feel overwhelmingly anxious at the thought that this might not be where Sam is. Then what will I do?

I rush in and look around. There he is. Sitting at a corner booth. He looks good. His reddish-brown hair has gotten a little long, and it is wavy and soft looking. I have an urge to touch it. As I approach the table, I notice how brown his eyes look next to his tan sweater. Why did I need a disguise to be turned on? He is so handsome.

"Hi," I say, taking a seat across from him.

He glances up at me with absolutely no expression on his face, and I wonder in a moment of terror if he is capable of pretending he doesn't know me. But then his bushy eyebrows come together and his mouth purses. He looks around like he expects someone to be just waiting there with my picture to identify me, and then him. When that doesn't happen, he looks back at me.

"I told you that I was going to eat dinner alone tonight," he says through clenched teeth. "You are not welcome at this table with me."

Apparently he hasn't started to work through any of this like I was hoping, because his anger is not dissipating—it's on the table next to his pint of Guinness. I sit down across from him.

"Sam, we have to talk," I say as calmly as I can. "Please, Sam, nobody is looking for us here."

He nods, then sits back, and I feel a little encouraged. But he doesn't say anything.

"Can we please talk?" I plead.

"I have to decide what to eat first," he says coldly.

"No," I say, realizing for the first time how his always directing the meal gives him something to hide behind. "Let's talk."

"I'm so mad," he starts. "Over and over I have talked to you about how important it is for me to remain unknown so that I can do my job. My job! I ask you simply to stay away from people associated with restaurants and to keep yourself out of the public eye. And what do you do? You go and make best friends with a restaurant owner. You start hanging out with a waiter. You go back to a job that throws you right into everyone's view. And now, apparently, you are having rendezvous in the park with your little waiter friend. What are you going to do next?" Sam looks around again to see if anyone is looking at us. But of course nobody is.

"Sam, that is not what happened. I didn't plan to meet Sebastian yesterday—we just ran into each other," I say. *Don't be defensive*, I remind myself. "And, as far as my friends go, you know that I knew

Maureen already; we were in school together." I take a deep breath. We have been through this so many times. "And Sebastian, well, I just like him. Sometimes you just can't help the people you like," I say. "Sometimes you like people who are inconvenient."

"Blah, blah, blah," Sam says with a dismissive tone. "We're adults here. We have control over the people we socialize with."

"Sam," I say, notching up to defensive. "I cannot live in a box. You were reluctant to meet our neighbors; you don't want me to work. The way I see it, this is your fault. You made me desperate!"

Just then the waiter dares to approach us. I could see him watching our table, waiting for a break in our heated discussion to take our order. We haven't even discussed the menu, but I'm glad to have Sam be distracted at this moment. He looks at the waiter, rattles off a bunch of dishes, none that sound particularly good to me, and the waiter leaves.

"When I said some people are inconvenient, I wasn't only talking about Maureen and Sebastian. I was talking about you, too," I say, breathing hard. "You take yourself so seriously. Not everybody hangs on your every word, you know. I've run into lots of people who don't even read your reviews."

Sam looks at me, and I worry I've gone too far. It isn't even true. I don't talk to enough people to have any sense of who does and who doesn't read his reviews. But I want to hurt him. We sit in the loudest silence I have ever heard for what seems like a long time. I can't think of anything to say that won't just make Sam more angry, and I guess he still has no interest in talking to me. The waiter finally puts a big juicy-looking cheeseburger in front of Sam, and he pushes it away, almost spilling the French fries onto the floor. We glare at each other. The waiter carefully puts down the other dishes and backs away from our table. I couldn't care less about the food.

"Say something," I growl through my teeth, trying to keep my voice down.

Sam continues to glare, turning strange shades of red. I go from not hungry to nauseated.

"Say something?" Sam finally says, maybe as mad as I've ever seen him. And then suddenly, it seems that the anger drains away. And he looks pale and sad. "All I can say right now, Lila, is that I don't trust you, and that is really scary to me. I just don't trust you."

He sits back.

"Oh," he says, sitting forward again, the anger coming back. "The most ironic thing in all of this is that you bill yourself as a crisis manager. The funny thing is, you don't seem to manage our crises particularly well. If anything, you cause them."

Is this the man I married? That Sam, the one who killed bugs for his elderly neighbor and made blueberry pancakes for me, was so easy to talk to, would never throw something like my career back in my face.

"I was pretty great at managing crises until I met you," is the only thing I can think to say. Sam just looks at me.

Okay, I can't help it; I am starting to cry. I try really hard to stop, even though I think this might soften him. But as the tears stream down my cheeks, he continues to glare at me hatefully. *Come on, this is me. You love me. Be nice to me.*

But my thoughts don't get through to him. He looks at his food, pulls it closer. He picks up his burger and starts to eat. He looks all around the room but will not look at me. I am breathing heavily; I want to scream, throw my chair to the floor. I have to get through to him.

"Sam," I say, hiccuping a little. "Please."

"Lila, I can't stand it," he says. "I get enough crying from the kids. Can't you hold it together better? I'm going to eat now."

He takes big bites of the burger and smacks his lips. Juice dribbles down the corners of his mouth, but he doesn't stop to wipe it away. I watch him eat. Something cold rushes through me.

I stand up. He barely looks at me. I put down my napkin. I get my jacket. I pick up my purse, and I turn away from the table. I wonder for a second if he will stop me, but he doesn't say a word. He didn't want me here in the first place. I head for the door. I have never walked away from him like this before. What am I doing?

The woman at the hostess stand smiles at me, and I try to smile back through my tears. I turn my head slightly, and out of the corner of my eye I can see Sam staring off, still eating that stupid burger. He isn't even watching me. How can he eat now? I face the exit, and for a minute the door seems way too heavy to manage myself, but I push it open and walk out into the beautiful late-summer night. I don't stop. I walk south to Walnut Street. People are looking at me because I'm crying so hard. At a stoplight an older woman offers me a tissue. I take it gratefully. When I reach Walnut, I head west toward Rittenhouse Square.

I see the big wooden door of La Noix. Without even thinking, I put my hand on the oversize silver walnut and pull the door open, stepping inside. Quiet. The hostess here does not smile at me. I glance at myself in the mirror behind her and see that my face is red and swollen, plus I'm not dressed for La Noix. But then a waiter who knows me walks by, does a double take, and rushes off somewhere.

"May I help you?" the tall woman asks. I wonder what Sam is doing now. Is he sorry I left? Is he still eating that burger? Then I remember what he said to me, and I try not to care about what he's doing.

"Do you have a reservation?" The woman tries again, clearly more annoyed.

"Oh, no, I don't," I say quietly. "But I was wondering if Sebastian is working tonight?"

"I am," a deep voice says, and I turn to see a confused but friendly face. "Lila, are you okay? Are the kids okay?"

I nod, but I start to cry so hard I can't speak. Sebastian nods to the annoyed woman, who makes a motion to him that he should take me outside. But instead, he leads me through the main room of the grand restaurant. I try not to make too much noise as we pass the fancy diners eating Dover sole and filet mignon. I glance at all the tables that Sam and I occupied on our various dinners here. Over there is where we sat just before Henry was born. And that is where we sat on my thirty-fifth birthday.

"Come on," Sebastian says gently. He leads me up a staircase to a small, empty banquet room. He nudges me into a chair at a big round table, sets my place properly, and walks away. A few minutes later he is back with a tall glass of Sprite, a straw, and a huge piece of my favorite walnut sour cream coffee cake. I try to smile.

"I am so sorry," I sob. "I know now that you would never have taken the picture. But I had to ask, I had to . . ."

"Is that what this is about?" Sebastian asks. "Because—"

"No, actually. I have to say, when you walked away, I wasn't sure if you would ever speak to me again. Hazel told me what you said to her. But this isn't really about that. This is about Sam."

"Okay," he says warmly. "I have a ten-minute break now, and then I'm off in less than an hour. And for the record, I knew we would talk again. But I had to walk away from you, or I was going to say some things that I would regret. I mean, my friendship is with you and has nothing to do with Sam. You could be married to anyone for all I care. I don't even like Sam that much; he's never been very nice to me. But I didn't want to say any of that to you. If you want to complain to me about Sam, I'm all ears, but I didn't want to complain to you, or suggest he was behind your accusation." He takes a deep breath. "Anyway, talk."

So I do. I tell him about meeting Sam at the pub, about what he said to me. About how much trouble my recent friendships have caused. I tell him about Sam's questioning my trust. And Sebastian listens. For nine minutes. Then he says he'll get me a real drink and that I should wait until he's off and we'll talk more. He comes back with a pitcher containing a yellow liquid and pours some into a crystal glass for me. I take a sip and am surprised to taste Malibu Rum and pineapple juice.

"How did you know I like this?" I ask.

"Just drink," he says.

"No, really; I have to know."

"You order it a lot."

"But not here."

"Well, I know lots of guys at other restaurants. People talk about what you and Sam like. Everyone wants to get it right. I personally have never uttered a word." He flashes me his warm smile and I sink back in the chair and relax. I believe him.

"I'll be back before you know it," he says. He pats me on the shoulder as he walks toward the stairs.

For a few minutes I think about leaving, about retracing my path and finding Sam. But I don't. I sit in the elegant banquet room of La Noix and drink my Malibu Rum cocktail. I stare at the painted mural of ferns and flowers and trees dancing on the walls, all green and pink, and I think of Willa's fairy party. For a minute I want to disappear into the painting. But thinking of Willa makes me feel a little better.

I know Sunny will stay, and eventually Sam will go home and relieve her. He'll take care of the kids. If Henry wakes up, Sam will have to offer him some formula or something. Poor Henry. In a little while Sebastian is back.

"Bruno is going to cover for me," he says. "Let's go."

We walk down the stairs and through the emptying dining room. Sebastian places his hand softly on my waist. I like it, but I glance around anyway, of course, hoping there are no gossip spies in the room.

"Good night, Glenda," Sebastian calls to the annoyed lady at the front. I don't even look at her.

"Where to?" Sebastian asks, once we are on Walnut Street.

"I don't know," I say.

"Do you want me to walk you home?"

"No, I don't want to go home," I say. "Let's go to a hotel."

Sebastian looks at me with feigned shock.

"I don't mean it that way," I say, really smiling for the first time since I left Sam. "I want to go to a hotel alone, but maybe you could walk me there."

"It would be my pleasure."

We are quiet as I steer us to the luxurious hotel that houses one of Sam's favorite restaurants. I don't want to go to an Addison.

When we walk through the glass doors, the lobby is serene and welcoming. The flowers are even more beautiful than I remembered.

Sebastian gestures to the reception desk, raises his eyebrows.

"Do you want to check in?" he asks.

"Let's just sit here for a minute," I say, flopping into an extremely soft leather chair. Sebastian sits down across from me. I catch a glimpse of us in a large mirror across the room. We look like an ordinary couple. Appearances can be so different from reality.

"Maybe I can just sleep here," I say, closing my eyes for a minute.

"I think that's what they call loitering," he says. I open my eyes.

"Maybe Sam won't even miss me," I say.

"He will," Sebastian says confidently.

We are quiet for a minute, and I watch people checking in. A lady with a drag-along suitcase. A young couple.

"Tell me things about Sam. Tell me about your first date. Tell me about when you met," he says.

"No," I say. "That's the last thing I want to do."

"Please," he insists.

"Okay, let me think," I say. "The first time I met Sam he was wearing a mask and he told me what to eat. Ha! I had no idea that it would be a pattern for the rest of my life," I say, but for some reason the thought makes me smile. *At least he's consistent.*

"Hmm," Sebastian says. "That's pretty funny. How did he ask you to marry him?"

"I got pregnant," I say, and Sebastian nods. "We hadn't really talked about getting married. I was so busy with work, and I think Sam was avoiding whatever it was that made his mother unhappy. She left Sam and his father when Sam was young."

I stop. I feel dizzy. I try to take deep breaths.

"What is it?" Sebastian says. "What's wrong?"

"I'll be right back," I say.

I walk to the bathroom. I know where it is from my dinners here, so I get there fast. I go into a stall and lock it, sit down on the closed toilet lid. I try to calm down so I can decide what to do, but I already know. Sam didn't want to marry anyone because he was afraid his wife would walk away someday, just like his mother did. He was terrified that he would settle into a life that he liked, but his wife would reject. Is that why he's so focused on his work? So if I do leave, he'll still have something to care about? I reel back a tiny bit and have to steady myself. That's exactly what my mother has been talking about all these years in her own way. And is that what Sam thinks is finally happening now? I walked away from him; I left him at the restaurant. All the other stuff with the birthday party and the gossip columns can be forgiven, I think. This seems borderline unforgivable. I have to go home.

As I head back to the chairs where Sebastian is waiting for me, I pick up my step to the tune of "When the Saints Go Marching In," and then I realize it is my phone ringing. As I reach into my bag to try to grab it, my first thought is that it must be Sam, or maybe Sunny. It's Maureen. I lean up against the wood paneling of the bar entrance and answer.

"Hello?"

"It's me," Maureen says quietly, but sounding like herself. "I saw you tonight walking on Walnut Street and you were crying some lady gave you a tissue I wasn't going to call but I miss you so much and I worried you were crying about me were you?"

"What?" I say. I can't make sense of what she is saying.

"Were you crying about me?"

"No, well, maybe a little, but not directly," I say suspiciously. Can I trust her? "Why are you calling me?"

"I wasn't going to Mike would kill me but I have to tell you something okay?" she says. As usual, there are no punctuation breaks. I have missed that so much.

"What do you have to tell me?"

"I never wanted to stop being your friend I was always your friend it was Mike who wasn't we're having some trouble that I won't go into now but he told me that I couldn't see you after the review and then when I made that plan anyway he said that he has a picture of you from Pamela's party and he threatened to send it around if I saw you that's why I left like that." She stops, takes a breath. "He can't know I'm calling you but please know I was always your friend here he comes."

The line goes dead. I stare at my screen for a second before turning my phone off.

"I'm going home," I say when I reach Sebastian.

"Okay," he says, sitting up, surprised by my abruptness. "I'll walk you."

"No," I say quickly. "I'll be fine. I just have to get home to Sam."

I start to walk toward the door, pause, and then I go back to Sebastian. I sit down next to him, leaning my head against his chest.

"Thank you," I say, grinning at him as I get up. "You are my good friend." I look back at him before I go out the door.

He grins back and waves. I walk through the door and into a cab. I glance at my watch: midnight. How did it get to be this late? What if Sam never went home, assuming that I would? What if Sunny is still waiting there for someone to relieve her? When the cab turns onto Colonial Court, I crane my neck to see if there are lights on. I can't pay the cabdriver fast enough, so I stuff a handful of money in his hand and jump out. I find my keys and open the door.

Sam is in the living room with Henry on his lap. At the sound of the door they both turn to me. I get a good look at Henry, and I can see his eyes are swollen, with pus in the corners. He looks so sad. He starts to wiggle when he hears me, and I go over and gently take him from Sam. I hug him close. He smells good.

"Apparently he was fine when he went to sleep, but he woke up a few minutes after I got home," Sam says flatly. "It must be pinkeye. I called the nurse hotline, and she called a prescription in to CVS. But that's as far as I got. I didn't want to wake Hazel, so I couldn't leave the house . . ."

Welcome to my life, I think. But I'm tired of being combative, so I don't say it. Henry starts to pull my shirt and bump his head into my breast, so I sit down and nurse him. I was gone for about five hours, but now I'm back. This is where I belong.

"Russell had pinkeye, and I think they played with the same ball the other day," I say. Sam nods, in a daze. This is easy. Maybe we can just take care of Henry and never mention any of the bad stuff again. "You can go get the drops now."

Sam walks to the back door. As he passes us, he leans down and gently brushes the hair back over Henry's forehead. Then he gets on his bike and goes to the twenty-four-hour CVS on Chestnut Street. While we wait, I rock Henry, who is so quiet. I hug him and kiss his small head. When Sam gets back, we give Henry a dose of the drops; then I nurse him to sleep. By the time I get to our room, Sam has dozed off. I go to his side of the bed to turn out the light. He opens his eyes, then sits up.

"Where were you?" he asks. "With Tom?"

I'm taken aback, by both the fact that Sam was listening when I talked about Tom and the fact that he thinks I went to him when I was so mad. But what will he think of what I really did? *No more lies,* I say to myself.

"No, at first I was walking aimlessly, but then I found Sebastian," I say.

"At the restaurant?" he asks, and I wonder if he is going to yell at me, but he looks so tired.

"Yeah, but it wasn't too crowded," I offer. Sam just shrugs. "Actually, I didn't really see Sebastian much all summer. I guess I worried a little that he was involved in the mysterious plot of the Sam Soto picture. All of your paranoia is rubbing off on me," I say. I look at Sam and see what I can only describe as a glimmer of hope in his eyes. I can't help but smile. Then I clear my throat.

"But the truth is that I missed him . . . Sebastian," I say, not daring to look at Sam now. "Then yesterday I ran into him and asked him about the picture. He said that he didn't have anything to do with it, and I believe him. He was pretty mad that I accused him of it."

"So what did he say?" Sam asks.

"When? Tonight? Oh, he was nice. I think he knows how hard this has been for me, for us. He asked me about when we met and when we got married, and it made me realize that I wanted to come home to you. He helped us. And then, the weirdest thing: Maureen called—she saw me crying on the street—and she said Mike said she couldn't be my friend anymore, that he threatened to release a picture of me if she was," I say, leaning back on my fluffy pillows.

"That's crazy," Sam says. "Hey, at least I'm not *that* bad."

"No, you're not. That occurred to me after I talked to her," I say, smiling. "But you have made things hard for me. It's been hard to find my place here—with friends and everything. I've been lonely."

"I can see that," Sam says. "But I always tried to give you space when we knew there were no restaurants involved. I didn't give you a hard time about seeing Tom. That's something," he says.

I look at him for a minute. That never occurred to me.

"I just thought you weren't listening to me, as usual. I couldn't understand why you didn't care," I say.

"I listen to you, Lila," Sam says. "I understand this has been hard for you. I even understand that your crazy friendships have developed out of desperation and loneliness, and not because you are out to get me. But even though a part of me wondered if you had gone to see him, I don't really worry that you are going to have a romantic encounter with Tom. We're married, Lila. That means something to me. Actually, it means more to me than I express, I know that. I just wish you could be a little less—I don't even know what the word is—insecure? Sometimes I feel like you're jealous of my job or something. You never used to need constant assurance. We're not dating anymore. If I'm distracted by my job, can you try not to take it so personally? Having said that, I guess I do finally understand where all of that is coming from. Sorry it took me so long. Without the other stuff, your work and friends and everything, I guess, you need this stuff more." He points to himself, then makes a bigger sweep around the room, indicating the whole house.

I just stare at him. I didn't know he had thought this through in that way. Actually, I'm kind of impressed.

"Okay?" he asks.

"Okay," I say.

"And that's why I am going to try to support your going back to work," he says. "It's almost September, and that's when you wanted to go back. I still worry about a lot of it, but if it's what you have to do, we'll do it. I do not want you to become unhappy like my mother did."

"Actually," I say, sitting up again and facing him. "I have been racking my brain to find a way to go back to work without it being so public. I'm playing with a few ideas. I know I want to do something. I am definitely better when I am doing something."

"That sounds great to me," he says, picking up my hand. "Look, I know we've had a hard beginning. But I decided when we got married that I couldn't be on edge about us every second, the way I think my father was. For some reason, I think, he was always so afraid my mother was going to be unhappy. He was always on top of her, getting her reaction to things. I really have no idea if that's what made her go, or if he was right in worrying and she was going to go anyway one day, but I knew I didn't want to live that way. I couldn't."

I smile at the idea that Sam thinks we are still at the beginning. Suddenly I see the old Sam sitting across the table from me on Burdette Street in New Orleans. He has just placed a china plate of blueberry pancakes in front of me. He watches, wanting me to like them, wanting to nurture me. And I want that, too. His face is open to me, then and now. I lean into him, smell the pine scent of his deodorant.

"For the record," I say, looking up at him, "I'm not sure anymore why I crave drama to manage. I can't think of a more crisis-ridden position than mother."

"I guess that's true. Hey, I have an idea," Sam says, nuzzling my ear. "Why don't I call Willa and Jake and invite them out to dinner with us. Everybody likes a review dinner, right?"

"Really, we can do that?" I ask. "Can we call them now?"

"Why don't we wait until the morning," he says, laughing.

Sam strokes my hair and it feels good. I don't want to fight anymore; I don't even really want to talk anymore.

I hear Henry shift in his crib over the baby monitor, and I hope he doesn't wake up. I want to stay where I am right now, at least for a little while longer. Sam is kissing me. He helps me pull my nightgown over my head and enters me. He moves slowly, teasing me. I want him in farther. I grab his back and try to push him inside as far as he'll go. *So this is what it used to feel like.* And then Sam isn't teasing anymore; he is as excited as I am.

I let everything fall away and will myself to put my brain in park. The important things are in place, I tell myself. I will make it work with Sebastian and Ed, as best I can. Sam and I will have plenty of time to hash out the details. We'll be discussing them for the next sixty years—if I'm very lucky.

I stop moving for a minute and look at Sam. I ease myself out from under him, a little afraid that I am going to break the spell, and go to the bathroom and put in my diaphragm. When I get back, Sam is waiting for me, and we have the best sex we've had since we were in Sam's old house with the purple door. No disguises needed.

Henry wakes up a few hours later. I am naked, and my nightgown is on the floor. Sam is nestled next to me. I gently push him over, put on my nightgown, and go to Henry, who is clearly uncomfortable. I spend longer than usual in his room, and when I come back, Sam is snoring. I climb in bed and take his hand again.

The first thing I do when Sam leaves for work the next morning is call Sunny to cancel. Then I get the kids ready, we take Hazel to school, and Henry and I set out to meet Tom at the Addison Hotel. Sam knows about our meeting.

I have Henry in the front carrier, and I'm wearing jeans and a long-sleeved yellow T-shirt, despite my previous fantasies about wearing a business suit or a dress. I have earrings on, and a touch of lipstick, but I am a far cry from made-up. I feel lighter than I have in a long time.

I walk through the hotel's revolving door with Henry trying to reach the glass wall with his feet. He screeches when I move to step out, so I go around one more time, and when we come back to the lobby again, Tom is right there.

"I thought you'd changed your mind and you'd decided to leave," Tom says, fiddling with his belt buckle.

"Oh, no—Henry loved it and wanted to go around again," I say. Henry is so quiet. Tom looks at him, then back at me.

"I thought you were going to get a sitter," he says in a perfectly friendly voice.

"Well, I was going to, but then I decided that I wanted you to meet him. Hazel is in school," I say.

"Okay," he says. Then he says to Henry, "Nice to meet you." I smile.

"I was thinking we could go to this breakfast place a few blocks away. They have great cranberry pancakes," I say.

"The coffee shop here is fine, if that's easier," he offers.

"Oh, no; the food here is awful."

Tom follows me into the revolving door, and Henry squeals with delight; then we walk the few blocks to the Hatchery. It's a weekday, so we get a table right away. Henry goes willingly into his high chair. I pull a plastic Elmo out of my purse and hand it to Henry. He takes it and starts chewing on it.

"You have to get the cranberry pancakes and the apple-smoked bacon, and we have to make sure we get the whipped butter and the real maple syrup," I say. "If you don't ask, they bring both in the little plastic tubs with the peel-off lids."

"I'm not that hungry; I was thinking more like a piece of toast," he says.

"They really are the best pancakes. You can have toast anytime," I say.

When the waitress comes to take our orders, Tom asks for the pancakes, and he defers to me to ask for the special butter and syrup. The waitress smiles knowingly at us.

"Since when do you care about food?" Tom asks. It is at that moment that I know I sounded just like Sam. So I tell him everything—about Sam's job, about our lives, about moving to Philadelphia—leaving out the bad stuff. It's easier to talk to him than I expected, and I quietly accept the fact that there are just some people I will always have a strong connection to. But I don't long to touch him, or wish that I could be here without Henry, without looking like a mom.

When the waitress brings the syrup in a little blue ceramic pitcher, Henry immediately knocks it over. Tom lets out a little yelp, but I scoop it up before too much spills, pull a few wipes out of my bag, clean the table and Henry's hands, and go back to what we were talking about.

Tom tells me about his work, which I have always found pretty boring, and goes through the long list of women he dated after me. He met someone recently and hopes she might be the one.

While I listen, I enjoy every bite of my pancake and sop up the syrup with my pieces of bacon. When I pour the last drop of syrup from the pitcher and the waitress rushes over with a full one, I know I have been recognized. I hope Tom notices. But he doesn't. He eats but doesn't seem to enjoy it much. *What a shame,* I think.

Then Henry gets a little fussy, and Tom looks around uncomfortably, so we get the check and head back to the hotel.

I don't plan to go inside, but Henry squeals again when he sees the revolving door, so I follow Tom in. We take a seat on one of the plaid couches in the lobby. Tom says he has about ten minutes before his next meeting.

"The thing is, Lila, I was hoping you might be able to help me," he says.

"With what?" I ask, surprised.

He glances at Henry, then back at me. "Well, just with some insight—I mean, I really like this woman I met. Do you have any idea why I keep getting, you know, dumped?"

I look at him, and he is handsome enough, strong looking, well dressed. I know he's smart. I think about telling him he has annoying habits, that he should think before he speaks sometimes, maybe open up emotionally. But I know none of that really matters.

"If she's the right one, then it will work out," I say.

"But, Lila, I've thought I'd met the right one before, and—"

"I know, but that's really what I think," I interrupt. "And I hope this one is Mrs. Right. If she is, she'll be able to forgive or ignore what everybody else couldn't. I promise."

Tom wants to keep talking, but I don't have anything else to offer him, and I'm completely bored. I glance around and notice mothers with strollers coming in, sitting for a minute, going out again.

Sometimes it's one mother with a baby, sometimes a group of two or three. I feel a kinship to them. I know that feeling of wandering around with no place to go, looking for civilization. And I know without a doubt that I am on to something with my idea. I want to get home and start working on it, draw up proposals, eventually talk to Ed. But first, I say good-bye to Tom, putting him and the old me in the past where we belong.

FALL, AGAIN

CHAPTER SIXTEEN

From behind the purple velvet–curtained entrance, the delicious smells and French music beckoned. And so we entered the Starlight Lounge, where, in the soft light of this bustling Center City bistro, Charles Trenet sang about his one true love.

—Sam Soto

When Hazel is in school and Henry naps, I go back to work. Well, nobody is paying me for it, and nobody actually knows I'm doing it, but I am. I sit at the computer and write outlines and descriptions; I think about timing and cost and refreshments and potential clients.

It is time that I call Ed. This is, after all, when I said I would be ready. But I'm not quite, and I worry that he has given up on me. So I put it off some more. I keep busy with the kids. I see my mother whenever she wants to visit. I enjoy Sam's company when he is present and try not to take it personally when he is more interested in chestnut fettuccine or braised artichokes than he is in me. We meet Sebastian and Charlotte in the square, with Sam's reluctant stamp of approval. And whenever I can, I work.

One day in September we are all playing outside. The big topic of conversation on the block now is Janie, who is a week overdue. Up until her due date she was out here with us, talking and playing with the kids. But that day came and went without a baby, and since then we haven't seen her much.

"I'm really worried about her," Willa says, as we watch Hazel and Russell search the street for goblin sticks (tiny twigs with a *v* at the top). They are finding a good number, and I can't help but wonder if Willa planted them here. "It's like she has postpartum depression before the postpartum."

"Well, hopefully it will be soon," I say, spotting what looks like a goblin hat made out of an acorn, and I know for sure Willa was involved. I smile at her. "She's been through so much. Did you know that she hasn't driven in months?"

"Yeah," Willa says. "Actually, that doesn't surprise me so much. Considering . . ."

Janie's door swings open. We both look, but no one comes outside. It slams shut. Then it swings open again, and Janie steps out, looking ragged and clutching her huge stomach. She is just about to go back inside when I call to her.

"Hi," I say, waving. "Is everything okay?"

She takes another step out onto her stoop. She does not look good.

"I haven't been feeling right since last night," she says. "But I was pretty much fine. Ben went to the train station to pick up his mother—oh, that hurts; wait a second." She leans over. I run to her and take her arm.

"Do you want to sit down?" I ask.

"Maybe, I don't know," she says, recovering a little. "I thought we would have plenty of time. But my water just broke and—oh God that hurts; wait a second." She stops.

I am about to ask her if there is anything I can do when something clicks inside me.

"Willa, go get that big folding chair you have and bring it out here," I command. Willa moves immediately toward her door. I keep my eyes on Janie, who seems to be between contractions, and walk to the house two doors down. I knock. Thankfully, Kate, the one teenager on our block, answers.

"Hi, Kate," I say. "I need your help. Can you please come gather the kids and bring them all to my playroom? The door is open. Janie is in labor and she needs help."

"Sure," Kate says, pulling earbuds from her ears and looking a little surprised. She slips her feet into shoes and comes right out. Willa is just returning with the chair, which we unfold and ease Janie into.

"I know they'll be here any minute," Janie says somewhat hysterically. "Her train was due in at 3:45. I'll be okay. They'll get here and we'll go. No problem—oh my God!" she screams. Daisy pokes her head out.

"Call 911," I yell to Daisy.

"No, I don't think—" Janie starts to say, but can't finish. Daisy disappears back inside to get her phone.

"Go and get Janie's phone for me," I say to Willa. She does. When she hands it to me, I say, "Now we need a cab. Go to Eighteenth Street, and do not tell the driver that you have a woman in labor. Go, quick."

"I know I should have gotten in the car a half hour ago," Janie says to me, clutching my arm. "But I couldn't, I couldn't."

"No," I say soothingly. "You did the right thing."

Suddenly Janie looks terrified.

"I have to go to the bathroom!" she screams. "Get me to a bathroom!"

"It's okay," I say. "We are going to get you to the hospital."

Letting Janie continue to clutch my arm, I dial Dr. Berri's number. Presumably an ambulance and a cab are on their way, but I think the baby might get here before they do. I push number one—the one you are supposed to push if you are in labor. I never had to push it because of my scheduled C-section. I always wondered what happens when you push number one. Not much.

It rings twice and a woman picks up. I can hear Janie screaming; then she turns her head and throws up.

"My name is Lila Soto," I say quickly. "I'm a patient of Dr. Berri's. I'm not in labor but my neighbor is, and she's one of his patients. We called 911 but the baby is coming. Who should I talk to?"

Just then I see Daisy come over with the phone. She must still be on with 911. I think she didn't realize how desperate the situation is, and now she is yelling into the phone. Through the phone I'm holding, I hear some rustling, a muted conversation. Then there is the miracle of Dr. Berri's voice.

"What's going on?" he asks.

"Dr. Berri, it's Lila Soto. Thanks for talking to me," I say. "Your patient Janie Burns, my neighbor, is in labor here, at home. We need help. Can you help us?"

"Did you call 911?"

"Yes," I say. "A few minutes ago. But now she's saying she has to go to the bathroom. I think the baby is here."

"Okay, see if she can hold off on pushing," he says. "Do you hear a siren?"

"Not yet," I say. "And she just threw up."

"Lila, you might have to deliver this baby," he says in such a way that I believe I will be able to. "Babies are slippery, so you're going to need gloves, and towels or blankets, and maybe even something to clamp the cord."

"Go inside," I say to Daisy. "I need gloves, towels, and—" I think for a minute. "Chip clips, bring me chip clips."

Daisy looks at me, then starts to go inside Janie's house.

"No," I yell. "It will take too long to find stuff. Go to your house."

"Okay," I say into the phone just as I hear the first notes of a siren. What took so long?

"They're coming," I say gently to Janie, hoping it is true. "I think I hear the siren," I say to Dr. Berri.

"Good, but I'm going to stay on the line," he says. Then I hear him shout orders to someone to be ready for Janie, to meet her at the ambulance bay.

The ambulance turns onto Colonial Court and comes to rest in front of Janie's house.

The medics come right over to me and ask questions. I fill them in, and they seem happy with my answers. One of them gets on the phone with Dr. Berri. I hear them discuss which hospital. I step back as they check Janie, apparently deciding there is enough time to get her there because they load her up. Then they drive away.

Daisy runs out of her house with her arms full of garden gloves, towels, and bright-yellow chip clips. She stops and watches the ambulance drive away.

"Thank you for calling 911, and for gathering all that," I say. "She should be okay now."

She nods, out of breath.

"What were the chip clips for?" she asks.

"You don't want to know," I say.

I see Willa walking toward us, looking defeated.

"I had to go to Lombard to try to get a cab," she says. "But I was so panicked nobody would follow me. I should have pretended it was for me and just given Janie's address. Why didn't I do that?"

"It's okay," I said. "The ambulance is better anyway."

Then Ben, Janie's husband, drives up. He and his mother take in the scene.

"She's okay; she's on her way to the hospital," I say gently to him. He gets back in the car.

"Did Janie have a bag packed?" I ask.

"Oh yeah," Ben says. "Right inside."

I sprint up the stoop and find a bright-pink suitcase to the left of the door. I grab it and hand it to Ben. He tries to place it on the floor of the passenger side, banging his mother's knees.

"Here, give it to me," I say as soothingly as I can. He thrusts it toward me. I take it and put it in the backseat. He smiles, shuts his door, and drives away.

Carol comes out and looks up and down the street. Then she narrows her eyes.

"What was all the commotion?" she asks in her raspy voice.

"Janie went into labor," Daisy answers politely.

"Oh, that," she says, with a dismissive swipe of her hand.

"You were amazing," Willa says, looking at me with wide eyes. "I had no idea."

"Huh," I say, smiling at her. "You just got a glimpse of the old me."

"Or the new you," she says, smiling back.

I call Sam to tell him about the excitement. He asks if I want him to come home, if I'm okay.

"I'm great," I say, reassuring him that I do not need him to come home. "I feel like I really did something great today."

"Lila, you do something great every day."

Later that night we learn that Janie made it to the hospital and had a healthy baby girl, whom she and Ben decided to name Colleen, a nod to their love of Colonial Court. A few days later they are back, and Janie can finally parade her daughter up and down the block with the rest of us. And it occurs to me that my neighbors do not have babies to add to their collections; they just want them.

Finally I feel confident enough to call Ed.

"Lila, I thought I'd never hear from you," he says, but his voice is warm.

"I'm sorry, Ed," I say. "I really am. This has been much harder than I thought it would be. And I think you aren't going to like what I have to say."

"I think you aren't going to like what I have to say on this end either," he says. My heart sinks. "You go first," he says.

"No, you," I say. "Please."

"Okay, here goes," he says. "You are one of the best. The greatest. The champion. But, we couldn't wait forever. Plus, I heard the distress in your voice when we last spoke. I am no longer in a position to offer you your old job back."

"That is probably for the best," I say after a moment. "I don't think I wanted it back."

"So, Lila, here's the good news," he says. "With the new hotels opening in Philadelphia, there will be a need for a few new regional managers, and—"

"Ed," I say, cutting him off. "I have a proposal for you."

"Okay," he says. "Lay it on me."

"Here goes. I've noticed that mothers with young children are often desperate—for company, for a place to go, and for something to do. And mostly, all the kids need is a big space to run around, maybe some activities. So why doesn't Addison start an Afternoon Vacation program for mothers with their young kids? We can start here, and if it takes off, make it a national program. We'd have it in the ballroom, which is a big, safe space. We could offer activities, maybe for both mothers and kids, and maybe some food. It could be a monthly event, or more frequent, depending on the response. I was even thinking I could contact Kraft to see if they want to cosponsor. I mean, what kid doesn't like macaroni and cheese?" I stop, realizing Hazel hasn't touched macaroni and cheese since we got back from our week at the Shore. "On second thought, it might be easier to stick with the hotel food. We can invite not only local women, but also women who might be staying at the hotel. It could have great appeal for women bringing their kids along on their husbands' business trips, or for men tagging along on their wives' trips, for that matter. I don't mean to limit this to only women, of course. Parents. It would be for parents. It might make people choose an Addison over another hotel, at least as much as a celebrity weekend does. What do you think?"

Ed is quiet for a minute and I wait. I want this to work, and I honestly believe it would be good for the hotel and the community.

"Whoa, Lila—there you are," he says finally. "I knew we'd get you back. I love it. I want the proposal sent to me within the month. And I'll have a contract drawn up and sent to you about the other stuff. Can we count on you for maybe twenty flexible hours a week?"

"I think you can," I say, smiling bigger than Hazel did when Willa handed her the fairy dust.

I spend October playing with the kids, getting ready for Henry's birthday party, which will be the traditional Colonial Court block party, and putting together a wonderful, creative, informative proposal for Ed. I tell Sam about my idea, and he loves it, as long as I promise not to do any of the press interviews and consider wearing a wig when an event is going on.

And then it starts to get colder, everyone stays inside more, and I begin to dread the winter and long for the blossoming cherry tree. But at least this time I know we'll be invited to the snowflake crafts circles and the hot chocolate parties. And now I have my work again.

Sam and I have offered to host our Thanksgiving feast this year. And of course, Sam takes this all very seriously.

"I have to cook," Sam says sternly when I try to ask him what he wants for lunch. It's the day before Thanksgiving, and I can almost see his mind working: *stuffing, gravy, bread, corn muffins*. Once again I have lost Sam to food. But I don't really mind; at least this is for us.

We have fifteen people coming for dinner, and I know it's a big deal. It is the first time we have ever hosted a holiday family dinner. My mother will be here. Sam's dad is coming. Aunt Gladys offered to bring the flower arrangements. We haven't seen her in months, but she calls to check on us and, despite my disastrous visit last winter, she still begs us to come again. We have also invited a bunch of random cousins who can't go home for one reason or another.

My big victory has been talking Sam into having a nontraditional dinner. Somehow I could not stand the thought of a typical roasted turkey, stuffing, and cranberry sauce. Too much has happened this year. So we decide on a New Orleans feast complete with oyster dressing, sausage and cornbread stuffing, and a turducken—which is a turkey stuffed with a duck stuffed with a chicken.

Sam spends the day prepping for tomorrow, when he is really going to have to cook; he cleans, chops, gets the turducken ready for the oven. I try to clean up, but mostly I play with the kids. After lunch I hear people outside, so I pull open the door. It is unusually balmy for late November. I see Willa and Russell, and the twins, who are both walking now. I call to Hazel, grab Henry, and we head outside.

"We can't wait until dinner next week," Willa says when I walk over to her, referring to the review dinner that she and Jake will be joining us on. "We're very excited."

"So am I," I say, meaning it.

"Will Sam wear a disguise?" she asks.

"I don't know, maybe," I say.

"That would be fun," she says. I laugh. Then she grabs my arm.

"Hey, did you see the moving truck yesterday?" she asks.

"No," I say.

"People moved into 1830," she says, very excited. "Do you know what this means? It means you aren't the new people anymore!"

"That's a relief," I say.

Eventually Sam comes out. He is wearing his chef's shirt and white apron.

"I was thinking we could have an early dinner, get the kids to bed, and then I can keep cooking," he says. "Let's order something for dinner."

"Okay," I say, thinking about the possibilities.

We order dinner from an Italian place on Twentieth Street. They have a new chef, and Sam wants to try the food. I get fresh linguine with tomatoes, Sam orders a veal chop, we choose lemon chicken with risotto for Henry, and Hazel just wants plain pasta with butter. We laugh every time Henry shoves a fistful of fancy asparagus risotto into his mouth. I cut the chicken into tiny pieces, but he shoves them in so fast they make one big piece anyway. He loves it and flashes his jazz appreciation smile.

I force Sam to go to sleep by midnight; otherwise he'll never make it through the next day. We turn out our lights, and Sam starts to snore immediately. But he quickly becomes more and more restless. At various times during the night he yells out, "Gravy!" and "Where's the okra?" and "No, don't eat that!"

The next morning we eat our breakfast while Sam starts the desserts. He is making pecan pie and bread pudding. He had the pecans flown in from New Orleans, as well as flaky French bread that he had to have for the bread pudding. And he ordered special cinnamon and vanilla from a catalog.

"Happy Thanksgiving," I say.

Sam looks at me like I just wished him a happy Fourth of July. He goes back to his chopping.

I open our door at around eleven o'clock. The air is even warmer than yesterday, and it lures me out. Sam comes out with the kids a few minutes later.

"It is so nice out here," I say, breathing it in.

"I'll just stay out here for a second," Sam says. "I need a tiny break."

Willa opens her door and waves to us. Then she motions for us to stay right where we are and runs back inside. A minute later she appears with a Minnie Mouse Dixie cup full of cranberry sauce. She crosses the street and hands it to Sam.

"I made this," she says. "Would you mind tasting it for me? I'm afraid it's too orangey."

"Sure," Sam says. He scoops a little onto the tiny spoon that she offers him, and he puts it in his mouth. He moves it around a little, makes smacking sounds.

"Nice texture," he says. "But it's a bit acidic. Add a little sugar and a splash of port. It will be perfect."

"Thanks," Willa says, going back inside. "Really, thanks a lot."

About two minutes later Daisy pokes her head out.

"Would you mind?" she asks, handing Sam a small Tupperware full of stuffing.

"No, I don't mind," Sam says. He takes the container, plucks a small amount with his fingers, and pops it into his mouth. He concentrates for a second.

"It's good," Sam says. "I like it."

"Not too salty?" Daisy asks.

"No, just right." Sam hands back the container.

"Great," she says, eating the rest of the stuffing. "Thanks."

"You should start charging for that," I say, after Daisy closes her door. "You could be a cooking consultant."

Sam laughs. Then he goes back inside. Carol comes out, and I wonder what her plans are for the holiday weekend.

"Did you notice how bright the streetlights are?" she asks, pointing up. "I called the city and told them the bulbs were too dull. We need bright lights. They came and changed them the other day."

I haven't noticed anything, but I smile. That's just like her, taking credit for the strangest things.

"Thanks, Carol," Willa says in her gentle way.

I have an urge to tell her she makes my blood boil, or ask why, if she bakes so much, she isn't better at it. But I don't. She turns to Willa and starts to describe the pain in her lower back. I walk over.

"Carol, do you have plans for dinner tonight?" I ask, not quite believing my own words.

She turns away from Willa and hesitates for a second; then she smiles brighter than our streetlights have ever been.

"My plans just fell through," she says. "I was just defrosting some turkey loaf."

"Well, why don't you join us, then," I say. "Come by around six."

"Great, I'll bake something," she says.

"That would be nice," I say.

She waves to Willa but doesn't finish her story about her back pain. She'll have people to talk to later; she doesn't need to get it all out now. I watch as she almost sprints up her steps. Then she stops, turns, comes back to me.

"Can you come inside for a sec?" she asks roughly, then looks up and down the street. "Please?"

"Sure," I say to Carol. "Willa, can you watch them for a minute?"

"Will do," Willa says, moving closer to the group of kids who are trying to bounce a tennis ball off of Daisy's house, but they are not quite strong enough to do it, and it just keeps rolling away.

I follow Carol up her stoop and into her strange-smelling house. She points to a dirty couch, and I sit on the edge so I won't have to touch too much of it.

"Something's been eating at me," she says quickly. She's still standing, and I am about to stand up when she holds her hand up, telling me to stay put. She lumbers up to the second-floor landing, where I can see her desk piled high with papers, newspapers, magazines. She rifles through some drawers. I hear rustling, and at first I think it must be Carol, but then I hear it again, and I know it is coming from somewhere next to me. I jump up. I wonder if it's a mouse. Maybe she nursed that mouse from my house back to health and made it her pet. I twist around to see if I can find it, but there's nothing there. When I turn back, Carol is right in front of me. She thrusts something in my face, narrows her eyes.

I take it from her and see it's a picture of Sam. I look closely at the wrinkled rectangle and know instantly that it is an image of Sam at our wedding. He's sitting alone at a table, smiling. His tuxedo jacket has been removed. It's a great photo, but the very top of his head is cut off, so I decided to toss it when I was organizing, or trying to organize, our pictures. When was that?

Before I have a chance to say anything, she pushes another photo into my hand. This one is of me, also at our wedding. I am standing up talking to someone I worked with at the time. You can see my face clearly, and I look pretty, but I didn't know the person I was talking to well enough to keep it. There were so many photos. So I threw that one away, too.

"Where did you get these?" I demand. Carol bends forward a little and backs into a gray chair that I think was once yellow. She keeps her head down.

"Where?" I ask again.

"From you," she says quietly.

"From me? I didn't give them to you," I say.

"No, I mean, from your garbage," she says. "You know how the garbage is always being torn open by mice and squirrels and rats and people." She says this last word with disgust. "You hadn't been here that long when your trash was strewn all over the street. There were pictures. I have friends, you know, a good friend who works at an Italian place in South Philly. They're having a hard time, and I thought I could help them. Willa was out there rebagging everyone's garbage. She was very serious about it, wearing gloves, sweeping it up. But the pictures had blown all the way to the corner. I picked them up, put them in my purse. When I got home later, I scanned them in and e-mailed them to my friends."

I sit back down on the couch. I can't believe it. My first thought is that Carol cannot come to our Thanksgiving dinner and sit at our table. She will infect it, infect us. In fact, it would be better if she didn't live on our street. Then I realize that I was the one who threw those pictures out, just put them whole in the trash without even using the shredder Sam had bought. I look over and see Carol is crying.

"I didn't know that you had such nice kids, or that you were going to be one of the few people here who is nice to me," she sniffles, and her voice sounds raspier than ever. "And those idiots! They knew Sam was there, and they still couldn't get it right. Then they passed his picture around to their friends. Idiots."

I glance down at the pictures and think about Sam's walking into a restaurant, having the owner or server or greeter reach into a pocket and subtly pull out the images. *Aha,* they must have thought, *we've got him.*

"I don't talk to them anymore," Carol says. "I didn't realize they were going to pass the e-mail around. I think they even sent it to that guy at the tabloid, Sy Gold?"

"Sy Silver," I say quietly. That explains that.

"But the worst part was that they blamed *me* for the bad review. *I* didn't have anything to do with it," she says.

I can hear the kids cheering outside, and I want to get back to them. I look out Carol's front window and see Sam has come out and is showing them how to bounce the ball. He must wonder why I'm here. What am I going to tell him? I look at Carol, who is wiping her nose with her sleeve. She looks up and holds my eyes.

"Sorry," she says loudly. "I am very sorry."

I take a deep breath. I've done things I'm sorry about and been forgiven. Just recently, in fact. And she did get that mouse for me, and gave me awful baked goods. I guess she isn't the worst neighbor a person could have.

"Do you have any other pictures of us around?" I ask, only half kidding.

"No, really, and I could barely stand having those," she says. "Stupid," she mutters.

"Fine," I say, standing up. "I'll see you at six."

"You will?" she says, then gathers herself. "I'll try to be on time."

I walk out the door and watch the kids from the stoop. I know I'm not going to tell Sam about this, not now anyway. And I vow to always, always use the shredder.

Finally, we welcome our guests. My mother gets a kick out of the New Orleans theme. When we have a minute alone, I fill her in about my work situation.

"I'm proud of you, Lila," she says, surprising me. "None of what you've done in the last four years has been easy, and yet, you have managed to make it work. I have no doubt in my mind about your success."

"But I thought you'd be disappointed with me," I say. "I always thought that you thought a life without work was useless."

"I'll let you in on a little secret," she says, leaning closer to me. "Life without love is useless. Work is important, and I do think it's a good way to stay happy, but for me it is a defense mechanism. When your father died, I had nothing—well, I had you, of course, but nothing that was my own; that's really where all that came from. And the good book by your bed . . . Well, I do like a good read, but now you can probably guess what that was a substitute for."

I laugh, realizing I figured that out in the hotel bathroom the night Sam and I had the big fight. The doorbell rings. I open the door to find Edgar dressed in what looks like a new suit. He is polite and clean shaven. The kids are thrilled to see him. He and my mother, who until this minute I would say have had absolutely nothing in common, spend a good part of the evening talking about winter gardening.

And Aunt Gladys and Carol hit it off. By the end of the meal I hear Aunt Gladys inviting Carol out to Swarthmore for tea.

"It's hard for me to get on a bus these days," Carol rasps. "The bumps kill my back. But I might be able to take a train."

"I know just what you mean about your back," Aunt Gladys answers. "I have very comfortable chairs with that in mind."

"Well, I think I'm free next Thursday," Carol says. "I'll bake a chocolate dump-it cake."

"That sounds delicious," Aunt Gladys says.

Sam was not happy when I told him I had invited Carol. He's still mad at her for saying those mean things we heard over the baby monitor, probably always will be. I'm glad, for now at least, that I didn't tell him about the picture. Maybe someday. When he asked why I invited her, I told him she's a sad, lonely lady who was going to eat turkey loaf alone. I told him that Aunt Gladys could use a friend. I told him that I invited her because it is Thanksgiving.

I sit back and look around the table. I'm finally starting to understand that nobody is just one thing. Carol is harsh and mean and a little scary, and she is helpful and giving and vulnerable. My mother is both steadfast and flexible, strong in her beliefs but open-minded. She is thoughtful and interesting, selfless and selfish. Willa isn't just a seemingly perfect mother, as I first thought. She is creative and caring and funny and kind, and sometimes unsure of herself. Edgar is not just a somewhat crazy Grizzly Adams wannabe. He is also surprisingly tuned in and often quite reasonable. Sam is the restaurant critic and my husband and Hazel and Henry's father. He's loving and giving and obsessed and preoccupied. Why have I spent my whole life putting people in categories and not letting them out?

And what about me? I'm not just a former corporate-hotel crisis manager or just a mother or just a wife. I'm a good friend, an old friend, and, in some cases, a former friend. I'm a patient mother and an exasperated mother, probably within the same hour. Hopefully I will still be a good employee for the Addison hotels. Hopefully I can make Sam more happy than angry. Hopefully the good stuff will outweigh the bad.

"Sam, I hope you know how sorry I am," I hear Carol say. I tense up. Did she think I told him about the picture? I see a flash of confusion pass over Sam's face; then he looks at me, and I shrug. He looks back at Carol, trying, I know, to act like he didn't miss something, wasn't being too distracted. Or maybe he thinks she is apologizing for the blood-boiling comment.

"That's okay," he finally says, and is instantly focused on the tur-ducken, making sure he carves it properly so that everybody can get a little turkey, duck, and chicken.

"Good," I hear Carol say under her breath. "Now I can put that behind me."

I smile at her, and then I smile at Sam, watching as he helps serve the food he cooked.

And I feel the absence of my father more tonight than I have for most of my adult life. I would like him to see my kids, sit at this table, and eat Sam's spectacular food. I feel my eyes well up a little, and I look at my mother, who I now know misses him this much every day, and I have the craziest thought of all. I think, suddenly, that my own lack of desire to settle down had less to do with me and my need to work, and more to do with losing my father. I didn't want to find something I needed so much that I couldn't stand the thought of living without it. That already happened to me when he died. And I know my mother has never gotten over it; she's moved on, but she will never stop longing for him. There was always another hotel or crisis. But there will never be another Sam or Hazel or Henry.

I excuse myself from the table, kissing the top of Sam's head as I pass him, and go upstairs. I open the closet door and look at Sam's olive-green duffle bag next to Hazel's Care Bear backpack. Then I go to our bed, get down on my stomach, and fish my suitcase out. I carefully unwrap the plastic and unzip it. I lean over and smell the inside, but the jet fuel is long gone. If anything, there is a slight powder smell from the diapers I once put in here. I zip it up and put it, unprotected by plastic, in between the other two bags. It looks good there.

I stand still for a minute, listening to the voices downstairs. I think about how my bag used to look when it turned the corner in baggage claim. How I would lift it off the conveyor belt like it was a long-lost friend and drag it behind me to the hotel, where I would sometimes order room service, sometimes go to bed without any food at all. I lean over and touch my bag's shimmering exterior. Then I close the closet door and go back downstairs for another piece of Sam's pecan pie.

ACKNOWLEDGMENTS

It's hard to know whom to thank first with this book, but I think that honor goes to my agent, Uwe Stender, who is truly unflagging in his enthusiasm and persistence. An old draft of this book brought us together years ago. He promised me then that he loved the book and would never give up on it. He meant it. I would also like to thank Laura Crockett, Brent Taylor, and Mallory Brown, Uwe's team at TriadaUS.

Thank you to my insightful editor, Jodi Warshaw, at Lake Union Publishing for choosing *The Restaurant Critic's Wife*, and for understanding Lila and appreciating her story. Thank you also to Kelli Martin, my developmental editor at Lake Union, for smartly and kindly working with me to make the novel as good as it can be. Thank you to Kristin Carlsen, my superhero-like copyeditor. She noticed things I never would have thought about. I am so grateful. I feel the same way about my amazing proofreader Rebecca Jaynes. Thank you to Emily Mahon for designing a great cover. And thank you to the rest of the team at Lake Union including Gabriella Van de Heuvel, Christy Caldwell, Tyler Stoops, Karen Upson, and Brent Fattore.

Thank you to my great friend Jennifer Weiner, who was the first one to read a very early draft of Lila's story, followed by many subsequent drafts, and has always given me her full support. One time she even delayed getting on the road in a snowstorm to talk through one of the points in this book. Thank you also to Petula Dvorak for all our lunches at the Plantation Coffeehouse in New Orleans, when we talked about our writing dreams, and for being a great friend for all these years since then. Thank you to Ivy Gilbert for reading this book numerous times, and for your incredible generosity. Thank you to Simona Gross, Nika Haase, Mary McManus, Dawn Davenport, Meghan Burnett, Melissa Cooper, Melissa Jensen, Doug Cooper, and Leah Kellar for reading or brainstorming at different points in the process, and for your consistent encouragement. Thank you to Avery Rome for your thoughtful help with the early stages of the manuscript.

Thank you to Dr. Drew Mellen, the best ob-gyn in Philadelphia, possibly the world. Thank you to Angie Benson, the best babysitter my kids could have ever had. And thank you to all the servers, chefs, and restaurateurs in Philadelphia, New Orleans, and beyond, who help to make our restaurant lives so rich.

This book wouldn't exist without my husband, Craig LaBan, who brings excitement, adventure, love, and great food into our lives every day, and has always been open to my writing a novel about a woman who is married to a wacky restaurant critic. For the record, Craig is not *quite* as obsessive or controlling as Sam—and he didn't even tell me to say that. I want to thank my amazing kids, Alice and Arthur, for believing in me and for making me laugh. Thank you to my family for your love and confidence: Joyce and Myron LaBan, Patty Rich and Terry LaBan, Amy LaBan and Eric Meyers, and Fran Whitehall.

Finally, I wish my parents, Barbara and Arthur Trostler, could be here to read this book. I would never have reached this point without their unwavering love and guidance.

ABOUT THE AUTHOR

Photo © Andrea Cipriani Mecchi

Elizabeth LaBan lives in Philadelphia with her restaurant critic husband and two children. She is also the author of *The Tragedy Paper*, which has been translated into eleven languages, and *The Grandparents Handbook*, which has been translated into seven languages.